FILTHY RICH SANTAS

EVA ASHWOOD

If you're looking for "that smutty Christmas romance with the TVP scene in it,"
I've got good news.

You've found it.

1

LANA

My heart races as I look around the club. Radiance is everything I expected an upscale sex club to be, and yet somehow, it's still more than I imagined.

The decor is sleek and modern, but with a touch of sensuality and, in honor of the season, some tasteful holiday decor. Low music plays from hidden speakers, and there are couches and comfortable-looking chairs throughout the space, all dark red and brown leather. Some of them are so big and wide, they're more like beds, a few sitting empty but most with people in various states of dress and undress lounging on them.

"And this is the tame part of the club," I whisper to myself, a hot flush moving through me as I think of the introductory packet I was given after completing the lengthy vetting process.

There are other rooms here. Rooms with BDSM equipment, sex toys, and all sorts of sexy possibilities that have my stomach filling with jitterbugs. The thought of exploring further has me so nervous that my hands are sweating... but those nerves feel a lot like the thrill of excitement too.

"Two sides of the same coin," I whisper to myself, knowing that no matter what happens tonight, I'm proud of myself for making it this far.

I'm ready to explore some new sides of myself, and if not now, when? And if I deliberately picked *this* club to start doing some of that exploration at, well, I won't get my hopes up. But that doesn't mean I can't stay open to possibilities, right?

I head toward the bar, telling myself firmly that I'm not keeping an eye out for the three men who own the place—my older brother's best friends. After all, it's one thing to stay open to possibilities, but it's something else entirely to wish for impossible things.

I still need something to calm my nerves, though. And even though I know they don't serve anything alcoholic here, having a glass of seltzer water in my hands will give me a little more of a sense of belonging. If nothing else, it should help me stop fiddling with the yellow wristband I chose when I arrived.

Which I'm doing again.

I force myself to drop my hand, biting my lip as I second guess whether I should have taken red instead. Yellow tells the other guests that I'm open to meeting them, but not ready to be outright propositioned. Red would have been a hard no on being asked to... *do* anything.

And green—well, no matter how interested I am in exploring the interests I've only recently admitted to myself that I have, I'm definitely not ready for green. In fact, the club rules about the wristband system are clear. They don't even allow it for a first-timer like me, since I'm here on my own and not even a full member.

Which doesn't mean I can't still play if I find someone interested.

And, of course, find the courage to do it.

"First time here?" a deep, baritone voice asks from my left after I've placed my order for a seltzer water.

My heart jumps into my throat as I turn to him, then look up. He's a little taller than my 5'6", even with the extra few inches my heels give me tonight.

Not as tall as Beckett, Tristan, or Ryder, though.

Which, I remind myself firmly, isn't relevant. I'm not here for them. And even if I was, it's not like I really expect any one of them to suddenly decide I'm more than just my brother's baby sister, just because I'm here.

The man who approaches me smiles, and the way he's leaning against the varnished oak bar, letting his gaze lazily roam over me in a way that's flattering but not sleazy, has a giddy, nervous laugh bubbling in my throat. Not just because he's attractive, although he is, but because even if my hidden desires about what might come of showing up here aren't likely to come true, I'm still following through with my commitment to start exploring who I really want to be.

I'm really here, and I've actually captured someone's attention.

"Yes," I admit to the guy, knowing my pale skin is probably showing my feelings the way it always does as I feel a blush heat my cheeks. "It's my first time."

My pulse starts to race as he starts to make small talk, his gaze pausing for a moment on my yellow wristband before respectfully coming back up to my eyes.

"I take it it's not *your* first time, though?" I say, daring to be flirtatious even though it has my stomach feeling jittery again.

His eyes dart down to my wristband again. "That's right," he says as the bartender returns and slides my seltzer water over to me.

I pick it up gratefully, taking a long sip, and remind myself that I'm here to explore things. To be bold. To finally learn what it is to be the person I want to be.

And even if I don't end up doing any of that with this particular man, his obvious interest definitely helps drown out the ugly voices in my head that I had to overcome just to walk through Radiance's doors tonight. The voices that sound an awful lot like my parents', and constantly remind me of all the ways I don't live up to conventional beauty standards.

All the freckles.

My generous curves.

The million and one imperfections that have been pointed out to me all of my life... and of course the new one that, thankfully, isn't outwardly visible.

My admirer shifts a little closer, his thigh brushing against

3

mine. "If you're interested in being shown around the club," he offers, carefully skirting the *no propositioning* rule my yellow wristband holds him to, "I'd be more than happy to introduce you to some of my favorite activities here."

I have no idea if he's actually someone I want to explore the world of kink with, but as anxious as I am about trying something so different and new, I feel safe here at Radiance. My brother's friends have created the perfect environment within the four walls of the club, and it makes me feel empowered to see where things might go if I really let myself explore my interests here.

"Tell me more," I murmur, sipping my drink again to combat the flush in my cheeks.

He brushes a long strand of hair off my cheek, tucking it behind my ear, then lets his hand linger as he leans in to murmur softly in my ear. "I could, but showing is often so much more rewarding than telling."

My nerves fire up again. Before I can convince myself that it's really just another taste of excitement, a hand falls on my admirer's shoulder. A big one, with thick, blunt fingers and all-too-familiar tattoos on the knuckles.

My breath hitches.

It's Beckett Stone. One of my brother's best friends. One of the reasons I came here tonight.

Beckett yanks the guy off me, and a flash of irritation crosses the man's face, his lip pulling back in a snarl for a split second before he sees who it is looming over him. Then he blanches a little, his expression smoothing out into something more respectful.

I can't really blame him. I have no idea if the man knows that Beckett is one of Radiance's owners, but even without taking that into consideration, Beckett is huge. His muscular 6'5" build is intimidating enough on its own, but combined with the scowl under his dark, messy hair and the fire in his dark green eyes as he glares down at the guy, anyone would think twice about getting into it with him.

"This one's off limits," he says gruffly, his eyes flickering to me for a second before zeroing back in on my admirer.

4

Well, former admirer. The man obviously wasn't that invested in getting to know me since he mumbles a quick apology in my direction, then scoots around Beckett's tattooed bulk to disappear back into the depths of the club.

Beckett turns to watch him go, standing like a brick wall between me and everything I came here to experience.

I really, really want to be irritated about that. But who am I kidding? Having Beckett not just notice that I'm here, but actually take an interest in what I'm doing is like the start of the dream I keep trying to convince myself there's no use in having.

Although I guess choosing the club he owns with my other two fantasy men, Ryder and Tristan, is all the evidence I need that I'm not doing a great job of pretending I don't want what I want.

Beckett growls something under his breath at the man scurrying away from us, and the waves of dominance rolling off him have heat pooling between my legs.

Thankfully, his back is still turned to me. Although I secretly hoped I'd run into my brother's friends tonight, now that one of them is right here, I'm not sure I'm actually ready for him to notice the effect he has on me.

Not after so many years of hiding it.

For most of my life, my older brother, Caleb, was practically joined at the hip with Beckett and his two other best friends, Ryder and Tristan. I'm friendly with all of them too, but I'm also very firmly in the "Caleb's little sister" category for each one of them. It's why all three of them make a point of checking up on me now that I'm living out here in Los Angeles where they all settled.

Somehow, I run into one of them every few weeks. It happens often enough to make me wonder if Caleb asked them to keep tabs on me, because Los Angeles is so huge that it can't be an accident.

I've never called them on it, though, because it's nice. Still, running into one of my brother's best friends while I'm getting groceries or grabbing a coffee is one thing. Having to face Beckett and all his lickable tattoos while I'm wearing fuck-me heels and a yellow "yes, I might be interested" wristband at a kinky sex club is another thing altogether.

But there's no getting out of facing him eventually. As soon as my former admirer is out of the picture, Beckett grunts something at me with another scowl. Wrapping one of his strong hands around my arm, he drags me away from the sweating glass of seltzer water I set on the bar.

"Come with me," he rumbles, pulling me into a dimly lit hallway behind the bar that I hadn't noticed before. Probably because the entrance is neatly camouflaged to blend into the decor.

I drag my feet, biting my lip as I look around. "Are we even allowed back here?"

It's a stupid question and I know it. Obviously, Beckett can go wherever he wants. It's his club. He, Ryder, and Tristan aren't just co-owners. From everything I've heard, they're actively involved in every aspect of running it.

Beckett doesn't even bother to answer. He just drops my arm and crowds me back against the wall, caging me in with both hands flattened to it on either side of my head.

"What the fuck are you doing here?" he demands.

My pulse starts to race again, but unlike with my former admirer at the bar, this time, there's no question about whether it's due to the man in front of me or not.

I may still be uncertain about where exactly my recently acknowledged interest in kink will take me, but the way my body reacts to Beckett's natural dominance leaves no doubt that I want to pursue more of it.

I lift my chin, reminding myself that I've known Beckett for half my life. I may be attracted to him, but I've never been intimidated and don't plan on starting now.

"Why does anyone come here?" I huff. "You do own this place, right? Which means you know what people come here to do?"

The pained look that crosses his face might have made me laugh if I wasn't strung so taut on nerves, excitement, and my body's reaction to his nearness. "And *you* know that Caleb would kill all three of us if he found out you were here."

I smile a little when he says "all three of us." I can't help it. And maybe that's the reason I can't settle on just one of these men to crush on. Through thick and thin, they've always been a unit. My brother too, of course, but now that he has to travel so much for his career in the NHL, I know that a certain amount of distance has grown between him and the other three men.

Beckett isn't wrong, though. Caleb would definitely have *feelings* if he found out I'd come to a kinky sex club tonight. Even one, or maybe especially one, where his friends were there to look out for me.

But I'm a twenty-six-year-old woman, single and free, and finally living far enough from my family to start exploring things that I know they'd disapprove of. If I was going to let my brother's *feelings* stop me from starting to live the life I really want, I never would have walked through Radiance's doors.

"This isn't any of Caleb's business," I tell Beckett, poking his rock-hard chest for emphasis.

He gives me a flat stare, ignoring my finger. "You're his sister."

"And a grown-ass woman! I can do what I want."

"Lana..." Beckett growls.

"Beckett," I say back, trying for sassy but ending up sounding hopelessly breathless instead.

Not my fault. Sassy isn't really who I am, and besides, he's standing too close. I can feel his body heat. Smell the cedar and leather scent that's uniquely his. And all that rumbling displeasure of his literally makes the air between us vibrate.

"I was having a perfectly nice conversation with the man at the bar," I start.

"No," Beckett cuts me off.

I blink up at him. "What?"

"I said no."

I give a disbelieving laugh, shaking my head. "Just... no?"

All three of my brother's best friends have always been incredibly protective of me, but even if they'll never see me the way I want them to, I still have every right to be here. Every right to explore my interest and try to discover if kink is right for me.

"You heard me," Beckett says, something dark and a little dangerous flaring in his eyes.

7

The sight of it makes my breath hitch, touching on the hidden part of me I'm yearning to explore here. So of course I attempt to poke him again, or maybe push him away from me.

Too bad for me I accidentally end up stroking the heated planes of his solid chest instead.

Again, not my fault, though. He's wearing a tight black shirt that's molded to his muscles and feels sinfully soft. Possibly silk? Whatever it is, it fits him like a second skin and feels like pure pleasure.

He captures my hand, holding it against his chest. He frowns down at me, his eyes narrowing. "You shouldn't be here, little menace. Where's your boyfriend?"

I snatch my hand back, his use of that stupid childhood nickname reminding me of where I'll always stand with my brother's friends.

Even when it's bubbling just under the surface, I can't quite admit to myself what I was really hoping for by coming to the club that *they* own. But Beckett's reaction to finding me here makes it clear.

I will always be Caleb's little sister to this man. I know it's the same with Tristan and Ryder too.

And if that isn't enough to kill my hopes, along with my libido, the fact that Beckett brought up my ex definitely is.

I guess he hasn't heard.

"Wade broke up with me—a month after proposing to me, actually. Apparently, 'chubby girls aren't wife material,'" I mumble, certain that my skin is broadcasting my emotions again as I feel my face flush with embarrassment.

Not that I miss my ex-fiancé. I don't. But it would be nice, just once, to be... enough for someone.

Or just enough, period.

"Shit," Beckett mutters, his hard demeanor instantly softening.

That just makes it worse.

I swallow and look away, my stomach dropping, but of course Beckett can't just leave it at that.

He tips my face back up, staring intently into my eyes. "Are you okay?"

"Yes," I whisper, getting a little lost in the intensity of his gaze before I catch myself and remember why I came. I shake it off and make myself grin up at him, tilting my head to the side. "Why do you think I came to a place like this? I'm free and single now! And I want to get back out there and have some fun."

Beckett's expression hardens so fast it's like someone dropped a steel shutter in front of his face, and suddenly the little bit of space that had opened up between us is *gone*.

"I'm sorry that piece of shit dumped you, but trust me, none of the men here are good enough for you," he growls.

There's something hard and almost possessive in his words, and, for just a second, the words *you are* flicker through my mind, making my heart skip a beat.

We stare at each other without blinking, so close I can feel his breath on my lips.

I can barely catch my breath, my body reacting to him in ways that are completely out of my control. He's so close, I feel like I'm wrapped in sex pheromones, his cedar and leather scent almost overwhelming me. He's an inked up muscle-bound god that any woman would get wet for, but it's more than that. It's his sheer presence, dominating not because it's a kink, but because that's who he *is*.

"You're right," I breathe out without meaning to. The guy hitting on me at the bar wasn't good enough, none of them are, because *this* is what I came looking for.

I want Beckett to crush me against the wall and kiss me.

I want him to see me for who I truly am. As more than Caleb's little sister. As more than I've ever let myself be.

I want him to see, and then *take*.

But of course he doesn't. He just blinks, shuttering the burning intensity I thought I saw in his eyes for a moment, then backs away from me, finally putting a little space between us.

Then, with another panty-melting glower, like he's trying to torture me with what I can't have, he crosses his massive arms over his chest and stares down at me. "Of course I'm right."

I sigh, feeling an unsettling mix of foolish and grateful. I love the way he's so protective of me. I don't even really mind how over-bearing he, Ryder, and Tristan can occasionally be, since it's not like they normally interfere in my life, tonight notwithstanding.

But wishing for Beckett to notice me as a woman? To *kiss* me?

I need to face facts. It's never going to happen.

None of my brother's best friends have ever seen me as anything but Caleb's nerdy, chubby little sister. The four-inch heels I'm wearing tonight and the leather halter top that made me feel so sexy and daring when I chose it aren't going to change that. Nothing will.

Beckett suddenly cups my cheek, the rough, callused feel of his fingers on my skin making goosebumps break out. "Are you sure you're okay, little menace? If you really want a tour of the club..."

His frown deepens, and I swear I can see the battle happening in his head as his voice fades away. It's a war between the thought of getting stuck hovering and growling around me all night like some kind of guard dog, just to let me have my fun, and the idea of having to explain all this to Caleb at some point.

I lean into his palm, letting myself enjoy this one single thing before I call it a night.

Then I straighten up and nod, smoothing my hands over the flowing pants I actually felt kind of sexy in when I left the house earlier, overly abundant curves or not.

"No, it's fine," I tell him. "I should go anyway. I have to work tomorrow."

It's clear that I'll just have to work out some other way to explore my interest in kink. One that doesn't include pining over men I'll never have.

"Are you parked in our lot?" he asks, his relentless protective-ness making me grin.

His eyes drop down to me—not my lips. Of course not. He's probably looking at the annoying little dimple in my cheek that just emphasizes how very *not* thin and svelte I am.

I pat his chest, only letting my fingers linger on that sinful black silk for a moment.

Then I make myself pull my hand off him again, automatically reaching for my phone before remembering that I had to check it before entering. Club rules.

"I took a cab. I'll just call another one as soon as I retrieve my phone and my coat."

"No," he says, wrapping his hand around my arm again and pulling me along like he did before.

"Bossy, much?" I mutter under my breath.

Beckett slants a heated look at me. "Yes. I'm calling you a car."

I duck my head, hiding my smile. Even if I'll never have the men I've always wanted, at least I know that I wasn't wrong about one thing. Dominance with a side of possessive overprotectiveness really does do it for me.

Still, I'm not a damsel in distress.

"You don't have to do that."

His grip tightens on my arm, and for a second, I see that flash of *something* in his eyes again. "Yeah, little menace, I do. I need to know you're safe."

I nod and let him do it, not arguing when he waits with me so he can vet the driver, then ushers me into the back seat and tells him where to take me with another one of those menacing glares to let the guy know I'd better arrive in good condition.

I even smile at him when he pats the top of the car to send me on my way, giving him a jaunty little wave that hides the dejection creeping over me as the town car pulls away from the curb.

Of course Beckett wants me to be safe. It's in his nature. It might even be some kind of bro-code promise he made to my brother.

But in the three months since Wade broke up with me, I've slowly been figuring out who I really am. Or at least, who I think I want to be. And playing it *safe* isn't really a part of that picture.

I want to paint my life with bold colors now.

I want to not just make peace with all my imperfections, but find a way to celebrate them.

I want heat and passion and something wild, like the fantasies I had about tonight would play out.

I sigh, using my finger to draw a row of interlocking hearts in the condensation on the town car's tinted window before leaning my face against the cool glass to watch the city pass by. This was my last chance to really feel like *me* before heading back east to spend Christmas with my family. At least, the version of me that I want to become. And it's only now, driving away from Radiance with nothing to show for my night except my dreams going up in smoke, that I can admit the truth to myself.

My fantasies about tonight *did* include the three men who own the club. But my fantasies were just that. Fantasies.

The reality is that even though it was only Beckett I ran into tonight, I know that all three of them see me the same way. As someone to protect, care for, maybe even coddle. But never as someone to love. Not the way I want them to.

And never as someone to do all the wonderfully filthy things that those fantasies of mine are made of.

2

RYDER

"You really don't mind me taking the whole week of Christmas off, sir?" one of our bartenders asks, lingering by the exit as I finish the final security check of the night.

"Of course not, Miranda," I reassure her, sending her a warm smile. "You've earned it."

Our employees tend to gravitate to Radiance because they're part of the kink community too, and I have no problem feeding her need for reassurance since her "Daddy" isn't around at the moment to handle that.

Not my kink, but I'm definitely equal opportunity.

She finally leaves, and with the club shut down for the night, I head toward the back office. Co-owning a kinky sex club with two of my best friends is probably the best thing that's ever happened to me. Financially, it's done incredibly well for us, but that's not the real perk. It's not even that I get to spend the majority of my time in a place that caters to my chosen lifestyle, with an unlimited buffet of play partners readily available. The real perk is being in business with two of my favorite people in the world.

"All good?" Tristan asks, looking up when I enter the office the three of us share.

"Peachy," I say, sprawling out on one of the expensive, wide leather chairs we chose for the office, to make our "business meet-ings" a bit more comfortable.

Beckett may be the true beast out of the three of us, size-wise, but equally matched at 6'2", even if he is a bit leaner, Tristan and I aren't small men either. So the chairs are less of an indulgence and more of a necessity.

Especially because gathering here for a drink at the end of the night whenever more than one of us is at the club has become a bit of a ritual. And sure, we do occasionally discuss business as we unwind after hours, but that's the beauty of owning the place. The only schedule we actually have to stick to is the one we make for ourselves, and building a life where I get to stay close to the guys who are practically like brothers to me is by far the best perk owning Radiance offers.

Not that I'm ever going to say shit like that out loud, of course.

"Too much Christmas cheer?" Tristan asks with an innocent look on his face that I don't buy for a damn second. He tends to be the quietest of the three of us, but that doesn't mean he can't dish it out.

I make a rude sound in response, and flip him off. From a busi-ness standpoint, giving in to the staff's enthusiasm for putting up some holiday decor and planning a few Christmas-themed events over the next few weeks made sense, so I accept that. The members eat that seasonal shit up, and even better, it boosts our employees' morale. But with Tristan and Beckett, I don't have to hide my real feelings on the overblown holiday, so I don't even try.

Tristan chuckles softly at the one-fingered salute I sent him, the light reflecting off his glasses for a moment and obscuring the blue-gray eyes that I just know are dancing with humor at my expense right now. He's not a sadist, though, so after reflexively patting down his short brown hair—something I'm pretty sure he does subconsciously to try to cover the scars that snake from the back of his scalp down the side of his neck and parts of the left side of his body—he sets aside whatever he was doing on his phone and grabs the bottle of top shelf whiskey we keep back here.

He pours us each a double, and hands mine over. "Don't worry, it will all pass soon enough. Just like it does every year."

I snort, then take a long swallow. "Thank fuck for that."

"Careful," he teases me. "If your latest play partner saw this Grinch act, she might not be so quick to drop to her knees for you. I overheard her talking to some of the staff about how excited she was for the holidays."

I stare blankly at him for a second, then mentally catch up. "Oh, you mean Camila?"

Tristan laughs, sprawling back in his own chair and raising his whiskey to me. "Ah, I see."

I narrow my eyes at him. "See what?"

"That it's over."

I shrug. He's not wrong. He's just making it sound like it was more than it actually was. "It was just sex, not a relationship. You know I don't want anything serious."

"And she did."

I shrug again. He didn't phrase it as a question, because he didn't need to. "I never misled her, but it was time. She was starting to get a little more invested than was good for her."

"So ending things was for her own good," Tristan says, his lips twitching like he's trying to hold in a smile. "How altruistic of you."

"I mean, you're not wrong," I say, taking another long swallow of my whiskey and sighing with contentment as it spreads exactly the right kind of cheer through my body.

Fuck Christmas. Good whiskey, though? Now that is definitely worth feeling merry over.

"You're never going to commit to any of them, are you?" Tristan asks, lifting an eyebrow at me.

"Oh please," I shoot back. "You know you and Beckett are just as bad. At least I actually date."

Tristan grimaces a little before he can hide it, but doesn't try to deny it. And there's nothing wrong with the way he—and Beckett too—choose to limit their play time to simple sexual encounters and carefully scripted scenes here at the club. I do find that I like a little more with a woman, though.

The problem is that, like Tristan just pointed out, no matter what kind of expectations I set going into a new relationship, no matter how clear I am that while I want it to be exclusive, I also have no intentions of it ever becoming more than casual, at some point, they always want more.

And that's just never going to happen.

Tristan uses his chin to nod toward his phone. "Have you seen the numbers from the Shibari event last week?"

"Not yet, but damn. Adding the suspension demo was a good call. I haven't made it through all the new member applications that flooded in after that, but assuming I'm able to vet even half of them, it's going to get us close to the benchmark goals we set for *next* year."

Tristan gives me a quick grin, acknowledging the well-deserved praise. I may not have the same affinity for rope play that he does, but I'd be lying if I said the event he set up wasn't hot as fuck.

"You know you don't have to get through them all before we leave," he says, his grin taking on a hint of evil. "A little denial can do wonders under the proper circumstances."

I raise my glass in salute to that. The appeal of a needy sub, writhing with desire but unable to do anything about it until their Dom gives them permission, is something we can definitely both agree on. Forcing that same kind of delayed gratification on the new member applicants doesn't give quite the same satisfaction, but it still carries a hint of the power exchange that both of us—all three of us, if I include Beckett—thrive on.

Besides, I've never been one to choose work over pleasure. Unlike *some* people. I'm more than happy to put off dealing with the rest of it until after the holidays.

"You know we're going to have to pry Beckett away from this place," I remind Tristan.

He rolls his eyes. "We already agreed that we're taking the time off, and you know Grandma Meg is expecting us. He's just going to have to deal."

I grin. Beckett and I both love Tristan's grandmother as if she was our own.

I know he promised her that all three of us would head back to New Hampshire to spend Christmas with her. It may not be my favorite time of year, but it means something to her. And since she's one of the few people in the world who means something to *me*, it's going to happen. Even if we have to pry Beckett's fingers away from the door frame to get his workaholic ass out of this place.

"Yeah. He'll deal," I agree.

"In his defense, he just wants to make sure everything here runs smoothly," Tristan says diplomatically.

I snort, then down the rest of my whiskey and gesture to Tristan to pass me the bottle. "That excuse is no longer valid. We hired good people. The club runs like clockwork. I get that he's protective of it, but we didn't spend as long as we did building our team just to turn around and micromanage them."

"I know," Tristan says as I pour myself another inch of golden heaven. "But you know how he is. He always wants to do a little more. Make it a little better here."

I shake my head. "Yeah, well, if we're really going to move on the new property, he's going to have to get used to the idea of letting our team do their jobs here with him overseeing everything. The next few weeks are a test run of that. He needs to take a step back."

"Uh huh," Tristan says, his eyes glinting behind his glasses.

"What?"

He laughs. "You know you're preaching to the choir here. It's Beckett you have to convince."

"Convince me of what?" Beckett asks in that deep, rumbling voice of his that makes submissives want to roll over and beg for him.

He makes a gimme gesture toward the whiskey bottle, and I top mine off before passing it over.

"Convince you not to be so damn controlling," I tease him, getting exactly the cold, hard, completely unimpressed look I expect for that comment.

"Not gonna happen," he states flatly, making me almost waste good whiskey by choking on it as I laugh.

"Yeah, I didn't think so," I admit once I can breathe again. All three of us enjoy the dynamics of a power exchange, but if anyone was born dominant, it's Beckett.

"I know you two aren't in here trying to figure out how to talk me out of being a Dom. So for real, what's up?" he asks, dropping into the third chair with a sigh.

"We were discussing the holidays," Tristan says. "You know Grandma Meg's expecting us."

Beckett raises an eyebrow. "Yes?"

I snort. "He means we were discussing your micromanaging tendencies, and trying to figure out what it's going to take to get you to actually leave this place alone for a few weeks, as planned."

Beckett's lips twitch, but he doesn't deny it. "Fair," he says with a shrug, pausing to drain his glass and pour himself another. "But someone's got to keep an eye on things around here. You won't believe who showed up tonight."

"If it was Ryder's latest submissive, that's old news," Tristan says, shooting me a look. "They're already over."

Beckett shakes his head, his face turning a little stormy. "It was Lana Reeves."

"*Motherfucker*," I curse, almost choking on my drink for the second time in a row.

"Lana?" Tristan asks in a tight voice as I grab a bar towel and clean myself up. "She's not a member here."

"Trial guest pass," Beckett growls, glaring at me. "I checked after she left."

"Fucking Christ," I say, scrubbing a hand over my face. "Are you serious? Maybe I should rethink how much I delegate."

My friends both snort at that, and I roll my eyes. Beckett may be a workaholic, but unlike him, I've never really had a problem delegating. I pull my weight, of course, but I also fully see the value of letting our staff do their jobs.

"I thought we agreed membership was something we'd continue to handle personally," Beckett says.

"I *do* handle it personally," I snap, as thrown as they both are at the idea of Lana Reeves showing up here.

We've known her since she was in pigtails, and her brother, our fourth brother-from-another-mother, would fucking kill us if he found out.

"But that's full membership," I go on a little more calmly, reminding myself that these two are not my enemy. I'd take a fucking bullet for either one of them. We're all on the same side here. "Trial applications are a step below that, and Benny handles those. But he knows our requirements. Hell, he's even stricter about enforcing them than we are."

Beckett stares at me hard for another second as he considers my words. Benny, the manager in training that the three of us personally vetted, isn't the type to get sloppy, and we all know it.

Finally, Beckett huffs out a breath and nods. "Yeah. On paper, she passes all our security checks. It's understandable that she was allowed in."

"But this is *Lana*." Tristan's voice is still strained. "Did she... play with anyone while she was here?"

"No," Beckett says, a muscle in his jaw ticking.

Tristan visibly relaxes, and I'm right there with him. Something obviously went down though, because Beckett still looks like he wants to take a flogger to someone without a safe word.

"What happened?" Tristan asks, idly rubbing at some of the ink on his left arm—a swirl of color that covers a few of the thicker scars from the accident that almost killed him years ago.

Beckett tells us about his encounter with Lana in short, precise sentences, his irritation with the whole thing bleeding through loud and clear.

I get why he's so on edge about it. All three of us have always been protective of her. Maybe even more than her own brother.

My private opinion is that it's because both Tristan and Beckett have always had a bit of a thing for her. Not that they could ever act on it, of course. Caleb would end them, for one thing. And besides, none of us can offer Lana the kinds of things she deserves, so it's a moot point.

I've never asked either of my friends how they feel about her, and I've definitely never admitted my own attraction to her out loud. It's better this way... even if it *has* been low-key torture to see her shackled to the slimy, waspish piece of shit she started dating once she moved out here to L.A.

"Wade didn't deserve her," Tristan says, unknowingly echoing my thoughts.

"No fucking shit," Beckett grits out. "But she also didn't deserve to be dumped by him like he didn't appreciate what he fucking had, either."

"What did he do?" I demand.

Beckett looks murderous for a moment, then sighs, shaking his head. "I don't know exactly how it went down, but it couldn't have been pretty."

My hands close into fists without me meaning to. I don't know what exactly Beckett saw on Lana's face when she told him about it, but I can imagine. She's always felt things too deeply, wearing her heart on her sleeve for anyone to see who's willing to look.

I'm pretty sure it's part of the reason we all feel as protective as we do. She's like a rare jewel, a ray of fucking sunshine, and she should be cherished and treasured at all costs.

None of which that Wade fucker ever seemed to understand.

"I never liked him," I admit. "And if he fucking hurt her..."

"If he did, it's no wonder she's rebounding or rebelling or whatever it is that brought her here tonight," Tristan finishes for me. "Isn't that what people do when they get shit on by an ex?"

Probably, not that the three of us relationship-averse people would know. Still, while Tristan's point is valid, it's not really the direction *my* thoughts had gone.

Not that I don't think they're both right there with me when it comes to the lengths we'd go to when it comes to taking care of anyone who does Lana wrong.

And privately, I have to wonder if that's part of why she kept it to herself.

All three of us have made it a point to keep tabs on her ever since she moved to the city. Keeping it low key, but making it clear to her that she's not alone out here. That all three of us will always have her back. But just as low key has been her obvious desire to make it out here—away from the constant oversight of the parents who were always up in her business back east—on her own.

"I wish she'd fucking told us that the piece of shit had ended things with her sooner," I grumble anyway. "I don't like the idea of her..."

I flounder for a second. What, on her own?

Actually, I do like that idea. Much better than dating Wade Bradshaw.

Obviously, I don't like the idea of her here at Radiance though, becoming the plaything of one of our members. None of us do, even though that's literally why we created a safe place for people in the lifestyle to participate in consensual kink.

But Caleb's little sister is different. And even if I'm not willing to look too deeply into why that is, I know something else the three of us can agree on.

"We should do something about this," I say, meeting Tristan's eyes, then Beckett's.

"Deny her membership?" Tristan asks dryly.

Beckett's huffs a half laugh. "I think he meant we should make sure she's okay after the breakup."

I nod. Sure. That's what I meant.

At least, it's all I'm ever going to admit to.

3

LANA

I GLANCE AT THE PRETENTIOUS, ornate wall clock hanging over the door to my boss's office, my pencil tapping on the edge of my desk. Ten more minutes until I can officially step away for an hour.

As if summoned by my glance, my boss's door swings open.

"Any word on the Wallington case, Lana?" he asks, striding across the room to loom over my desk.

I sit up a little straighter, scooting a file folder over the edge of my planner to hide the sketches I've been doodling. Not because I think Mr. Sanders will either notice or care, but a lifetime of listening to my parents demeaning comments about my "useless hobby" didn't only kill the ambition I had when I was younger to be an artist, they left a permanent emotional scar that I doubt will ever be exorcized.

Just one of many, but I'm working on that.

I push away the thoughts of exactly how I tried to work on that last night when I went to Radiance, and focus on what my boss just asked me.

"I forwarded their counsel's latest filings to your inbox this morning," I remind him, doing my best not to let my eyes stray back to the clock while he's hovering like this. "Would you like me to print out a hard copy for you as well?"

"Please do," he says with an impatient frown that has me stifling a sigh.

Of course he wants a hard copy. He's not *that* old, he's a friend of my father's who was in the same class at Harvard as Dad was, but apparently, since Mr. Sanders' family started this law firm back when dinosaurs still roamed the earth, it means he only trusts paper documents.

In triplicate.

He starts rattling off a list of tasks he needs me to take care of after my lunch break, and I can't resist. I glance at the clock again.

Two more minutes until my hour of freedom.

And yes, I'm very aware of the fact that me looking forward to lunch as much as I am, when the only thing I have waiting for me is a bland, unseasoned chicken breast and some equally boring steamed vegetables, pretty much says everything about how fulfilling I find working here as an executive assistant.

It doesn't matter how prestigious my employer is, or how pleased my parents are that I landed a job with what they consider "potential." The work is completely uninspiring, and being here means constantly worrying about living up to all the same standards my parents always held me to.

All the ones that make me feel like I'm slowly drowning in a sea of conformity.

But just because I don't love what I do for a living doesn't mean I'm not good at it.

"Are you getting all this, Lana?" Mr. Sanders asks, with a pointed look at my planner.

"Yes, sir," I say, dutifully flipping to a clean page and listing out his requests, even though I've already got most of them already accounted for in my online schedule. "I'll take care of it."

"See that you do. Especially since you'll be taking extra time off this month."

A lifetime of hiding my real emotions serves me well, and I manage to give him a bland smile. I may not love my job, but I do want to keep it. And I also understand exactly what that takes, including all the office politics that make me want to bury my face in a pillow and scream sometimes.

"Thank you for authorizing my vacation days, sir."

The vacation days that I've earned, per company policy, and almost never take. And yet of course he's made it an issue. Especially after I let it slip that part of the reason I put in for as much time off as I did was because I won't be flying back east, but driving.

I guess he sees it as a weakness, and it probably is. Still, I've been terrified of flying ever since the one and only time my parents forced me onto a plane when I was younger, then handed me off to a flight attendant to "deal with" when I started to have a panic attack. And since it's bad enough that I'm going to have to spend the holidays with them, there's no way I'm planning on trying to overcome that fear to get back there even faster.

"Yes, well, be sure to wish your father a merry Christmas from Martha and me," Mr. Sanders says with a distracted smile. "I'm sure he and your mother are pleased to be hosting you and Mr. Bradshaw this year."

My smile almost drops at the mention of my ex, but I hold it together out of habit.

"Actually, Wade won't be able to join me," I murmur, not really expecting my boss to push for more information but dreading the chance all the same. Wade does travel in the same circles as the Sanders and my parents, after all. It's why they like him so much.

It's also why I haven't been able to tell mine the truth yet. They know he's not coming for Christmas, of course, but I haven't admitted to them that we broke up. I just don't want to deal with their disappointment in me. Again. As always.

I nod along, making appropriately encouraging sounds, as Mr. Sanders thankfully gets back to business and wraps up the long list of assignments for me. At least half of which—like handling his dry cleaning—are definitely not in my job description, but still expected.

Thankfully, it doesn't actually take that much of my attention to follow along, though. After last night's embarrassingly disappointing end to my big attempt to explore my options at Radiance, the reminder that I wasn't good enough for Wade, either, stings more than I'd like it to after all this time.

The man asked me to marry him. And even if saying yes to him felt a little bit like I was sinking under a heavy weight, it was also really validating in ways I'm not sure I'm proud of to know that someone like him wanted me forever.

Until he didn't, of course.

He broke it off only a few weeks later, after I found out—

Well, I don't want to think about *that* right now, either. It's just one more thing I'm not ready to share with my family. Although in the case of my engagement to Wade, at least I dodged that bullet.

Sure, they'll be disappointed when I finally have to confess that we're not together anymore, but we were going to announce the engagement at Christmas, since both our parents are back in New Hampshire. This way, at least, mine will never realize how close I came to making them proud by marrying the man they practically hand-picked for me, only to fail once again.

"I'll be sure it's waiting on your desk when I get back from lunch," I tell Mr. Sanders as he ends his monologue with another request for a hard copy of the latest filings in the Wallington case.

"Good. See that you do," he says crisply, as if I need the reminder.

I'm always on top of things with my job. *Always.* But I shake off my irritation as he walks away, because I'm finally free. At least for an hour.

And honestly, after I got over my hurt at how abruptly Wade dumped me, I have to admit that *finally free* is also how I feel now that he's out of my life.

It definitely left me reeling at the time, and it took me a little bit to find my bearings after the path I'd been following all my life— well, sort of just plodding along on, really—suddenly blew up around me with no warning. But with the distance between me and my family limiting our contact and Wade out of the picture, I realized I could just be *me* for once.

As soon as I figure out exactly who that is, of course.

I head to the pretty little rooftop alcove that gets too much wind but has a fantastic view of the city, and unpack my low calorie lunch, munching through the sandwich as I stare out over the valley. I've had a lot of time to think about all the ways I want to reinvent myself over the last few months, and last night was supposed to be a part of that.

It's pretty obvious that if I'm going to explore kink, I'm not going to be able to do it at Radiance, though. The thought leaves me feeling just as embarrassed and dejected as I did last night when Beckett sent me off in a car instead of ravishing me the way he would have if fantasies actually came to life. But that's the problem with looking too closely at fantasies in the hard light of day. They really don't hold up.

"Kind of like these," I say with a little chuckle as I poke at the vegetables that I steamed last night, causing them to fall apart on my fork.

I sigh and shove them back into my lunch container, deciding to just skip it. Or maybe head down to the cute little coffee shop on the ground floor and treat myself to a cinnamon muffin?

Before I can decide whether to break my diet or not, my phone pings with an incoming message, saving my waistline.

"But not my sanity," I whisper under my breath in a sing-song voice when I see that it's from my sister.

> VIVIAN: Please remember that we all agreed to wear red for the family Christmas photo. Carmine, not scarlet. A photographer will be coming to the party on Christmas Eve, so pack accordingly.

I roll my eyes. "We" didn't decide anything. My mother dictated it. And I honestly don't know the difference between carmine and scarlet, other than vaguely thinking they're both darker shades of red. Or brighter, maybe?

Either way, I'm sure the dress I'm planning on bringing will be deemed the *wrong* shade, but finding something flattering for my shape is challenge enough. The red I found will just have to do.

> ME: Thanks for the reminder! I've already packed a red dress for the party. :)

Her reply comes back almost immediately.

> VIVIAN: A dress, Lana? Really? An accent piece in red is enough. You don't want to draw too much attention. Maybe go with black as your base, since it's more slimming.

"Damned if I do, damned if I don't," I murmur, doing my best to ignore the pang in my chest over yet another reminder that my choices are always the wrong ones. At least, according to my family.

> ME: Thanks for the advice. See you soon!

I brace myself for her next jab, but am pleasantly surprised when she lets it go.

> VIVIAN: I'm looking forward to it.

Not overflowing with sisterly love, but I'll take it. I'm even feeling a bit of a warm glow as I pocket my phone, gather up my lunch, and start to head back inside.

So of course my mother has to call and ruin it.

I almost don't answer, but good manners and familial expectations are too deeply ingrained in me. Besides, I've technically still got ten minutes of my lunch break left.

I sigh, then paste a smile on my face and turn back to face the gorgeous view as I answer. I read once that it's possible to hear a smile in your voice, so I figure I might as well stack the deck.

"Hi, Mom," I say brightly.

"Lana," she says, already sounding impatient. If I had to guess, she's definitely *not* smiling. "I know you'll be leaving soon, but I hope you haven't finished packing."

I make a non-committal sound and just let her talk. She just told me she hopes I haven't finished packing, and yet if I were to admit that I haven't, I'm sure she'd find something wrong with my procrastination.

"You need to find something presentable to wear in red," she goes on. "We'll have a photographer here for the annual Christmas party, and it's important that the whole family coordinate."

"I know, Mom. I've already got it covered."

She sniffs. "Do you? *Carmine* red, Lana. I don't want to have to pay extra to have the photos touched up. Although, if you've fallen off your diet—"

"Vivian just messaged me with a reminder," I cut in quickly, not sure I'm up to hearing where she's bound to go with that comment. "I'll be ready for the party."

"And Wade?" she asks, making me wince. "He should have something subtle, but it should tie in with the family theme. A tie in carmine would be too garish. But maybe a festive silk pocket square?"

I clear my throat. "Actually, remember when I told you that he probably wouldn't be able to make it this year?"

"No," she says sharply, and I can tell by the tone of her voice that she's not denying that she remembers, but refuting what she can tell I'm about to say. "He *must* join us. What would it look like if you were abandoned on Christmas by your beau?"

She titters out a laugh, and my stomach ties itself into a knot.

"Sorry, Mom," I murmur, clutching the phone a little too tightly as I stare at the horizon. "He really won't be able to make it, though."

It's smoggy today, because L.A. always is, but I can still see the ocean out there, which always uplifts my spirits. Maybe because it's an ocean that's three thousand miles away from everything my family expects of me.

"Well, you'll just have to talk to him," my mother says firmly. "Or maybe I should give his parents a call? I just ran into them at the country club last weekend. If I'd known he was thinking of changing his holiday plans, I would have brought it up then."

"No, Mom, really," I say quickly. "Please don't get involved. This is between Wade and me."

"Well, see that you don't embarrass us," she says after a slight pause. "Now, have you forwarded your flight itinerary to your father and me?"

I take a deep breath. Then another. "You know I plan on driving out."

She makes a disgruntled sound, annoyed as she always is when reality doesn't match her expectations or dares to inconvenience her. "It would be faster to fly, darling. Safer as well. It may be perpetual summer over there, but winter roads in the northeast are nothing to trifle with."

"I'll be fine. I learned to drive on those northeastern roads," I remind her.

"But you might be delayed," she says sharply. Then, after a beat, "You know we'd all hate for you to miss out on the festivities due to poor road conditions."

"I'll be there in time for Christmas, I promise."

"Well, we'll need you here a bit earlier than that," she huffs. "The party is, as always, on Christmas Eve, and we have several other social engagements we'd like you to be present for before then."

My chest feels constricted, like I can't draw a full breath. I rub it absently, silently reminding myself that it's only a few weeks. Well, really much less than that, if I count the time I'll actually have to stay under my parents' roof, with the drive time both ways.

"I've mapped it out and I'll stick to the main highways, Mom," I reassure her. "They'll be kept clear enough, and I'm already planning on leaving a few days early so I'll have buffer days of travel, just in case, okay?"

"Well, I suppose it has to be," she says, sounding exasperated but also a little distracted, like she's already mentally moving on to whatever is next on her agenda after this conversation. "But if you come to your senses, we'd be happy to book a flight for you, even if it means paying last minute prices."

"I'll keep it in mind," I say, just to keep the peace. She's never had any patience for my fear of flying, and that clearly isn't going to change any time soon.

But thankfully, after a few more reminders about holiday expectations, she lets me end the call.

I sigh, lowering my phone but not moving. I probably just have a few minutes of my break left, but I just need a moment to look out at the view. To see the whole world, or at least all of Los Angeles, spread out before me, and beyond that, the endless-looking ocean.

Free. That's what a long view like this makes me feel. And like I can breathe again.

"Are you planning on driving all the way to New Hampshire by yourself?" a voice behind me asks, making me jump.

I whip around, my heart in my throat, then immediately feel a flush rise in my cheeks.

It's Tristan.

"What are you doing here?" I blurt out, my heart pounding as he saunters toward me. He might not be as physically intimidating as Beckett or as traditionally handsome as Ryder, but the scars from his childhood accident speak to his strength, and the quiet, deliberate way he always holds himself, blue-gray eyes the exact color of the ocean I was just admiring, piercing me from behind the barrier of his stylish glasses, is sexier than I'm prepared to deal with in the middle of a random workday.

I swallow hard as he reaches me, stopping just out of arm's reach and smiling down at me with the same intensity he brings to everything he does.

"You're going to drive all that way by yourself?" he repeats.

"Um, yes?" I clear my throat, embarrassed that it sounded so uncertain. I go on quickly, hoping he won't notice how flustered he's making me. "I'm heading home for Christmas, and I'll be driving alone, but it will be fine."

He frowns a little, looking just as doubtful as my mother sounded.

The last thing I need is one more person who doesn't believe in me, so I go on the offensive before he can say anything about my travel plans. "What *are* you doing here? I don't think most of the people I work with even know that we have rooftop access, so I'm not sure how you found your way up here."

He grins, and my breath hitches. He really is unfairly attractive. "You don't think we can keep track of you?"

I bite my lip to hold in a smile. "You, Ryder, and Beckett? I knew it wasn't just coincidence that I'm always seeing you guys around the city."

He shrugs, but then his smile fades a little. "I came to make sure you're doing okay."

I swallow, the genuine concern in his eyes doing something to me. "Oh, um, yeah. Like you probably heard me tell my mother, I'm sure they'll keep the highways clear, and—"

He reaches out and brushes a stray piece of hair off my cheek, his fingers lingering for a moment and his touch rendering me mute. "No," he says after a moment, letting his hand drop. "Not with the drive. Beckett told us you were at the club last night. And about the breakup."

Shame rushes through me. I may have convinced myself I'm better off without Wade, but I can't help it. For this man, for all three of them, to know I wasn't enough for my ex is more embarrassing than I think I can stand.

But I have to, so I lift my chin and smile, putting on a brave face. "I'm fine."

Tristan looks at me so warmly that it almost feels like he's touching me again, even though his hands stay firmly at his sides this time. "You don't have to pretend for me."

For a split second, my chin trembles, and I want to tell him everything. All my doubts and insecurities. The hopes and dreams and how hard it feels to let myself actually reach for them.

That's way too much, though. I have no doubt at all that he cares about me. They all do. But he's just checking in, not inviting me to bare my soul to him.

I smile at him again, meaning it a little bit more even though it also takes more effort than usual to keep my true feelings under wraps.

"I really am fine," I tell him, daring to brush my fingers over the back of his hand. "It's been three months, and trust me, I don't miss Wade at all. But I *do* have to get back to work. My lunch break is over."

He stares at me hard, then gives me another small smile. "Okay. I'll let you go for now."

Before he can step back, I surprise both of us by lunging forward and hugging him. "Thank you," I whisper, meaning it. "I do appreciate you checking in."

"Always," he promises, only hesitating briefly before wrapping his arms around me too.

For a blissful moment, I'm completely surrounded by strength and acceptance, his lean, hard body molded to mine and his amber and spice scent filling my senses.

Then I go up on my toes to press a quick, chaste kiss to his cheek before making myself pull away. "Merry Christmas. Please say hello to your Grandma Meg for me."

"Hmm," he says, looking at me thoughtfully. Then he smiles. "I will."

Something about the way he's looking at me has me feeling a little too vulnerable and exposed, his gaze more perceptive than I know what to do with. So I mumble another comment about needing to get back to my desk, and hurry off.

But as I head back into work, I'm hit with a little rush of nerves. I was quick to brush off my mother's and Tristan's concerns about my upcoming trip, but the truth is that I've never done the long drive between here and New Hampshire by myself before, and I'm a little nervous about tackling it given the recent diagnosis I was given.

But then I take a deep breath and straighten my spine. Even if Wade couldn't handle my illness, I can. I have to. I'm finally figuring out who I want to be, tasting a hint of freedom for the first time in twenty-six years, and I'm not about to let anything stop me from reinventing myself.

The trip will be fine. Everything will be fine. It has to be.

All I have to do is make it through Christmas.

4
LANA

I PULL out a couple of sweaters that I never wear out here in California, a knot forming in my stomach as I carefully fold them and add them to the open suitcase on my bed.

"It's just clothing, Lana," I lecture myself, trying not to let myself dwell on the stifling feelings that heading home always brings up. There's no denying that there are sections of my closet I only touch when I have to head back east, though.

I know how my parents expect me to present myself, and it's just easier to go along with it than invite even more criticism. Of course, I'm sure they'll find something wrong with my wardrobe anyway.

My phone pings with a text, and I grimace a little when I scoop it up and see that it's from her.

"What, are you psychic now?" I mumble to myself as I swipe open the notification and tell my phone to read it to me.

> VIVIAN: We think Oliver might be lactose intolerant, so please avoid milk chocolate if you're bringing any treats for him. Dark is fine, though. Preferably at least 85% cocoa, for the antioxidant benefits.

I snort, shaking my head. My nephew is five. He doesn't need antioxidants. He needs sugar.

But I just send back a thumbs up.

Of course Vivian can't just leave it at that, though. She follows it up with a whole list of reminders and tips about what to bring and not bring. If I didn't already know that she was slowly but surely turning into a clone of our mother, I'd almost think Mom hacked her phone and was pranking me. Not that our mother would ever stoop to doing something like that, of course. She has no problem just lecturing me herself.

My phone pings a few more times while I finish packing, but I'm sure it's just more of the same, so I crank up some holiday music and sing along to try and push down my annoyance. Unlike me, Vivian has always seemed totally in line with our parents, living up to each and every one of their expectations with ease. I bet she's actually looking forward to spending the holidays at our family home.

Not that I'm completely dreading it. I do love my family, even if it feels like I have to walk on eggshells around them to avoid doing the wrong thing. It will be nice to see Caleb, though. I don't want to say I have a favorite sibling, but he's the golden child for a reason. Everyone loves my older brother, including me.

Everything always seemed to come easy to Caleb when we were all growing up. Not only did he have this great group of friends, but he did well in school too. Not as well as with sports, though.

He's always been athletic, and when his coaches started singling him out for his innate talent, my parents couldn't have been prouder. They were happy to let his academics play second fiddle, and they love that he's a professional hockey player now.

I just love that he's living his dream. Even Vivian is, I suppose, since the sum total of her goals and aspirations seem to be becoming the perfect politician's wife.

Not that her husband, Kyle, holds office, but he's the son of the mayor and it couldn't be any clearer that he's being groomed to follow in those footsteps.

I pull out the red dress I'm planning on wearing to my parents' annual party, biting back another sigh. It's actually quite flattering on me, but now I can't get my mother's and sister's comments out of my head.

No surprise. Unlike my siblings, I don't think I've ever made our parents proud in my life.

I grimace. Well, maybe when I started dating Wade. And even if breaking up with him currently feels like the best thing that could have happened to me, I know that when I eventually have to confess it to my family, it will just be one more way that I disappoint them.

One more area of life where I lag behind my golden siblings and fail to live up to the Reeves' family expectations.

"Annnnnd that's enough of that," I tell myself firmly, shaking out the dress and then carefully laying it out in my garment bag.

One visit home is not going to derail my quest to reinvent myself. I won't let it. Even if I'll never be exactly who my parents want me to be, I'm determined to become the person I want to be.

Besides, I may not be as enthusiastic as I should be about home for the holidays, but I do love Christmas.

"And if I have to be at that stuffy party full of uptight people, I'm going to do it in a loud, red dress that makes me feel like a queen," I murmur to myself as I zip up the garment bag and then look around to make sure I haven't forgotten anything.

I tuck an extra sketch pad into the side pocket of my suitcase, attach the garment bag to the handle, and park them both just inside the door to my apartment before heading back to my room for the bag of gifts I wrapped for my family.

A knock sounds as I pluck the bag from the closet, and I almost trip over my own feet in surprise as I head back to the door to answer it. I really haven't had time to make a lot of friends here in L.A. yet, and since I'm not expecting any delivery, for the life of me, I can't think who it might be.

My heart stutters a little when I pull open the door. Of course, the three men waiting on the other side of it have always made it do that.

"What are you guys doing here?" I ask, feeling unaccountably breathless.

Ryder and Tristan both grin at me, while Beckett stands with his arms crossed over his chest behind them.

"I've got that," Ryder says, plucking the bag of gifts out of my hand instead of answering my question.

Tristan's big body brushes up against mine in the doorway as he leans past me and grabs my packed suitcase from behind me. "Is this all of it?"

"All of what?"

"Everything you're taking."

It takes me a beat, but then I remember that I did mention this trip to him, the other day when he surprised me at work. Well, he overheard.

"Yes. Well, mostly," I say, snatching up my keys, purse, and headphones from the little table I keep by the front door. I jiggle the keys at him. "As you can see, I'm about to hit the road."

Ryder smirks. "So are we."

"And I'd really like to beat traffic on the 101," Beckett grumbles, making me feel guilty for a second before I remember that they're the ones who decided to stop by and see me on their way to wherever it is they're going.

"Come on then," Tristan says cheerfully, heading down the hallway with my suitcase.

"Wait," I say when Beckett turns and follows him, quickly locking up my apartment then hurrying after them. "Where are you guys going? You don't have to carry my stuff down. I—"

Ryder's low laughter from behind me makes me stumble. He steadies me with a hand to the small of my back. "Slow down, love. We're all headed to the same place. No one's going to leave without you."

My cheeks blaze at the endearment, but I ignore the little leap my heart takes when I hear it since that's just the way Ryder is. He's always been a charmer, and I have no doubt at all that any woman he speaks to is instantly his "love."

It's the other thing he said that piques my curiosity. "What do you mean we're all headed to the same place? The parking lot?"

He laughs again and urges me forward with the hand he still has on my back, the bag of gifts still tucked under his other arm. "No, to New Hampshire."

I stop completely, turning to face him. "But... what? You're all headed back home for Christmas too?"

He nods. "Yep, and you heard Beckett. We don't want to get stuck in traffic."

"Are you guys headed to the airport?"

He grins down at me as we catch up with the other two, standing next to Beckett's oversized SUV. Beckett is already in the driver's seat, and Tristan is in the process of wedging my suitcase into the back, beside three others.

"We're driving with you," Ryder says, tossing the bag of gifts he carried down for me in too, just before Tristan closes the back.

"But—" I start, my heart racing.

"No buts," Tristan cuts me off, opening the front passenger door. "You want shotgun?"

"I, um... wait. The three of you really want to drive all the way across the country with me?"

Tristan grins at me. "Absolutely."

"Sounds like a good time," Ryder adds, making butterflies erupt in my stomach.

Beckett leans toward the open door, sounding impatient. "You know Caleb would kill us if we let you travel alone, little menace. Now get in so we don't get stuck with the morning commuters."

My spirits droop a little at his gruff tone, but I scramble into the backseat after Ryder does, leaving the front to Tristan.

Of course they're just doing this for Caleb. I still can't find it in me to reject their offer though. And despite knowing that it's more of an obligation than an adventure for the three of them, I can't help feeling a little excited as we hit the freeway.

I'm still stunned it's happening at all, but a road trip with three hot men I may or may not have been secretly crushing on forever sounds infinitely less boring than driving on my own with nothing but audiobooks and podcasts for company. In fact, for the first time since making plans to head home for Christmas, I'm actually looking forward to the trip.

Well, this part of it, at least.

"What's got you looking so happy?" Ryder asks, nudging me with his shoulder.

I blush hard, happy beyond measure that he can't read my mind. Thankfully, he doesn't call me on it, moving right along without actually making me answer. As we head out of L.A., his warm, familiar banter puts me at ease, and if I can't help notice the warmth of his body radiating into mine from how close we're sitting, I'm the only one who has to know that.

"So, what were your holiday plans before you all decided to escort me back to New Hampshire?" I ask the three of them when there's a lull in the conversation.

Tristan turns around to grin at me. "I was going to end up there anyway. You know Grandma Meg wouldn't let me spend Christmas anywhere else."

His words are full of affection, and I can't help feeling a little jealous of how close he is with his grandmother. On the surface, I could say the same thing. My family won't let me skip out on spending the holidays with them, either. But I've known Grandma Meg practically my whole life, and she's the warmest, kindest person I know. I'd bet anything that Tristan's Christmas with her will be everything the holiday is meant to be.

"Don't you usually fly home?"

Tristan shrugs. "Sure, but this is a much more fun way to get back there."

I bite my lip, holding in a smile. Even knowing Caleb probably put them up to this, it's nice to hear.

"Were all of you already planning on heading back to New Hampshire?" I ask.

"No," Beckett says, his eyes trained on the freeway ahead of him. "I haven't been home for Christmas in... fuck. I don't know how many years."

"I'm sorry," I say with a wince, some of my good cheer evaporating. Hearing it doesn't really surprise me since I know he doesn't get along with his father. I just feel bad that I'm the reason he feels like he has to do this.

Beckett grunts, shrugging, and Tristan elbows him in the side. "Don't be an ass."

"What?" Beckett asks, his eyebrows scrunching together. "What are you talking about?"

Next to me, Ryder rolls his eyes. "I mean, I wasn't gonna go home for Christmas either, Beckett. It's a pointless holiday. But you don't hear me bitching about the road trip."

"I'm not bitching about the road trip," Beckett grunts.

They start to bicker, but I'm still stuck on what Ryder said.

"Pointless?" I blurt out, interrupting them.

Tristan snickers, and I see Beckett's eyebrows go up in the rearview mirror. Ryder just shrugs, though. "Uh, yeah? I mean, it's an over-commercialized excuse to profit by pulling on people's heartstrings. I'm not gonna fall for that."

I blink at him, aghast. "But Christmas is *wonderful*. It's the best holiday ever!"

He gives me a slow, teasing smile. "Oh? Give me one good reason."

"Christmas carols," I reply promptly. "They're cheery and fun and festive and nostalgic. You can't tell me you don't like any of them."

"Nope. None," he says, an amused note in his voice that makes it clear he's baiting me.

I don't care. I'm right, and I'll prove it. "Okay, what about... *All I Want For Christmas Is You?*"

I start humming the tune, then sing a few of the lyrics, ignoring the way my cheeks heat up when both Beckett's and Tristan's deep voices join in for the chorus.

Ryder grins. "Not ringing any bells."

I narrow my eyes. "*Jingle Bells?*"

"Not a fan."

"*Winter Wonderland?*"

"I'd prefer to stay indoors."

39

"In other words, sitting around a cozy fire with snow falling outside and the scent of cinnamon and pine in the air sounds good to you?" I ask triumphantly.

"Sure, but it doesn't have to be Christmas for that."

"Hot chocolate," I say, starting to tick off some of my favorite things about this time of year on my fingers. "Presents. Mince pie. Eggnog! Oh, and what about gingerbread? I can't think of a better cookie flavor, and Christmas is the only time anyone bakes it."

"Okay, fine. Those are all great things, and I can agree that they make December a fun month."

"Exactly!"

He smirks. "But you have to admit that a lot of them are a little more about the season and less about the holiday itself. I just don't see any reason to get excited about it. It's why I don't usually head back home."

"There wouldn't be a season without the holiday! Besides, surely you've gone home with a girlfriend for Christmas or something. Even if you're determined to be a Grinch, you wouldn't have imposed that on any of your exes."

He laughs. "I don't have to. I don't really do relationships. So, nope. No one's ever dragged me home to meet the family for Christmas."

My heart squeezes with something a lot like disappointment at his easy dismissal of being in a relationship, but that's silly, so I ignore it. I've got better things to do than pine over men I can't have.

Like help Ryder see the light about my favorite time of year.

"Come on, back me up here, guys," I say to Tristan and Beckett.

Beckett just snorts, but Tristan grins at me. "I'm with you. I've always liked Christmas. The world just feels a little friendlier this time of year."

"Exactly! I think it brings out the best in people." I grimace without meaning to, thinking of my own family, and quickly add, "Well, most people."

"Not to mention that it's the best eating you'll get all year," Tristan says helpfully.

Ryder scoffs. "Are you forgetting about Thanksgiving?"

"Oh please," Tristan says, adjusting his glasses. "I'm not saying Thanksgiving isn't great, but it's only one meal, and it's basically always the same food. Turkey. Gravy. Stuffing."

"Pumpkin pie," Beckett rumbles from the driver's seat. "Sweet potatoes."

I bounce in my seat. I can't help it. "Oh, don't even get me *started* on sweet potatoes. My mom makes this sweet potato casserole for Christmas every year that's to die for."

"You've had one sweet potato casserole, you've had them all," Ryder says with a smirk, clearly trying to bait me again.

And, once again, it totally works.

"No," I tell him earnestly, adjusting my seat belt so I can turn toward him and resting a hand on his arm as I stare into his eyes. "You don't understand. This is the kind of casserole that makes you want to have its babies. It has marshmallows and brown sugar and spices. I can never convince her to give me the recipe, but the smell alone is divine, and it literally tastes like heaven."

"Literally?" Ryder teases me. "And what, literally, does heaven taste like?"

I close my eyes, my mouth watering as I sink into the memory. "Like warm, gooey marshmallows. Like sweet, sticky brown sugar. Like all the spices from the holidays wrapped up in one perfect dish."

I sigh happily, my whole body tingling with the visceral memory of sliding that first forkful into my mouth every year.

"Well, damn," Tristan says in a husky tone that has me snapping my eyes back open.

All three of the men are staring at me. Even Beckett's eyes flick back and forth from the road to the rearview mirror, and I swallow, feeling suddenly self-conscious.

I may have... moaned a little while describing it. But in my defense, it really *is* that good.

Ryder clears his throat, and I realize I'm still groping him. Or resting a friendly hand on his arm, at least.

I snatch it back, embarrassed. "Um, anyway, what are your favorite holiday foods?"

"Pretty sure it's sweet potato casserole now," he tells me, giving me a heated look that makes me want to squirm in my seat.

Then he blinks, clearing his throat again, and looks away. "We over the state line yet, Beckett?"

I bite back a smile. It sounds an awful lot like the grown-up version of "are we there yet."

Beckett just grunts in response, then suddenly veers onto an off ramp, the momentum flinging me against Ryder's body.

"Gotta gas up," he says, his eyes flicking back to us just once as Ryder helps me right myself.

Tristan raises his eyebrows. "We did that on the way to Lana's house. We can't have burned through more than a quarter of the tank yet."

"We're taking a break," Beckett says gruffly. "I think we all need to get out of this fucking car for a second and quit thinking about fucking casseroles, okay?"

My cheeks burn with embarrassment again, but Tristan just chuckles, shaking his head. "Ah, gotcha. Yeah. Let's do that. I'm sure the fresh air will do all of us some good right now."

I hope he's right, because we've still got a *lot* of miles to go to get to New Hampshire.

5

BECKETT

I PULL into the first gas station I see off the highway, and I have the door open and one foot on the asphalt before the engine stops ticking.

I surreptitiously adjust myself in my jeans, biting back a groan. Fucking hell. Listening to Lana make those noises about a damn casserole was driving me crazy.

"You actually gonna fill the tank up?" Tristan asks, smirking at me over the hood of my SUV. "The whole, what, half gallon of gas we burned?"

I flip him off, and he laughs, then pats the hood and turns to head into the convenience store attached to the gas station.

"I'll grab some beef jerky," he calls over his shoulder.

Tristan's not wrong that we don't really need gas, but I stick the nozzle into the SUV anyway, gritting my teeth as I try to get my cock to go back down.

Ever since the night she came to the club, I've been having a hard time getting thoughts of Lana out of my head, and it's starting to become a problem. The kind of problem that's making it difficult to remember she's Caleb's little sister.

"Do you want any snacks, Beckett?" she calls out from the other side of SUV, walking backward toward the convenience store with a wide smile on her face that brings out the tiny dimple in her left cheek.

I shake my head, waving her off, and next to her, Ryder laughs.

"He's lying," I hear him tell Lana as she turns back around and follows him into the store. "He'll be jonesing for some beef jerky in ten miles."

I grunt. He's got me there, but beef jerky isn't the problem when it comes to jonesing for things.

Lana was just so fucking sexy the night she came into Radiance, all wide-eyed and breathless. It caught me off guard, and I fucking hate being caught off guard.

But not as much as I hated seeing that man put his hands on her.

That shit sent the kind of fury racing through me that I haven't felt since my teens. And when I had her boxed in against the wall, trying to get her to leave, it took all of my self-control not to do something very, very stupid. She was gazing up at me through her lashes, and the look on her face... *fuck.*

It was far too easy to picture that same look, but with her on her knees for me.

The gas pump clicks, my tank full, and I shake off the image in my head. She'd be fucking gorgeous like that, but it doesn't matter. She's still as off limits as she's always been.

I head into the store for a quick restroom pitstop, passing my friends as they head back out with enough road trip snacks for the next five hundred miles. I snort, shaking my head as I try to ignore the sound of Lana's laugh. Ryder, naturally, is still teasing her while Tristan watches with a small smile on his face.

The three of us have always been united in our desire to look out for her. I don't even want to think about what my friends would have to say if they knew how fucking attracted I am to her, not to mention the fact that Caleb would kill me.

I've done my best to shove it aside for years, but it's never gone away.

And it should.

It needs to.

There's no fucking way I can have her. And even if I could, I shouldn't. *Wouldn't.* I don't do attachments, and I have no interest in all the things a woman like Lana wants and deserves.

Like a family.

"Jesus," I mutter, staring at myself in the mirror after doing my business. "Get a fucking grip."

I shake my head and brush those thoughts away, washing my hands and heading back out to the SUV.

Tristan's already behind the wheel with Ryder next to him, leaving me no choice but to get in the back with Lana.

"Got enough room?" she asks me with a smile, resting her hand on my leg for a second.

"It's fine," I say curtly, the soft weight of her touch almost undoing all my earlier efforts to get my cock under control.

I move her hand back to her own lap, annoyed with myself. I usually have impeccable control.

Ryder turns around to face Lana from the front seat, sending a brief pulse of gratitude through me for keeping her attention diverted. I stare out the front windshield, ignoring her soft laughter as he teases her.

At least, until he brings up her visit to the goddamn sex club.

"Was Radiance your first choice, or have you been doing some comparison shopping with the other clubs around town?" he asks.

"Oh my god," she groans, covering her face as her skin flushes pink. "Can we please just all forget that happened?"

I'm pretty sure that's impossible. I sure as shit haven't been able to.

"What?" Ryder raises his brows. "Are you saying we've got competition?"

"No, no, of course Radiance was my first choice," Lana says, laughing despite her obvious embarrassment.

She's so fucking sweet. Always has been.

"Why, um, why did the three of you decide to open it?" she asks. "I've always kind of wondered that."

I'm pretty sure she means she wants to get the conversation off of her recent visit.

"It was Tristan's idea," I say, happy to go along with avoiding that topic and more than happy to throw my friend under the bus to make that happen.

Tristan meets her eyes in the rearview mirror with an easy smile. "That's right. I mean, I knew we all had an interest in kink—"

"Sure, you knew *eventually*," Ryder cuts in with a laugh before turning back to Lana. "We each fell into kink separately, and it wasn't until a certain night that included far too many shots of Patron that we all realized we had that in common."

"So the three of you, um, all have the same kinks?" Lana asks hesitantly.

"No," Tristan says without elaborating, "but it's a big enough part of each of our lives that it made sense to open a place like Radiance."

Lana smiles. "I have to admit, it's not what I would have guessed you'd do. I always thought... well, I guess I just never imagined a sex club."

"You thought I'd aim for a professional hockey career, like Caleb?" Tristan asks, a hint of strain in his voice that I only recognize because of how well I know him.

Empathy flashes over Lana's face. "You seemed to really love it," she says softly.

"I did," he says, his smile turning a little easier. "And you're right, I definitely had NHL aspirations back when Caleb and I used to play together. There was just no way after the accident, though." He grimaces, reflexively rubbing at some of his scars. "I could still play, and I do still like to get out on the ice sometimes, but the rods in my leg are never going to be as stable as they'd need to be for me to go pro."

He hardly ever talks about the car accident that took his mother's life and left him to be raised by his Grandma Meg. I know he worked his fucking ass off in rehab to regain mobility, and I respect the hell out of him for making that happen. And Lana probably doesn't realize it, but it says a lot that he's opening up to her even this much.

"Anyway, after I made peace with giving up hockey, I needed something else to focus on."

"And you chose a business degree," Ryder cuts in, rolling his eyes. "Fucking boring."

Lana laughs. "Well, I'm sure it serves you well as a business owner, right?"

"Right," Tristan says, grinning at her in the rearview mirror. "I wasn't actually sure what I was going to do with it at first, but—"

"But then after trying to demonstrate some knots for us after half a dozen shots of Tequila..." Ryder waggles his eyebrows.

"Knots?" Lana asks.

"Shibari." Tristan brakes a little when a Prius changes lanes in front of us with no blinker. "Asshole," he mutters before glancing back at Lana in the rearview mirror again. "It's Japanese rope bondage."

"I know." Lana's cheeks go pink again. "I mean, I've... I've seen some videos. It looks, um, interesting?"

She bites her lip, that pink flush spreading down her neck, and fucking hell. Bondage isn't really my kink, but I'd suddenly give anything to see her lush body wrapped in Tristan's silky ropes.

I subtly adjust my cock again, glad her attention is so fully taken by Tristan at the moment.

"So the three of us basically came up with a business plan—"

"The night you were drinking Tequila?" she asks with a cheeky grin.

Ryder laughs. "You know it. We've still got the napkins these two sketched out the initial ideas on."

He jerks a thumb in my direction, and Lana looks over at me. "So you jumped right in?"

I clear my throat. "Tristan asked for my opinion about opening a club. I heard him out, and just pointed out that the three of us don't just have different kinks, we also have different strengths that could all benefit the venture if it was something we wanted to get into together."

"Which of course we did," Tristan says, glancing over his shoulder at me for a second to shoot me a smile.

Ryder laughs. "Pointed out? Quit underplaying it, Beckett. Those napkins are basically a full-blown business plan. Tristan knew what he was doing when he brought the idea up to you. Business is in your blood."

That's true, and of course I'm glad my background has helped make Radiance successful for the three of us. I still scowl at him though, because I have no interest in being associated with my father's business empire and could do without the reminder of how I earned my business education.

Not the degree I eventually got, but the *real* education.

Not that I can ever forget the weight of expectation I grew up with. It was always understood that I'd carry on the family business. I was groomed for it from birth, and it really is in my blood. But no matter how much I excelled, there was never any pleasing the asshole whose name I carry.

My father's relentless criticism and general toxicity were a dark weight I shrugged off as soon as I was old enough to make my way in the world, and cutting ties with him and everything he represents is the best thing I've ever done.

"Well, that's probably useful," Lana says gently, resting a soft hand on my arm for a second.

The touch zings right to my dick, and I grunt, subtly moving away from her. "Sure. I needed something to build toward and work on," I say with a shrug that completely downplays how fucking important the club has been in my life. "I was kind of aimless after turning down a position with my father's company."

It's a pretty tame way of describing the brutal argument between us that finally led to me walking out and never looking back, but Lana doesn't need to hear all that. Hell, the gory details aren't something I've dumped on Tristan, Ryder, or Caleb, either.

In my experience, some things are best dealt with by shoving them out of sight and keeping them permanently out of mind.

The look Lana gives me almost makes me think she sees some of that anyway, and for a second, I have the strangest feeling that she's using her artist's eye to see right into my fucking soul.

Then she smiles at me and the tension breaks.

48

"What about you, Ryder?" she asks, leaning forward just enough that the soft weight of her thigh presses against mine, activating my cock again.

He grins. "You don't think I could let these two start something up without me, do you? Can you imagine? They both take life too damn seriously. It would have been no fun at all if I hadn't thrown in with them to get the club off the ground."

My lips tilt up a little without my permission. Ryder isn't exactly wrong.

"It definitely wouldn't be the same without you," Tristan says to him, chuckling. "Best choice I ever made, going into business with you two."

"Aw, you *lurve* us," Ryder jokes, batting his eyelashes in an exaggerated way that makes Lana laugh.

Even though he's joking, he's right. These two are closer to me than brothers, and we've seen each other through a lot over the years.

We've had each other's backs through all of it, so starting a business together was easy, despite our differences. Actually, maybe because of them. We all bring something different to the table, balancing each other out in ways that only strengthen what we've built together.

And it certainly helps that kink is a shared interest we all have. Radiance is more than a business venture; it's something each of us is passionate about. It gives us all purpose. And I'd like to think that creating a safe space for the lifestyle makes a difference in the lives of our members too.

"So, um, if you don't all have the same kinks..." Lana starts to ask, her face flushed.

Ryder smirks. "Are you asking us what we're into?"

"That's probably pretty personal," she says, fooling no one. "I just wondered, um, how you decided what to have at the club."

"Radiance caters to all kinds of clientele," Tristan tells her before Ryder can jump in to tease her over her interest again. "And you're right. It is really personal. What gets you off is unique to you, but as long as it's safe, sane, and consensual, we try to provide an environment where our members can explore it."

She bites her lip, her face still a beautiful shade of pink, and nods rapidly. "Oh, that makes sense, and I've only heard good things."

"Only *heard* them?" Ryder quips, still half-turned in his seat so he can face her. "You mean to say that Beckett found you the other night before you got to do any exploring of your own?"

"Ryder," I growl, this entire conversation testing my control. The last thing I need to do is have Lana tell us in detail what it was she was hoping to find at our club. My mind is far too eager to supply images of what could have been, all on its own.

Ryder just laughs, of course, but thankfully, he also turns the conversation in a different direction. Toward me.

"Take Beckett here," he tells Lana. "I'm sure it won't surprise you to hear that he's a Dom."

I glare at him, silently daring him to out my kinks to her and see what happens.

Lana's tinkling laugh derails my anger, though. It's a beautiful sound, and it's the first time I've heard her sound truly carefree in quite a while.

"Yeah, no, that's no surprise," she agrees, grinning at Ryder. Then she rests her hand on my arm for a moment, sending me a warm look that I'm not sure what to do with. "But I'm sure if he wanted me to know his kinks, he'd be the one to tell me," she says softly, speaking to Ryder but still looking at me.

I grunt an affirmative, and she gives me a small smile that brings out her dimple.

"I enjoy Shibari," Tristan says. "Among other things."

"It's always the quietest ones who are the most kinky," Ryder says, nudging him.

The two banter for a minute, Ryder teasing Tristan about what an ideal playground the club is for his voyeuristic tendencies, but I can't take my eyes off Lana. She's listening avidly, her breathing quick and shallow. The color on her creamy skin is pure temptation, and I discipline myself hard to shut down thoughts of touching it. Licking it. Tasting the heat that I can feel radiating off her curvy body as she unconsciously sways closer to hear more.

"What did you think of the club when you stopped in?" Tristan asks her, looking back at her again in the mirror.

"I... didn't see much," she admits, "but it looked really nice. Very upscale but welcoming. I thought it might be more intimidating, but I, um, I could see myself spending time there."

She shoots him a look that makes me grit my teeth and force my gaze away. "No," I snap.

"What Beckett means to say," Ryder inserts with a grin, "is thank you. We've all worked our asses off to make it into what it is, and it's great to hear that you felt comfortable there."

"I mean, I wouldn't go as far as to say *comfortable*," she says quickly, laughing softly. "But that's on me, not the club. It really is nice, though."

"Beckett gets a lot of the credit for that," Ryder says. "We all play our part, but he's really made it his baby."

I shrug. "It's easier to take care of than a real baby. Not that I plan on having any."

Lana glances over at me, her eyebrows shooting up as a look I can't interpret crosses her face. "You don't want to have kids?"

"No." I clear my throat, suddenly feeling a little awkward. "Do you?"

She beams, her expression brightening. "Yeah, I think so. I've always thought it would be amazing to be a mom."

I nod, not surprised in the least. It's just one more reason to kill off, or at least quarantine, the interest I've got in her. Lana is one of the best people I know, and unlike my own piece of shit father, she'd be a fantastic parent.

I spent plenty of time at her house when I was younger, hanging out with Caleb, and from what I saw of their parents, most of Lana's sweetness is all her, not something she inherited from her folks.

That's not always the case, though. Most of the time, the apple doesn't seem to fall far from the tree, and there's no way I'd ever put a child at risk of having *me* for a father. Not when I have no way of knowing if I'd be any better at it than my old man.

Thankfully, before the conversation can go any further down the current path, Lana's phone rings. I relax a little, thankful for a break from talking about things that I'd rather not think about, but then tense up again when she pulls it out and frowns at the screen.

"Problem?" I ask, my protective instincts roaring to life.

She looks up at me with a quick smile that doesn't reach her eyes. "Oh, no. It's nothing. I mean, it's my mom. It's fine."

That sounds an awful lot like protesting too much, but she answers the call before I can decide what to do about it.

"Hi, Mom... no, I'm on the road already... yes, I remembered... I packed it... uh huh... yeah... yes, I already... okay."

I can't hear what Mrs. Reeves is saying, but from Lana's side of the conversation, it sounds like the woman isn't letting her get a word in edgewise. And from the look on Lana's face, I'd guess that she's either berating her or rattling off a list of demands and reminders that Lana neither wants nor needs.

Another pattern I remember well from when we were all younger.

Lana shrinks in on herself as the conversation drags on, her side of it devolving mostly into versions of "yes" and quiet sighs.

She picks at a napkin from the gas station we stopped at as the miles pass, and I nudge her hand, then pass her a ballpoint pen I keep on me for business.

She flashes me a quick smile that brings back a hint of her usual exuberance, and just like I suspected, immediately starts doodling as her mother drones on in her ear. It's something I remember her doing a lot when she was younger, and it soothes some of my protectiveness to at least be able to provide her that small outlet.

When the conversation finally ends, she hangs up and tosses her phone onto the seat next to her and blows out a breath. "Sorry, guys."

Tristan looks back at her. "For what?"

She shrugs, looking embarrassed. "Um, the four of us were talking, and..."

52

"Mothers," Ryder finishes for her when she trails off, loading the word enough that she finally laughs.

"I know, right?" She shakes her head as she wads up the napkin and tosses it on top of her phone.

I pick it up as the two of them banter a little, flattening it out and smoothing it over my knee.

Lana has always been artistic, but damn. The call couldn't have lasted more than a few minutes, but the sketch she whipped out is beautifully done. Obviously fast and with a distinct style that I've got no name for—but whatever it is, it makes the image feel vibrant and alive. With just a few lines, she brought to life the moment we all stopped at the gas station.

It's like a snapshot, but better.

More personal.

"You gonna keep this?" I ask, running one of my fingers over the image.

She glances down at it, surprise on her face. "That?" She laughs, waving a hand at it. "Definitely not. It's nothing. Just put it with the trash from our snack wrappers. Oh! But here's your pen back."

I take it from her, but when she looks away, I slip the napkin into my pocket along with the pen.

It's not nothing. I'm not sure what it *is*, but "nothing" is definitely a word that doesn't apply. Not when it comes to Lana Reeves.

6

LANA

"Is THAT IT?" I ask when Tristan puts on the blinker for an exit a few hours later, peering at the brightly lit sign for a familiar hotel chain.

"Sure is," he says, making me sigh in relief.

Ryder catches my eye and raises his eyebrow, obviously having heard.

"Tired of us already?" he jokes.

I grin at him. Nothing could be further from the truth. "Just ready to stretch my legs."

Next to me, Beckett huffs out a breath and if I'm not mistaken, actually almost smiles.

"Tell me about it," he says, not quite grumbling.

I bite my lip as I let my eyes shamelessly wander over his huge frame. He's got a point, and I'm sure we're all more than ready to stop for the night.

This road trip has already been more fun than I'd hoped for when I thought I'd be doing it with just my favorite audiobooks for company. But still, being trapped in a car with the three of them for so many hours has been its own form of torture.

Spending so much time in the back seat, pressed up against one or the other of their large bodies, has had me fighting not to notice how good they each smell. And after the conversation drifted to kink, raising the temperature in the car by several degrees, I need a little breathing room for sanity's sake.

After we park outside the hotel, Beckett steps up to handle the check-in process. As he turns away from the desk, he hands me a little plastic card.

"Here's your key, little menace. You're in room 1304."

"Just me?" I blush when the question makes him give me a strange look.

He nods. "We're in 1306 and 1308. So we'll be close if you need anything."

"That's great," I say quickly to hide my embarrassment over ever thinking we'd somehow all be rooming together. Heck, even with the three of them, they're splitting into two rooms, so of course it's crazy of me to have been low-key expecting, or at least hoping, that we'd end up in some kind of intimate sleeping situation.

As we all head to the elevators, I notice the guys talking quietly amongst themselves about something that sounds like it has to do with their club.

"Ten minutes?" Tristan asks the other two as we reach our floor.

Beckett is already headed down the hall, but Ryder nods at him, then slings an arm around my shoulders when he catches my curious look.

"We've got a little business to do," he explains. "A video conference we scheduled with some of our key employees, since we left L.A. earlier than expected."

I stop in my tracks. "You did what? But I thought you said you were already headed back to New Hampshire! Please tell me you didn't all take extra time off just because Caleb guilted you into looking out for me."

"We didn't all take extra time off just because Caleb guilted us into looking out for you," he quotes me, making me laugh and lightly punch his arm.

He grins down at me, giving my shoulders a quick squeeze before dropping his arm and moving farther down the hall, turning to walk backward as he moves away from me, so that he's still facing me.

"Yes, we were already planning on heading to New Hampshire," he says, easing some of my guilt. "We just moved the date up a little. No big deal, but this meeting might take us a while, so don't wait for us, okay? Go grab yourself some dinner if you want."

"Oh." I tamp down a surge of disappointment. "By myself?"

Ryder spreads his arms with an apologetic look. "Or order in if you're too tired? Because you know Beckett will turn into a drill sergeant in the morning and insist we hit the road early. He doesn't just reserve his Dom tendencies for the club."

Beckett can't defend himself since he's already gone into one of the rooms, and Tristan, who's using a keycard to open the other door, overhears Ryder's words and snorts a little. The three of us share a look and then all burst out laughing, because if there's one perfect word to describe Beckett, it's "bossy."

I'm still smiling when I enter my room, but the emptiness of it drains the moment of good humor. It's silly, honestly. I expected this trip to be a solo one, so it doesn't make sense that I'm feeling bummed just because I actually *am* going to be on my own tonight.

I settle in, drawing for a while before my stomach starts grumbling enough to remind me that Ryder was right. I should definitely get something to eat.

I glance at the room service menu but decide I want to be in the company of other people, even if they're strangers, so I head down to the front desk to ask for some restaurant recommendations. The concierge points me toward a bar just down the street, selling it to me when he mentions that they've currently got Christmas themed cocktails that are to die for.

I really do love this season, and the minute I step into the lively bar, I know I've made the right decision. Upbeat Christmas music plays in the background, seasonal decorations give it a festive feel, and it's busy enough to tell me the food must be good.

I decide to eat at the bar since I'm on my own.

"Have you seen our cocktail menu?" the friendly bartender

asks me after I've placed my food order, almost like he's reading my mind.

I grin at him. "I *do* deserve a treat."

He chuckles, tapping his finger on one of the listings. "Then you definitely need one of these Christmas Cranberry Cosmos. Unless you want something warm. Then maybe the Gingerbread Hot Toddy?"

"The Cosmo, please," I tell him, and end up ordering a second one before I'm done with my meal, because just like the food, they really are that good.

"I don't suppose you'd let me put that on my tab," an unfamiliar voice says from just behind me when the bartender hands me my second drink.

I swivel around on my stool to face the man who just spoke.

"Too late," I tell him, taking a sip and feeling more flattered than I'd like to admit at the attention when I see how good looking he is.

He grins at me. "In that case, maybe the next one?"

"Maybe," I agree, flirting back a little as the drink loosens up my inhibitions enough to let the new, bolder version of myself that I'm trying to become rise to the surface. I know nothing will come of it and I'm totally fine with that, but it's fun to have a little admiring attention on me.

Especially since I'm tipsy enough that the voices in my head that usually remind me of all the ways I'm not enough are quiet for now.

The guy sits down next to me and orders himself a Scotch, neat. Then he sees the shocked look I'm giving him and raises his brows. "What is it?" he asks.

I pick up the cute, laminated cocktail menu that lists all the seasonal drinks. "With all this to choose from, *that's* what you're going with?"

He chuckles. "It's a classic."

"But it's not very fun."

"You've got me there." He swivels his stool around to face me more fully. "Is that what you came here for tonight? Some fun?"

I pick up the last thick-cut French fry on my empty plate and hold it up, grinning. "Actually, I came for this."

"Ah. A good choice. They're delicious. But that's not all this place has to offer, you know."

I tap the cocktail menu again. "That's what I was trying to tell you!"

He laughs again. "Then I definitely need to buy you another."

Before I can decide if I want him to or not, my phone vibrates on the bar top where I have it lying next to my second empty Cosmo glass. The man I'm chatting with signals the bartender, pointing to my drink, as I pick up the phone to see a text notification in the group chat the guys insisted we set up earlier today.

> TRISTAN: Just wanted to make sure you got dinner. We're still in our meeting, but we're about to order something to be sent up. Should I send something to your room too?

"Aw." I smile down at the message. "That's so sweet."

"What's so sweet?"

I look up, belatedly remembering the man I was just chatting with. "My friends are checking up on me. One sec."

I type out a quick reply.

> ME: I'm fine, thanks! I just ate, am having some amazing drinks, and even made a new friend.

I look up to find the bartender handing me a fresh Christmas Cranberry Cosmo.

"Oh! Thank you," I say, confused until I catch my new friend smiling at me.

"I did say I'd get the next one," he reminds me.

I laugh. "Touché."

I take a sip as my phone dings again. This time, it's Beckett.

> BECKETT: Who's the friend?

It's all too easy to read that one in the deep growl he would

58

have used if he was asking me in person, and I bite my lips to hold in a smile as I imagine it.

"Who are you?" I ask the man next to me, the third drink making me feel flushed and free. "My friends would like to know."

"Shane Ostrander," he says, holding out his hand like it's a formal introduction. "Cocktail snob."

I laugh, shaking his hand. "Lana Reeves. Christmas junkie."

"I never would have guessed," he deadpans, making me laugh again.

My phone catches my attention with another ding. I haven't answered Beckett's question yet, and now the other two guys have also chimed in to find out who I'm chatting with.

"Oops." I hold it up. "I need to report back."

> ME: His name is Shane Ostrander.

TRISTAN: What does he want?

> ME: Scotch, neat.

RYDER: Boring.

> ME: Right??

BECKETT: What does he really want?

I look over at Shane, holding my phone up like it's a microphone, then pointing it at him. "Tell me what you want. What you really, really want."

He grins. "Just to buy you a drink."

I text that his answer to the guys, adding in that Shane's mission is now accomplished, and get another message back right away—another one that I once again read in a certain someone's favorite gruff, growly tone.

BECKETT: I thought you already had one.

> ME: No, I already had two!

I giggle as I send that one off, feeling pretty proud of my own humor. Then I remember that I'm actually on my third now, so quickly send a follow-up text with the correction.

> RYDER: What are you drinking?

> TRISTAN: Only accept it if it's in an unopened bottle.

> BECKETT: Where are you?

> TRISTAN: Or if the bartender handed it to you directly.

I reassure Tristan that he did, then finish off my Cosmo as the music changes from Christmas songs to current ones.

"I love this song!" I tell Shane, somehow accidentally swiping the little microphone icon on my screen that picks up my voice and sends it as texts as I fumble my phone in my enthusiasm.

> RYDER: What song?

"Oops," I say when I see Ryder's question. "Let me ask my phone."

That gets sent off to the guys too, and I fuss with my settings for a minute, trying to remember how to get my phone to do the thing where it recognizes the song currently playing. It keeps vibrating with more texts from the guys while I do that, and once I finally figure it out and send it back, the group chat feed is full of new messages.

> BECKETT: What's the name of the bar?

> RYDER: I've got a great drinking game you can try. Too bad for Shane Bystander, though. It can only be played back at the hotel.

> RYDER: Wait, are you at the hotel?

> BECKETT: Lana, tell us where you are.

> TRISTAN: When you say "new friend," just how friendly is this guy trying to be?

I shake my head, grinning down at my phone.

I send that one off after I see the wall of text, just so they don't think I'm ignoring them, then scroll back up to read through everything I missed.

"What was that?" Shane asks, leaning in as I snap a pic of the cocktail menu and send it off to the guys.

There. That answers Ryder's question about what I'm drinking *and* tells Beckett where I am, since it's got the bar's name at the bottom.

I look up at Shane again. "I said, I love this song!"

I didn't, but I should have, because I totally do. And when Shane points out that the little bar has a dance floor, I completely blame the Christmas Cranberry Cosmos for the way I slide off my stool and convince him to finish off his boring Scotch and come dance with me.

For once, I'm not even self-conscious about it. I'll never see this man again, I'm full of cocktail confidence, and most importantly, I'm a brand new me. One who actually manages to live that old cliche, dance like no one's watching, for once.

At least, for a minute or two.

Then heavy hands fall on my hips, and I open my eyes to the reminder that I invited Shane out onto the dance floor with me.

He smiles down at me, and I almost feel bad for instantly comparing his attractiveness to the three guys I'm road tripping with.

Beckett? Hotter.

Tristan? Also hotter.

Ryder? Yep, still hotter.

Shane leans in. "That smile of yours is amazing. What are you thinking about right now?"

"Um," I stall, feeling a little guilty. Not to mention a little too tipsy to come up with white lie on the fly.

Before I have to, Shane is suddenly yanked backward, breaking us apart.

"Hey!" he shouts as another set of hands stabilizes me when I stumble.

"Hands off," someone tells him. Someone who sounds a lot like Ryder.

"You're a goddamn magnet for this shit, little menace," a familiar voice growls in my ear at the same time.

"Beckett?" I ask, twisting to look up at him. "I was just thinking about you!"

"The lady was dancing with *me*," Shane says, sounding a little belligerent.

I turn back to him and realize that Ryder really is here. Tristan too.

"Hi," I tell them, my stomach fluttering. "Is your meeting over?"

"Get lost," Tristan tells Shane with quiet authority when he tries to move toward me again. "*Now*."

I blink, swaying a little. The guys seem a little tense. I'm still really happy to see them, though.

Shane doesn't seem to feel the same way. He grumbles at them for a second, but then turns and leaves.

"You should dance with me," I tell Beckett, since he's still right behind me. I grab both his hands when the beat picks up, wanting to share the fun, happy feeling I'm floating on with him, but the stubborn wall of muscle refuses to move.

I frown at him, then turn to Ryder and Tristan. "Come on! *No* one can resist Shakira on the dance floor."

Ryder grins at me, matching my rhythm for a minute, but when I hip-bump Tristan, he shakes his head. "We should get back to the hotel."

"No, we should dance!"

"We've got to get an early start in the morning," Beckett insists, grabbing on to my arm.

I catch Ryder's eye and we both laugh. And then, because I'm suddenly a *much* more coordinated dancer than I ever have been before—thank you, Christmas Cranberry Cosmos—I use the hold Beckett has on me to swing myself around and shimmy up against him.

"Lana..." he growls, his grip tightening on my arm.

"Beckett..." I tease him, resting my hand on his massive chest as I mimic his tone.

He sighs, but I swear I see his lips tug upward a little.

"We really should get back," he says, somehow managing to maneuver me off the dance floor before I realize what's happening.

I whine in protest, and someone groans, but none of them agree to stay and dance, and by the time we get back to the hotel even I can admit that those three cocktails packed a punch.

"Do you need help getting to bed, love?" Ryder asks once they get me to my room.

"Yes, please," happy-drunk me says, leaning my head against his shoulder and breathing him in.

Cinnamon and bergamot. *I'd drink that cocktail.*

"What cocktail?" Ryder asks.

I blink up at him, realizing I must've spoken aloud. "What?"

He shakes his head, smiling down at me. "Never mind. Let's get you some water before you lie down."

"On it," Tristan says, handing me a bottled water from the room's mini fridge.

I shake my head and push it back at him. "Nuh-uh. They over-charge for those."

He smiles, opening the top and holding it out until I take it. "We can afford it."

"Thank you." I take a sip. Then another.

It's heavenly.

But it's also washing away some of that lovely, happy feeling and turning me a little melancholy.

63

"You left your meeting early for me," I murmur drunkenly as it hits me, looking at the three of them. They're all here in my room taking care of me instead of doing the business they said was so important. "I'm sorry."

"Don't be." Beckett gives me an intense look. "It's fine."

I sigh. "I just wanted to have a little fun. Go out and be the new me."

Beckett's eyebrows shoot up, but it's Ryder who asks, "Who's the new you?"

I shrug. "I don't know. That's what I'm trying to find out. I just know that I've been trying to reinvent myself ever since Wade and I broke up. Shake off other people's expectations and figure out what my *own* are. What I really like. Who I actually want to be."

"And who you want to be is someone who gets groped by strangers?" Beckett asks, glaring a little.

I stick my tongue out at him, and Ryder snickers.

Tristan elbows Beckett in the ribs. "I think that sounds pretty fucking healthy, to be honest, Lana. But just so you know, who you already are is pretty fucking great."

I blink up at him, swaying a little. "Really?"

He gives me a small smile, brushing a strand of my hair off my cheek. "Really."

"Thank you. I just... I feel stuck? I want *more*."

"More what?" Beckett asks, crossing his arms over his chest as his eyes narrow a little.

I wave a hand vaguely, knowing I'm oversharing but unable to stop it after all the cocktails I had. "More... everything! More excitement! I want to know what kink is like! I want to know what *good* sex is like, because honestly, with Wade..."

I bite my tongue, not finishing that thought.

But all three men are staring at me now with undivided focus, and it's as if their gazes pull the truth right out of me.

"I just want to explore," I admit, plopping down on the edge of my bed and looking up at them. "It's why I went to Radiance. It wasn't a mistake, you know," I add in a whisper. "I knew it was your club. I picked it on purpose."

Beckett frowns. "You wanted us to see you getting hit on by other men?"

I shake my head. I can't tell if I'm blushing or if I'm just flushed from drinking. "No, I wanted..."

Them.

Any of them. *All* of them.

My breath hitches, and a thick heat pools in my core as I look up at the three men who've starred in so many of my secret fantasies.

It's a truth I'd be a fool to admit. Even drunk, I know that. But the loaded silence as they loom over me, all three of them staring down at me like I'm a puzzle they're just now starting to piece together, makes me think that even without saying the words out loud, I just admitted to something I didn't mean to.

I groan, flopping backward on the bed. "Ugh. I should've stopped after the first Cosmo."

Tristan's lips tilt up, and he leans down, brushing my hair back and pressing a chaste kiss to my forehead. "It's okay. Get some sleep. You're allowed to have a little fun."

"Not with strangers," Beckett grunts under his breath, sliding off my boots and then pulling the blanket over me.

I close my eyes, sleep starting to tug me under. I can hear them murmuring quietly to each other, and then the gentle click of my door as they leave.

And then I'm out.

7

LANA

My mouth tastes vaguely like Christmas and regret when I wake up, and I shake my foggy head, trying to clear it and figure out why.

"Ow." I wince when the motion only intensifies the throbbing at my temples.

I squint in the early morning light, rubbing the center of my forehead. I'm definitely a little bit hungover, and everything that happened last night suddenly comes back to me in a rush.

"Oh god," I groan as I remember telling the guys that I basically went to Radiance looking for *them*.

True? Yes.

Embarrassing? Also yes.

But not nearly as embarrassing as the memory of the way all three of them just *looked* at me after I blurted it out, not saying a word.

Just thinking about it makes me flush with heat, and not the fun kind. It's not that I'm shocked they don't want me. I already know that their protective, attentive natures come from me being Caleb's little sister, not from anything more personal. And despite the internal pep talk I used to get myself to show up at Radiance in the first place that night, I know that each one of them is out of my league too.

They're like three different flavors of sex-on-a-stick, and I'm a work in progress who's never lived up to anyone's expectations. Not my parents', not Wade's, and certainly not whatever expectations Tristan, Beckett, and Ryder must have for the kind of women they're actually interested in.

I sigh, then grimace as my head starts to throb a little harder now that I'm actually awake.

I throw an arm over my eyes, blocking out the morning light, and allow myself one more second of self-pity.

I can't even imagine how awkward the rest of this trip is going to be now that I've admitted why I really went to the club that night. But I can't hide forever, so I throw off the covers and head for the shower, berating myself the whole way for not stopping at just one drink last night.

I'm honestly a little shocked I actually got drunk. I'm not usually like that, even if letting loose the way I did felt like I was following through with my promise to reinvent myself at the time.

Unfortunately, in retrospect, it feels more like a mistake.

"Well, at least I can fix one part of that mistake," I mumble under my breath when I reach the bathroom.

I fish a small bottle of painkillers out of my toiletries bag and swallow down two of them. It's been a while since I've had a hangover, and the reminder of my overindulgence last night has me worrying about what other effects I might have to deal with.

I've never been a big drinker, so I have to admit I sort of glossed over it when my doctor told me I'd need to limit alcohol from now on, given my condition.

I stare at myself hard in the mirror, for once, not cataloging all my visible imperfections, but trying to see a little deeper. To find some evidence of the *invisible* one.

Lupus.

I squeeze my eyes closed for a second, shaking my head in denial. Pointless, but I can't help it. It's overwhelming. I honestly didn't even know what the disease was before getting my diagnosis, and part of me wants to pretend I still don't. I know it's not smart, but I can't deny that a huge part of me just wants to act like an ostrich and put my head in the sand, ignoring the whole thing.

And I guess, in a way, that's exactly what I did last night when I ordered those cocktails against my doctor's orders.

It's just... it's not *fair*.

"As if I need one more imperfection to add to my lifelong list," I mumble, staring into my own eyes again. Then out of sheer habit, letting my eyes drift down over familiar territory.

Round face.

Rounder body.

I'm working hard on loving myself even if others don't, but I still can't erase all the voices in my head that love to remind me that, no matter what I do, I'm never quite pretty enough, or slim enough, or put together enough.

I'm never quite *good* enough.

And I'll be damned if I'm going to give anyone more reasons to think so by telling others about this stupid lupus.

Especially after it already drove away the one person I shared the news with.

"Enough," I tell myself firmly, turning away from the mirror. "I'm *glad* I don't have to deal with Wade on top of this diagnosis."

I flip the shower on, biting my lip as I adjust the water temperature. I have no doubt at all that my family will see lupus as just one more of my personal failings, just like Wade did, if I were to bring it up during this visit. So I won't. Just like I obviously won't bring up my interest in exploring kink, or admit that I still love to draw, or share any of the other things I'm learning about myself the more time I spend away from their oppressive, judgmental expectations, either.

I laugh wryly as I step under the spray of water. At this point, I'm keeping so many secrets from my family that there won't be a lot I *can* talk with them about over Christmas... so I guess it's lucky for me that my folks aren't big on heartfelt conversations.

I hear my phone chime with an incoming text just as I'm stepping out of the shower, and as I go to check it, I take a cleansing breath.

The hangover, thankfully fading now, stole some of my natural optimism this morning, but it's time to shake that off and remember who I actually want to be. And that's definitely not a cynical Grinch.

The text is from my brother, and I grin at the screen. I may not be looking forward to this holiday visit, but I *am* looking forward to seeing him.

> CALEB: Hey, sis! I hear the guys decided to drive out with you this year. I'm glad you'll have the company. Can't wait to see all four of you!

I smile, my heart already lighter as I type out a reply.

> ME: I'm excited to see you too!

> ME: Almost as excited as you looked when you scored that winning goal against the Bruins last weekend. I hope you know your victory shimmy is a trending meme now.

He sends back a row of laughing emojis, then a three-second video of him, which he must have just recorded, given the bad case of bedhead he has. He's shaking his hips the way he did on the ice after that goal, and it makes me laugh out loud for real.

It's not until I'm dressed and headed out of the hotel room to find the guys that it occurs to me they must have reached out to Caleb last night to tell him they're on this road trip with me.

Oh shit. I hope like hell that's *all* they told him.

I know all four of them are still really close, and I'd die of embarrassment if Caleb knew what I said to the three of them last night. Although I also can't imagine a world in which they told Caleb and he didn't lecture me about it instead of sending me a silly video, so maybe I'm safe.

The guys are all waiting for me near the hotel's buffet-style breakfast offerings, and to my horror, I feel myself blushing all over again at the sight of them.

"Good morning, love," Ryder says cheerily, as if I didn't imply last night that I'd happily climb any one of them like a tree if given the chance.

I mumble an awkward reply, not sure what to say to get things back to normal.

The guys don't help. Beckett is his usual gruff self, Tristan looks completely engrossed in waffles and coffee, and while Ryder has always been able to carry a conversation all on his own when needed, I can't seem to shake the dread that they're all secretly looking at me with pity now, knowing how badly I want them.

By the time we finally head out to the SUV, I can't stand it. I have to say *something*.

"Thank you guys for coming to rescue me last night," I blurt, my cheeks warming.

Beckett grunts something unintelligible and takes my suitcase from me, tossing it in the back, and Tristan gives my shoulder a friendly squeeze.

Ryder is right next to me, keys jingling in his hand, and he tips my chin up so I have no choice but to look into his warm brown eyes.

They've got little flecks of gold in them, and when he smiles enough for them to crinkle at the corners, it takes him from gorgeous to unfairly attractive.

"We'll always come rescue you," he says softly, making it sound so sincere that it banishes some of my awkwardness.

"Thank you," I say, letting out a little breath as the knots in my stomach unwind a little. Then, before he can react, I snatch the keys out of his hand and slip into the driver's seat. "I'll take the first leg of driving."

Ryder leans in through the still-open driver's door, shaking his head. "You don't have to do that, love. We've got this."

"No," I insist. "I want to pull my weight."

He almost looks like he's going to argue again, but then Beckett slips into the passenger seat next to me and growls something under his breath that sounds like *little menace*, and Ryder laughs and backs off.

I press my lips together to hold off a smile as he slides in next to Tristan in the back and we hit the road. It's nice to feel like Beckett has my back.

I mean, it's also nice that Ryder wants to coddle me a little, but while I like the idea of being spoiled by hot men as much as any woman would, feeling competent—and like *they* know I'm competent, especially after the fool I made of myself last night—feels even better.

GPS guides me as I navigate away from the hotel, and just as I hit the freeway, Tristan chuckles from the back seat.

"Holy shit, Caleb's a meme now!"

"What?" Ryder asks as Beckett huffs a breath that almost sounds like a laugh.

I flick my eyes to the rearview mirror and see Ryder reaching for Tristan's phone.

We all roast my brother for a bit, and I show them the "live replay" he sent me this morning before the guys in the back both settle down with other distractions on their phones, and Beckett pulls out—

"Is that yarn?" I blurt, not sure what I'm seeing.

He raises a single eyebrow at me, then produces a pair of knitting needles to go with it. "Yeah."

That's all he gives me before turning his attention to the long, fuzzy... scarf, maybe? It looks like it's about half finished, and his large hands wield the knitting needles dexterously as he gets to work on it.

I press my lips together so hard my cheeks ache, but it does absolutely nothing to stop the charmed grin from spreading across my face. "I didn't know you knit."

He makes one of his trademark grunts but doesn't pause the steady clacking rhythm of his needles. Or answer me.

I mean, I guess technically I didn't ask a question, but he's delusional if he thinks I'm going to let go of something as adorably sexy as a big, gruff man knitting a fuzzy red scarf with a white snowflake pattern worked through it.

"Where did you pick that skill up?" I ask.

He shrugs.

"Have you been knitting for long?"

He glances over at me, then back at the scarf-like thing magically growing beneath his huge hands.

"A while."

"And is the scarf a Christmas gift? Who is it for? It looks so soft."

"Scarf?" he says, actually pausing for a moment to give me a flat look. "This is gonna be a sweater. You can't see that?"

He holds it up.

"I, um, oh?" I stutter, looking over again and seeing nothing but a long, thin... scarf. "It's lovely," I add quickly, not wanting to offend or discourage him from his hobby.

But honestly, I don't see how he's going to take *that* and make it into anything other than what it already looks like.

It's already too long, for one thing, and for another—

Beckett chuckles, his handsome face breaking out into a grin that's so sexy it should be illegal.

Realization dawns on me suddenly. "You were *teasing* me, you jerk."

I smack his shoulder, which is like smacking a warm brick wall, and he shrugs unrepentantly before getting back to it.

"You're the one who fell for it. Of course it's a scarf."

I reach over before I can help myself and run a hand over it, sighing happily. It really is as soft as it looks.

"Cashmere?"

He snorts. "No way. That shit is too expensive for this."

I arch an eyebrow, unable to stop myself from fishing a little. "Are you saying she's not worth it? Or whoever it's for."

He slants a look at me without breaking his knitting rhythm. "Of course they're worth it. I donate them to the pediatric ward of the children's hospital on Sunset. You know the one?"

I blink. "Oh. That's kind of amazing."

He makes another grumbly sound, shrugging off the compliment. "It's nothing. Just something I do to help me relax and organize my thoughts. Tristan's Grandma Meg taught me one summer when we all took turns looking out for her while she recovered from a broken hip."

"I remember that. I didn't realize you flew back to New Hampshire to help out, though. Weren't you all out in Los Angeles by then?"

He nods, then shrugs again. "We all flew back."

He must mean him, Ryder, and Tristan. I was away at school when it happened, and Caleb had already been drafted by the NHL, but I do remember hearing how Tristan had to fly home to care for his grandmother at the time.

I just didn't realize that Ryder and Beckett went too.

They really are close.

I reach out and pet the scarf he's making again, my heart fluttering a little at the knowledge that not only does this huge, tattooed man knit, he does it for the sweetest reason.

"This really is nice of you. Even if L.A. winters don't get as cold as back home, I'm sure the kindness will be very much appreciated."

"It doesn't feel cold to you or me, maybe, but those kids feel the chill a little more what with all the crap they're going through."

I grin at the slightly defensive note in his voice. Sure, I've been crushing on him—on all three of them—for longer than I'd ever care to admit to, but there are layers there that I never knew about, and I'm instantly hungry for more.

We talk a little more about some of the projects he's knit and the children he's met through the pediatric hospital. The other two men chime in after a while, and the conversation switches to silly car games and random banter.

As the miles pass by, something inside me slowly relaxes, and I realize that I'm having a really good time.

Maybe, since none of them seem to feel as awkward as I do about last night, I can let it go too and enjoy this trip for what it is. Not the wicked fantasy of my dreams, but at least a chance to satisfy a different kind of yearning for these three men. I want to learn everything I can about them.

And when I see what's waiting for us just off the next exit, I decide that the new, reinvented me isn't going to shy away from letting them learn a little bit more about me, either. Even the ridiculous parts.

I flip on the blinker and move over into the right lane.

"Gotta pee, love?" Ryder asks from the backseat.

"No. Did you not see the sign?"

I'm practically bouncing in my seat as they all exchange a look.

Tristan is the one who answers me. "I think we all missed it. Snacks?"

I shake my head, grinning. "Better."

"Ready to take a break from driving, little menace?" Beckett asks as he packs away his knitting.

"Maybe once we get there," I say as I take the exit, pointing toward the gloriously tacky billboard guiding us in the right direction.

Beckett scoffs when he sees it, then folds his arms over his chest. "No."

"Yes!"

"It's... a dragon," Tristan says hesitantly, like he's not sure if he read the sign right. "Made of license plates?"

I smile at him through the rearview mirror. "Uh huh."

"But why?"

"Why not?" Ryder answers him with a grin before I can speak. "What's a road trip without roadside attractions?"

"Efficient," Beckett grumbles.

"Bo-ring," I correct him in a sing-song voice that makes Ryder snicker.

Tristan stays quiet, but he's smiling gently, looking a little bemused. I take that as full endorsement from the backseat.

"Come on, Beckett," I plead, even though I've got all the power since I'm at the wheel. "It will be fun, and it's only a *little* detour."

"It's three point eight miles from the highway."

"Exactly!"

He huffs again, but by the time we make it to the site where the dragon is located, park, then wander around until we find it, we're all having fun.

"Aw, look," I point out, reading a sign planted in the ground in front of it. "The artist named it 'Dad.'"

"That's weird," Tristan says, pushing his glasses up when they slip as he leans down to read over my shoulder.

Ryder squeezes in for a selfie, dragging a still grumbling Beckett in so it's all four of us. Then, at my insistence, Ryder helps me balance on one of the dragon's knees so I can reach up and pretend I'm kissing its cheek while Tristan snaps another pic.

On my way back down, I wobble a little as a wave of dizziness overtakes me.

"You okay, love?" Ryder asks, stabilizing me when I tumble against him.

I nod. "I just slipped."

He looks a little skeptical, but Beckett distracts him before he can push me about it, saying something about getting back on the road.

I don't argue. I'm *still* dizzy, and a deep fatigue is starting to work its way through my bones, making the short trek back to the SUV feel daunting.

"Running out of steam?" Tristan asks with a quiet smile, giving me a friendly shoulder bump as we get there.

I reach for one of the rear doors. "Just ready for a break from driving."

He nods, letting it go as he slips in beside me. This time, Beckett takes the wheel, but I tune out their banter as he steers us back toward the highway and the three of them start to debate the merits of roadside attractions.

Now that I'm seated, the dizziness seems to have settled down, but I'm still tired. Far too tired to blame it on not sleeping well last night.

This is the lupus. Thanks to my doctor, I know all about the effects it might have on me.

That it *is* having on me.

I look out the side window, blinking away the sting in my eyes as it starts to feel all too real.

Thankfully, before I can get too lost in my head about it, I doze off for a bit. When I wake up, I feel a little more refreshed, and the rest of that day's drive passes quickly.

I opt for room service once we reach that night's hotel, still a little emotionally unsteady even though the fatigue has passed, and as soon as I'm done eating, I wash my face and change into my pajamas, then go to bed, hoping my body will cooperate tomorrow and not try to ruin the fun I've been having with the guys.

But before I can make it that far, I'm sucked into a dream that has me waking up in the middle of the night with a gasp, my heart racing and the memory of it already fading even though the emotions remain lodged firmly in my chest.

It wasn't a dream. It was a nightmare. One where I was following the signs for another roadside attraction, but not in the car. I was wandering down white, sterile corridors that twisted together like a maze. I could hear the guys laughing and having a good time, but could never find them, and every time I thought I'd reached the right room, I'd open it only to find it dark, empty, and barren. Filled only with the echo of my mother's voice, criticizing the red dress I was wearing, the one I'd chosen for the Christmas party.

I felt inadequate. Like I had no control over the situation and couldn't reach what I wanted, even though I was following all the signs.

I sit up and flick on the light, swallowing hard. I just need to see that I'm here, in this bland hotel room, not there. Except once I do, it's still not good enough. It doesn't slow my racing heart. I still feel just as alone and abandoned as I did in the dream.

So I don't think; I just act.

I stumble out of bed, then out into the hall, knocking sharply on the door of the room next to mine without giving myself a chance to overthink it. I know the guys have the rooms on either side of me, and I think this one is Tristan's.

I hope it is, because I need to not be alone. And even if these men don't *want* me, I know they won't let me down. Like Ryder said the other day, they'll always be there to rescue me. And right now, I need that.

I need to be rescued from *myself*, and from this disease I don't even want to admit to having, much less know how I'm going to handle living with for the rest of my life.

8

TRISTAN

I BLINK INTO THE DARKNESS, not sure what it was that woke me up. Then it comes again—a knock on my hotel room door. When whoever it is knocks for a third time, I finally get over my groggy confusion and grab my glasses to check the time.

It's 2:20 in the morning. That gets me moving. Ryder and Beckett are in the other room we booked, and I'm already envisioning an emergency at the club that one of them has come by to bring me in on.

I don't feel awake enough to work out why they wouldn't have just called, so it takes me a minute to process my surprise when I open the door to find out it's not what I was expecting.

"Lana?" My voice is raspy from sleep, but I'm suddenly wide awake when I realize she's upset. "What's wrong?"

"Can I come in?"

"Of course."

I step away from the door, worried over the hitch I hear in her breath. I didn't bother to turn on the lights, so the room is too dim for me to see her well, but it's obvious by her loungewear and mussed hair that she came straight from her bed.

"Did something happen?" I ask.

She stands awkwardly just inside the door, shifting from foot to foot and looking up at me with big, glassy eyes. The protective instincts she's always inspired in me rise up instantly at the sight of her like this.

"Um, no. I mean, yes. But nothing real."

She looks down, obviously embarrassed, and I step closer, tipping up her chin. "Tell me."

"I had a bad dream," she blurts out. "And I just... didn't want to be alone."

"Okay."

Tension flows out of her body, and she sways on her feet. "Okay? Really? That's not weird?"

"No," I tell her simply, shoving away the memories that try to rise to the surface.

She called it "nothing real," but I suffered through enough bad dreams after the accident that took my parents' lives to know that "real" can be very subjective.

And no one should have to go through that kind of suffering alone.

"So, I can stay with you?" she asks. "You really don't mind?"

I'm surprised to realize how much I don't. Maybe it's the dark, or maybe it's just that it's her, but the usual reluctance I feel to have someone in my private space, much less sharing my bed when I'm dressed only in a pair of boxers with most of my scars fully exposed, just isn't there.

"I don't mind," I tell her honestly, leading her over to the bed and pulling the covers back for her.

It's only after I crawl in next to her that I realize that, just like the room Beckett and Ryder are in, mine is a double too. I could have put her in the second bed, but damn. I really don't want to. Not just because I've always been attracted to her. I've long known that nothing can come from that. But because those instincts of mine are only getting stronger.

I want to comfort her, protect her, be the wall between her and all her fears tonight, whatever those may be.

Lana doesn't complain about sharing my bed, so I set my

glasses back on the nightstand and pull the blankets over the both of us after settling onto my back, careful not to touch her. That's not what she asked for, so I leave a good amount of space between us, hoping my presence here will help.

"Okay now?" I ask, staring up at the darkness.

"Uh huh," she says, her breath still ragged and shallow in a way that I don't like. Then after a minute, she adds a soft, "Thanks," followed by a quiet sniffle.

Then it comes again, as if she's fighting to hold off tears, and it breaks my resolve to keep my distance.

"Lana," I mutter, rolling toward her and pulling her into my arms.

She stiffens in surprise, almost making me second guess my instincts, but before I can, she melts against me, her soft breath fluttering against my chest.

I've hugged her before, but this is something else. She feels incredible against me, all warm curves and plush softness. If I wasn't so worried about her, it would be a hard temptation to resist.

Instead of letting myself think about that, I wrack my brain for something that could have upset her like this. She seems to be over her shit-head ex, and I know we got to the bar the other night before the man who was plying her with drinks could do anything we would've had to hurt him for, so I'm at a loss.

"Want to tell me about the dream?" I ask, my lips brushing her hair a little as I speak. She smells like cherry blossoms and honey, and it takes an act of will to keep my cock from stirring in response.

Lana shakes her head, her breath still stuttering and short.

I stroke her arm, hoping to soothe her, and feel something warm in my chest when she finally starts to calm down.

"Sometimes it helps to talk about it," I try again.

"I'd rather not," she says quietly.

I don't like the idea of her keeping her fears to herself. If I don't know what's wrong, I won't know how to fix it. But I do know something about the painful process of working through things that are hard to share with others, so I decide not to push her.

That's not why she came, and it's clearly not what she needs.

But I can also tell by the tension still present in her body that she's not going to be falling asleep any time soon, so maybe talking about something else will help calm her down.

"It's been a while since you've been back home, hasn't it? Are you excited to see your family for Christmas?"

She laughs softly. "Yes. But also... no."

"Oh?" My brows rise. "I know Caleb is looking forward to seeing you."

She sighs. "I'm looking forward to seeing him too. It's just complicated. He's really the only one I fit in with."

"Hmm."

I can feel her smiling against my chest at my non-answer, but just like I hoped, it encourages her to go on.

"I do love Christmas, but you know how my parents are. They don't really celebrate the things that I love about it. They expect perfection, and that's just not something I'm capable of giving them."

"Bullshit."

Her soft body tenses up, but then she laughs, relaxing even more. "You know what I mean."

I really don't. But I do know that her parents have rigid ideas about the kind of image they expect their family to project.

"I never got the sense that their expectations were that demanding," I say, thinking of all the things Caleb got away with.

Lana gives a delicate snort. "Not if you're my brother."

I lean back a little so I can see her face, but the little bit of moonlight coming through the window isn't enough to show me her expression. "What do you mean?"

"He's the golden boy in our parents' eyes, so of course he feels that way. They don't think he can do any wrong. It's the opposite for me, though. I've spent most of my life trying to live up to their standards, but all I hear from them is how I'm failing at it. I love my brother, and he's the one family member who doesn't ever make me feel that way, but he also doesn't get it. He does everything right in their eyes without even trying."

I'm not sure what to say to that. I agree that Caleb excels at not just hockey, but almost anything he touches. But fuck, so does Lana. It's hard to imagine anyone finding fault with her. As far as I'm concerned, she's pretty much perfect.

But what I really hear is that she doesn't feel like she belongs. That she feels separate from the rest of her family in some way, even when she's surrounded by them.

Despite the close ties I have with my best friends, I know what it feels like to walk through life not fitting in.

I rub slow circles against her back. "What about your sister?"

"It seems easy for Vivian. Everything my parents expect just comes naturally to her. It's..."

"Lonely?" I offer.

"I guess," she says with a sigh. "I love them. But it's just hard to be around them sometimes when I can never seem to measure up. You're lucky you were raised by someone like Grandma Meg."

I smile in the darkness, because I know she's right. My grandmother is the best. But then Lana suddenly stiffens with a little gasp, her soft hand landing on my cheek.

Right over my scars.

"Shit, Tristan. I'm sorry. That was horribly insensitive to say."

It's my turn to stiffen. I don't particularly like to be touched, and I especially avoid letting anyone touch the damaged parts of my body.

But then I realize that's not entirely true. Not right now.

Holding her here in the dark, with most of our bodies touching, is something I like a little *too* much.

I cover her hand with mine, letting it stay where it is.

"I know what you meant," I reassure her. "And of course I regret losing my mother, but you're right. Grandma Meg is great."

"I remember when it happened," she says softly. "She never left your side at the hospital."

She means the accident. I nod. if I let myself, I can still remember too much of it—the shocking abruptness of the impact, the overwhelming, disorienting terror as the car rolled and rolled and *rolled*, the pain—but almost nothing at all about the weeks immediately following it.

I've never been sure if the gap in my memory is due to a trauma response, or to how drugged up they kept me for all the surgeries, but when I started to become more conscious, Grandma Meg was there.

"When the accident happened..." I start, the words surprising me. I never talk about this.

Lana makes a quiet sound of encouragement, inviting me to continue.

"It was obvious that she couldn't have survived," I say after a second, my voice raspy, "but she was my *mother*, so it also felt impossible that she could be gone. When I woke up in the hospital, I kept thinking it hadn't been real. Grandma Meg insisted to the doctors that I hear it from her, not them. It can't have been easy on her, but I... I've always appreciated that."

Lana hums quietly under her breath. It sounds like empathy, not pity, thankfully. I hate that. But I guess I knew I wouldn't get it from her, or I never would have opened my mouth.

"She was different before the accident," I go on, not sure why I'm telling her all this. "Grandma Meg, I mean. She was stricter when I was a little kid. A little more like your parents, actually."

"No way." Lana gives a disbelieving laugh. "Grandma *Meg*?"

I chuckle softly. "I know, but it's true. She told me once that losing her daughter changed her whole perspective on life. She thought she was going to lose me too. The two of us were her only living family."

"Everyone said it was a miracle you survived," Lana whispers.

I tighten my arm around her. "Everyone was right."

"I'm glad you did."

I close my eyes, a shudder going through me. "There was a time I wasn't. But I am now. And honestly, that has a lot to do with being raised by my grandmother. She told me once that sitting next to my hospital bed all those weeks, not knowing whether she'd lose me too, made her realize that none of the things she used to think mattered were actually important. That all she wanted, if I lived, was for me to grow up and be happy, whatever that meant for me."

"Even if it means owning a kink club?" she teases.

I laugh. "Even that."

"Wait." Lana half sits up, her silhouette backlit by the faint moonlight. "Don't tell me she *knows*."

I grin, reaching up to push the curtain of her hair back, even though her face is still in shadow. "Of course she knows."

"Holy shit." Lana laughs, collapsing back down onto the bed, her head resting on my chest. "I literally can't imagine."

I shrug, still grinning in the dark. "She's never judged me for any of my choices, and she doesn't judge me for that. She's the most supportive person I know. You were right. I *am* lucky she raised me."

Lana's fingers trail over my chest in a way that feels far too good. I don't even think she's aware of it.

After a minute, she asks, "Is she really okay with it, though? Even something like that?"

"There's nothing wrong with being kinky," I tell her firmly. "As long as it's safe, sane, and consensual, it's a healthy way to express your sexuality."

"Is that what you told Grandma Meg?"

I laugh. "That's what she told *me*. And believe me, if you think getting 'the talk' from a parental figure is bad, it's nothing compared to the version you get if you admit to unconventional interests."

"But you were able to admit it to her," she says quietly. "That's kind of amazing."

"We don't keep secrets from each other. We're all that we have."

"No, you've got my brother. You've got Ryder and Beckett too."

I smile, the tightness on the left side of my mouth from my scarring not bothering me for once. "True."

She shakes her head with another soft laugh, one that gets swallowed up by a yawn. "I still can't believe she knows you three own a kink club."

"She knows. And she's proud of us. Proud of *me*. Not just for making a successful business, but for fulfilling her one wish for me."

"To be happy," Lana repeats softly. "I love that. I can't imagine hearing anything like that from my family. I can't remember them ever telling me they were proud of something I've done."

My heart twists. I hate that her family makes her feel like their love is conditional. I know Beckett went through the same thing with his father, and I've seen up close and personal how much it fucked him up.

Lana doesn't deserve that, and I can only assume that Caleb doesn't realize how deeply she feels it, because he *does* love her. He wouldn't want her to have that kind of pain.

Neither do I. It hits me suddenly that she hasn't shared these feelings with him, her own brother—but she just shared them with me. That thought makes my heart twist in an entirely different way.

I kiss the top of her head, holding her a little closer. "For what it's worth, *I'm* proud of you."

"You don't have to say that."

"I know, but it's true. You've built an incredible life for yourself. Graduated with honors. Are great at your job. Had the good sense to say fuck off to that piece of shit you were dating..."

She laughs, lightly smacking my chest. "Stop" Her voice softens as she adds, "Thank you."

I kiss the top of her head again, breathing in cherry blossoms and honey.

"Do you remember the winter the ice rink flooded?" she asks out of the blue.

I chuckle softly. "Of course I do."

"Caleb was so mad. He never would tell me where you guys ended up going to sneak in your practice while they were fixing it."

"That's because we were all sworn to secrecy," I say as she yawns again. Then I go ahead and tell her anyway as she snuggles deeper into my arms, because the dark has already stripped away a few secrets tonight. What's one more?

Halfway through the story, I realize by her steady breathing that she's fallen asleep.

I keep talking anyway, my voice getting softer and softer, just because I like it.

Talking to her.

Holding her.

Having her in my bed.

I like it far, far too much. And it takes me a lot longer than it should to finally fall asleep.

9

LANA

I FEEL so warm and safe when I wake up that it takes me a moment to realize I'm not alone. There's a hard body behind me in bed.

My heart rate doubles, but then memories of last night start to bubble up through my sleep-fogged brain.

It's Tristan, and he's not just behind me. It's more like he's wrapped as completely around me as one person can be, spooning me in a way that makes me feel utterly cherished.

And unlike last night, when he was a total gentleman, his hands definitely wandered while we both slept, one wrapped around my waist but with his hand under my cami top, against my bare skin, and the other cradling my shoulders.

My heart skips a beat, and I can't help pressing back against him a little as I stretch lightly.

I'm still half asleep, and I close my eyes and just let myself bask in this feeling for a moment. Strong arms around me. Soft breath ruffling my hair. That unique amber and spice scent of his overlaying the chemically clean genericness of the hotel sheets.

His cock is hard, the thick line of it pressed against my ass, and I can't help squirming against it a little more.

My subtle movements pull a low, sexy sound out of Tristan as he begins to wake up. He starts grinding against me a little, making heat build in my core. It's sleepy and sensual, our movements almost instinctive as our hips undulate together.

A soft sound escapes me, and he nuzzles my neck. He groans, so quietly that I feel it more than hear it, and it feels so fucking good that I whimper, arching my back and spreading my legs.

Tristan rolls me onto my back and looks down at me. His eyes are still foggy with sleep, but they're warm and hungry in a way that makes the spark of heat in my belly flare into a bonfire.

He looks different without his glasses. Softer and more open. Then his lips tilt up in the smallest smile, and he runs a finger over the bridge of my nose.

"You have freckles," he murmurs.

I wince and put a hand on my cheek, embarrassed. "I usually cover them up."

He shakes his head, wrapping his hand around mine and pulling it away from my face.

"You shouldn't," he says after a moment, his voice low. "They're gorgeous."

Something in his tone makes my stomach flutter, and I don't think either one of us blinks as our gazes lock. I'm drowning in his eyes.

Gorgeous.

I've been told I'm cute before, but that's thanks to my dimple. I've also been called pretty from time to time. But no one has ever called me *gorgeous* before.

"You think I'm gorgeous?" I whisper.

"Jesus Christ. *Yes.*"

Tristan's voice drops on the last word, and the soft flutter in my stomach turns into the flapping of a dozen butterflies. My breath hitches as his hand tightens on my hip. His gaze drops to my lips, and it hits me in a rush.

He's going to kiss me.

My heart slams against my ribs, my eyelids fluttering shut as I lean up to accept, wanting it so badly I can almost taste it already.

But then he suddenly goes still. With a soft curse, he rolls off me and slides out of bed, getting to his feet.

I scramble upright, pushing my hair out of my face. "Tristan?"

His back is to me, but he turns just enough that I can see his cock straining in his pants.

"We'll have to hit the road soon," he mutters. "I should take a shower."

Then he disappears into the bathroom without another word, and I'm left feeling like I have whiplash as I stare after him. I woke up with his hands all over me, and less than a minute ago, I felt his breath against my lips as he hovered over my willing body.

And now I'm all alone in his bed, completely confused.

I hear the shower turn on, and it feels like a slap in the face. I'm *not* imagining what just happened between us. He wanted it just as much as I did. He almost kissed me. And he already knows that I want him too, thanks to my drunken confession to the three of them the other night.

I fight back the hurt, gritting my teeth as irritation washes through me. I've accepted that my crush on Tristan, Ryder, and Beckett isn't going to be returned. I even fought through my humiliation after telling them about my reason for showing up at Radiance that night. But I'm sick and tired of rejection. Of not being good enough. I get plenty of that from my family, and had more than enough from Wade.

I thought Tristan was different.

I take a deep breath when my eyes start to sting, then suck it up and throw back the covers, prepared to head back to my own room. But I freeze in place when I hear a quiet groan from the bathroom.

My stomach flips.

It comes again, and there's no mistaking it. Because it's not the only sound I hear over the water.

Tristan is in there, jerking off.

I get up and go over to the bathroom door. I thought he'd shut it, it *looks* shut, but once I'm standing in front of it, I can see that the latch didn't take. There's the smallest crack still open, letting out warm steam and the scent of body wash.

And through the crack in the door, I can hear the wet, rhythmic sounds of him stroking his cock.

My stomach swoops, my pulse starting to race as I squeeze my thighs together. I really, really should leave. Especially knowing he chose this over what could have happened in bed with me.

But then I hear another sound.

"...Lana."

He mutters my name, so softly that there's no way I would have heard it if I weren't standing right by the door.

My eyes fly wide open, and before I can stop myself, I push the door open wider and step into the bathroom.

The shower stall has a clear door, with only the steam from the hot water obscuring Tristan's body from me. The haze of steam almost makes it feel like I'm watching in a dream, which is as good an excuse as any for why I'm here ogling his naked, muscled body when he clearly told me without words that he wasn't interested.

Except... he is.

He *has* to be.

He said my name.

His head is thrown back, his mesmerizing storm-colored eyes closed and his soft brown hair looking like dark chocolate now that it's wet.

He's so self-contained, quiet and deliberate in his normal, fully clothed life. It's almost shocking to see him like this. Water dripping down lean muscles that stand out in stark relief as he jerks himself off, quickly and harshly, almost like he's angry at himself for needing the release he's so clearly chasing.

And his scars. My eyes widen, a soft sound escaping me. He shared some of his emotional pain with me last night, and of course some of his scarring is always visible—on his face, and sometimes peeking out from his sleeve or the collar of his shirt. But I've never seen the full extent of them, jagged lines and deep furrows that tumble down the left side of his body.

My eyes trail down from his handsome face to his neck, his left arm, torso, upper thigh... it's as if a violent beast ripped into him, a sight all the more shocking because of how calm and contained Tristan always is.

I can't even begin to imagine how much strength it took to heal from all that, and the simmering arousal I woke up with suddenly bursts into something much hotter and more urgent. Not because of how he looks or what happened to him, but because of who he *is*.

And then his eyes open, his movements shuddering to an abrupt stop as he sees me.

"Fuck, Lana. You shouldn't be in here," he rasps, his voice harsh and strained.

I cross my arms. "Liar."

He huffs out a surprised breath, his hand still wrapped around his straining cock. "What?"

"You said my name. If that's not an invitation to come in, then I don't know what it is."

"Lana..." He drags my name out in a warning tone that almost makes him sound like Beckett.

I don't know where my boldness comes from, but instead of scampering back to the room, I stand my ground, crossing my arms.

"Why did you get up so fast? Why did you leave?"

"That's irrelevant."

I stare pointedly down at his cock. "It looks pretty relevant to me."

"Lana," he straight-up growls this time. "Get the fuck out of this bathroom."

I open my mouth to argue again, his intensity only turning me on even more, but then he slaps his free hand against the wet glass, startling me, and I spin on my heel and stomp out, restless and unsettled.

I almost leave. I should leave. But knowing he was thinking of me while doing what he was doing makes me feel wild and reckless.

And still so turned on that I want to scream.

My nipples tingle, the soft silk of my cami almost too much to bear, and without letting myself overthink my actions, I crawl back into his bed instead of leaving the room the way I'm sure he expects me to.

"Tristan," I whisper as I slide a hand down my body and slip it under the sleep shorts I'm wearing. Turnabout is fair play, after all.

91

I brush my fingers over my clit through my panties, imagining that it's Tristan's hands on me, bigger and lightly callused.

My body responds immediately, my legs spreading as if they have a mind of their own and my body arching up as I rub against myself faster.

I whimper, my arousal escalating so fast that it makes me feel a little crazy. This is wild and impulsive, but I'm beyond caring about that right now. Slipping my fingers beneath the waistband of my panties, I lose myself in it. My soft whimpers speed up in time with my hand as I think of Tristan's desperate-looking motion in the shower. The low need in his voice when he said my name. The feel of him when he was behind me, on top of me—

I suck in a sharp breath when I hear a heavy thump, my eyes flying open.

Tristan is standing at the foot of the bed, his skin still wet and flushed with the heat of the shower and his eyes, dark and hungry, locked on my body.

He's got a towel wrapped around his waist, but it's beyond obvious that he hasn't come yet, his cock tenting the material in a way that has me whimpering again. But then nerves rock through me as the audacity of what I'm doing hits me.

I walked in on him naked.

I watched him jerk off.

And now I'm touching myself in his bed, moaning his name.

For a moment, shame and embarrassment threaten to swamp me, but then his eyes flick up to mine, and the raw heat I see there burns it all away. I want more. I want a reaction from him. I want to push every button he has so that it's impossible for him to walk away from what we both clearly want.

I run my free hand over my chest, brushing against my pebbled nipples through the soft silk. It feels incredible, every sensation heightened from the intensity of having his eyes on me. I lean into it, moaning with abandon as I start to rub my clit again.

Harder.

Faster.

My gaze stays locked on him as the flush I thought was from

the heat of the shower spreads up his body. His thick cock twitches under the towel, but he makes no move to touch himself again.

He's holding back, and I hate that.

I spread my legs and let go of all my inhibitions, rocking against my own hand as I let my body's needs guide me, racing toward the release I crave.

"Lana," he grits out in that same warning tone as before as his eyes bore into me.

My thighs tremble, my core clenching tight as I stare right back at him. "*Tristan.*"

His jaw clenches, then he moves so suddenly it's like a predator being unleashed onto its prey.

"Fuck it," he mutters, closing the distance between us so fast it makes me dizzy.

He crawls up onto the bed, then pushes my legs open even wider and kneels between them, the heat from his body like an electrical charge pulsing between us.

"Keep going," he growls.

It's not a request, it's an order, and something in his tone sends fire licking through my veins. The interest in being dominated in bed is what sent me to their kink club in the first place. And the fact that it's *Tristan* bossing me around right now makes it so much better.

"What else?" I pant, not looking away from him. "Tell me what to do. Please."

His cock jerks again under the towel, and with a low grunt, he rips it away and fists himself. "Tell me how wet you are, gorgeous."

A shiver runs through me, and I dip my fingers deeper into my panties. "*So* wet. Sopping."

"Why?"

"Because of you."

His eyes are hooded, his fist picking up the same rough, almost angry rhythm as before as it moves over his cock. "I can smell it. You're usually all honey and sweetness. Now you're cherry blossoms and sex. Fuck yourself with those fingers for me. Show me how you like it."

93

I writhe on the bed as I follow his commands, my insecurities temporarily drowned out by the ease of just doing what he wants me to.

"Oh fuck," I gasp as my climax builds inside me. "I'm—"

"No," Tristan says sharply, pulling me back from the edge. "Don't come yet. Take off your clothes first. I want to see you come undone. And you want me to, don't you? You want me to watch. It's why you're in my bed. Why you were waiting for me, putting on a show you knew I couldn't resist."

"You can't resist me?" I whisper breathlessly.

His stormy eyes become almost black. "You fucking know I cant. And you don't want me to."

I lick my lips. "I don't."

"You want me to watch."

A twinge of anxiety threatens to interrupt the fantasy. I can't help feeling self-conscious at the idea of baring my less-than-perfect body to him, but then my eyes catch on his jagged scars, the physical evidence of the pain he shared with me last night, and I push aside my reluctance.

"I... I do," I pant, pinned in place by the heat in his gaze. "Watch me, Tristan. Let me show you how good I can be for you. Tell me what to do."

His lips spread in a wicked smile, the approval on his face making my breath hitch.

"That's right, baby. You're going to be good for me now and do what I already told you to. Take off those pretty things you're wearing and show me that lush body of yours. I want to see your wet pussy dripping for me. Show me what you like to do to it. Let me hear you pant my name as you touch yourself."

I moan, my self-consciousness slipping away as he strips me bare with his words. And I give him everything he asks for, tugging off my sleepwear and sliding out of my panties. His gaze roams over every inch of me as he murmurs low words about how beautiful I am, how soft my skin looks, how lush my curves are.

By the time I'm naked, I'm blushing and trembling and so

damn turned on that it feels like I'm about to shatter into a thousand pieces.

I lie back, completely revealed, biting my lower lip as my neglected clit throbs. I don't even realize I'm waiting for his direction until he gives it.

"Touch yourself."

Instantly, I reach between my legs, only to be stopped by a sharp click of his tongue.

Heat bursts through my core, the almost impersonal command in the sound making me feel owned in a way I didn't even know I craved.

"Not there. Not yet. Touch your breasts, gorgeous. Lift them up and stroke them."

I pant as I do it, unable to be still as my body writhes.

"Roll your nipples between your fingers. Fuck, they're incredible." He takes a deep breath, his nostrils flaring. "Pinch them for me."

I do it, and although satisfaction flares in his eyes, he shakes his head.

"Harder."

I gasp, my clit throbbing.

"Please," I beg, spreading my legs. "Let me... I need to... *Tristan*."

His hand starts flying over his cock again, and something flares in his eyes as his gaze drops to my pussy. "Jesus fuck, Lana. You're pierced."

I moan, my hands still on my breasts despite the aching need in my core. "Yeah. It's new."

Part of my reinvention. Something I did after Wade broke up with me.

"You're the first one to... to see it," I admit, shamelessly pushing my hips up like I'm presenting the small jewel decorating the gold ring in my clit hood as an offering.

Tristan's eyes snap up to mine. "The first?"

I lick my lips. "The only one to see it so far. The only one who knows."

Something almost feral crosses his face, and he stops stroking himself abruptly, squeezing his cock so tightly that the head turns purple. "You told me you wanted to be good for me, but as sweet as you look, this is who you really are, isn't it, gorgeous? A dirty little thing, deep down where it counts. A bad girl beneath all your sweet softness and smiles."

I whimper, heat pulsing between my legs as the need in me builds to unbearable portions.

"Please, please let me touch myself."

He starts to stroke his cock again, hard and fast. "Do it. Tug that little ring. Play with it, baby. Use it the way you know you want to."

I do, both hands diving between my legs as I rub myself desperately, using the little ring to heighten the sensation and shoving the fingers of my other hand into my pussy as I stare at Tristan's cock.

He's dripping for me. His thick length swelling before my eyes. He's going to come soon, I know it.

"*Please*," I gasp, my voice breathy.

"Come for me."

The command strips away the whisper-thin barrier holding back my orgasm, and pleasure slams into me so fast that I cry out, throwing my head back and grinding up against my hand.

"Fuck," Tristan groans, practically leaning over me when I force my eyes back open, still shuddering in the aftermath of my release. "Again."

"Wh-What?" I stutter, by body throbbing at his demand.

"Do it again. I want to see another one."

"I can't!"

Tristan's eyes turn molten. "I thought you said you wanted to be good for me."

"Oh god," I moan, tugging on my clit piercing as he taps right back into the kink I'm discovering. "I do."

"Show me."

My body takes over, arching up to meet his demands, taking the swirling eddies of my arousal and whipping them into a frenzy.

My fingers fly over my clit again, my thighs shaking as I push up against my hand.

"Faster."

I whine, but I do it.

"Fuck, you're gorgeous. *Faster.*"

My pulse is in overdrive. Chasing that peak a second time has me almost sobbing, needing something more.

"Please," I gasp out, not sure what I'm asking for until Tristan gives it to me.

With a groan that seems to come from somewhere deep inside him, he knocks my hand away and drags his rough fingers through my slick folds, then slips the tip of his finger into my piercing and tugs.

I tumble over the edge, crying out his name as the second orgasm hits me like a tsunami.

"Fuck," he grunts as I ride it out.

He keeps stroking himself hard, and a moment later, thick cum splashes over my stomach as he follows me over the edge, leaning over me as he milks out every drop.

10

LANA

"Oh fuck," I pant, goosebumps springing up over my skin. If I thought Tristan was hot before, it's nothing compared to how he looks when he loses that calm control he always holds on to so tightly.

His eyes bore into mine as I stare up at him, breathless as I watch him wring out the last of his orgasm.

I've fantasized about things like this, but my imagination fell short. He hardly touched me just now, and yet this is the single hottest thing I've ever done in my life.

I reach for him, needing more.

I need to taste him. Kiss him. Feel him.

The heat in his eyes warms into something softer as he leans in —but just before our lips touch, he freezes.

"Tristan?"

He turns his head to kiss my palm, but then pulls back, regret in his eyes.

I swallow, not liking that look on his face at all. It's as if, now that the heat of the moment has passed, he's come to his senses. Realized what he just did, and who he did it with.

Remembered that I'm still Caleb's little sister.

He gets off the bed before I can think of what to say, and I raise myself up on my elbows, watching as he crosses over to the small bathroom without a word.

He comes back with a towel, steaming from the warm water he obviously wetted it with.

"You should clean up," he says, holding it out to me.

I blink but don't take it from him. My emotions are getting whiplash right now.

After a moment, he sighs softly and sits on the bed next to me, starting to clean the cum off my stomach himself.

I swallow, something twisting in my gut. I'm lying here naked, and what he's doing is definitely intimate, but everything has changed from the passion we shared a few minutes ago.

The way he's touching me now feels clinical and removed, and I hate it.

I'm also not willing to be some passive little thing who lets someone else decide things for me anymore. He doesn't get to share that kind of moment with me and then just shut down without a word.

I grab his hand as he finishes, not letting him pull away again. "What's wrong?"

He stares at me for so long that I actually think he might try to get away without answering at all. But then he sighs, pulling out of my hold and standing up again.

"It was a mistake. We shouldn't have done that."

It's not exactly a surprise to hear with the way he's acting, but even if I half expected it, it still hurts. Maybe even more so because I never truly expected anything like this to happen between us in the first place, so when it did...

I swallow hard, disappointment spreading through my body and tainting the afterglow.

"I'm sorry."

"Are you?" I snap, some of my hurt spilling over. "Because you missed a spot." I brush my fingers over the little triangle of trimmed hair on my pussy, getting them wet with the last of his cum then holding them up for him to see. "If you're trying to clean up all the evidence, you should make sure to do a better job."

He grimaces, looking away. "That's not what I was doing."

I scoff and roll off the bed, done with lying naked in front of him when he considers me a mistake.

I scoop up the silky shorts and camisole I slept in.

"There. Happy? It's like it never happened now," I say sharply once I'm dressed again, balling up my panties in my fist since I didn't bother putting them back on in my haste to cover myself again.

He pinches the bridge of his nose, looking oddly vulnerable without his glasses on. "We both know it happened."

"And that you regret it."

A pained look crosses his face. "I didn't say that. I said we shouldn't have." He swallows, his Adam's apple bobbing. "You're Caleb's little sister."

My hurt feelings morph into anger. "So? You're Meg's grandson!"

He blinks, rearing back a little. "What? What does that have to do with anything?"

"Nothing! That's my point! You're more than who you're related to, and so am I."

Tristan shakes his head. "You're comparing apples to oranges. You don't have the same relationship with my grandmother as I do with your brother."

"And what about your relationship with *me*?" My voice is rising, but I can't help it. He's infuriating. "Am I supposed to only be defined by who I'm related to? Because I'm pretty sure I'm a whole person. One who makes her own decisions."

"Of course you are."

"Am I, though? To you? Because it sounds like I'll never be a woman in your eyes. Not if all you see when you look at me is Caleb's little sister."

"That's not all I see," he says after a minute, his heated gaze raking down my body. Then his eyes meet mine again. "But it's still true," he says with a sigh. "Caleb trusts me. He's one of my best friends. I can't just pretend that being his little sister isn't *part* of who you are."

Even though the rational part of me knows it's different, I suddenly flash back to Wade. He defined me by my family ties too. By who I was related to, what kind of connections he thought I could help him with, and the expectations he put on me because of that.

It's everything I wanted to walk away from, and it's suddenly too much to feel it from Tristan too.

"I never asked you to pretend," I tell him stiffly, the fight going out of me. "But I'm more than that too, and someday I'd really like to meet a man who can see that."

He looks like he wants to say something else, but honestly, I think he's said enough, so I don't wait around to hear it. But it's just my luck that the moment I open his door, still in my silky little sleep set and no doubt looking as well-fucked as I felt for those few blissful moments on the bed before reality crashed back down, Ryder and Beckett both step out of the room they've been sharing next door.

They freeze when they see me, their eyes widening in a way that would be comical if I were in a different mood. But I'm not, and my cheeks flame with embarrassment as I lift my chin in a small show of defiance, then quickly slip back into my own hotel room before they can say anything.

I head straight to the shower, but as good as it feels to step into the cocoon of hot steam and white noise, it does nothing to quiet my racing mind. I hate that I'm still turned on, even after the emotional ringer I just went through.

Of course, I'm still stunned that anything happened between us at all, and despite how upset I am about the aftermath, I can't help replaying it in my mind as I soap myself under the water.

I've always liked Tristan. Not just the way he looks, but also the way he *is*. Smart. Quietly funny. Kind. But I feel like he just pulled the curtain back and showed me an entirely new part of himself. One that was filthy in all the ways I crave, and commanding too.

I've never been talked to the way he talked to me, and it's that that got me off as much as what we actually did.

And I want more of it.

My hands go still, fingers buried in the lather I'm working through my hair, and something inside me deflates.

"It's not going to happen though, is it?" I whisper to myself, the one memory I'd rather *not* replay in my head suddenly front and center.

Tristan thinks it was a mistake, and nothing I said changed a damn thing.

I squeeze my eyes closed, breathing through the fresh wave of disappointment, then suck it up and finish my shower, not letting myself dwell on it anymore. There's just no point.

I find a text waiting for me in the group chat when I'm done, and as soon as I dress and repack my suitcase, I follow its instructions and meet the guys downstairs for breakfast. It's awkward, but I've pulled up my big girl panties and accepted the way things are, so I get through it with a smile that's only a little bit fake.

Once we all pile into the car, though, there's no denying the tension going in every direction.

"Do you want the front?" Tristan asks me politely after Beckett gets in the driver's seat.

"No, go ahead," I tell him, equally polite.

For a second, just like back in his room, he looks like he wants to say something else, but once again, I don't give him a chance. I hop in the back next to Ryder and pull out a sketchbook as the three of them discuss the route and who knows what else for the first few minutes of the drive.

All around, everything feels weird. I expected it between me and Tristan, and I'm not all that surprised that the casual ease I've felt for the last few days with Ryder and Beckett is gone too, since they caught my walk of shame, but it's definitely not all centered around me.

I can tell that there's strain between the two of them and Tristan, and I can't help wondering if they—if *he*—talked about me.

But I try very hard not to wonder about that, because it will drive me crazy if I do.

I start randomly sketching, but I have trouble focusing, and it's not until I realize I've started drawing a rough outline of Tristan in the shower this morning that I give up with an annoyed huff and slam my sketchbook closed, tossing it onto the seat.

"Writer's block?" Ryder asks with a small smirk.

"I'm drawing, not writing."

His smirk turns into a full grin. "Actually, it looks like you're *not* drawing."

That gets a laugh out of me, which I can tell by the glint in his eye was kind of the point, but just as I'm enjoying the tension relief, he ruins it by clearing his throat and bringing up the one topic I was hoping we could all spend the rest of our lives avoiding.

"So, why were you in Tristan's room this morning, love?"

"She had a bad dream," Tristan answers from the front seat, too quickly for me to decide what I want them to know.

And honestly, that's probably what I would have gone with too. It's not just the truth, it feels far less embarrassing than admitting that Tristan considers me a *mistake*. But now that he put it out, any lingering embarrassment is completely overshadowed by how annoyed I am at the way he tried to backtrack so hard after the fact.

He came all over my body. He was so hungry for me that he broke his own rule and touched me after he said he wouldn't.

It was the best orgasm of my life, and something bold and reckless rears up inside me, refusing to let him downplay how fucking good it was.

"The bad dream is why I was in your room *last night*," I remind Tristan, giving him a sweetly murderous smile. "But that's not what Ryder asked, is it? He wants to know what I was doing there this morning."

Tristan clears his throat. "Well, you slept over. I was... happy to comfort you."

"Thank you."

He's hoping I'll leave it at that. The silent eye contact I'm getting from him couldn't be any clearer. And why that turns me on even as it sort of pisses me off, I've got no idea.

I'm not sure I care, either. For better or worse, the emotional roller coaster this man is putting me on is exhilarating.

But if he thinks I'm letting him off the hook, he's wrong again.

"And are you going to tell them what else happened?" I ask him, arching an eyebrow.

Tristan's lips tighten, emotions I can't identify flashing across his face.

Ryder looks between the two of us like he's watching a ping pong match, and I catch Beckett's gaze in the rearview mirror a couple of times too.

"Well?" Ryder finally asks, breaking my stare-off with Tristan. "Are you going to tell us?"

"No," Tristan says.

"Sure," I answer at the same time, feeling bolder than I ever have before, as if every mile of this road trip shakes loose another inhibition. "We both woke up in a certain mood, but Tristan decided to take care of that by himself in the shower... at first."

He groans quietly, shaking his head at me.

I smile at him, holding his gaze as fresh arousal pools between my legs. "I heard him say my name, so naturally, I went into the bathroom when he called me."

"I wasn't *calling* you. I told you to get out."

I lick my lips. "And I did. But you still had me in a state, Tristan."

"What happened?" Beckett demands, the quiet growl ratcheting up my arousal to a whole new level.

I break eye contact with Tristan, feeling a flush spread over my skin as I briefly meet Beckett's eyes in the mirror. "I decided to take care of things myself, just like Tristan was. I went back to the bed and got comfortable. Then I started... touching myself."

Next to me, Ryder groans softly, and I'm suddenly intensely aware of the heat of his thigh, pressing against mine.

I shift slightly to face him, my heart beating faster as I look into his eyes while telling them the rest. "I was so turned on that I probably would have come in minutes just from picturing how sexy Tristan looked, jerking off in the shower. But then he decided to join me—"

"Lana," Tristan rasps softly from the front seat as Ryder's pupils expand, his eyes still locked on to mine. "*Fuck.*"

"A fuck? I wouldn't have said no," I tease him a little. "But the way you took me apart with just your voice alone was honestly better than any fuck I've ever had."

"Jesus," Beckett mutters quietly.

"That's what I said," I admit with a breathless laugh, pressing my thighs together. "He told me exactly how to touch myself. Where I was allowed to, and how hard he wanted me to do it, and when I had permission to come."

Ryder's eyes are still locked with mine, and the filthy, appreciative smile he's giving me answers the question I just asked myself—I definitely don't regret this. Not a single second of it.

No matter what Tristan said, *none* of this has been a mistake.

11

BECKETT

My grip is so tight on the steering wheel by the time Lana finishes talking that I'm a little shocked it hasn't cracked in two. But if it does? That shit will one hundred percent be Ryder's fault.

I send him a quick glare through the rearview mirror, but of course he doesn't see it. His gaze is still locked on Lana like she's the second coming of his dick's messiah, too enthralled by her recap of what went down between her and Tristan earlier to notice the silent message I'm currently sending him.

I jerk my eyes back to the road as he prods her for more details. That fucker just can't let things alone, always jumping in to talk about shit that anyone rational would ignore or shove under the rug like a normal person.

We both saw Lana come out of Tristan's room this morning.

We both saw how well-fucked and gorgeous she looked.

Was goading her into spelling it out for us like this is really necessary, or does the man just have a death wish? Because hearing the details in that breathy voice of hers is seriously fucking with my ability to focus. So if I wrap the four of us around a tree while she goes on and on about how hot Tristan made her this morning— once again, it will be Ryder's fault.

"What kind of piercing?" he asks her, the question breaking through my ability to block the conversation out for my own sanity.

Tristan groans so softly I would have missed it if he wasn't right next to me.

"It's a hood piercing," Lana answers in the backseat, a gorgeous pink flush on her cheeks when I dart a glance back there via the mirror.

"Sounds fucking hot," Ryder tells her with a grin, making her bite her lip like she's trying to hold in a smile.

"It's new, but so far, I really like it," she says, making me picture something I really fucking shouldn't.

I've got no doubt at all that her pussy is the exact same lickable color as her lips, and thinking of it wet and swollen from attention with a sexy-as-fuck little... barbell? Ring? Horseshoe? Fuck, imagining any kind of metal there at all is something my mind is having a much easier time visualizing than it should.

I reach down and subtly adjust my cock. The sexual tension in the car is thick enough to cut with a knife.

"How about you, Tristan?" Ryder says from the back. "Did you like Lana's new piercing too?"

"What do you think?" Tristan replies, his jaw tight.

Lana huffs out a breath. "Well, since you said it was a mistake that shouldn't happen again, I think you must not have been as much of a fan as I thought."

The tension surrounding all of us shifts into something a little less playful for a moment, but then Ryder cracks a joke that has Lana's pretty skin flushing pink again, and Tristan rolls his eyes, and the conversation thankfully moves the fuck on.

For them.

I don't have much to say as Lana whips out her phone a while later and starts going on about other roadside attractions along our route, because I still can't stop picturing the blow-by-blow recap she gave us, and it's driving me crazy.

"The world's largest ball of twine is in Kansas," Lana says. "Are we driving through Kansas?"

"What even is twine?" Ryder asks. "Rope? String? Cording?"

"Cording isn't actually a word."

"The fuck it isn't." He laughs as I tune out their banter,

rubbing the center of my chest, where a shit-ton of feelings are churning, and then dropping my hand the minute I realize what I'm doing.

I scowl at the highway ahead of us, trying to make sense of what it is that's got me worked up. Besides the obvious, of course. Because despite the half hard-on I'm still sporting, there's definitely something more happening inside me, and when I cut my eyes over to Tristan—who's engrossed in his phone in the seat next to me—those feelings take a turn I'm not sure I like.

It was hot as fuck to hear about what he did with Lana, and normally the only thing a story like that would have me feeling about him was happy to hear he got some. I'm not sure if it's being part of the kink community or just the bond I've got with my closest friends, but no matter who any of us has hooked up with in the past or what kind of kink any of them have shown an interest in, I've been supportive no matter what.

And no matter who they've hooked up with, I've sure as hell never been *jealous*.

But goddammit, I'm rubbing at my chest again before I realize it, unable to deny that that's exactly what this shit-storm inside me feels like right now.

"Okay, B?" Tristan asks, glancing up from his phone to send me a concerned frown.

"Heartburn," I mutter, grabbing the wheel at ten-and-two to keep my hands occupied the way they should be right now.

Without a word, Tristan rustles around in the center console and passes over two Rolaids, and I grunt my thanks as I pop them into my mouth. I chew the chalky things as my penance for lying, wishing they'd work for whatever the fuck it is that I'm actually feeling.

I refuse to let it be jealousy, because that's bullshit, especially between us.

And Tristan shut things down between them anyway.

I don't love how unhappy Lana sounded about that, but it's still for the best. I'm not shocked that he went there, because I'm pretty sure any of the three of us would if circumstances were different, since Lana is pure, dimpled temptation. But they're not, and it would get too fucking messy given our relationship with Caleb and how understandably protective he is of her.

A soft hand touches my shoulder, claiming my attention, and my eyes snap up to meet Lana's in the mirror. She smiles, and a whole fucking cascade of filthy images flicker through my mind, the kind of shit that I've kept under lock and key around her up until now.

Exactly the reason it would be best to just slam the lid shut on that particular Pandora's box before it even opens.

"Hungry?" Lana asks, the tone of her voice clueing me in that maybe it's not the first time she's tried to get my attention. "We were thinking it's about time to stop for lunch."

"Sure," I say, forcing my eyes back to the road.

"There should be an exit in two miles with some options," Tristan says from next to me.

I take it when it appears, barely paying attention as they direct me toward the diner they've picked out. Then I follow the three of them inside, still feeling tense as all fuck.

Lana ends up sitting next to me in the booth, with Ryder and Tristan across from us.

It's fucking torture.

"Good burger?" she asks me at one point, her soft thigh pressed against mine and the honey-sweet scent of her body products more mouthwatering than the fried food we're all devouring.

"It's fine."

I take another bite, keeping all my attention focused on it, and after a moment, she gets caught up in conversation with Ryder again. It's not until Tristan gets up to pay for our meal that I realize I've got no fucking clue what they've been talking about, lost in my thoughts this whole time.

As Tristan is paying, Ryder makes a comment about needing a pit stop before we get back on the road and heads toward the sign for the restrooms in the back of the diner. When we're alone at the table, Lana puts her soft hand on my arm again.

"Are you..."

She bites her lip a little shyly, and I tense up, hoping I haven't somehow given away the kind of shit I've been thinking about her.

"What?" I ask when she just leaves the words hanging.

"I was just wondering if you're upset."

"No," I say, more curtly than I mean to.

Lana gives my arm a little squeeze. "Are you sure? Something has seemed weird with you all morning."

"Everything's fine."

She nods, looking at me like she's not quite convinced, then sighs and removes her hand, giving me a tiny smile. "Okay. I just don't want things to be awkward on this trip."

"Nothing is awkward."

I hold her gaze, hoping she'll believe it, since it's true. I may not be able to name the riot of emotion still broiling in my chest, but awkward isn't a part of it.

This time, the smile she gives me is a little more real, one that draws my eyes to the dimple near her mouth. "Good. It's really freeing to be able to be myself around you three. Wade was just so vanilla, you know?"

I give her a non-committal grunt. I *don't* fucking know, nor do I want to know anything about her piece of shit ex.

"He always made me feel weird if I ever wanted to try new things in bed," she goes on, wreaking havoc on the tight control I'm using to keep myself from picturing what she told us in the car. "It didn't take me long to realize I shouldn't even bring certain things up."

I want to know what kind of things. I want to hear every fucking one. I want to dominate her, insist she tell me in vivid detail, then show her what *true* pleasure can be.

Instead, I double down on my control and keep my response to the basics.

"He's a motherfucking prick. He didn't deserve you."

She laughs softly.

"It took me a while to see that, but you're right. I think that's why I wanted to reinvent myself after he broke up with me. I never wanted to be the person he would have been happy with, and with him out of the picture—well, that's part of the reason I got my piercing. It's something just for me. And it feels like the *real* me, if that makes sense."

I force out another grunt to let her know I'm listening, but fuck, she's seriously trying to kill me with all the shit she's saying.

Her cheeks turn the prettiest shade of pink with this latest confession, but the way she keeps her shoulders back and her head high anyway, refusing to be ashamed of her sexuality, is so fucking attractive that it sends all my blood south.

She starts nibbling her lip again, a hint of uncertainty passing across her face when I don't say anything. "*Does* it make sense?"

I nod at her, not trusting myself to open my mouth right now. But it must be enough, because she gives me another of those devastating smiles in return.

Thankfully, Ryder and Tristan both rejoin us a minute later.

"Want me to take a turn at the wheel?" Tristan asks, holding his hands out for the keys.

I shake my head. I could use something to focus on besides my chaotic thoughts, so I tell him, "Nah. I can do another shift."

He raises his eyebrows, giving me a curious look. "Got something on your mind?"

"I'm good."

He snorts but doesn't push it, leaving me to my thoughts as we all pile into the car and get back on the road. I grip the wheel tightly, doing my best to ignore the temptation in the back seat and keep my mind from obsessing over things it shouldn't.

There isn't anything to question here. I know that when it comes to crossing lines with Lana, there's no way in hell I can ever let myself go there.

Not with her.

We'd never work.

Outside of kink, she wants things I just don't.

Kids. Family. The kind of relationship I'm just not fucking built for.

And none of this is news to me. The raw truth is that her hot-as-fuck story this morning didn't spark something *new* for me, it just unlocked the door to the craving I've already got for her, and it's taking all I have to slam that fucking door shut again.

But I have to.

I can't touch her. Can't ever let myself have her, even if I find myself in Tristan's shoes one day.

Because if I do?

I know myself too damn well, and one taste would never be enough with Lana. If I ever did cross that line, I'd never be able to get on the right side of it again.

And if I ever completely fucked up and actually *fell* for her, even knowing all the reasons it's a bad idea, there's no fucking way I'd ever be able to let her go.

12

LANA

I GET a little lost in my thoughts once we're on the road again. I'm not sure what came over me with Beckett, but it felt good to just open up like that. It felt like maybe I really am becoming the bolder, more authentic version of me.

But if I'm really honest, that's not the only reason I can't stop thinking about the conversation we had at the diner. I don't quite know what was going through his head, but there was something in his expression that made my heart beat a little harder.

I don't think I was intentionally taunting him, talking so freely about my sex life like that. But I'd be lying to myself if I didn't recognize that choosing that particular subject created something electrical between us.

Unless I'm fooling myself.

I don't really know where things stand between all of us right now. We're not even halfway across the country, and already, so much has happened that I didn't expect.

I bite my lip, my breath hitching a little as a few of those *unexpected* moments replay in my head, but when my eyes dart toward Tristan in the front passenger seat, Ryder catches my gaze instead.

"All good, love?" he asks, throwing his arm over the seat behind me and grinning at me in a way that makes me feel things, especially given where my thoughts just were.

"Yup," I answer, pulling out my sketchbook. "I just need to..."

I trail off, letting some of my flustered thoughts take shape on the paper. It's just doodling, but it settles my mind. I'm not even sure how long I've been sketching when I realize Ryder is still watching me.

I look up, feeling a little flustered when I see his expression.

"They have the best hot chocolate there, don't they?" When I don't answer right away, he taps the page. "That's Caldwell's, right? On Fourth? Back home?"

I glance back down, and he's right. I was just letting my hand run away with me. Drawing the same snow that's started falling outside our windows. Adding in some holiday decorations because of course. And when I added in the three of them, the rest of the scene just sort of took shape all around... and it *is* Caldwell's. One of the nicer restaurants in our hometown, but one that was always warm and inviting around Christmas, not pretentious like most of the places where my family preferred to dine.

I shrug, blushing for some reason. "I didn't really think about it. It's just doodles."

Ryder scoffs, pushing my hand to the side when I reflexively cover the page. "Are you kidding? You got Beckett's scowl down perfectly! It's really good."

I shake my head. "Just something to occupy my hands."

He pins me with a look that's almost serious for him. "It's a lot more than that. You've been drawing as long as I've known you, but it's been a while since I've seen your work. Why didn't you ever do more with it?"

I laugh. "With what, this? I *am* actually an adult now," I tease him. "I think I've been a little busy with real life things like a job and all."

For once, Ryder doesn't laugh with me. "Sure, but why not a job you love? Like making art."

My heart skips a beat. All I've ever heard from the people closest to me is what a waste of time my little hobby was, and that I need to be serious and put my time into things that matter.

"I used to want to," I whisper, gripping my pencil a little tighter when I realize my fingers are trembling a bit.

Ryder smiles. "Yeah? Be a professional artist, you mean?"

I nod, my pulse racing.

He glances back down at the scene I sketched, reaching out to trace some of the lines. "It's so full of life. Not totally true to life like a photo, but... something more? Something better?"

He laughs, and I grin before I can help it.

"Yeah, yeah. I don't know what I'm saying," he says, nudging my shoulder with his. "I sure as shit don't know art terms. But I don't just recognize what you drew. I *feel* it. You didn't even draw in the details, but I swear I can almost taste that cocoa they had just from looking at this picture." He looks back up at me. "You've got an amazing talent, Lana. You know it's not too late, right? If you really want to do this, you should go for it."

I stare back at him, a little overwhelmed. I don't quite know what to do with what he's saying. I've never had anyone encourage me like this, or say something so moving about my stupid little sketching hobby.

Wade knew I liked to doodle, of course. But just like my parents, he'd get impatient with me wasting my time on it, so I kept my art supplies out of sight and hopefully out of mind for him for the most part.

It never occurred to me to show him any of my drawings, and I know for sure if I'd ever so much as hinted that I sometimes thought of quitting my dreary office job to pursue it, he would have...

Well, I'm not sure what. I know he wouldn't have liked it, though.

And he *definitely* never would have encouraged me. Not like Ryder is right now.

"What's the style called?" he asks, tilting his head like he's trying to get a different view of my sketchpad. "Like, not realistic but, uh, there's gotta be a word for it, right?"

I laugh, releasing some of the build-up of unfamiliar feelings inside me. I'm not sure if he's playing up his cluelessness or really wants to know, but I'm always happy to talk about art, so we do for a bit.

"Wait, his name is really Hunter Greene-Paige?" he asks me, laughing. "A little on the nose."

I pull out my phone and find the artist's Instagram. "I know, but it really is his given name, so I guess he just went with it? It's become his signature color."

Ryder flips through Greene-Paige's work, pausing on an abstract watercolor. "I don't get it. But I like it?"

"Oh, good eye." I chuckle, leaning in. "But I'm biased. That one was inspired by one of my favorite artists."

"Oh? Who's that?"

I tap the screen and pull up a different page. "Emilia Rossetti. She's *amazing*."

I may be fan-girling a little, but it's well-deserved.

"Huh." Ryder scrolls through a few images. "Kind of reminds me of your style."

My eyes go wide, then I laugh and punch his shoulder. "Shut up."

"Hey, I may not have any artistic skills of my own, but come on. I know what I'm looking at here."

He's still got me laughing. "You literally just said you didn't know."

He shrugs, and my stomach flutters. There are definite vibes between us, and even though he's always been charming and warm with me, this feels like something else.

His eyes drop to my mouth, and I bite my lip as my heart stutters.

"I could teach you," I blurt suddenly.

Ryder's eyes jerk up to mine. "Teach me?"

"To draw something," I clarify, flipping to a clean page in my sketchbook. "You can't be *that* bad."

Tristan twists around a little in the front seat. "Oh, believe me, freckles. He can."

"Freckles?" Ryder repeats while I send Tristan a dirty look.

"Quit outing me." I make a face, wadding up a piece of paper and throwing it at him. "I wear makeup for a reason, you know."

Tristan's eyes flare with heat, then he blinks and they're back to normal as he gives me a tiny smile. "You look gorgeous either way."

I look down, feeling flustered all over again.

"Come on," I say to Ryder, handing him the pencil. "Just try."

Beckett scoffs, the only sign that he's listening with his eyes glued to the road, and Tristan nods.

"Are you sure you want to suffer through this?" he asks, adjusting his glasses with that same small smile hovering on his lips.

Ryder flips him off, then shoots me a wicked grin as he takes the pencil and draws a circle. I mean, sort of. "You want art? I got art," he says, adding a line connected to the circle. Then he draws a couple more lines, and...

"Ryder!" I laugh, bumping my shoulder into him again. "A stick figure doesn't count!"

"Hey, I saw some of that Greene guy's work. It was all lines!"

"Yeah, but those were..." I search for the right word, then give up. "Let me show you."

"You're wasting your time," Tristan jokes.

"You're just jealous that you're stuck up there while I get free art lessons," Ryder shoots back, trying and horribly failing to copy the technique I show him.

"For whatever good they'll do you." Tristan snorts. "We should switch spots."

Ryder smirks. "Pretty sure you already got plenty of time with Lana this morning."

Heat pools in my core, making me squeeze my thighs together, and the unspoken tension in the car spikes from every direction. We're *all* thinking about what Tristan and I did this morning now.

But of course it's Ryder who comes right out and says something. Again.

He adds a few blobby shapes near the head of the stick figure he drew. "Want to know why I'm crying, love?" he asks, tapping the blobs.

I grin, shaking my head. "Those are tears?"

"Of course they are. Because you ran to Tristan when you had that nightmare instead of coming to me."

"You were rooming with me," Beckett grunts from the driver's seat.

"And?" Ryder throws back. "You know we both would have been there for her."

Beckett grunts again, and that heat inside me burns a little hotter. "I would have been glad to have you, um, comfort me," I tell him, suddenly a little breathless. "But Tristan's room was closer."

Ryder's eyes lock onto mine, something wicked glinting in their depths. "Yeah? But just think, love. If you'd gone just a little bit farther, you would've woken up sandwiched between me and Beckett."

My stomach flips, my heart starting to race at the innuendo. There's no mistaking it, and no second-guessing that he's flirting. This isn't Ryder teasing Caleb's little sister. This is one of the sexiest men I know suggesting that he would have welcomed me into his bed.

His *and* Beckett's.

"Maybe I wouldn't have minded that," I murmur, finding a level of daring I didn't know I had.

Ryder gives me a slow, sexy smile that suddenly makes all sorts of things seem within reach. "You like that idea, huh?"

"Just think what we could save on hotel room costs," I say, making him laugh.

"Definitely something to consider."

I lick my lips, a little surprised by how confident and sexy I feel as we banter back and forth. "It's not *just* about the money. I do get kind of cold at night too."

His eyes drop to my mouth. "Is that so?"

"I mean, it is the middle of winter."

He chuckles, but this time there's a husky quality to it that has my breath catching as tingles spread through me.

He reaches out and runs the backs of his fingers down my cheek. "Good point. We've all gotta do our part to keep you warm, right? But I draw the line at cold feet." Without taking his eyes off me, he tosses a comment at Tristan. "Is that a problem, Tris? You can tell us. Do her toes turn into ice cubes at night?"

"No," Tristan responds, biting off the word.

Both Ryder and I startle at his tone, turning to face him.

He's looking out the front windshield, brows drawn low as Beckett navigates through the densely falling snow.

It's getting dark out, and visibility is so low that it's only the faint glow of someone else's red taillights up ahead that reassure me we're actually still on the road.

"Wow," I say with a wince. "I didn't realize how bad it had gotten out there."

"We'll be fine," Beckett assures me gruffly, even as he slows the SUV down even more when the brake lights up ahead flare brightly.

I trust him, because the way he commands the vehicle is exactly the way he commands everything else in his life. With a kind of absolute authority and assurance that in other circumstances I find sexy as hell.

But right now, it's the *other* cars still on the road that I'm not sure I trust, not in weather like this, and by silent agreement, we all stay quiet so Beckett can focus. It's only when he has to tap the brakes a few miles later, causing the wheels to slip a bit, that I realize I'm gripping Ryder's hand.

"Shit," Beckett mutters softly. "Was that an exit sign?"

"Yeah," Tristan replies, already looking down at his phone. "Two miles up."

Beckett nods, carefully navigating into the right lane. "We need to get off the road."

"Fuck, there's not much availability," Tristan mutters, swiping through a few screens on his phone.

Ryder squeezes my hand once, then extracts his so he can pull out his phone. "You're checking hotels?" he asks Tristan, opening an app to do the same.

Tristan mumbles a reply, and I pull my phone out to help too. The conditions are so bad now that Beckett has us slowed down to a crawl, and I've got no doubt that everyone else out here tonight is doing the same thing we are. It would be crazy to keep going until the storm passes, so it's no wonder everything nearby is booked up.

"Got one," Ryder says after a few minutes, naming a familiar hotel chain. "It's a little farther off the highway, but all they've got left is the executive suite."

"Grab it," Beckett grunts, tension in his voice as he throws his blinker on and finally exits the highway.

Ryder nods, tapping his screen a few times. "Already on it. Take a right and head under the overpass."

He continues to direct Beckett to the hotel, and once we get there, we leave everything that's not essential in the SUV, all four of us hurrying inside as the snow whips around us.

"My toes are definitely ice cubes now," I joke weakly, shivering as we crowd together at the reception counter since I didn't stop to put on my coat.

Beckett grunts and tugs me against his side, his body heat thawing me out a little while Ryder finishes checking us in.

It's not until we finally get the key cards and make our way up to the suite we'll all be sharing that it really hits me what Ryder said back in the car.

One suite. The only one left. The one we'll all be sharing tonight.

And it's almost like all that heated banter wasn't just flirting or foreplay, but actually prophetic, because when we get there we realize that the suite is plenty big enough for the four of us to share. It's a large space with a little living room area and a kitchen too.

But only one bedroom.

And only one bed.

13

LANA

My heart thuds at the sight of the king-sized bed. It's large enough for all of us to fit on, and after the way Ryder was teasing me earlier, my heart races at the thought that it's no longer just teasing.

We'll have to.

Something coils inside me at the thought, but I force my shoulders to relax. There was too much tension between all four of us this morning, the much-less-fun kind of tension, and the truth is, we don't *have* to.

"I, um, I can sleep on the couch," I stutter, nervously running my hand over the back of it.

All three men turn to face me.

"No way." Tristan shakes his head. "We'll figure something out."

"What's to figure out," I say, shrugging. "I'm the smallest."

"And that thing is tiny." He gives the couch an assessing look. "We're not letting you sleep there." Then he smirks slightly, adding, "Especially since I know you didn't sleep very well last night."

Warmth floods my chest. He hasn't explicitly said what my other options are, but just the fact that he's looking out for me heals some of the cracks inside me from the way we left things this morning.

He holds eye contact, and I finally smile.

"Okay," I say softly, getting a smile in return. "We'll just figure it out?"

He nods when my voice lilts up at the end, making it into a question that I'm not sure how to ask, and something settles between us.

"Shit, it really is bad out there," Ryder declares from over by the window, breaking the moment between me and Tristan.

I hurry over to join him, pushing the curtain open to see a solid wall of white. I have a fleeting thought of how my mother will react if the storm delays us past tonight, but I shake it off, a grin spreading over my face before I can stop it.

Next to me, Ryder snorts. "What?"

"It's snowing!"

He raises his eyebrows. "Yes? And?"

"Oh, come on." I beam, lifting my eyebrows. "It's almost Christmas! It's beautiful, isn't it?"

"Now that we're not driving in it," Beckett mutters, wandering closer.

"Exactly! And just look at this suite. It's really nice, isn't it? And what's better than being all warm and cozy inside in winter?" I pull the curtains open wider. "It's like we're inside our own personal snow globe!"

All three of them shoot me extremely unimpressed looks, their expressions so similar that I burst out laughing.

"Really, guys? Where's your holiday spirit?" I turn back to look at the falling snow. A subtle rainbow of blurry lights is visible through the tumbling flakes from the nearby buildings that are decorated for Christmas. I sigh happily. "This reminds me of winters back home, you know? Whenever it would get really bad outside like this, I'd curl up on that padded window seat we had. You guys know the one, remember?"

"Down the hall from Caleb's room," Tristan murmurs.

"Yup. I'd curl up there with a cup of peppermint hot chocolate and a plate of frosted gingerbread cookies, watch the snow fall outside, just like this, and dream of..."

I shrug, smiling as bits and pieces of memories flit through my mind.

"Dream of what, love?" Ryder asks, putting his arm around my shoulders as he looks out the window with me.

"Oh, I don't know." I shrug. "So many things, but also nothing really specific. Just a happy life, you know? This time of year kind of makes it impossible not to daydream like that, don't you think?"

Ryder hums softly under his breath, which isn't a no. But knowing his distaste for this season, it's not a yes, either.

That's okay. I love *Christmas*. And there really is magic in it, as far as I'm concerned. Even if you have to find it in small moments most of the time, not in big, flashy miracles.

"Shit, I think I left my charger in the car," Tristan says, digging through the small bag he grabbed when we all came inside.

"I'll grab it," Beckett grunts, keys jingling in his hand. "I've gotta step out anyway. I'll be back in a bit."

He nods at us, then leaves the room.

I shiver as cold seeps in through the window, and Ryder rubs my arm briskly, then steps away. "Let's turn up the heat."

"I think I'll grab a quick shower too," I tell them, needing to warm up.

Ryder tosses me my overnight bag, and I head into the spacious bathroom, sighing contentedly when I finally step under the water a few minutes later.

I do love winter, and snow really is one of my favorite things. But getting warm again after spending a little time in it? That's its own kind of miracle, and I stand under the rainfall shower head and let myself relax and enjoy it.

As I close my eyes and tilt my head back, the sound of the water hitting the glass enclosure suddenly takes me back to this morning. To Tristan. To watching him touch himself, hearing him groan my name, seeing his head fall back with pleasure.

I gasp and open my eyes again, reaching for the scented body wash provided by the hotel. Rubbing it over my skin tempts me to follow Tristan's example and touch myself a little more intimately.

But I don't. Not with the three of them—well, maybe just two if Beckett isn't back yet—out there possibly listening.

Or maybe I don't because the idea of these men out there listening makes it a little *too* tempting.

I bite my lip, then shake my head and rinse off quickly without giving in to that temptation. I'm not sure what's happening between all of us, or between any of us, but I do know that I don't want to figure it out in here all on my own.

I turn off the water and towel myself off, then moisturize with the high-end lotion I'm addicted to and put on a fluffy robe, compliments of the hotel.

It feels amazing against my bare skin, but my enjoyment is cut short when my phone rattles against the counter where I left it. I've got it muted, and when I pick it up, I realize that I missed a call and several texts about Christmas from my mother.

I blink, surprised to see them. Not because the urgent tone over mundane matters is out of character for her, because it's not. But because for a moment, I almost forgot what this road trip is really about.

For another moment, I very, very briefly consider continuing to forget, just for a while, but then I shake that bit of foolishness off too and quickly tap out a reply to her repeated requests for confirmation of my arrival time.

She's already going to be annoyed by the update I'm sending, letting her know that we've run into bad weather. Annoying her further by delaying my reply would just make my life that much more miserable.

I got a response almost instantly.

MOM: I hope you're not using that as an excuse to spoil our holiday plans. You have obligations as a member of this family, Lana.

My stomach tightens unpleasantly, but really, what did I expect? Concern over the safety of the roads?

> ME: I'll be there. Depending on the road conditions tomorrow, I might arrive a bit later than I expected to, but I budgeted extra time anyway, so I'm not too worried about it.

> MOM: Maybe you should be a little more worried. We've invited people who will expect to see you on the 24th. Don't disappoint me.

I bite back a sigh, knowing there's no point in wishing she'd want me there because she misses me, or because she's looking forward to all of us being together at the holidays, rather than just appearances and expectations.

> ME: I'll make it in time for the Christmas Eve party.

> MOM: This wouldn't have been a problem if you'd flown. Where are you now? If the weather hasn't cleared tomorrow, we should look into flights local to you.

I sigh. It doesn't matter how many times I explain how uncomfortable with flying I am. She *always gives me a hard time about it.*

> ME: I really don't want to fly. There's still plenty of time to make it on the road. I'll be there. I promise.

It takes me another minute or two of going back and forth before she finally lets me be, and I set my phone back down on the counter and decide to leave it there as I head back out into the suite.

If she really needs to say anything else to me tonight... well, it can wait.

I pull the luxurious robe around me more tightly and step into the living room just as Beckett returns to the room. He pauses by the door, brushing some snow off his shoulders and the oversized paper bag he's carrying.

"Did you grab my charger?" Tristan asks.

Beckett nods, fishing it out of his pocket and tossing it to him.

Ryder jerks his chin toward the bag. "What else did you get?"

"Went to that bakery we passed."

Ryder's eyebrows go up. "We passed a bakery?"

Tristan nods, following Beckett to the table as Beckett sets down the bag and carefully pulls a drink carrier out with four steaming travel cups in it. "It was on the corner a couple blocks back. With all the Christmas lights. You didn't see that?"

Ryder shrugs.

"I walked over," Beckett informs us, pulling a take-out box from the bag, then folding the bag flat and setting it aside. He glances at me, his lips tilting up ever so slightly on one side. "Just like being in a snow globe."

That startles a laugh out of me, and something warm and a little bit wonderful spreads through my chest.

"Colder than one, though," I whisper.

Beckett grunts, then hands me one of the travel cups. "Yeah, but this will warm you up. Peppermint hot chocolate, right?"

I nod as I take it, that warmth inside me starting to glow.

Ryder pops open the take-out box, then grins up at me. "And Christmas cookies!"

"Gingerbread ones?" I ask, a little stunned.

"Frosted," Ryder confirms, shoving one into his mouth with a grin as Beckett gazes down at me.

His handsome face is ruddy from the cold, and I reach up to rest one of my hands on his cold cheek, my other hand warmed all the way through from the drink he went out of his way to get.

"You didn't have to do that. You're freezing."

"Winter will do that. But someone told me that it just makes things feel more warm and cozy inside."

I'm definitely feeling warm and cozy inside, and for a moment, I can't look away. It's not just that he remembered what I said, and it's not even the unexpected thoughtfulness of Beckett going out of his way to fulfill one of my favorite holiday memories.

It's how *seen* I feel.

"Peppermint hot chocolate, huh?" Tristan says, pulling one of the cups out of the travel carrier and sniffing it.

Beckett chuckles, pulling my hand from his face and giving it a quick squeeze before turning back to Tristan. "Not for you. One of them should be that Chai shit you like."

Tristan grins as Ryder turns on the gas fireplace, and we all settle in to eat the treats Beckett brought back for us. It really is cozy, and as I curl up on the couch and listen to the three of them tease each other with the familiarity of lifelong friends—including me in their banter as naturally as breathing—it hits me that I'm happier than I can remember being in a long time.

And a little bit nostalgic, too... even if it's more of a wistful longing for the happy future I used to dream of than actual memories of Christmases past.

"These are almost as good as the ones Grandma Meg makes," Tristan groans as I relax into the plush couch.

He holds up a gingerbread man currently missing its left leg.

"You'd better not let her hear you say that." Ryder chuckles as Tristan bites the right leg off too. "Remember that year she made a whole batch with their heads missing?"

Beckett cracks a smile, and Tristan laughs hard enough it's a holiday miracle that he doesn't choke.

"What happened?" I ask, grinning as I look between the three of them.

"It was Caleb's fault," Beckett says. "We should probably leave it at that."

I lean forward. "Oh no, you don't! You've got dirt on my brother? I need it."

Ryder chuckles. "He used to play hockey without a helmet sometimes, and Grandma Meg wasn't having it."

"She does have a way of making a point," Tristan says with a grin. "Although I don't think I've ever seen a hockey player take a hit quite as bad as she was implying with those headless cookies. Speaking of hockey, do you remember that time—"

Beckett cuts him off. "Nope. We're not talking about that."

"How do you know what he was going to say?" I ask, laughing as I look between the three of them.

Tristan smirks. "Oh, Beckett knows because he was the one

who broke my grandmother's favorite reindeer Christmas ornament with a hockey puck."

"Allegedly," Beckett says, pointing a cookie at Tristan, then swinging it around to aim at Ryder. "And you do remember who came up with the great idea to play hockey in the living room, don't you?"

"Hey, that was Caleb's idea, not mine!" Ryder defends himself, grinning.

"Oh, I see." I smirk. "You're all going to blame everything on my brother since he's not around to defend himself."

Tristan shrugs. "To be fair, he *was* the one who was always saying we should get in more practice."

"And look where he is now," Ryder points out. Then, after a moment, he adds, "Rest in pieces, Rudolph."

All three of them snicker, and that leads to a few more stories about trouble I never realized the four of them got into back then.

"A total hot chocolate ban?" I ask at one point, laughing so hard my cheeks start to hurt. "That sounds extreme."

Ryder shrugs. "I mean, it *was* a lot of snowballs."

"And let me guess. That was Caleb's fault too?"

Beckett and Tristan both nod solemnly, Tristan's eyes glinting behind his glasses. But then Ryder leans forward.

"I'll tell you a secret," he says in a conspiratorial voice. "Caleb may have been the master strategist, but Beckett was the one who came up with the idea to add the food dye."

Beckett chucks a pillow at him. "Traitor. If I remember that night correctly, we all swore an oath of secrecy about that shit."

Ryder grins. "Eh, I'm pretty sure the statute of limitations on that has expired."

"Oh really?" Beckett drawls, looking more relaxed than I'm used to seeing him and dangerously attractive as he gives Ryder a sly grin. "So we're free to tell each other's secrets now?"

"I'm here for it," I tell them, wiggling into a more comfortable position.

I pull the plush robe I'm still wearing around me as I rest my head on the arm of the couch, the dancing flames in the fireplace giving everything a cozy feel.

"You want our secrets, freckles?" Tristan asks softly, looking over at me with a small smile.

I guess I'm a little *too* relaxed, because I have to bite my tongue to keep from saying something along the lines of *I want everything*.

"I want to hear yours if you're gonna hear ours," Ryder tells me. "Something good. Something you've never told anyone before."

"Um, are we all playing by that rule? One secret we've never shared before?"

Something shifts in the air at my question, and all three men look at me with heated intensity before Beckett breaks the electric tension.

"I'll go first," he rumbles. "Remember Jonathan Hawkins?"

I frown, surprised. Jonathan was a couple of years younger than my brother and these three, and a grade ahead of me in school. He used to tease me relentlessly, with a biting humor that played on every one of my insecurities.

I never complained about it because I was too embarrassed, but I used to dread seeing him.

Until he changed.

Beckett's eyes flare with something sharp and dangerous when I give him a cautious nod, then his lips spread in a fierce grin. "He was a little shit, but he eventually learned to treat you nice, didn't he, little menace?"

"Yeah," I admit, laughing a little awkwardly. "My junior year of high school. He must have had a personality transplant or something. He became almost *weirdly* nice to me."

It was a lot better than the way he used to tear me down with his taunting, but it was definitely jarring the way he did such a one-eighty, going out of his way to be nice to me all the way up until he graduated.

Beckett holds my stare for a second, then gives a single sharp nod. "Good. I had a talk with him. Glad it stuck."

My heart trips in my chest. "You talked to him?"

Ryder snorts. "I'll bet you anything that their 'talk' involved the threat of bodily harm."

My eyes go wide. "Wait. You threatened him?" I ask Beckett. "For me?"

"I heard some of the shit he said to you once. He fucking deserved to feel a little fear over that."

I'm a little embarrassed that he knew how Jonathan was treating me, but I'm also so touched that he decided to do something about it.

"Thank you," I murmur after a moment, trapping my bottom lip between my teeth. "I didn't realize you even paid attention to me back then. Did Caleb ask you to look out for me then too?"

He holds my gaze for a moment, then shakes his head. "No."

"Oh," I breathe, the word barely a whisper.

"I've got a secret," Ryder says, breaking the gathering tension. "I hate Christmas."

Tristan laughs, adjusting his glasses. "Sorry, Ryder. That's no secret."

"It *is* a shame, though," I add. "It's such a magical time of year."

Ryder loses a bit of his perpetual cheer, a bleak look crossing his face as he brings his cup to his lips. It's got to be empty by now. Or if not that, his drink must be cold, because we've been sitting here for a while.

It's just a stalling tactic, though, and he finally sets it aside. "I guess it used to be fun. Presents, you know. The works. But when I was ten, it hit me... it was all just for show. It wasn't—"

He swirls his hand in the air, a meaningless gesture, but somehow I feel like I know what he's trying to say. Or maybe I'm just projecting some of what I used to feel growing up, since I know a bit about Ryder's family.

"It wasn't as warm and wonderful as you always see in the feel-good holiday movies?" I say softly. "With the families that come together and..."

I make the same swirl with my hand, and he gives me a lopsided smile.

"Yeah, that." He clears his throat. "I think that was the year my parents decided to go to Bali for Christmas. Or maybe Aruba? Whatever it was, they left me with the nanny, in our big-ass house that had been professionally decorated with enough holiday 'cheer' to choke all the fucking reindeer and Santa too. And I realized it was all for show."

"Ryder," I murmur, scooting closer to him and resting a hand on his arm. "That's awful."

He shrugs. "It's fine. They didn't give a shit about me. They never had, not really. That just happened to be the year I figured it out. Right before they'd left, we all had to get dressed up and do these family Christmas photos for some magazine spread. It was why the house was decorated to the nines like that. But it was all for show. The holiday cheer bullshit was all a lie."

My heart aches at his words. And while I love Christmas, I understand a little too well what he's saying.

It often feels like it's all for show in my family too. I still think the holiday *is* magical. But I also think some of us have to seek out that magic. To choose it, search for it, and hold on tight to all the little moments it's hiding in, even when the people who should have been a part of making the magic happen didn't do it.

I still have my hand on his arm, and I slide it down and lace our fingers together, squeezing his hand. "I knew you weren't close with your folks, but I didn't realize it was so bad. I wish..."

I stumble a little, not sure if it's my place to criticize his parents no matter how shitty it is that they put their own child second to their selfish needs.

"What?" he asks.

I'm about to brush it off and say it was nothing, but I feel closer to all three of these men right now than I have to anyone in a long time. And while I know I'll have to go back to censoring myself once the road trip is over and I'm around my family again, right now I want to be real, just like Ryder was brave enough to be.

"I wish they hadn't ruined Christmas for you. I wish they had put you first," I tell him, squeezing his hand again before I start to let it go.

131

But he doesn't let me. He squeezes back tighter, tugging me a little closer to him.

"Thank you, love," he murmurs, pressing a chaste kiss to the top of my head. Then he looks up at Tristan, something close to his usual grin back on his face. "Your turn."

Tristan nods, but instead of spilling a secret, he takes his glasses off and carefully cleans them, then puts them back on his face, adjusting the fit for a moment.

Stalling.

"Should I go?" I offer, trying to give him a way out.

But he surprises me, shaking his head and pinning me with a look I can't quite interpret.

"No," he says. "Ryder is right. It's my turn." He takes a breath, exhales, and then says, "I lied to you."

I blink. "To me?"

He nods, and a little ball of anxiety starts spinning inside me.

"Recently?" I whisper, my mind racing.

What did he lie about? I'm not sure I'll be able to take it if he tells me that he was faking his attraction to me this morning or something. He did call it a mistake, after all.

Tristan nods again. "This morning—"

I suck in a sharp breath, and Ryder wraps an arm around me, his body heat unwinding the knot in my gut a little.

Tristan's cheeks flush, but he holds my gaze as he finishes. "This morning I told you that what happened in my room was a mistake. But that wasn't true."

"You... lied about it being a mistake?" I ask over the pounding of my heart, my anxiety from a moment ago doing a one-eighty as the atmosphere in the room shifts.

Tristan nods again, and just to be sure, I murmur, "So... you liked it. You wanted me. You enjoyed what we did."

His eyes flash with enough heat to burn away my doubts, but he answers me anyway. "Yes."

My pulse picks up at the implications of that word. It wasn't a mistake. I can think of dozens of reasons why he could have gotten gun shy this morning, starting with my brother and ending with my own insecurities, but the way he's looking at me now puts all of those to rest.

He means it.

He wanted me.

He *still* wants me.

I'm not even drunk, but I almost feel that way. Each one of these men has opened up to me in ways that have rocked my understanding of who they are tonight, and fundamentally shifted all my own assumptions about my relationship with each one of them. And while I know none of them will pressure me if I don't want to go there, they're all looking to me for *my* secret now.

I swallow, my blood burning in my veins and a riot of emotions swirling inside me. Almost like I really am in some kind of magical bubble. A snow globe of possibility.

Tonight feels like the kind of night where I can either take the leap... or let it pass me by.

"My turn," I whisper, licking my lips. "Did you all hear what Ryder was teasing me about on the drive? About waking up sandwiched between him and Beckett?"

I get three nods. Three stares hot enough to make me combust.

And I leap.

"That wouldn't be quite what I want," I confess, my eyes darting toward the single bedroom and the king-sized bed before I admit the truth. "What I'd really want is to wake up in bed with all three of you."

14
LANA

I FEEL the weight of each man's gaze on me, the room so silent that I can hear my own heartbeat. I'm breathing too fast, both nervous and excited.

Finally, Tristan speaks. "What are you saying?"

The low rasp of his voice plays over my skin like fire, distracting me from the question for a moment. But then I realize he's going to make me explicitly spell it out, and I flush with embarrassment.

"The three of you own a sex club. Don't tell me you've never shared a girl before?"

"Not a girl like you," Tristan says, adjusting his glasses as he gives me an enigmatic smile.

I'm not sure what he means, but I've come this far. I'm not going to give up this chance without a fight.

I lift my chin. "Don't think that just because I'm not like the girls at the club, I can't be kinky. I like..."

I flounder for a second, losing a little steam as my inexperience catches up with me.

"Tell us, love," Ryder says in a low voice, his eyes burning into me. "What do you like?"

"I, um, okay. I don't know exactly what I like yet, but that's the whole point! I want to explore, to figure out who I am and what turns me on."

My heart is racing. The way the three of them are watching me, hanging on my every word, has the flush of embarrassment I felt a moment ago fueling the desire that's making me bold.

"I want to know what *really* turns me on," I go on in a whisper. "Not just what I think my partner wants to see. I've had my fill of faking it and then having to finish myself off later."

Tristan makes a low sound in the back of his throat, and I laugh, pressing my hands to my heated cheeks as I shake my head.

"I don't mean with you! What happened between us this morning was the hottest sex I've ever had." I look at Ryder, then Beckett. "And I want..."

I bite my lip, the tension in the room so thick that I can barely catch my breath.

"What?" Beckett growls. "Say it."

"I just want more," I whisper. "I want everything."

"So to be clear," Ryder says, giving me a heated smile. "By everything, you mean kink. You want the three of us to help you explore that?"

I nod.

"Do you trust us?" Tristan murmurs. When I nod again, his gaze sharpens, reminding me of how he took control this morning. "Then I'd like to propose a deal."

I toy with the plush softness of the robe I'm wearing. "What kind of deal?"

"Yeah, Tristan. What kind of deal?" Ryder echoes, his eyebrows going up.

"While we're on this road trip, let's forget that she's Caleb's little sister," he answers Ryder before turning his attention back to me. His voice drops lower. "We'll put all that aside for now, okay? And all four of us will be free to do whatever we want to."

"With each other?" I ask, my breath hitching.

"That's right. But when we get to your parents' house, it stops."

"Okay," I agree quickly, barely able to believe this is happening.

Tristan looks to his friends. "Are you both in?"

Ryder grins. "Whatever we want as long as we're on the road? Fuck yes, I'm in. We both are, right, Beck?"

Beckett stays silent, his gaze locked on mine until Tristan prompts him again.

"Beckett?"

He blinks, looking torn, then finally gives a curt nod. "Agreed. But if we're really going to help Lana explore kink, we need to talk about safe words."

A rush of excitement has me clenching my thighs together. "Can we just use the stoplights?"

"Tell me you understand them," he demands, suddenly all Dom.

I nod, my nipples pebbling. "If I need whatever we're doing to stop, I'll say red. If I'm not sure, or I just need to slow down, I can say yellow."

Finally, he smiles. A slow, sensual one that heats me from the inside out. "Good girl. And what does green mean?"

"That I'm all in," I whisper.

"And right now?"

"Green."

The three men share a look, silently communicating, then Tristan speaks. "Come here, freckles."

I blink, then draw in a shuddering breath, feeling like I'm waking up from a trance.

This is really happening.

"Lana," Tristan says, a note of authority in his voice. "Come here. Now."

I nod, pushing myself off the couch, and go over to him.

He pulls me down onto his lap, my back to his chest.

"Do you know how jealous Beckett and Ryder were, knowing I got to touch you this morning?" he asks, sliding one hand around me and slipping his hand through the opening in my robe. "That I'm the one who got to see all your gorgeous curves laid bare?"

His voice rumbles against me, the heat of his body like a drug and the words he's saying even more of one.

Or maybe it's the way the other two are looking at me while he says them.

Like Tristan is right.

Like they both want me too.

"I think we need to show them what they missed," Tristan whispers in my ear, his fingers stroking my stomach under my robe. "What do you think?"

I part my legs, letting my head fall back on his shoulder. "Please."

"Gladly," he says, a smile in his voice as he tugs on the sash of my robe, letting it fall open.

A low groan from Ryder has heat pooling between my legs, and the intensity of Beckett's gaze, sharp and hungry as Tristan bares my body to them, has arousal pulsing through my veins like a heartbeat of its own.

Then Tristan's hands are on me again, first lifting the heavy weight of my breasts and toying with my nipples until I'm panting, then sliding down over my stomach, heading toward my pussy.

"I love how fucking soft you are," he murmurs, kneading the soft flesh around my waist.

I tense up, then force myself to relax. Mostly.

"Definitely soft," I agree, turning my face to tuck it into the crook of his neck, hoping it will hide the flaming blush there.

I both love and hate having their eyes on me. It's hot like fire... but like Tristan said, I'm not exactly svelte.

He leaves one hand cupping my stomach, his fingers brushing the neatly trimmed curls at the top of my pussy, and uses his other hand to turn my face back toward Ryder and Beckett.

"No hiding, freckles. You're fucking gorgeous. They already missed out this morning. Don't deny my friends the right to see how sexy you are when you come."

"Am I going to come?" I ask breathlessly, half teasing him, half turned on.

He chuckles but doesn't answer me in words. Instead, he starts brushing his fingers back and forth over my clit while he pushes the fingers from his other hand into my mouth.

"Suck these for me."

My core tightens as I wrap my tongue around them and then moan when he pushes them deeper. It's enough to distract me from the last of my insecurities, and it doesn't take long before the teasing touch he's using on my clit has me squirming on his lap.

He groans, scraping his teeth across the sensitive spot under my ear again. "Love those moans, but they're not good enough. Not if we're going to figure out what you like. Get specific. Communication is key when it comes to kink, so tell me—and I mean use your words—do you like it when I do *this*?"

He pinches my nipple hard on the last word, the sharp burst of pain like nothing I've ever felt before. It lances through my body like a lightning strike, landing right between my legs, and I cry out, clenching my thighs around his hand.

"Yes! *That*. I liked that."

"A little pain?" Ryder rasps, his eyes burning into me.

"I... I guess?"

Tristan nudges my legs open again, grinding the heel of his hand against my clit with his fingers still buried inside me. "No hiding. Let them see."

Another bolt of desire rocks through me.

"That too," I whisper shamelessly, my inhibitions falling away as I make eye contact with Ryder and Beckett. "And I like knowing you're watching. Both of you. *All* of you."

Beckett holds himself so still I'd almost think he was uninterested if it weren't for the dusky red flush creeping up his neck. *Desire.* It's almost intoxicating to know how much he's enjoying this.

And Ryder's eyes, glinting with something hot, are practically eating me alive, creating a feedback loop with my own lust that just sends it higher.

Tristan pulls his fingers out of me, moving his hands to my hips and rearranging me so I'm spread open even more. Fully on display for all three of them.

"If you like being watched so much, how about we give them something to see then?" he murmurs in my ear, his big hands controlling my hips, subtly rocking me back and forth over his cock. "Touch yourself, freckles. Give Ryder and Beckett the kind of show you gave me this morning. Show them that pretty little jewel you've got."

He means my hood piercing, and even though I'm no stranger to pleasuring myself, when I slip my pinky through the little ring and tug on it, moaning as it stimulates my clit, this feels different.

Ryder's and Beckett's attention makes every sensation even more intense as pleasure builds inside me. Being the focus of all three of these men gives me a heady, electric thrill.

The more they watch, the more I love the feeling of being exposed. Of having them see me like this, even the parts of myself I used to try to hide.

I speed up my attention to my clit and slide my other hand between my legs too. I run my fingers up the sensitive skin on my inner thighs, rubbing my slit, then plunge two of them inside.

"You're so fucking wet, love," Ryder groans, his gaze locked on my hand as I move faster, playing with my piercing. "Feel good?"

"*So* good," I gasp.

"And so fucking pretty," he adds, his erection straining against his pants. "You're close, aren't you? Close to making yourself come. Close to showing me and Beckett what we missed this morning?"

I am. It usually takes me a little more to get there, but everything feels heightened with all three of them.

"What did I tell you about not keeping things to yourself?" Tristan rumbles, his cock pulsing under my ass as he pinches one of my nipples again. "Ryder asked you a question."

"Yes." I arch, pushing my pussy against my hand. "So close. Please..."

I'm not sure what I'm asking for. It's my own fingers inside me, my hands between my legs, but my orgasm feels like it belongs to them.

"What do you need, love?" Ryder growls.

"I don't know. I just..."

I gasp, letting my head fall back onto Tristan's shoulder as I frantically rub my clit, so close to coming.

"It's not your job to know," Beckett growls. "It's your job to do as you're told right now." He pauses. "As long as you're still green."

"Green," I breathe. "Yes. Tell me... tell me what to do."

"Stop."

I freeze. "What?"

Beckett's voice is dark, his eyes locked on my clit ring. "Take your hand away from your pussy. I want to see that piercing again."

I do it, squirming on top of Tristan's cock.

Ryder's eyes flare. "Are you trying to get Tristan off, love? Because I don't think that's fair, do you? After this morning?"

Tristan chuckles, then slides his hands beneath me, gripping the backs of my thighs, and spreads me open even wider. "He's right. They want to see *you* come, freckles. Now be good and show them. One hand on your gorgeous tits, the other back on that pretty jewel."

"Yes, sir," I whimper, the honorific instinctively falling from my lips, and Tristan makes a low sound in his throat.

"Such a good girl."

The words make me melt, and when Beckett growls, "Now," I do exactly as Tristan commanded, playing with my tits and my clit until the world narrows to the pleasure they're giving me.

I'm close.

So fucking close.

I bite my lip, moaning as the pressure inside me builds.

"Look at her," Ryder groans. "So fucking sexy. So responsive. Is this how she was this morning, Tristan?"

"She was perfect," Tristan says, and I don't know if it's hearing those words from him, or the way illicit thrill of hearing them talk about me like I'm a sex toy for them to enjoy, but I cry out as my pleasure starts to crest, writhing on his lap.

His hold on me tightens, holding my thighs in an iron grip as his hips surge up beneath me, the feel of his hard cock making me feel almost frantic.

"Oh fuck," I moan, arching my back and grinding my ass down, riding him without shame.

"That's right, love," Ryder encourages me. "Fuck, you're beautiful. Now come. Do it. *Come.*"

The order sends me over the edge, like my body was waiting for it, and I cry out, shaking as my orgasm rolls through me like a tidal wave.

Someone groans. Hell, maybe it's all three of them. And then Tristan releases one of my thighs, moving his hand down and plunging his fingers inside me again.

"Fuck, you feel so good," he rasps, the rough stubble on his jaw scraping against my neck as he nuzzles me. "Tight and sopping wet. Do it again."

"Wh-what?" I gasp.

"I know you can handle more. You gave me two orgasms this morning, one for me and one for you." He rolls my clit piercing with his fingers, making me whimper. "But now there are three of us watching. I think you can give us each one, don't you?"

"Yes..." I moan.

"That's right."

He keeps fucking me with his fingers, thrusting deep inside and curling them inside me, applying pressure to my G-spot in a way that feels incredible.

"Oh fuck, yes," I repeat, writhing on his hand.

It's not always easy for me to get there from penetration alone, but somehow, that doesn't seem like it will be a problem. Not when these three are in charge. Not when I get to give up control like this.

"Good girl," Tristan praises, thumbing my clit. Then he pulls his hand away again. "But this is your show."

He doesn't even have to encourage me this time.

I'm already riding the wave of the first orgasm when Ryder groans, "You're so fucking hot, love. Do it. Give us another."

I obey without thought, grinding down on my clit and coming again with a choked sob.

"Fuck yeah." Beckett's voice is gravelly. "How did that one feel, little menace?"

I drag my eyes open, not even sure when they closed. "Amazing."

His eyes flare with heat, and his hand twitches in my direction before he controls it.

"You deserve amazing," he says. Then he smiles, slow and a little bit evil. "But I'm pretty sure I heard Tristan tell you we need at least three. Can you come from nipple play alone?"

"I... I don't know."

"With amazing tits like that, my guess is hell yes," Ryder says with a grin. "Push them together."

I do, my skin flushed and overly sensitive, making it feel so good to handle myself this way.

"Now thumb your nipples. No pinching. Not yet. Just rub them for us."

I do what Ryder tells me to as Tristan's hands tighten on my hips, his breath hot and ragged against the back of my neck.

"God, yes," Ryder grunts, rubbing himself through his pants. "Keep going. You're sexy as hell like this."

"She's sexy as hell all the fucking time," Beckett says, his hand moving again like he's struggling to maintain that iron control over himself.

Then his control breaks. He curses, shoving open his pants enough to free his cock.

"Fuck," I whimper, my mouth watering as I stare at it. "Beckett..."

"Put your fingers back in that pretty mouth," he growls. "Get them wet, then tug on your nipples the way Tristan was. Imagine he's sucking on them. Imagine it's me. Do you want to feel my lips on your skin, Lana? All over your skin."

My breath hitches. "Yes. Oh fuck, yes."

I'm panting, and with the way he's guiding me, it really does feel like he's sucking on me when I roll them between my wet fingers. I tug on the little buds, imagining Beckett sucking hard on them while the other two fuck and finger me.

But that's not going to happen. Not yet. I can tell not one of them will touch me until I give them what they want. Another orgasm.

But I don't know if I can get there with nipple play alone.

"Please," I gasp, pinching hard enough to send a bolt of pleasure through me. "*Please*. I need to touch my clit. I need something in my pussy."

"You sure about that?" Beckett asks. "Because I don't think you do. Not this time."

The commanding timbre of his voice awakens something new inside me. It's the same something that attracted me to kink in the first place.

Domination.

And the sweet release I've never felt with anything else when I give myself the freedom to submit to it.

"Okay," I breathe out.

"Good girl." He strokes himself slowly, staring at me without blinking. "Squeeze those pretty thighs together and clench your pussy tight. Pulse your inner muscles like you're trying to milk one of our cocks. Then pinch those gorgeous nipples again."

"Do it," Ryder groans, finally pulling his cock out too. "Beckett has the *best* fucking ideas."

"You see what you're doing to them, freckles?" Tristan murmurs. "You've got them all worked up, just like you got me this morning."

I've got my legs pressed tightly together, just like Beckett told me to, but Tristan tugs the robe up to my waist, leaving me bare right over his lap, and pulls my ass cheeks apart.

Then he grinds his cock between them. His pants don't allow him to penetrate me, but the hard ridge of his erection is so hot and thick that it turns me on anyway.

"*Tristan*," I gasp, lost in sensation as he bucks up against me.

"Keep touching yourself," Beckett growls, the head of his cock slick with precum as he works his fist over it. "Get yourself there. Show us how obedient you can be. You said you wanted this, that you wanted *us*. Prove it."

I nod frantically, abusing my nipples until I'm practically

sobbing. I grind down on Tristan's cock, clenching my legs together and tightening my core over and over in a frantic rhythm that really does almost feel like I'm getting fucked.

"Please," I whimper, so close again that I can almost taste it. "*Please*, I need to..."

It's Ryder's groan that sends me over the edge. Tristan is so hard beneath me that I can feel each pulse of his shaft, and the sight of Beckett clenching his jaw as he strokes himself makes my heart race.

Each one of them is totally focused on me, just as turned on as I am.

For *me*.

It's every one of my fantasies coming to life in the hottest way possible, and it slams into me so hard that my body arches off Tristan's lap.

"Fuck," one of them mutters almost reverently.

My climax seems to go on forever, and I finally collapse back into Tristan's hold as a few aftershocks roll through me.

"Lana," Beckett says after a moment, using that commanding Dom voice.

I drag my eyes back open, my gaze meeting two ravenous sets of eyes.

"Color?"

I lick my lips, my brain a little slow on the uptake thanks to the blissful haze I'm floating in.

And then it clicks.

"Green," I whisper.

They're not done with me yet.

15

LANA

I ALMOST FEEL greedy as arousal pools in my core while I watch Ryder and Beckett jerk off. They just gave me three orgasms, and that's true even if it was my own hand that delivered them.

I feel sated. Boneless. More satisfied than I can ever remember being after sex.

But I still want more.

"What do you want now, freckles?" Tristan whispers in my ear, his hands moving lazily over my body. "Tell us."

His cock throbs under my ass, and a mouthwatering image flashes through my mind.

One that makes me blush.

"Um, you decide."

Beckett's eyes flare with heat and Ryder's grin turns absolutely wicked, but Tristan just chuckles.

"I am deciding," he says. "We're supposed to help you figure out what you like, so you have to tell us what you want. Don't be shy. You already told us that you're green for more, but that's not good enough. Not when it comes to kink. Not when we haven't already negotiated your limits for this scene."

I lick my lips. "This, um, this is a scene? It's not real?"

"Scenes are real," Beckett says in that gruff voice of his.

145

"They're agreed upon interactions where everyone gets what they need."

"Which brings us back to communication." Tristan's thumbs brush over my nipples, sending a cascade of desire through me. "Good kink requires good communication. Being clear about what everyone involved actually wants isn't just the best way to get it. It's the only way. That's when we have a green light."

He rolls my nipples, then pinches them, and I arch up with a moan.

"Fuck, that's hot," Ryder grunts, squeezing his cock.

"So, are you ready to tell us now?" Tristan asks. "What is it you want right now?"

"I want to go down on you," I admit, feeling a little emboldened now that he's spelled it out for me.

Tristan's hands drop to my hips, and he pulls me down as he thrusts up against me. "You're going to have to be more specific with that 'you,' freckles. There are three of us here to choose from."

I lock eyes with Beckett. "I mean you."

He groans so softly I would have missed it if I wasn't staring at him, but I'm still feeling greedy, and Tristan told me I needed to communicate my wants and needs clearly, so I look at Ryder, my pussy clenching as I whisper, "And you." Then I twist around to face Tristan. "And you."

"Fuck," he mutters, fisting my hair and grinding against my ass. "Greedy girl."

"*Yes.*"

"Our favorite kind." Ryder starts to stroke himself again. "You gonna start with Tristan, love?"

"You decide," I repeat, because that *is* what I want.

Tristan's eyes flare. "Then get on your knees like a good girl," he says, spreading his thighs and pushing me to my feet.

My heart starts to race as I stand up. Tristan keeps ahold of my robe as I do, and it slips off my shoulders, leaving me naked.

I inhale slowly, feeling both vulnerable and powerful with all three mens' eyes on me, and when Tristan smacks my ass, sending a bolt of lust straight to my core, my arousal drips down my thighs.

But then a wave of self-consciousness washes over me.

The last person I was completely naked in front of was Wade, and when memories of some of the comments he used to make about how curvy I am start to intrude, I instinctively move my hands in front of my body, trying to cover up a little.

Beckett's voice stops me. "No."

The command in his tone is undeniable, and I immediately drop my hands.

"That's it, love," Ryder murmurs. "We want to see you. Still green."

"Still green," I whisper, mustering my courage as their eyes roam over me.

I turn and face Tristan, who's rubbing the thick bulge of his cock through his pants as he leans back, watching me with hooded eyes.

He dips his chin toward the floor, a reminder that he told me to kneel, and I drop down and reach for his zipper, then hesitate. I'm not even sure what I'm waiting for until Tristan speaks again, giving me permission.

"Take me out," he rasps. "I've been craving you all fucking day. Thinking about what you looked like in my bed this morning. Remembering those sexy noises you made."

His hand covers mine, rubbing it over his cock. Then he moves my fingers back to his zipper.

I lower it, and he groans when his cock finally springs free, lifting his hips to help me get his pants down.

"That's it. Good girl." He puts a hand on the back of my head, guiding me forward. "Now take what you asked for. Suck me."

My eyes flutter closed as the salty taste of him hits my lips, and I run my tongue around his cockhead—just as greedy as they accused me of being—before letting the heavy weight of his shaft slide over my tongue.

"Oh damn," Tristan says, his thighs flexing under my hands.

"How does her mouth feel?" Ryder asks from behind me.

"Better than I imagined." Tristan's grip tightens, his fingers tunneling through my hair. "Can you take a little more?"

I look up at him, my lips stretched wide, and instead of trying to nod, I push closer, not stopping until he hits the back of my throat.

"Fucking gorgeous," he murmurs. The praise sends heat through my veins as he cups my chin with his free hand, still holding me in place with the grip he has on my head.

I blink up at him, loving the way he's taking control almost as much as I love how he's staring down at me.

I bob up and down on his cock, feeling held in place just as much by his gaze as I do by his hands. And then, when he hits the back of my throat again, he holds me there for a moment.

"Good girl. Now swallow it. Let me into your throat. Can you do that? Breathe through your nose. That's it. Fuck. Deeper."

The command makes my pussy clench. It's such a wonderfully filthy feeling, and I obey, relaxing my throat as he pushes my head down. My stomach flutters as I take him all, until I feel his balls on my chin and have my nose pressed to his neatly trimmed hair.

"Jesus Christ," Beckett grunts, the sound of his hand moving on his cock a reminder that I'm being watched.

"*Fuck.*" Tristan's thighs turn to steel under my hands. "Do it again."

I do, gagging a little, and his hold tightens as he slowly pulls back, then thrusts in again.

"That's perfect. Fucking perfect," he praises, his voice husky. "Do you want my cum?"

I moan, blinking away the tears that spill out of the corners of my eyes and hoping he'll see the *yes* I can't speak right now.

He does.

"Take it, then," he orders. "Suck harder. Swallow me down."

He pumps his hips, thrusting his cock in and out of my mouth, and I feel it when his control slips, his cock jerking. He holds me down again, and when his cum starts to spurt down the back of my throat, a bolt of pleasure ricochets through me, making me moan again.

"Holy shit," Ryder mutters from behind me. "That's fucking hot. I can see your pussy clenching, love. You like that, don't you? Is

148

it sucking Tristan's cock that's turning you on so much? The taste of his cum? Knowing you pleased him? Or is it the way he's holding you down and making sure you don't miss a drop of what you earned?"

I shudder with lust, wanting to answer *all of it*. But I still can't, and somehow, that's almost better.

I blink up at Tristan, not moving until he finally lets me.

"Green," I whisper once his cock finally slides out of my mouth, my voice a little hoarse and my pussy so wet that I know the view Ryder and Beckett have right now must be obscene.

"Good girl," he murmurs, his thumb brushing over my bottom lip. "Who do you want next?"

"You know the answer to that," Ryder answers before I can. "She wants us to decide. Come here, love. I know you like to tease me, but seeing you like this is a special kind of torture, so let's not keep me waiting."

I stand up on shaky legs, looking over at him.

The smile he gives me is pure fire.

He squeezes his cock as I walk over to him, my eyes stuck on the sight. It looks even harder and angrier than before, and seeing how I affect him drives home a truth I've heard about BDSM.

That it's the submissive who has the power in every power exchange.

"May I?" I whisper once I'm in front of him.

He releases his shaft and cups my face. "You're fucking killing me here."

Then he spreads his legs and pushes me down to my knees, bringing my face to his bulge.

"So open and honest with us." Ryder shifts his hips, rubbing himself back and forth over my lips. "You really are a good girl, but you're dirty too, aren't you?"

"She likes it filthy," Beckett rumbles as Ryder thrusts forward.

"I think you're right," he says with a groan as he tightens the grip he still has on my hair to hold me in place. He thrusts forward, his eyes going hooded when I gag, but doesn't stop until he's filled my throat. "Fuck, that's tight." He pulls back, then thrusts in again. "Now make me come while Beckett and Tristan watch you work."

I moan and suck hard, bobbing my head up and down and proving them both right. It's not just dirty, it gets wetter and sloppier as my own arousal starts to peak again.

I shove a hand between my legs, clenching my thighs around it, and Ryder suddenly yanks on my hair hard enough to sting.

"None of that, dirty girl. Not quite yet. I said make *me* come."

I sink into a warm haze, following his directions and riding the high of his praise as I suck and moan, bob and swallow, over and over while the heat of all three men's eyes on me sends me flying.

"Oh fuck, that's it." Ryder's grip suddenly tightens again, his cock swelling in my mouth and pulsing hard as he fills my mouth with his salty spend. "But don't swallow. Not until I say so."

I choke a little, my throat convulsing, but I manage to do what he says, holding it in my mouth until he finally pulls me off, his cock sliding from my mouth and leaving a trail of cum and saliva dripping from my lips.

"You're so damn sexy," he says, pushing it back inside with his thumb. "That was perfect, love. Your mouth is even better than Tristan said it was."

"Only because words don't do it justice," Tristan murmurs as Ryder stares down at me, slowly sliding his thumb out and gripping my chin instead.

He tugs it down. "Now show me what you saved for me."

I open my mouth and stick out my tongue, trying to curl it a little so I don't lose any. It doesn't quite work, and Ryder groans as it spills down my chin.

"Beckett was right. You're fucking filthy." He leans forward and kisses me, groaning into my mouth as he tastes himself there, then shoves his cum deeper with his tongue. "Now swallow," he says when he finally pulls back, his voice husky and his eyes filled with heat. "Swallow what I gave you, then go show Beckett how good you can be for him."

I do as I'm told, turning to find Beckett staring at me without blinking, cock still in hand. He's on a leather chair near the fireplace, legs spread wide already, but when I go over to him, he stands up before I can crawl between them.

"Stop."

I bite my lip, shuddering a little at the pure dominance in that single word.

He points to the floor at his feet. "Kneel."

I slowly lower myself in front of him, keeping my eyes on his as my skin prickles with awareness. He looms over me, masculine and solid and gorgeous, making me feel small in the best possible way.

Then my eyes drop to his cock.

It's pierced. A Jacob's ladder. His shaft so thick and long that it fits eight rungs. Eight sets of stainless steel balls running up the center of his cock that I want to worship with my tongue.

"*Beckett*," I whisper, squeezing my thighs together as a rush of heat floods my pussy.

I part my lips as I sway forward and reach for it.

"No," he says sharply, causing my eyes to jerk back up to his as I freeze in place.

He doesn't smile, but something in his stern expression still feels like praise.

I lick my lips. "I want to, um, to please you."

A *sir* almost comes out on pure instinct alone, but I swallow it down at the last second, not sure if that's okay since we didn't "communicate" about that sort of thing, and feeling all too aware of how inexperienced with kink I am.

Beckett's eyes bore into me for long enough that I start trembling.

Then he nods, just a fraction, and his lips tilt up. "You do please me, little menace. I'm pretty fucking sure you can't do anything else."

My breath hitches in my throat, warmth spreading through me like a drug.

I lift a hand again toward him again, but then drop it when he raises a silent eyebrow.

"Good girl. Shoulders back. Keep your eyes on me. That's it."

My nipples harden as he stares down at me, and when his eyes drop to my lips, I lick them, already greedy again. I need to know his taste too.

"I'm not going to use your mouth," he rumbles.

I suck in a sharp breath, but the intensity of his gaze burns away any disappointment before it can take root.

I swipe my tongue across my lower lip again, tasting Tristan's and Ryder's cum and imagining his. Beckett grunts, then drags his gaze up to meet mine again.

"I want you to stay right there on your knees while I jerk off on you," he says, starting to stroke himself again. "I'm going to come all over that pretty face of yours, and those perfect fucking tits. I want to see it dripping down those gorgeous curves, filthy girl."

Heat races through me, my stomach swooping. I want to touch myself again. I want to touch *him*.

His thick fingers play up and down his double row of piercings, then circle his fat cock head before he thrusts almost violently into his fist again. He fucks his fist brutally, almost like he's punishing his cock, and the rough grunts he makes with each stroke ratchet my arousal even higher.

I'm mesmerized. Entranced. And so damn turned on that it feels like if I twitch, I'll come.

"Fold your arms behind your back."

I moan, my body obeying him instinctively and then shuddering as the position makes me feel even more exposed.

I'm a blank canvas, waiting for him to paint me as he will. Waiting for him to make me *filthy*.

My pussy clenches tight, my eyes fluttering closed before I remember that Beckett wants me to keep my gaze on him.

I snap them open, and he groans, slowing down and squeezing his length in a long, slow glide. "You're so fucking desperate for it, aren't you?"

"Yes," I whisper.

"Look at you. Greedy for cock. Panting for my cum, even though you've already had a double mouthful. You can't fucking get enough, can you?"

I moan, and he makes a sharp sound that has my core tightening.

He stops stroking. "When I ask you something, you answer."

"Yes."

"Yes, you *can* get enough?"

"I mean, no," I pant, my whole body vibrating as I hold the position he wants me in. "I can't. It's not enough. I want more. I want *yours*." I lick my lips, then whisper the word I want to. "Sir."

His fist tightens around his cock again, his whole body freezing for a second. Then, with a groan that vibrates the air between us, he starts violently jerking his cock again.

"Such a pretty little slut for it. You want it? It's coming. But I need something from you, first."

I nod, lost in my arousal and unable to deny him anything. Anything at all.

"Give me another orgasm."

I nod again with a breathy little gasp, but wait until he tells me how.

He smiles. It only shows in his eyes, but the praise still rolls over me like a crashing wave.

"Touch yourself."

"Yes, sir. Oh god. Yes..."

My hand delves between my legs, and it barely takes a moment before I'm shuddering, my body pulsing as pleasure slams through me.

"*Fuck*," Beckett rasps, his hand flying over his cock while his other one reaches out, grabbing my hair.

The sharp sting as he uses the grip to tilt my head back takes the aftershocks of my orgasm and sends them into a tailspin, driving my pleasure even higher.

"Beautiful little menace."

He grunts the last word as the first hot jet of his cum hits my chin.

He aims the next one at my cheek, then aims his cock at my chest and milks out the last few spurts onto my chest, as promised.

"Fucking filthy," he mutters almost tenderly, breathing hard as he slowly strokes himself a few more times. "A perfect, filthy little slut."

I keep my gaze locked with his, the invisible tether between us pulled taut, and when I feel his cum sliding from my cheek toward my mouth, my tongue darts out, catching it and tasting him at last.

His eyes darken, and he finally releases my hair and tucks away his cock, then crouches down in front of me. His gaze drops to my lips for a split second, and for a moment, I think he's going to kiss me.

"Color?" he asks instead.

"*So* green," I whisper.

"Good girl. You were perfect," he murmurs, giving me a smile in return. A small, private thing that almost makes it feel like he kissed me after all.

16

RYDER

I STARE up at the dark ceiling as the quiet sounds of the night surround me, one arm under my head and the other curled under Lana where she's breathing softly next to me. But that's not what I'm listening to right now.

Every single one of the hot little moans she made earlier tonight is burned into my memory now, and I stifle a groan as they replay in my head on a loop that has my cock aching to be inside her sweet mouth again.

After she went down on all three of us, we got her cleaned up, put away the leftover food in the suite's compact little kitchen, and all piled in bed together by silent agreement. Not to fuck, unfortunately, since the trip, the sex, and hell, probably all the emotional sharing we did tonight too, seems to have knocked everyone but me out for the night.

I definitely could have kept going, the free pass we agreed to awakening a deep, insatiable hunger for her that I've spent years trying to deny. But she needs her rest after all the orgasms we just gave her. And while those alone probably would have worn her out anyway, this is also her first real experience with kink. The high can be intense, and I've got no doubt it took just as much out of her as the actual sex.

Which, let it be noted, was fucking phenomenal.

I grin in the darkness, my cock thickening as I let every second of that replay in my mind too.

I'm tempted to slide out of bed, head into the bathroom, and do something about my hard-on. Or, hell, just take care of it right here. But instead, I close my eyes and inhale cherry blossoms and honey, the soft weight of Lana's body next to me both soothing and arousing in equal measure.

Actually, that kind of sums up everything about Lana in a nutshell.

On the other side of her, I hear Tristan grumble in his sleep, then the bed shifts a little as either he or Beckett—who took the edge of the mattress on Tristan's other side—changes position.

Probably Beckett.

I frown a little, my libido cooling for a minute, because something was off with Beck tonight. He agreed to this, clearly enjoyed the hell out of it, and I know he would have said something if he hadn't wanted to be a part of everything that happened.

But he was also holding himself back. I could tell.

If I had to guess, Beckett doesn't want to let Lana get too deep under his skin, which is why he didn't even let her touch him. It's like he was being careful not to completely let himself go.

I huff a breath, shaking my head as I grin up at the ceiling again. Honestly, he's probably not wrong to be cautious. She's definitely addicting. But holding back would defeat the whole purpose of indulging ourselves like this, as far as I'm concerned.

Besides, the deal we made sets clear boundaries—this all ends when we get Lana to her parents' house in New Hampshire—so there's no actual danger of any of us getting too deeply involved. We've already agreed on that.

I close my eyes again. It's probably four or five in the morning by now, and even though I still feel wound up from our recent activities, I should probably try to get some sleep before we hit the road in the morning.

But next to me, Lana stirs. Then she quietly climbs over me, slipping out of bed.

I open my eyes again, rolling onto my side and propping myself up on one elbow to watch her. I can tell by the careful, quiet way she moves around the room that she doesn't notice I'm awake.

She slips the plush robe she was wearing earlier back on, grabs her phone, and leaves the bedroom.

I'm out of bed before the door closes, padding silently after her. I find her bent over in front of the open refrigerator, looking too tempting to resist.

"Good morning, love," I murmur as I come up behind her, stroking her hips.

She startles, gasping as she straightens up and whirls around to face me, catching herself with a hand in the center of my chest.

I capture it and hold it there, and she smiles, laughing softly as she murmurs, "Don't *do* that."

I shrug, grinning down at her. "Can't help it." I nod toward the open refrigerator. "Hungry?"

"Your fault." Her eyes gleam as she teases me. "But yes, I woke up starving. We have leftovers, right? Because I really need a midnight snack."

"You're a few hours too late for that," I tease her back. "I think the sun is about to come up."

Her fingers curl against my chest. "I think we still have time."

I nod, grinning. "Oh, there's always time for a midnight snack. Tristan and Beckett may not always understand that, but I'm a believer."

The three of us bought a house together when we opened the club, and my late night snacking habits are something they give me shit about on a regular basis. Lana clearly understands the importance of it, though. She pulls a few takeout containers from the fridge, hands me one, grabs forks for both of us, then leans back against the counter and devotes her attention to last night's leftovers like a woman truly after my own heart.

I follow suit, groaning at how good it tastes.

"I know," she says as I make another sound. "Mm, this tastes even better cold."

I bump her fork with mine. "Maybe it's the company."

She grins up at me. "Maybe."

I like how relaxed she seems, but the Dom in me still has to check. "How are you feeling, love?"

She raises her eyebrows, slowly sliding the fork out from between her plush lips as she looks up at me. Then she clears her throat. "Still a little hungry, I guess? Why, do you want to trade?"

She holds out the takeout container she was eating from, and I swap hers for mine. But the first rule of good kink is good communication, so I'm not going to let her dodge my question.

"I mean after last night," I clarify.

"Oh." She flushes. "Um, good. I don't think I've ever come that many times in a row before."

Hearing that is hot as fuck, but also somehow sweet, just like Lana. She's got an innocence to her that has nothing to do with her sexual experience or how new to kink she is. It comes from inside her, and combined with how eager she is to explore her interests, it's sexy as hell.

She rests her hand on my chest again, her expression softening. "You know, that's not the only thing I enjoyed about last night, though."

I grin. "I'm all ears."

"It was nice just spending time with you all. I mean, it's been nice during this whole trip, but I really liked sharing things." She pauses for a second, trapping her lip between her teeth. "But you know, I never really thought about why you spent so many holidays at our house growing up. You even celebrated a few birthdays at our place, didn't you?"

I shrug, the reminder dampening the playful, intimate mood a little. Not that they're bad memories, but I feel a bit exposed.

Lana smiles gently. "I guess I figured it was because you and Caleb were so close, but it was because your folks weren't around, wasn't it."

"Can't it be both?"

I'm joking to lighten the mood, and Lana laughs softly but doesn't let it go.

"I didn't realize things with your parents were that bad. Not back then. And I'm sorry about that. But thank you for opening up last night. It means a lot."

I almost make another joke, but maybe I actually don't mind that she's not letting it go.

"It did kind of suck that they weren't ever around," I surprise myself by admitting. "Not that I hated spending holidays with you guys, of course."

She laughs. "Of course not! But I get it." Her voice softens. "They were your family."

I nod. "Yeah, and I would have felt ungrateful if I'd complained about it since it wasn't like I had a rough life. They gave me whatever I wanted."

She cocks her head to the side. "You mean material things. But that's easy with the kind of wealth they have."

It's my turn to laugh, although I'm basically laughing at myself. Because of course she doesn't let me get away with downplaying my feelings. Not when she's been so brave about her own.

And maybe I don't really mind her pushing me on this, either.

"Right," I agree. "Material things. But all I *really* wanted was..."

"For them to be around," she finishes for me quietly.

"Yeah."

She holds my gaze, the warm blue of her eyes making it easy to get a little lost in them. It's peaceful, the quiet of the night around us broken only by the gentle hum of the refrigerator.

"They didn't deserve you," she says quietly.

"I've got money in a trust from them." I'm not sure why I'm telling her this. "Enough that even if the club failed, I'd never have to work again."

She smiles at me. "But you haven't touched a penny of it, have you?"

I'm not sure how she knows.

"Never. And I never will. You know what the best feeling in the world is?"

She blushes again, making my cock stir. "I think I might have some ideas about that."

I grin at her. "I'm happy to give you a few more. Anytime, love.

But I actually mean the feeling of knowing I've fucking done it. That I've been able to succeed in this world *without* their money, you know? Without having to take anything at all from them."

"You should be proud of that," she says fiercely. "Your family doesn't know what they've missed out on."

"Maybe, but I'm good without them." I lift her hand from my chest and press my lips to her knuckles. "I built a family of my own."

"Tristan and Beckett," she whispers.

I grin. "Hey, just because we don't see each other as often anymore, don't leave Caleb out."

A tender look passes over Lana's face, and it hits me that I just claimed her family as my own, connecting us.

"Can I kiss you?" she breathes.

"Are you asking if that's part of our arrangement?" I tease, cocking a brow even as heat surges in my blood.

She nods, her breath hitching as her pupils dilate.

"Yeah, love," I murmur, tugging her closer. "Kissing is allowed. For as long as we're doing this, *everything* is allowed."

She rises up on her toes and presses her lips against mine, and they taste so fucking good that I lose myself all over again.

"Fuck," I groan against her mouth, gathering her closer so I can get a little more. "I know you asked for help discovering your kinks, but I think I've just found a new one of my own."

"Yeah?" she asks, laughing breathlessly. "What's that?"

I fist my hand around her long, thick waves and tug her head back so I can drag my lips down her throat.

"Kissing you," I murmur against her impossibly soft skin.

She arches against me. "Does that really count as a kink?"

I smirk, slipping my hands beneath her robe and filling them with her lush curves. "What do you think?"

"I think I want to know *all* your kinks. What else do you like?"

"Hmm. Well, I liked knowing Tristan and Beckett were watching you get on your knees for me earlier," I murmur in her ear, slipping one hand between her legs and sinking my fingers into the wet heat there. "I like being watched."

"Exhibitionism?" she whispers, moaning as she spreads her legs for me. "I, um, I think that might be one of mine too."

"Yeah? You liked having their eyes on you while you sucked me off? Liked knowing I was watching when Beckett told you to touch yourself?"

A sound gets trapped in her throat as a gush of wetness coats my fingers.

I withdraw them and hold them to her mouth. "Lick."

Her tongue darts out, her eyes never leaving mine.

"You know what I was thinking about earlier, before you woke up? How much I wanted to sink my cock into you, love. Awake or asleep." I lean down to whisper in her ear. "But it would be *really* fucking hot while you're asleep."

Her breath catches. "That's... that's a kink?"

"Fucking you while you sleep? Playing with these amazing tits of yours while you're all soft and relaxed, your body mine for the taking? Getting you wet while you dream of me, then sliding my cock inside you so you wake up already coming?"

She gives a sexy little whimper, her skin flushing pink.

"Yeah, it's a kink, love. My kink. It's called somnophilia. Kind of goes along with one of my other favorite kinks. Free use." I push the robe off her shoulders, letting it pool around her feet and running my hands over her body when she offers it up to me. "Being granted unlimited access to fuck my partner, or use her for my pleasure in any other way I want, *whenever* I want."

"Ryder," she whispers, licking her lips. "I, um..."

"You what? You want me to keep touching you?"

"*Yes.*"

"Worshiping you?"

She makes a sexy little sound of surprise, and I lift her lush breasts, one in each hand, then bend down to suck one of her nipples into my mouth.

She moans, grabbing on to the back of my head when I release it, then gasping when I take the other one in my mouth. I could do it all day, but I want more.

And I can tell Lana does too.

I play my tongue over the tight little nub, then drag it up her throat and suck on the hummingbird-fast pulse fluttering at the base. "I want to fuck you."

"*Please.*"

I straighten up, sliding my hands around to her ass, and lift her up against me.

"Ryder!" She laughs, clutching me while also trying to squirm out of my arms. "Wait! Stop. I'm too heavy!"

"Liar," I murmur, kneading her soft curves. "You're not too heavy at all. Want me to prove it?"

She blushes again but wraps her legs around me, her warm pussy cradling my cock with only the thin material of the boxers I pulled on to sleep in between us.

"I want you to, um, to do anything you want."

"Good girl," I praise her, indulging in one of my other kinks as I set her on the counter. "That's what you are, aren't you? A dirty, perfect little thing, just waiting for someone to show you how filthy you can be. Now spread your legs."

She does, and I kiss her again, my cock nudging between her legs.

"Green?" I murmur, swallowing her moan. "Do you want my cock inside you, love?"

"Yes. Green. *Please.*"

"I can't fucking wait to get inside you," I growl, teasing us both by sliding my shaft through her slick folds. "Don't move. I'll be right back."

I start to step back and she grabs on to me. "Where are you going?"

"Just gonna grab a condom."

"No!" She wraps her legs around my hips, using them to urge me closer. "I, um, do we have to? I don't... I don't want to use one."

Fuck. My cock is already wet with her arousal, and the feel of it sliding against her soft inner thighs has me groaning.

Lana bites her lip. "After Wade, I got tested. Negative for everything, and I'm on birth control, so..."

My balls draw up tight, heat racing down my spine and swelling my cock until it aches.

"Fuck," I mutter, tightening my grip on her ass and resting my forehead against hers as I try to calm it down.

"Sorry," she murmurs, looking embarrassed. "Of course we can use one. I don't know what I was thinking, I—*mmph*."

I shut her up with a kiss, devouring her as I fight for and finally regain control.

"Yeah," I rasp, resting my fingers over her plump lips when they open again. "We can do that. I get tested regularly, love. Is that what you really want? You want me to fuck you raw? Fill you with my cum? Use your hot pussy to sheathe my cock, and take you bare?"

I'm a serial dater, but I'm smart about it. I've never gone without a condom, not for anyone. I've never even considered it.

But with Lana?

Fuck yes.

It's not even a question. I need to feel her, skin-to-skin, more than I need air.

Her breath starts coming hard and fast, and she makes another one of those sexy sounds that make me feel like a fucking caveman. Then she nods. "Please. Fuck me, Ryder. Take whatever you want."

I don't know whether I'm more stunned that she's asking for this, or that, despite having all but perfected the art of not getting close to women, at every point when I would normally push her away and keep my distance, all I want to do is bring her closer.

But then again, this is Lana. Everything is different with her.

I *want* everything to be different with her.

And until we get to New Hampshire, it can be.

"Lie back on the counter, love."

"Why?" she asks breathlessly, already doing it like the natural sub I'm pretty sure she is.

"That's it. Good girl." I ease her back and arrange her lush body the way I want it, then run my hands up her thighs and push her legs apart. "I want you just like this, so you're splayed out all

163

pretty for me. I want to see all of you. I want to watch you take every fucking inch of me."

"Anything," she whispers as I rub my cockhead against her piercing, then slot it against her hot, wet entrance. "Anything. *Green*. Take everything you want."

I groan. Everything I want?

She's a total fucking dream, and she couldn't have made her consent any clearer.

So I do.

17

LANA

"Oh fuck, love," Ryder grits out, his eyes glued to my pussy as he works his way into me with slow, shallow thrusts. "You're taking me so fucking well."

I don't know if it's the steady stream of praise or the way his thick cock forces my body to stretch and accommodate him that has my heart racing, but I'm already addicted to both.

Ryder is bigger than Wade. Bigger than the few other men I've been with too. And now that I know how good, how *overwhelming* it feels to be filled like this, I'm not sure I'll ever be satisfied with anything less.

It doesn't just make me want to let go. It forces me to.

"That's it," he murmurs. "Look at you."

A whimper gets trapped in my throat. I'm completely on display, and with him, I like it. I *want* him to look at me.

The counter is cold against my back, but the heat radiating off Ryder more than makes up for it.

He leans forward and braces his hands on either side of me, his cock pulsing inside me, and kisses me with a possessive thoroughness that has my whole body lighting up, and the last of my inhibitions falling away.

Then he lifts his head and locks his eyes on mine.

"Fuck, love, I can feel you," he murmurs. "Your pussy's begging for me. Every clench, every ripple, every spasm. I can feel how much you need this."

"Yes," I moan, my legs wrapping around him and my arousal mixing with a sweet ache as he teaches my body how to take him, how to adjust to his size, inch by inch until he finally bottoms out with a groan.

"So fucking good," he rasps, grinding his hips against me, in so deep I can almost taste him.

"Please," I beg, utterly shameless. "Fuck me."

His eyes close for a second, but he opens them again quickly, staring down at me like he can't get enough.

"Oh, I'm definitely going to fuck you, but you promised me anything I want, dirty girl. And I want something else first."

He splays one of his hands over my stomach, staring down at me as he slowly pulls back, then watches himself slide back in.

Once.

Twice.

And then on the third time, he buries himself to the hilt again and stays there, still flicking my piercing.

"Ryder!"

My inner muscles clamp around his thick shaft, instinctively trying to get more of him.

"Fucking hell," he mutters, tugging on my clit piercing again. "That's it. Your pussy's a greedy little thing, isn't it? Milk me, love. Work me over. I want to feel you come on my cock, just like this."

"Oh god," I gasp, arching my back and clawing at his biceps as I writhe on the counter.

"Not my name, but sure, I'll answer to that," he says with a sinful grin. "Ready to say a few more prayers?"

He doesn't give me a chance to answer before he starts playing with my piercing again, tugging and twisting it. Grinding his hand against my clit and then teasing it mercilessly until I have no idea what's coming out of my mouth.

I just know I need him to move.

I need him to fuck me.

I need to *come.*

"Ryder."

This time, his name comes out more as a whimper than a word, and the next thing I know, he's got his hand fisted in my hair and is kissing me with an intensity that makes me feel claimed, owned, almost possessed.

I squeeze my pussy around his shaft, and his cock swells to fill me even more as he groans into my mouth.

"So fucking good," he pants, grinding against my clit as he throbs inside me, his tight grip on my hair holding me in place as his free hand roams over my body, igniting every place he touches with a trail of sparks that have me burning for him.

"Please," I beg, completely shameless and so turned on I can't think. "Move. Fuck me. Take me."

"Not until you give me what I want." He straightens up and hauls me closer to him, then grinds against me until I'm a writhing, whimpering mess. "You can do it, love. You want to be good for me, don't you? You're a filthy little thing, but you need this. You need to come. I know you do. I can feel how hard your pussy is working for it. Come on my cock. Let me feel you fall apart for me. Come on, sweetheart. Do it. Let go for me. Give me your pleasure."

I'm so full. I've never been so turned on in my life. He's stretching me to my limit in every way, and the sweet, dirty things he's saying take me right to the edge, his possessive touch calling for my submission.

"Now," he demands, his fingers on my clit. "Come."

I moan, arching my back and grabbing on to his forearms when he tugs on my piercing again. And then, all of a sudden, it's there, a hot rush of bliss pouring through me that has me shaking as the orgasm he demanded slams through me.

Just as it hits, I remember that we left the other men sleeping and bite my lip, turning my head to muffle the sounds of my pleasure.

There's no way I can stay totally quiet, though. Not when Ryder groans and starts fucking me as if my obedience snapped something inside him, pounding into me while my orgasm is still rolling through me and pushing my pleasure even higher.

167

"Fuck, yes, just like that. Squeeze my cock," he grunts, his hips slapping against me as he picks up speed. "Milk my fucking cum out of me, dirty girl. Fucking gorgeous. Give me more. Give me fucking everything."

I feel boneless, exhausted and afloat on the afterglow of pleasure. I'm his to use, just the way I imagine it would be if he indulged his kink and fucked me while I was sleeping, my body craving more even while it still hums with the aftershocks of my first orgasm.

"You were made for this, love," he grits out. "Now open your mouth."

His eyes burn into mine, and when I obey, he slips two fingers between my lips, groaning as he fucks me faster.

"That's it. Suck."

I do, moaning as he drives his cock deeper, harder. His fingers play across my tongue, and the salty taste of his skin fills my senses. Pleasure starts to coil inside me again, the need for another release already starting to build.

My back arches as his other hand finds my clit again, and I curl my tongue around his fingers with a moan.

"Good girl," he murmurs, stroking my throat with his free hand and using the fingers in my mouth to turn my head to the side.

Tristan is standing in the doorway.

He smiles at me, his eyes hooded and the bulge of his cock clearly visible in his sleep pants.

"You look hot as fuck like this, freckles," he murmurs, palming his length. "Are you enjoying yourself?"

I gasp around Ryder's fingers, my inner muscles clenching as heat races through me.

"Fuck," Ryder groans, pulling his hands back and grabbing my hips as he pauses his rhythm to grind against me. "That's it, love. Just like that. But Tristan asked you a question."

I grip the edges of the counter. "I, um..."

I've never done anything like this before. Last night was different. They were all watching, but they were also all participating.

Now, though, even though Tristan's eyes burn into me, he makes no move to come any closer.

Or to leave.

I don't *want* him to leave.

"I'm... oh fuck... yes. I'm enjoying myself," I pant, holding his gaze.

His smile turns wicked. "Me too."

Ryder leans down, his hips rolling against me as he starts up a slower, deeper rhythm.

"You've heard of voyeurism, love?" he murmurs. I nod, and he drags his nose along my throat, then nips my ear before telling me, "One of Tristan's kinks is that he likes to watch. Should we give him a good show?"

"Yes," I breathe out, tightening my legs around his hips.

He pulls my upper body up, adjusting my ass so I'm sitting right on the edge of the counter. Then he starts fucking me again. Fucking me hard and fast while he whispers dirty things in my ear, while I cling to him and watch Tristan watching us over Ryder's shoulder.

"How does she feel?" Tristan asks, his hand moving lazily over his cock.

Ryder groans, slowing down and giving a slow roll of his hips, pressing deep. "Like heaven. Like her pussy was fucking made for my cock."

I flush, gasping as his thick shaft grinds against my g-spot.

Tristan makes a satisfied sound, and it feels like another touch, lighting up the part of me that was first drawn to kink, the part that was drawn to the desire to please and be praised for it.

"You know what else Tristan likes?" Ryder rasps, tugging gently at my piercing and making me moan. "Bondage. Ropes. Shibari. Would you like that, dirty girl? Do you want to be tied up like a present? Bound and constrained while he fucks you? While he passes you over to me, or to Beckett? Would you like that? Would you like to be our toy to share?"

I can't answer. All I can do is whimper as pleasure shoots

through me, as the thought of being restrained and at their mercy sends heat coursing through my veins.

"What color ropes would you use with our beautiful toy, Tristan?"

"Blue," Tristan replies, his voice rough and his eyes fixed on mine. "Like her eyes."

My nipples tighten. My pussy clenches. My body hums.

Then Ryder peels my arms from around his shoulders and pins them behind my back, forcing me to arch against him. Forcing his cock in even deeper. He grips both my wrists in one hand, holding them there. It's like a taste of the bondage they're discussing, and the way they're discussing me—as if I really am their toy to enjoy—has me starting to float on the spiraling pleasure, moving toward what can only be the bliss of subspace that I've read about.

"I love how soft she is," Ryder says, his free hand moving between us and rubbing over my breast. "I love these. So lush, so pretty. I could suck on them all day. But I especially love this," he continues, dipping his fingers into the wetness coating my pussy, then tracing his fingers up and playing them over my clit. "You need to try it, Tristan."

My breath catches. I'm so close. And I want them. I want everything he just said. I want them *all* inside me.

"She's so fucking wet," Ryder goes on, hooking his finger through the ring in my clit as he starts fucking me deeper. "She's dripping all over my cock. I think she likes the idea of letting you tie her up. Isn't that right, love?"

I whimper.

Ryder chuckles, his cock throbbing inside me. "I think that's a yes."

"Sounds like it to me," Tristan agrees with a hungry smile, and the heat in his gaze sets off a chain reaction.

My nipples pebble, my thighs quiver, and with Ryder's next thrust, I start to come, my body so overstimulated that it feels like being overtaken by a tsunami.

I gasp, my pussy clenching around Ryder's cock, my whole body shuddering as the pleasure roars through me.

"Yes," Ryder groans, fucking me through it. "That's it. Soak my cock. Let Tristan hear how much you love this."

"Jesus," Tristan rasps, the lust in his voice ramping me up even higher. "That's fucking beautiful."

Ryder grunts, his cock thickening as his fingers tighten on my wrists, his hips slamming against mine once, twice. Then, with a hoarse grunt and a final thrust, he comes too.

His shaft jerks and pulses inside me, filling me with a rush of cum.

My head falls back, but before I can hit it on the cabinet door behind me, Ryder's free hand catches the back of my neck. He pulls me forward and kisses me hard as I shudder, my inner walls rippling around him.

"Fucking addicting," he murmurs, smiling against my mouth.

And when he pulls away, still buried inside me, Tristan is right there.

"I want a taste."

He doesn't wait for permission, and I wouldn't deny him anyway. I just moan, opening my mouth and leaning forward. Tristan cups my jaw and slides his tongue between my lips, groaning as he licks his way inside me and stakes a claim of his own.

"Good girl," he murmurs against my mouth, and the praise has a fresh wave of arousal crashing through me. "Do you have any idea how hot that was?"

I do, and I can hardly believe it. It feels like I'm living in a dream. One where I get everything I want, and everything I didn't even know I wanted.

But if it is a dream, I don't want to wake up.

I reach for Tristan's cock, the filthy idea of taking it while I'm still full of Ryder's cum making my arousal spike all over again. But before I touch him, my phone pings.

All three of us look to my left, where I set it on the counter.

"It's Caleb," Tristan says, reading the notification on the screen.

We all freeze, then Ryder breaks the tension.

"Well, this is awkward," he jokes, grinning at me as he pulls back. A gush of his cum follows when he slides his softening cock out of my pussy. "At least it's not a video call."

"Oh god." I laugh even as the thought makes my stomach twist, shaking my head in denial. "Don't even say that!"

He grins at me. "Can we ignore him?"

Tristan snorts softly. "This is Caleb we're talking about."

Ryder chuckles. "Right." He hands me my phone. "You gonna say hi to your brother for me and Tristan?"

I blush, biting my lower lip. "What is he even doing up this early?"

"Hockey," the men both say as I swipe open the message thread with my brother.

I laugh, nodding, because of course they're right. We all know that.

> CALEB: I heard you hit some bad weather on your road trip. Everything okay, sis?

I bite my lip at the childhood nickname, smiling even though it feels almost surreal to have my brother call me that while I'm still full of one of his best friend's cum.

I send him a quick reply.

> ME: Everything's great!

Tristan kisses my temple, then steps away, and I try to ignore the sinking feeling that it's kind of prophetic. The minute the real world intrudes on this kinky bubble we're in, it pops.

Caleb sends back a thumbs up and another message.

> CALEB: Good. It sounds like you've got a lot of snow.

> ME: It's beautiful.

> CALEB: Of course you'd say that, LOL. But you're not driving in it, right?

He sends a string of emojis with that one—a cloud with snow falling, a car, and a red circle with a slash.

I roll my eyes, even though I'm still smiling. It may be overprotective of him, but it's still nice that he cares.

> ME: We'll wait until the roads are clear. We're all good. I promise.

CALEB: Good. I'm glad the guys are with you.

I blush. I am too. Not that I'm about to tell my brother exactly *how* glad I am.

Caleb and I chat for another couple of minutes before he tells me he has to head out for practice, but when I finally put the phone down, the mood between me, Tristan, and Ryder has shifted. Caleb's text was a stark reminder of just how temporary the agreement I've got with the guys is. No matter how incredible what we're sharing is, there isn't a future for us back in the real world.

Not that they'd even want one, of course. I need to remember that even if I wasn't Caleb's little sister, they've all been very clear about their feelings on relationships.

Tristan comes back over with a warm washcloth and hands it to Ryder, who uses it to clean me up before kissing me softly.

"We should go back to bed, love."

I nod, glancing out the window as he helps me down from the counter. Caleb was right, the snow is still coming down pretty heavily. And while too much of it will mean it really isn't safe to drive, I'm not sure whether to hope it clears up by morning or not.

18

LANA

I WAKE up to the sound of wind whistling outside, and my heart skips a beat. Padding over to the window, I push the curtain aside and let out a soft gasp. The world outside is a swirling mess of white, fat snowflakes dancing on gusts of wind that bend the trees nearly in half.

It's breathtaking, and I can't help the grin that spreads across my face.

By all rights, I should be tired. The clock on the nightstand tells me it's just past eight in the morning, and the ache between my legs is a visceral reminder of how late I was up last night.

But somehow, instead of wearing me out, being able to live out some of my deepest fantasies has only invigorated me.

I press my palm against the cold glass, my breath fogging it slightly, then let the curtain fall back into place, ignoring the echo of my mother's voice in my head. The one trying to remind me of my "obligations," and the importance of arriving in time for the Christmas Eve party.

I can almost hear her exasperated sigh, can picture the tight lines around her mouth as she inevitably scolds me for the delay. Because I'm sure the men will agree once they wake up; there's no way we should be driving in this weather.

But right now, wrapped in the cocoon of this hotel room, those concerns feel as distant and hazy as the buildings I can barely make out through the falling snow.

There's no way I can regret being stuck here a little longer. Sure, it means more time on the road. But that just means more time in this little alternate universe, where seemingly impossible things become possible. Where I can be bolder, braver, more authentically myself than I've ever dared to be before.

Where I get *them*.

For now.

I bite my lip to hold in my smile as I finish my morning routine, then wrap myself in soft, silky lounge clothes and head into the kitchen.

The dismay I felt in the middle of the night when it really hit me that this fantasy I'm living can't last is gone for now. Yes, it's temporary. And yes, if I'm being completely honest with myself, I wish there was a way to keep what I've found here with Tristan, Ryder, and Beckett forever.

But there isn't a way.

I can't keep them.

And I'm not going to let that stop me from wasting what I *do* have, from enjoying the fact that I have them right now. And for as long as that snow keeps falling.

My stomach gives a quiet rumble, and my phone pings, making me grin at the perfect timing. I ordered groceries after waking up, and it sounds like they're here.

When I get to the door, the delivery guy looks like he's battled the elements of a small apocalypse just to bring me my groceries.

"Thank you so much," I tell him sincerely as I accept the bags. "You're a lifesaver."

A lifesaver that I tip very, very well for braving the weather like that for me once I put the bags down in the kitchen.

As I start to unpack the groceries, I hear the rustle of sheets from the bedroom, and low murmurs that tell me the guys are starting to stir. Tristan wanders into the kitchen a few minutes later, his hair adorably mussed and his glasses slightly askew.

Gentle heat curls in my core as I smile at him, the intimacy of seeing his bedhead just as sexy as the kinks he's helping me explore.

"Good morning."

"Morning." His voice is still rough with sleep, and a thrill goes through me when he walks over and adds a casual one-armed hug to his greeting, kissing my temple. "What are you up to in here?"

I grin up at him. "Well, since we're stuck here, I figured we need breakfast. So, I'm going to make it."

He raises an eyebrow, looking both amused and a little concerned. "You cook?"

I laugh, swatting at him with a dish towel. "What has Caleb been telling you? I'm not completely hopeless in the kitchen, thank you very much. And I'll have you know, I make the best pancakes in the world."

I lift my chin defiantly, but instead of the lecture on the dangers of eating too many carbs I would have gotten from my mother, he just gives me another lazy smile.

"Mmm. I love pancakes."

I bite my lip to keep from blurting that I love how accepted the three of them make me feel. How validating it is to actually be myself and not hear any criticism about it.

That's too much, though, so instead I point toward the living room. "Out of my kitchen, mister. Go shower or something. I've got this."

Ryder's head pops around the corner, a devilish grin on his face. "Did I hear something about Lana's kitchen? Are you staking a claim here?"

I'd love to, but not the way he means.

"Don't even start," I warn him playfully, determined to keep things light. "This is a sacred space right now. You'll just interfere with my mojo."

"Your mojo?" Beckett rumbles, appearing behind Ryder and raising a single eyebrow. "Sounds serious."

I roll my eyes, fighting back a smile and secretly thrilled that Mr. Grumpy Pants is actually joining in the banter. "You're all impossible. Now shoo. Let me work my magic in peace."

They grumble good-naturedly but eventually clear out, leaving me alone with my ingredients and my thoughts. As I start mixing the batter, using the recipe I've perfected over the years, I hum to myself as I work.

The sex with these three has been mind-blowing, but it's the little moments like this that truly mean happiness to me. Snowed in like this, I've got no obligations right now other than relishing this quiet moment alone and looking forward to sharing the meal I'm making with the guys.

It may just be temporary, but it's perfect.

By the time I hear the shower shut off for the last time, I'm sliding the final pancake onto a towering stack.

"Breakfast is served!" I call out.

It doesn't take them long to wander in, each one of them looking freshly showered and irresistibly relaxed.

I try not to stare too obviously as I set the platter of pancakes in the center of the table. Just like me, none of the guys bothered to really dress for the day, and the soft sweatpants and snug t-shirts they've got on give them a casual kind of sexiness that has my heart racing a little.

"Holy shit," Tristan breathes, eyeing the stack with something close to reverence. "Those look amazing."

I beam at him, warmth blooming in my chest. "They taste even better," I tell him shamelessly. "Prepare to have your minds blown."

"You know, confidence is fucking sexy on you," Ryder says with a grin, making me blush.

I could really get used to this.

I serve them up, and as they all take their first bites, I hold my breath, watching their reactions.

They're not what I hoped for.

Instead of a chorus of appreciative groans or more of the praise that I'm admittedly getting greedy for, the kitchen gets quiet. All three men have unreadable expressions on their faces, and Beckett... well, he looks almost angry.

My stomach tightens, and I dart a worried glance down to my

own plate. Maybe I should have tasted them before inviting the men to dig in, just to be sure I didn't mess up the recipe by swapping salt for sugar or something.

But before I can spiral about it, Ryder stands up abruptly. He strides over to me with purpose, and before I can even squeak out a question, he's cupping my face in his hands and kissing me so hard that it bends me backward.

When he finally pulls away, leaving me breathless and dizzy, he grins down at me. "These pancakes are fucking amazing, Lana."

I blink, looking between the three of them as I try to process what just happened.

"You've found Ryder's weak spot," Tristan chuckles, adjusting his glasses. "The man is a sucker for a good breakfast."

Even Beckett's stern expression has softened. He pins me with an intense look that makes my toes curl as he murmurs, "They really are amazing."

I beam at them all, relief and happiness bubbling up inside me. "I'm so glad you like them."

As we finish eating, we all agree that we're not going to try to keep driving until the weather clears up, but it's not until Tristan is gathering up our empty plates that Ryder stretches and asks, "So, what's the plan for today? We're pretty much snowed in, but the local roads might be okay if we want to do some exploring. Should we try to go out and about?"

Beckett's expression is predictably serious. "We've got some club business to take care of, but that can be handled right here from the hotel room."

"Oh," I say, trying not to sound disappointed. "That's okay. I can keep myself busy."

"Don't get too busy," Ryder tells me with a grin. "The stuff for the club shouldn't take all day."

Tristan tilts his head, studying me. "And you could always hang out with us while we handle it, if you'd like. Maybe pull out your sketchbook?"

My heart skips a beat at the suggestion. "Are you sure? I don't want to be in the way."

Ryder cups my chin. "Trust me, love. Having you around will make boring business a lot more bearable."

I flush, deciding to take them up on the suggestion. A lazy morning curled up in an armchair in the suite's living area, my sketchbook balanced on my knees while the guys spread out paperwork and their laptops on the coffee table, sounds kind of perfect, actually.

They talk in low voices as they work, occasionally asking each other questions or debating some point I don't quite understand. But honestly, I'm not really listening. I'm too busy studying the lines of Beckett's profile, the way Ryder's hands move as he gesticulates, the furrow that appears between Tristan's brows when he's concentrating.

My pencil moves almost of its own accord, capturing moments and expressions as I lose myself in the act of creation, only vaguely aware of the passage of time. It's not until I feel a presence looming over me that I snap back to reality.

"I think we're done here," Tristan murmurs, resting his hand on my shoulder as I instinctively cover my sketchbook. "The weather looks like it's clearing too."

My stomach sinks slightly at the news, and when I glance out the window, I see that he's right. The snow has slowed to a gentle flutter.

Beckett is already shaking his head, though. "If we left now, we'd barely make any progress before having to stop again. We might as well wait till morning. We can get an early start tomorrow if the roads are clear."

Ryder grins, sprawling on the couch next to me and throwing an arm around my shoulders. "Oh no, whatever shall we do?"

I laugh, leaning into him. "Well, we can't just sit in this hotel room all day, as nice as it is here. There's got to be something to do around here, right?"

We all look at each other for a moment before Tristan suggests, "Why don't we ask at the front desk? They might know of some local attractions."

It's a great idea, and after quickly changing into more appropriate clothes, the four of us end up trooping down to the lobby to ask.

"Can I help you?" the clerk asks, looking up at us with a smile.

"We're looking for something fun to do in the area," I tell him. "Do you have any suggestions?"

He rattles off quite a few, but it's the three magic words he says at the end that have me perking up with excitement.

"A Christmas tree farm?" I repeat, smiling so hard my cheeks ache. "Really? Is it far? Is it open? Do they do tours? Tell me everything!"

The clerk grins, clearly amused by my enthusiasm, but I can't help it. Something like this is definitely a holiday experience I can't get back in L.A.

"It's only about a fifteen-minute drive from here," he explains. "They've got tree cutting, a little market, hot chocolate... I'm not sure of their hours, but it's quite popular this time of year, so I'm sure you'll have plenty of time to enjoy it."

I turn to the guys, practically bouncing on my toes. "Can we go? Please?"

"I suppose we could manage that," Beckett rumbles, sounding a bit put upon.

I don't buy it for a minute, though. I think I'm starting to be able to read the different versions of his resting grumpy face, and if I'm not mistaken, he's not as opposed as he's letting on.

Tristan agrees too, but Ryder, predictably, rolls his eyes.

"Christmas trees. Joy," he deadpans. "It's just what our hotel room needs."

"Oh, come on," I tease, poking him in the side. "It will be fun! And you did hear that they have hot chocolate, didn't you?"

He grabs my hand to keep me from continuing to poke him, pulling me close.

"I suppose I can endure it," he murmurs, his lips brushing my ear. "If it makes you happy."

I beam at all of them, my heart swelling with affection. "Thank you," I say softly. "This means a lot to me."

As we head back upstairs to grab our coats and scarves, I feel a little giddy. It's silly, maybe, to be so excited about something as simple as a Christmas tree farm. But after years of sterile, picture-perfect holidays with my family, the idea of tramping through the snow with these three men, surrounded by the scent of pine and the promise of hot chocolate feels like the start of a whole new kind of Christmas magic. The kind that Christmas is supposed to be about.

And that feeling only intensifies when we finally get there.

As we pull up into the lot, I gasp. The farm is laid out like a Hallmark movie set, with twinkling lights, evergreen scents, and velvety red bows and bells everywhere.

"Look!" I exclaim, pointing to a sign after we all pile out of the SUV. "They have a Christmas tree maze!"

Ryder groans, but I catch the hint of a smile. "A maze? Really?"

"Scared you'll get lost?" Tristan teases, nudging him.

"Is it fear?" Beckett deadpans. "Or just accepting the inevitable?"

"Oh, it's *on*," Ryder answers, his competitive spirit triggered. "Come on."

He drags us over to the maze, and the guys continue to tease him about his lack of sense of direction as we make our way through it, laughing every time we hit dead ends and have to backtrack.

It's all in good fun, though, and after we've wandered through it for an hour, I'm pretty sure we can all agree that *none* of us has a very good sense of direction. Not when all the trees look the same.

At one point, Beckett lifts me up so I can see over the trees, and I finally direct us out, feeling like a queen on her throne as the three of them praise me for saving them.

It's... *glorious*. And as we continue to explore the farm, I'm struck by how easy it all feels. We've crossed a line into new territory, but the banter and laughter flow just as naturally as they always have between us. Maybe even more so now that it feels like they've stopped treating me like Caleb's little sister; like they're really seeing me as a woman in my own right for once.

After a while, we come across a section of pre-decorated trees, each one a different theme. I'm admiring a whimsical Alice in Wonderland tree when I hear Ryder yelp behind me.

I turn to see him covered in snow, cursing colorfully at a laughing Beckett and Tristan.

"You assholes!" Ryder sputters, shaking snow from his hair. "You told me there was a squirrel under there!"

A laugh bursts out of me. "Oh my god, your face!"

Ryder narrows his eyes at me, a dangerous glint in them. "You think that's funny, do you, love?"

Before I can react, he scoops me up, threatening to drop me in a snowbank. I shriek with laughter, clinging to him.

"No, no! I take it back! You're very manly and not at all gullible!"

He sets me down but keeps his arms around me. "That's what I thought," he murmurs, his lips brushing my ear. "Now, did someone say something about hot chocolate?"

"They're serving it in the main building," Beckett notes, jerking his chin back in the direction of the parking lot.

The four of us head in that direction, and even before we reach the large barn that serves as the main building, I can smell cinnamon and chocolate wafting out, promising warmth and treats inside.

As we approach, my phone buzzes in my pocket. I pull it out, and my good mood falters when I see the name on the screen.

Wade.

There was a time, not so long ago, when seeing his name would have made my heart race with hope. I spent an embarrassing amount of time after the breakup longing for him to call and tell me he'd changed his mind, that he'd realized walking away from me was a mistake.

It wasn't, though. At least, not for me. It freed me.

And now, seeing his name on the screen just leaves me... not even cold. just indifferent.

"Everything okay, freckles?" Tristan murmurs, resting a hand on my lower back, the light pressure both comforting and reassuring.

Without hesitation, I decline the call and slip the phone back into my pocket. Whatever Wade wants, it can wait. Or better yet, it can stay in the past where it belongs.

"Everything is wonderful," I say sincerely, hooking a mittened hand through Tristan's arm with a smile.

I look up to see Beckett watching me, a question in his eyes. I give him a reassuring smile too, then think what the heck, and link my other arm through his.

"Come on," I say, tugging the men into the barn. "I smell hot chocolate calling our names."

Ryder is in front of us and turns to face me at that, grinning as he walks backward. "You *smell* it calling our name? That's a pretty impressive nose you've got there."

"If you think that's impressive, you should see what I can do with other parts," I tease him, my heart glowing as brightly as the massive tree in the center of the Christmas wonderland that we find inside the barn.

He laughs, heat in his gaze, and like a true Christmas miracle, he doesn't even grumble about the stalls selling everything from ornaments to gingerbread or the jolly Santa in the corner, surrounded by excited children.

Well, at least not much.

"This is amazing," I gush.

Ryder turns around, his eyes going wide. "Did Christmas throw up in here?"

There's no real bite to his words, though, and I laugh, feeling lighter than I have in years.

"Come on, guys. Let's get some hot chocolate and see what kind of trouble we can get into."

19

TRISTAN

AFTER SPENDING the last few hours outside, the warmth inside the barn envelops me like a blanket. The scent of pine and cinnamon fills the air, and Lana gasps softly in delight as we move deeper into the building, her eyes wide as she takes in the festive wonderland around us.

"Oh my god, just look at all of this!" she exclaims, her voice filled with wonder.

But she's a woman on a mission, and even though I can see that she's itching to stop and look at everything we pass, she makes a beeline for the hot chocolate station set up near the back of the building.

I smile as I follow. The barn is decked out in full holiday splendor, with twinkling lights strung across the rafters and displays of ornaments and decorations covering every available surface. Ryder wasn't wrong. It really does look like Santa's workshop exploded in here, but Lana's reaction makes wading through all the holiday cheer worth it.

The joy radiating from her is infectious, and I find myself wanting to bottle it up and keep it forever. It's a dangerous thought, one I shouldn't be entertaining, but between the agreement we all made to explore kink with her and being snowbound in this post-card-perfect town today, it kind of feels like living in a bubble, removed from the reality where I'd normally put the brakes on enjoying her company this much.

"Do you want whipped cream on your cocoa?" Ryder asks her gruffly once we reach the small concession stand.

Lana finally tears her gaze away from the decorations and beams up at him like he just offered her the moon. "Absolutely. And maybe one of those giant gingerbread men too?"

He nods, grunting in acknowledgment as he places the order and pulls out his wallet, and I have to bite back a grin of my own at the faint hint of color on his cheeks.

She's getting to him too. Not that I can blame him. Her smile is like a ray of goddamn sunshine, and none of us are immune to it.

Lana insists that we all get some hot chocolate, then laughs with joy when Ryder hooks his arm through hers and drags her toward a display of hand-painted ornaments. His Grinch-like tendencies are nowhere to be seen as he watches her trail her fingers over the ornaments almost reverently.

The soft glow of the Christmas lights illuminates her face, and I'm struck suddenly by how beautiful she is.

It's not a new realization. I've always known Lana is attractive. But something about seeing her like this, so open and joyful, hits me right in the chest.

"Earth to Tristan." Beckett chuckles, snapping his fingers in front of my face. "You want one of these cookies, or should I just eat the rest of them while you moon over Caleb's sister?"

I flip him off and grab a cookie, perfectly aware of what he's doing. I get it. Lana is off limits outside of this weird holiday bubble we're all in. But I've known Beckett long enough to see right through him, and it's not *me* he's trying to remind of that fact right now.

He starts grumbling about some of the club business we took care of this morning, slowly ambling along next to me as we follow Lana and Ryder, but I already know there's nothing urgent happening with Radiance, so I tune him out and let my gaze drift back to Lana.

She's moved on to a towering Christmas tree, decorated with

what looks like hundreds of ornaments. Her face is tilted up, eyes wide as she takes it all in, and I'm struck by the thought that for all the success I've had in my life, being a part of putting that smile on her face feels like my greatest accomplishment.

And temporary agreement or not, I want to *keep* doing it.

"Shit," I mutter under my breath, pushing the thought away fast. It's not possible. At least, not like this.

"Problem?" Beckett asks.

I shake my head, then laugh when Ryder glances back and sends the two of us a look of total dismay, mouthing a silent "save me."

Lana has managed to drag him over to the guy dressed up as Santa in the corner who's taking pictures with kids, and even Beckett chuckles when Ryder shakes his head emphatically after she gestures toward the short line of families waiting to sit on his lap.

"Come on," I murmur. "Bro code. We're going to have to intervene."

We catch up to them just as the last family finishes getting their photos and Santa turns his attention to Lana.

"Ho Ho Ho!" he says, playing it up like he's the real thing. He pats his lap. "Come on over and tell me what you want for Christmas, little lady!"

Lana's eyes go wide. "Me? Oh, no, I couldn't."

"Afraid you're not on the nice list this year?" Santa teases her, making me narrow my eyes when his own eyes flicker with interest, his smile just a little too wide in my opinion.

The white hair and beard are clearly part of the costume, and if I'm not mistaken, so is all the padding. This isn't some jolly old man. He can't be much older than we are, and even if the flirty banter he falls into with Lana is innocent enough not to get him in trouble in this family-friendly setting, I'd bet my entire share of Radiance that he'd be more than happy to put her on his own naughty list this year.

And dammit, he actually convinces her to pass her hot chocolate over to Ryder and go sit on his lap.

"Are you seeing this?" Beckett growls, pinning an intense stare on Santa as Lana perches on the asshole's knee.

"Fucking Christmas," Ryder grumbles, looking around the barn. "Come on, let's go look at that leather work."

Beckett actually perks up a little. "Where?"

Ryder points it out, and the two of them head in that direction. But I don't go with them, sticking close to Lana instead. I'm not leaving her side—especially while she's on another man's lap.

"What are you hoping to find under the tree this year?" Santa asks her, resting his hand on her knee.

Lana laughs, then leans in to whisper her answer in his ear.

It's perfectly innocent.

She's having fun.

I *know* that.

But something inside me snaps, and before I even realize what I'm doing, I've stomped over and tugged her off his lap.

"Tristan?" Lana asks, looking startled.

I tuck her against my side and glare down at the knee-groper. "Hands to yourself, *Nick.*"

A flash of irritation crosses his face, but then he obviously remembers where he is—which is at work, not at a pickup joint—and gets back into character.

"That's *Saint* Nick to you," he says with an exaggerated wink and another *ho ho ho.* "And what do you want for Christmas, young man?"

I can't help the smug smile when Lana melts against me. "I've already got it right here."

Lana laughs breathlessly as I pull her away. "What was all that about?"

"What did you whisper to him?" I ask instead of answering her question.

She purses her lips, shaking her head. "That's a secret between me and Santa. If I tell you my Christmas wish, it won't come true!"

"That's not how it works."

"I'm pretty sure it is," she jokes.

I grab her by both arms, swinging her around to face me. "No, freckles, it's not. If you're going to be sitting on someone's lap and spilling your secrets, it's going to be one of us."

"But what if I want presents?" she asks with a pretty pout, like she thinks I'm kidding. "That's Santa's job, not yours!"

"The fuck it's not."

Her eyes go wide, and I look around for some privacy, then pull her into a small alcove behind a row of themed Christmas trees.

"If you want presents, you tell me, Ryder, or Beckett. If you want something for Christmas, *we'll* make it happen. No sitting on anyone else's lap. No letting other men touch you."

"Tristan," she says softly, resting a hand on my chest. "I, um... I don't know what to say."

"I'm serious," I tell her, all the feelings that have been building up inside me today crystallizing into something I'm done denying. At least in this moment. "I know what we're doing is only tempo-rary, but while we're on this road trip, you're ours. And I've got no interest in sharing you with anyone else. Not even in little ways."

"Besides Ryder and Beckett," she murmurs, her cheeks flushing pink. "I'm, um, I'm all of yours for now."

"That's right."

I don't feel any of the sharp spikes of jealousy I just experi-enced when it comes to my two oldest friends. It feels *right* to share her with them. Not to mention it's hot as hell.

"Okay," she whispers, her eyes wide.

"Okay?" I repeat, cupping her jaw and stroking my thumb over her satiny skin.

"Yeah." She bites her lip, then smiles at me, her adorable little dimple popping out. "I'm very okay with that."

Something settles inside me, and I can't help smiling back at her. "Good."

Then I kiss her, because for right now at least, I can.

After we catch up with Ryder and Beckett and admire the leather crafts they found, Lana tries to excuse herself to "find the ladies room."

Ryder snorts. "You know you're not very good at being sneaky, right?"

She laughs, playfully smacking his arm. "Stop it! A girl is entitled to her secrets."

"What kind of secrets?" Beckett asks with a frown.

She gives an exaggerated sigh, rolling her eyes at him. "I'm just going to grab a few things before we go, okay? But none of you are allowed to peek!"

I chuckle as she scampers off. "She's buying us presents, isn't she?"

"She doesn't need to buy us presents," Beckett grumbles.

Ryder rolls his eyes, but he's grinning. "Try telling her that."

"I think you're wrong," Beckett insists. "She doesn't have any reason to buy things for us. We don't need any of this crap."

I raise my eyebrows, shooting a pointed look at the festive bag stamped with the tree farm's logo that he's carrying.

"That's different," he mutters. "That leatherworker was a skilled craftsman."

Ryder and I give him a little more shit for his shopping choices, then finally head back to the hotel once Lana rejoins us. None of us mention the fact that the weather has cleared up even more—or that, while it's too late to hit the road tonight, it's clear that we'll be able to continue traveling in the morning.

Lana vetoes Ryder's suggestion for take-out once we're back in our suite, whipping up a simple but delicious meal for us from the groceries she ordered earlier instead. A meal that she insists we eat while having a Christmas movie marathon.

Ryder, predictably, groans. "Do we have to?"

"Would it be mean of me to say yes?" she asks, shamelessly batting her eyes at him.

He folds immediately, making even Beckett chuckle, but passes on Lana's offer to let him pick the movie.

"Okay, well, which one do you want to watch first?" she asks, turning to Beckett.

He shrugs. "Anything is fine."

Lana narrows her eyes a little. "But which Christmas movie is your favorite?"

He grunts, and she turns the spotlight on me.

"Tristan?"

"Uh..." I try to remember what Grandma Meg used to put on while she made Christmas cookies. "The one with the angel?"

"You mean *It's a Wonderful Life*?"

"Sure."

"Oh my god," she says, throwing her hands up as she laughs. "You have no idea, do you? Come on, tell me. How many Christmas movies have you guys actually seen?"

The silence echoes.

Then Beckett breaks it. "I like *Die Hard*."

Lana's jaw drops. "Are you kidding me? That is *not* a Christmas movie! Okay, that's it. We're starting with *my* favorite, *Miracle on 34th Street*, and I'm not even going to ask if any of you have seen it or not, because I already know the answer."

I settle back on the couch as she sets it up, exchanging grins with Ryder as she huffs under her breath while she does it. I'm definitely not as sold on Christmas as Lana is, but even I can admit that her obsession with it is kind of adorable.

So is the way she recites half the movie's lines under her breath as she watches it.

Once we all finish eating, she puts on another one, something about an elf, and pulls out her sketch pad, curling up with her fuzzy-socked feet on the couch, tucked under my thigh, and her head on Ryder's shoulder as she divides her attention between drawing and the screen, tossing aside each sketch as she finishes it.

I've spent plenty of nights chilling at home with Ryder and Beckett, but something about having Lana in the mix makes this feel different. Just as comfortable, but also somehow better. And the way I keep catching Ryder smiling down at her fondly makes me think I'm not the only one feeling this way.

Beckett, on the other hand, seems a little tense as the last movie wraps up.

"We should clean up," Lana says, standing up and stretching as the credits start to roll.

I stand up too so I can block her before she can grab the scattered remains of the meal she made us. "Uh uh. You cooked. We'll handle the dishes."

"You're going to spoil me. But if you're sure, I wouldn't mind grabbing a shower."

"Go," I tell her as Ryder gathers up the dishes from the coffee table and takes them to the kitchen.

She goes up on her tiptoes and kisses my cheek, then heads to the bathroom. I turn to follow after Ryder, but then glance at Beckett and change my mind.

"You okay?" I ask.

He looks up at me like I've startled him out of his thoughts, then gives a single, short nod. "Fine."

I prop my hip on the arm of the couch and cross my arms over my chest. "Want to try that again? You've been tense ever since we got back from the tree farm."

For a second, he looks like he's going to close down on me. But then he sighs, looking away for a second. "I just don't think this is smart."

I don't have to ask what he means.

"It's only until we reach New Hampshire," I remind him. "Then everything will go back to normal."

He gives me a noncommittal grunt, and I huff in irritation. We don't have that many days left on the road, and as I realized after Santa put his hands on her, I don't want to waste them.

"Fuck, Beckett. It's *good*. You know it is. Just enjoy it. Lana is..."

Incredible. Sexy. Joyful. Addicting.

He raises an eyebrow at me when I trail off without saying any of that, not sure which adjective to give him.

But I'm not the only one who knows his friend well.

"Yeah," he says after a minute, the corner of his mouth tipping up. "She's all that. So do you really think we'll be able to go back to the way things were after this?"

"Sure," I lie, then have to look away, scrubbing at the faint ache in my chest.

Beckett snorts. "Want to try that again?" he asks, parroting the question back at me.

"It's complicated."

"No shit. And what happens if our relationship with her can't recover? You really think it's not gonna get awkward? Are you willing to lose her from our lives forever, just for a few days of fun?"

"It's more than that," I snap, then yank my glasses off to polish them so I don't have to see the sad smile on Beckett's face.

I can still hear him, though.

"Yeah, that's kind of my point," he says quietly.

My gut twists. I understand where Beckett is coming from. He's putting into words a lot of the same things that held me back when I first tried to ignore my attraction to her the night she came to my hotel room. And maybe he's right. Maybe it would have been better if we'd never started any of this. But that ship has sailed.

I slide my glasses back into place. "We're not going to avoid things getting complicated by ending things early."

Beckett gives me a long look. "It might help."

"No."

He huffs out a quiet laugh. "No, you don't think it will help, or no, you're not willing to end this before we have to?"

"Are you willing to do that?"

He frowns at me. "I should."

"But *are* you?"

"Fuck," he mutters, scrubbing a hand over his face.

"Yeah," I agree, laughing ruefully under my breath. "I don't have the willpower to stop either. Not now that we've started. But it *is* good. You know it is. And since we're not going to stop, it's okay to enjoy what we've got with her while we've got it."

He huffs again, shaking his head like he's not sure he agrees with me. But that's fair. It's not just complicated with Lana—it hit me earlier today that it's going to fucking hurt when we finish this trip and have to go back to...

Well, to whatever the new normal ends up being after our agreement comes to an end.

A warm wave of floral bath-product scent wafts out from the suite's bedroom. Lana must have finished her shower.

A moment later, she appears in the bedroom's doorway, leaning against the doorjamb in just a sexy-as-fuck pair of lacy panties and a matching bra.

"You two look serious," she says to me and Beckett, smiling as she looks between the two of us curiously. "Everything okay?"

Ryder emerges from the kitchen as if called by a siren. "Very fucking okay, love," he answers, striding over to her and pulling her against him. "You look gorgeous."

She makes a sexy little sound that goes straight to my cock, and Ryder kisses her, swallowing it down with a groan.

"Fuck," Beckett murmurs, so low that I'm probably the only one who hears.

I nod, but my attention is riveted to the sight of her clinging to Ryder's shoulders, her lush curves pressed against him like a dream.

They're hot as fuck together.

Ryder has one arm wrapped around her waist, and when he fists his hand in her thick, silky hair and tugs her head back, kissing his way down her throat, she gasps, making eye contact with me over his shoulder. Eye contact that looks a hell of a lot like an invitation.

I share a quick look with Beckett, the conversation we just had silently replaying between us.

I can respect his reasons for continuing to hold himself back, but I'm done with that. I may not know what the future will look like once this all ends, but I do know that the only thing I'll regret about tonight is not enjoying every fucking second we've still got with her while I can.

With a low curse, I get to my feet and stride over to join Lana and Ryder.

20
LANA

I'VE NEVER FELT as bold, as sexy and confident, as I did walking out of the bedroom in the most provocative lingerie I packed. But the best part is that the minute the men see me, I can start to let go of that and begin falling into submission, because Ryder kisses me exactly the way he did the other night.

He kisses me in a way that makes me feel not just wanted, but totally owned.

I love it. I crave it.

And then it gets even better when Tristan comes over and joins us, sandwiching me between the two of them.

When he takes over the kiss from Ryder, the sensation of being totally surrounded and controlled is intensified. My body feels electric, every nerve ending sparking. With two sets of hands and mouths on me, it's hard to keep track of which is which.

I love the feeling. It makes it the easiest thing in the world to just let go, to lose myself completely in the intensity of the sensations and just drift along in the pure, raw pleasure of it.

"You taste incredible, love," Ryder murmurs, pushing me back against Tristan and lifting my breasts in his hands as he drags his hot mouth down my throat.

His thumbs rub my nipples through the lace of my bra as

Tristan tips my head back and takes my mouth. I whimper, the combination of sensations sending my arousal ratcheting higher.

"Tell us what you want," Tristan murmurs, his fingers digging into my hip as he grinds his cock against my ass.

"You," I whisper, turning my head to capture his mouth again.

Ryder chuckles against my skin, nipping the swell of my breast. "More specific."

I groan. "I want... I want you both to make me come."

And I don't think I *can* get more specific than that. Not with the overload of pleasure that's already racing through my body.

Tristan kisses the back of my neck, the rough stubble on his jaw rasping across my skin. "I think you want more than just an orgasm though, don't you? You want to submit to us. You want us to decide how to make your body sing tonight. You want to give up all control and hand it over to me and Ryder."

"Yes," I gasp. "*Please.*"

Ryder groans, pushing my bra out of the way and sucking one of my nipples into his mouth as Tristan reaches between my legs from behind and slips his fingers inside my panties.

"She's wet, Ryder," he says. "Dripping wet and so damn tight. How many orgasms do you think we can get out of her tonight?"

Ryder answers him with a low chuckle, but I can barely process what they're saying, lost in the sensations as Ryder switches to my other breast and Tristan tugs on my clit piercing, working me higher and higher.

Then Ryder drags his mouth down the center of my body and gets on his knees, mouthing my clit through my panties when Tristan moves his fingers away.

"Open your eyes," Tristan whispers in my ear, cupping my breasts as he holds me against him. "Beckett is watching."

I cry out, pleasure spearing my core and rippling outward. I don't know if it's from Ryder's mouth, or the way Tristan is pinching and teasing my nipples, or from what he just told me.

But I do it. I obey him, forcing my eyes open to find Beckett's hot gaze locked on me.

He hasn't moved, hasn't come any closer, but even though

there's no expression on his face, the intensity radiating from him is obvious. He's hungry for me. And as soon as I realize it, I can't look away.

I want him too.

But then Ryder hooks his fingers in the edge of my panties and works them down over my hips, taking the ring in my clit between his teeth. I gasp and look down at him, his wicked eyes and his clever mouth mesmerizing me.

"Spread your legs," Tristan murmurs. "Ryder deserves a taste, don't you think?"

"Fuck, she's delicious," Ryder murmurs as I open my legs a bit, turning his head and sucking a bite into the tender skin of my inner thigh. "But as sexy as you look in these, I need them off."

He rolls my panties down even farther, inch by inch, and he follows their progress with his mouth until I'm panting, desperate to have his tongue back where I need it.

As if he can sense my rising need, Tristan captures my arms and folds them over my chest, then holds them there as Ryder finishes stripping off my panties. It reminds me of how hot it was last night when Ryder told me about Tristan's interest in bondage, but the reality of being restrained like this is even better.

I want to touch myself, but I can't.

I want to push Ryder's head between my legs, but they've taken that choice out of my hands.

"Green?" Tristan murmurs, as if he's reading my mind.

"Green," I whisper.

"Beautiful," Ryder murmurs, looking up at me.

The heat in his eyes makes me flush, and when he hooks one of my legs over his shoulder, the wave of heat that goes through me is so intense it has me moaning before he even puts his mouth back on me.

"I've got you," Tristan says, supporting my weight and keeping me steady even as he continues to restrain me. "Let yourself enjoy this. Let go and surrender all your pleasure."

It feels like I can't do anything *but* surrender. I feel exposed and vulnerable, but also cherished and safe.

And so incredibly turned on that I could go off with barely a touch.

"Please," I gasp, writhing in Tristan's hold.

"Keep begging," he murmurs in my ear, his hot shaft pushing into my back. "It's sexy as fuck."

"I agree," Ryder says with a wicked chuckle, sucking more of those hot, tingling love bites into my thighs and then, finally leaning in and dragging his tongue through my folds with a long, filthy lick that has me crying out and shamelessly pushing my hips forward.

He looks up at me with a smile that's pure heat. "You know what else is sexy? The way you taste, love. Fucking Christ. It's sweeter than dessert. I could stay here all night."

I don't have the words to respond, especially when he slides two fingers inside me, rubbing his thumb over my clit and making me writhe against him, gasping and begging.

Tristan groans, his fingers digging into my forearms. "Damn, I wish I had my ropes right now. I love how fucking wild you get, but be good and hold still for us. I want to see Ryder make you come."

"I can't," I pant, arching in his hold as Ryder sucks my clit into his mouth and does something magical to it with his tongue.

"Sure you can," Tristan says, his voice smooth as silk. "You're sexy as hell like this, but I know what you really crave is submission. And all you have to do is surrender to the pleasure. Not chase it, just accept it. Let us take care of you."

I moan, the sound welling up from my innermost core as his words tap into something fundamental and deep inside me. The same "something" that drew me to kink in the first place.

"Oh fuck," I whisper, melting back against him. "*Yes.*"

Tristan's lips curve into a smile against my cheek. "That's it, beautiful. Fuck, you're perfect."

He turns my head and catches my mouth with his again, kissing me like he's claiming me as Ryder groans against my pussy, sucking on my clit as he slips two fingers inside me and finds my g-spot.

I sob into Tristan's mouth, shaking as Ryder starts fucking me hard and fast with his fingers while relentlessly working his magic on my clit.

"Good girl, that's it, let yourself go," Tristan murmurs, brushing my hair back and then taking my mouth again. He doesn't rush, just kisses me deeply and thoroughly, letting Ryder drive me wild without getting distracted from the possessive, demanding way he owns my mouth.

The contrast between his restraint and Ryder's frenzied passion overloads my senses, and I fall apart in a shuddering orgasm, screaming my release into Tristan's mouth as I ride Ryder's face.

Tristan groans, swallowing my cries.

Ryder doesn't stop, and I have a second, smaller climax that leaves me floating before Tristan finally pulls his mouth from mine.

He turns me around to face him. "My turn now."

My knees give out, and Ryder rises to his feet quickly to catch me, holding me steady. "We should get her on the bed first."

"Mm, good idea." Tristan smiles, kissing the tip of my nose and then leading me into the bedroom.

I'm glad he and Ryder are helping, because I honestly don't think I can walk. My body feels like my bones have been replaced by sweet, warm syrup in the aftermath of my orgasm, but even better than the languid pleasure still sparking through me is knowing that they mean it. They really do have me. All I have to do is let them do whatever they want.

"Green," I murmur dreamily as they lower me to the bed, making Tristan chuckle.

Ryder gives me a sexy smile as he stands back and strips off his clothes, and when Tristan follows suit, my skin literally tingles, aching to feel them against me.

"I need to taste you," Tristan says, his heated gaze traveling the length of my body as I lay sprawled on the bed, still in my bra. "I want to feel that sweet pussy come all over my tongue."

I gasp as he grabs my hips and yanks me toward the edge of the mattress, then moan when he drops to his knees, his eyes burning.

"So pretty and wet," he murmurs, spreading me wide and

looking up the length of my body. "Ryder got you good and primed for me."

"Not a hardship," Ryder teases, kneeling on the bed next to me and palming one of my breasts. "But fuck, neither is this. She was made to be worshiped."

A hot thrill goes through me when they start talking to each other about me.

Tristan dips his head, kissing my inner thigh. "That's the truth," he agrees, dragging his lips upward until he reaches the juncture of my legs.

When he starts licking me, his tongue hot and sure, Ryder shifts his attention to the other breast, kneading and playing with it as he sprawls out next to me and kisses me, his cock hot and hard against my side.

I want it inside me. I want to be fucked so deeply that I lose myself.

But Tristan has me trapped, and the thrill of letting them have their way with me, letting *them* decide how to use my body, has my core tightening as Tristan's fingers and tongue work their magic.

"For someone so sweet, you're fucking dirty beneath, aren't you?" he murmurs, tugging on my clit piercing. "I love this thing. Love the way you react. Love how fucking hot it looks on you."

I moan, arching up against his mouth as Ryder matches his pace, sucking my nipples and stroking his hands all over my body, making me ache to be touched everywhere at once.

And with two of them focused on me, it makes it feel like I am.

Ryder kisses his way back up my throat and nips at my earlobe. "You're getting close. You love this, don't you, being held down and taken care of? Forced to come for us as many times as we want?"

I sob, nodding desperately.

"Say it."

The order lights up the dark places inside me and sends a wave of need crashing through my body.

"Yes!"

"Not good enough," Tristan says, raising his head and pinning his eyes on me. "You heard Ryder."

"I do. I love this," I gasp, squirming, aching, desperate.

Tristan rewards me by sucking my clit into his mouth and flicking my piercing with his tongue.

I wail, then gasp as I open my eyes and realize that Beckett has come to the bedroom door. He's leaning against the frame, watching me with a laser focus that has my core throbbing.

"I love being held down," I whisper, talking directly to him. "Being touched. Coming for you. For all of you. I want... I want all three of you to use me as much as you want."

"Just two for now," Ryder chuckles, rolling my nipples between his fingers.

Tristan lifts his head again, twisting a little to see Beckett behind him before he looks back and shares a look with Ryder.

"Beckett isn't ready to join in yet," he says, smirking.

"Is he, um, is he into voyeurism too?" I ask breathlessly.

Tristan chuckles. "Oh, I'm sure he's enjoying watching you, but no. That's not really his kink."

"He's a Dom through and through," Ryder says, both of them clearly goading Beckett on. "He likes to be hands on, likes to edge and push the limits of pleasure."

"Oh fuck," I whisper, staring straight at Beckett. "*Yes.*"

I can't manage anything more articulate than that, I just know that I want all of it, everything, from all three of them.

Beckett's jaw ticks, but he doesn't move. I don't feel rejected, though. I can't. Not when he's staring at me so intensely that it makes my heart race. His eyes are hard and his expression is fierce and primal in a way that has me imagining exactly what his hands and lips would feel like on me.

He would take me apart.

I gasp, and heat flares in his eyes.

"It's not you, love," Ryder murmurs, sliding his hand up my side and opening the clasp on my bra between my breasts, baring me completely to Beckett's gaze.

"Right now, Beckett's just being stubborn," Tristan agrees.

I don't know what he means by that, but I don't have time to decipher his words, because the next thing I know, Tristan is pushing my legs open even wider and fingering my pussy until I'm sobbing.

"Damn, you're incredible," he says, giving me a wicked grin. "But you can do better. Let's show Beckett what he's missing out on."

He dips his head down without giving me a chance to make sense of that, either, and then his mouth is on me again and I lose all sense of time.

Everything melts away, until there's only the sensation of Tristan's mouth and Ryder's hands on me, the sounds of their voices, their low, teasing laughter and their soft, filthy words.

And Beckett's heated gaze.

It's my anchor. I can't look away, and he doesn't either. He doesn't even blink.

And then I'm coming again. Arching up like a bow as the pleasure crests and breaks over me in a wave. I have a moment to realize that it's stronger this time, even more intense than my first orgasm, and then my mind blanks, lost in a storm of pure sensation as Tristan and Ryder work me through it, dragging it out until I'm a shaking mess on the bed, tears running down my cheeks and my heart thudding so hard I think it might beat right out of my chest.

When Ryder cups my jaw and tips my face toward him, I can't even focus on him, let alone kiss him. He smiles, looking satisfied, then kisses my forehead instead, brushing his thumb across my cheek.

"Such a filthy, kinky little thing," he says tenderly. "Do you like two men getting you off at the same time?"

"Yes," I whisper, the word coming out raspy. "It's amazing."

I can't believe what I've been missing out on all this time... or imagine how I'll ever go back to being satisfied without the perfect overload of sensation they're giving me.

Ryder smirks. "Do you want us to keep using you like this? To fuck your gorgeous body until we're all sated and spent? For both of us to take you at the same time?"

I suck in a sharp breath, my mind going wild with a whole montage of filthy scenarios.

Ryder fucking my face while Tristan buries his cock in my pussy. Tristan making me ride him while Ryder works himself into my untouched backdoor. Being sandwiched between them again, just like I was earlier, but this time, with *both* of them in my pussy.

I whimper at the thought, a needy sound escaping me.

"I think that's a yes," Tristan rasps, nipping my inner thigh as Ryder smirks and grips my chin, tugging it down.

I obediently let my mouth fall open, and he slips his thumb in my mouth, rubbing it back and forth over my lower lip. "We'll start easy on you, love. One cock in this plush mouth of yours, and one in the pussy you've gotten so nice and wet for us. How does that sound?"

I whimper, nodding.

I can't breathe. Can't move. But I want it. I want everything they'll give me.

I want that more than air.

2 1

LANA

Tristan crawls up my body and kisses me, and the taste of my arousal on his lips makes me moan.

"So fucking good," he murmurs. "You taste better with every orgasm."

Without thinking, I thread my fingers through his hair, pulling him closer. My fingers brush against a pattern of raised ridges on his scalp, and he suddenly tenses above me, freezing in place.

I blink, realizing in a rush that the ridges must be scars.

Of course they are. They cover most of the left side of his body, and since they snake up his neck, it makes sense that they don't just stop at the hairline.

I pull my hand back. "I'm so sorry. I didn't mean to hurt you!"

He gives me a rueful smile. "It doesn't hurt." He reaches up and takes one of my hands, bringing it down to his right shoulder. "Here, you'll like this better."

"*I'll* like it better?"

He shrugs, avoiding my eyes. "My scars are ugly, Lana. That's just a fact."

"And what's this?" I ask, pushing him back enough that I can grab my own soft stomach. "Is this ugly?"

His eyes go wide. "The fuck? No! You're gorgeous."

"You're pure fucking temptation," Ryder throws in. "So soft

everywhere. Such a luscious fucking body. And... fuck, love, I just need inside you."

I grin even as I blush. I need that too. But first, I need to set something straight.

"Well, 'gorgeous,' 'tempting,' and 'luscious' are not the words I've heard in the past. But I'm not in bed with any of the assholes who've had a different opinion about my curves, and if I'm not allowed to be self-conscious about my body, then neither are you."

Tristan gapes at me for a moment, like he's at a loss for words.

I tunnel my fingers through his hair again, running them over the scars on the back of his head, then following their trail and stroking down the left side of his neck, over his shoulder, his arm, and down his side.

Unbidden, my eyes burn with tears. Of course I know about the accident he got into years ago, but I'm not sure I've ever let myself really think about it. About the damage to his body. About the pain he went through. About everything he lost.

"These are beautiful," I whisper. "Every single one of these scars is a miracle. Don't you know that?"

He stares at me for a long moment, his eyes going bright, then swallows hard and gives his head a tiny shake.

No.

He doesn't know.

I drag my fingers over his ridged skin. "These are all the places your body patched itself back together, so that you could live. And I am really, really happy you're here. Living. With me."

I'm only speaking the truth, but it occurs to me after I let those uncensored words out that they aren't really in the spirit of this temporary arrangement between us. They're too raw. Too real.

But before I can backpedal or diffuse the intensity with a joke, a look passes over Tristan's face. Something I can't quite read but that pierces right into my heart.

Then he palms the back of my head and kisses me like his life depends on it.

"Fuck, that's hot," Ryder mutters.

"I need to be inside you," Tristan groans, his hands roaming over my curves in a way that takes everything I just said to him and cements it as truth.

I'm gorgeous. Tempting. Luscious.

And I need him to be inside me too.

"Condom?" Ryder asks as Tristan sits back, kneeling between my legs and lifts one to my shoulder.

He places a lingering kiss on my calf, eyes locked on me with a clear message: it's up to me.

And I don't want it.

Ryder laughs, low and throaty. "You want to take him bare, just like you took me, don't you, love?"

"Yes," I whisper, never breaking eye contact with Tristan... until Beckett makes a low sound from the doorway that shoots my arousal into the stratosphere.

I suck in a sharp breath, propping myself up on my elbows to see him over Tristan's shoulder.

His eyes burn into me, reminding me that he's not just here. He wants me too.

But for now, he's clearly only planning on letting himself watch, and I surprise myself all over again by how hot I find that idea.

With the position I'm in and the consent I've already given, I expect Tristan to drive into me immediately. Instead, he teases me, running his hands up and down my sides and kneading my ass.

"Hands and knees," he orders, giving me a heated smile that has my breath catching in my throat. "I've been fucking dreaming of this."

My entire body flushes as I scramble to obey him, silencing the voice in my head about how ungracefully I manage it in my enthusiasm. I can't lecture Tristan about accepting himself and then become a hypocrite in my own mind. Besides, the lust in all three men's eyes is unmistakable, and I don't plan on wasting a single moment of this amazing experience on self-consciousness.

Especially not when I'm too busy enjoying the butterflies in my stomach at the idea of taking both Tristan and Ryder at the same time. Being watched is one thing, but actually letting them share me is a whole other level of hot, and one I've definitely never tried before.

Tristan groans as I get into position, running his palm down my spine.

"What did it feel like when you were inside this perfect pussy, Ryder?" he asks.

Ryder smirks as he crawls onto the bed next to me, propping himself up against the pillows and palming his cock.

"Like heaven," he says. "Fuck, this is hot. That last orgasm is going to have her so soft and wet for you. Isn't that right, love? Is your pussy ready for Tristan's cock?"

"Yes," I gasp. "I want it."

I want both of them.

I want them to use my body to get off. To fill me up, raw and bare, with their cum.

Ryder grabs a pillow and helps prop me up, and then Tristan slides deep.

It's not a hard thrust, but I can't hold back the little sob that falls from my lips. He feels so good. And even though he's just started moving, he's already taking me higher and higher, my pleasure spiraling upward until I can't catch my breath.

"That's it," he growls, gripping my hips as he starts thrusting harder. "Fuck, how are you so tight after coming so hard for us already?"

Ryder smirks, lazily fisting his cock as he watches Tristan fuck me. "I told you. Tight. And wet. And fucking perfect."

"Fucking Christ, it's true." Tristan groans, leaning over my back and wrapping one arm around me, cupping my breast as his fingers toy with my nipple. "And all ours, aren't you? We can take this pussy any time we want. Can't we? Free use."

For the duration of the trip.

None of us voice that part, and his next thrust pushes it right out of my head.

"Yes," I whimper, barely able to hold myself up as the pleasure quickly mounts, his angle just right to my g-spot with every slow, deliberate thrust.

But not enough to take me to the edge.

He's toying with me.

"*Tristan*," I beg in a whimper. "Please. More."

"More?" he asks, as a wicked grin spreads across Ryder's face. "Sounds like she's begging for you to join in," he tells Ryder.

"Yes. *Please.*"

Tristan grips my hips and drives into me hard enough that the slap of our skin echoes through the room, and the moan that slips past my lips is loud and shameless.

"That sounds like an invitation," Ryder murmurs, getting to his knees in front of me and stroking my chin. Then he tugs on it, pulling my mouth open as I pant with my rising need and stare up at him. "Is this what you need?"

He guides his cockhead, already slick with precum, to my lips, then teasingly drags it across them, painting them with his salty taste.

"Yes." I'm completely shameless as I flick my tongue out and lick his slit. "I want it."

He hisses in a breath, his expression going dark and fierce.

"Fuck, she's sexy," Tristan growls, driving into me even harder. "Come on, give her what she wants."

"Don't worry," Ryder says, sliding his cock between my lips and groaning. "I plan on it. And you're going to be a good girl, aren't you, love? Going to come for us again while we fuck your mouth and that pretty pussy, as hard and deep as we want?"

I can only moan around him, which he takes for the enthusiastic yes it is. I've never had anyone truly fuck my mouth, and honestly, I'm not sure how I'll take it.

But I know he won't give me more than I can handle. He'll get just as dirty as I've always dreamed of, but he'll take care of me too.

As if to prove it, he cups my cheek, his thumb resting right under my ear, the position and angle allowing him to feel his own cock through my cheek as he slowly slides it across my tongue, easing me into it despite his wonderfully filthy promise to fuck my mouth.

"We're going to take good care of you," he whispers, looking me straight in the eye. "And you want to be good for us, don't you? You want to submit and surrender yourself, to take everything we give you tonight and show Beckett what he's missing out on."

I whine around his cock, my skin tingling at the reminder that Beckett's eyes are on me right now too.

"Fuck," Ryder groans, his cockhead hitting the back of my throat as the thickness of his shaft forces my jaw to stretch. "Your mouth is so fucking good, love."

The praise starts to send me into a state that almost feels like floating, and combined with the way Tristan is fucking me, it's a sensation I want to linger in forever.

Ryder thrusts deeper, his hands fisting in my hair. "Jesus," he mutters, staring down at me as he repeatedly pushes his cock as far as it can go while still letting me breathe. "She's got no gag reflex, Beckett. You have no fucking idea how hot this is."

I hear a grunt from behind me in response.

Tristan is breathing raggedly, hands tight on my hips and cock driving into me in a perfect, overwhelming rhythm. But that sound wasn't him. It was Beckett.

I moan, and Ryder hisses out a breath. "Yeah, love. Like that. Feels so fucking good. You ready for me to go deeper? I'm going to use your throat. Blink once if you're green, because it will cut off your air."

I've never experimented with breath play, but it's just one more way I can submit to these men completely. And I want that. I want every aspect of my pleasure to be in their hands.

I blink, and Ryder gives me a blinding smile filled with so much heat that my core tightens.

"Good girl. Okay, breathe in through your nose now, then hold it."

I do it, filling my lungs with oxygen, and on his next thrust, he shoves his cock all the way to the back of my throat.

But this time, without stopping there.

I feel a subtle pop in the back of my throat, like something painlessly giving way, and he slides home with a rumbling groan that sounds like pure sex. As his cock passes into the tight confines of my throat, cutting off my air just the way he warned me it would, I feel owned in a way that I've never experienced before.

It's utterly freeing.

My eyes water as I stare up at him, my nipples tingling and my pussy clenching around Tristan's cock as Ryder finally bottoms out, his balls a soft weight against my chin and my nose buried in his neatly trimmed pubes.

"Fucking hell," he mutters, and I'm gratified to see that his expression is just as strained as I'm feeling, his cheeks flushed and his brow creased as he struggles to maintain control. "So good."

I start to feel lightheaded as he holds himself there, but I don't want air. I don't want him to pull back. All the pleasure coiling inside me gets hotter, tighter as my throat convulses around him.

Then Tristan spanks me, and a jolt of sensation races up my spine and bursts inside my head, and my whole body tightens up.

"Fuck, yes," he grunts as my pussy tightens around his shaft, my orgasm slower to build this time after already coming for them, but feeling no less intense as it starts to creep up on me. "You love being filled by two of us, don't you?"

Ryder pulls back, leaving just the head of his cock on the tip of my tongue, and I suck in a breath and nod, panting.

Tristan kneads my ass as his thrusts slow a little. "You pink up so prettily."

He spanks me again, and I gasp—something that Ryder immediately takes advantage of by pushing back into my mouth.

"You should see this," Tristan mutters, spanking my other cheek, then going back to the first as his thrusts pick up speed again. "So fucking gorgeous. And tight. Fuck, your pussy feels amazing, just like your mouth did the other day. Makes me want to fuck all your holes."

I want to tell him he can. That I'm his. That if he wants to switch places with Ryder and use my mouth again, he can. Anything they want.

But I can't, because Ryder's eyes flare and he starts truly fucking my face, going in to the hilt on every thrust with short pauses in between to allow me to breathe.

Tristan spreads my cheeks, then presses a finger to the tight pucker of my asshole, and I cry out, the sound muffled by the cock in my mouth.

A moment later, something slick and warm dribbles down my crease.

Tristan's saliva.

It feels filthy and just a little bit forbidden, and when he rubs it around my back hole, I shudder, my arousal ratcheting up to the next level.

"*All* your holes," he murmurs as he works his fingertip inside me, starting to shallowly fuck my ass with it in the same rhythm as his cock.

I groan around Ryder's shaft, sucking him even more eagerly as my pleasure crests and I start to go into sensory overload.

"Yeah, just like that, love," Ryder says, his voice rough with his own arousal. "Such a good girl, letting us fill you up like this. Are you going to come for us? You're almost there, I can feel it. Your throat is squeezing the hell out of my cock, and the way Tristan's pounding into you, I'm guessing that sweet little pussy is getting damn tight too."

"Fuck yeah, it is," Tristan grits out. "It's already milking my cock. She's responsive as fuck to ass play. If we had lube on hand, I'd be tempted to switch holes. But fuck if I'm going to last long enough for that."

I can't respond. I can't even moan. I feel full in all the best possible ways, every part of my body an instrument of pleasure, humming and tightening with my imminent climax as they fuck me and toy with my most private places until I'm teetering on a knife's edge of shattering.

I've never been fucked like this before. Never been taken apart piece by piece and trusted that I can truly let myself go and count on them to catch me. It feels like true submission, the promise fulfilled of all the things that attracted me to kink in the first place.

The feeling of giving all my power away. Of trusting someone else to decide what's best for me. To push me, to test my limits, and to know when I need to be restrained and when I need to be freed.

To give me everything I need, even if it's not what I ever would have thought to ask for.

"Fuck," Tristan growls. "I need to see you come."

He pulls his finger out of my ass and spanks me again, making me moan, then warm spit dribbles over my back hole again, and he pushes two fingers in, timing it with his cock.

"Come for us," he demands. "Do it now. Squeeze my fucking cock and make Ryder come too. Let me feel your pleasure, freckles. Do it."

I sob, the orgasm he's calling for ripping through me so powerfully that my muscles seize up, and I'm lost to the waves of ecstasy as Ryder groans, his hips thrusting as he fucks my mouth faster.

"Fucking love the way you respond to orders," he pants, staring down at me. "You like knowing what's expected of you? You like being told what to do?"

I can't nod, but the pleasure still rippling through me intensifies even more.

"Fuuuuck," Tristan groans, and a second later, I'm suddenly so empty I'm gasping, the sound of his hand flying over his cock filling the room. "I want to see her looking like she belongs to us," he tells Ryder. "Come on her face. Mark her."

Ryder's eyes flare and his cockhead swells in my mouth.

"Oh, hell yes," he breathes out, thumbs tracing my jaw, then rubbing over my stretched lips. "Is that what you want? Do you want to be our filthy little fucktoy, with Tristan marking your ass while I paint your face with cum?"

"Mm-hm," I manage around his cock.

"Blink once for green."

I do it, my body quivering with the aftershocks of the pleasure they've already wrung out of me.

"Good girl," Ryder murmurs, gripping his shaft. "Open wide and look at me. Eyes open. I want to watch them shine when I claim this gorgeous face."

I suck in a breath, doing exactly as he says, and he pulls his cock from my mouth. The next moment, his cum is painting my lips and tongue, and my pussy clenches so hard with another tiny climax that it's like a lightning strike.

He growls, his fist working over his shaft and his eyes burning into me as I hear Tristan grunt behind me. A moment later, I feel his cum landing on my skin, hot and thick, and that sends me into another mini-climax.

I can't even scream with the force of it. The only sound I'm capable of making is a weak moan that ends up muffled by the cum still pooled on my tongue.

I can't even swallow it. My brain isn't working, and even though my muscles aren't seizing anymore, I'm still so overwhelmed that it feels like I'm floating.

Or maybe I'm just waiting for permission.

Ryder leans in and kisses my forehead, then drags his tongue through the mess on my lips.

"You can close your eyes now," he murmurs. "But keep your mouth open and don't swallow."

He holds his cum in his mouth and kisses me, our tongues tangling, his hand cupping my cheek.

"So fucking gorgeous," Tristan mutters, pulling me upright once Ryder releases me and then turning my head as he presses against my back so he can take my mouth too.

His kiss is even dirtier than the one Ryder just gave me, at odds with Tristan's usual restrained personality. I'm clearly not the only one affected by how intense this was.

"So sexy," he murmurs, licking the cum from my lips, then pushing it into my mouth again.

Ryder smirks as we pull apart. "Now swallow."

I do it, swallowing twice as the boneless satisfaction inside me starts to pull me under. I'm not just exhausted, I'm completely at peace in a way I can't ever remember being before.

And it's making it really hard to keep my eyes open as Tristan and Ryder murmur sweet, filthy things to me, passing me back and forth between them a few times before Ryder finally pulls me down on the bed, collapsing onto his back with me sprawled across his chest.

"So good," he mumbles, his eyes already drifting closed. "I'm just gonna crash right here."

"Same," Tristan murmurs with a low chuckle, crawling into position on my other side and making me feel so deeply content I have no words for it.

It's almost perfect, but as my eyes start to drift closed, I turn my head to see the doorway. I can't imagine Beckett would join us now if he held himself back from the sex, but once upon a time I never would have imagined any of this is possible, so the least I can do is ask.

But I don't get the chance.

He's gone.

2 2

LANA

I'm still sandwiched between Ryder and Tristan when the morning sun filters in through the blinds, waking me up. Both men are still asleep, and I sigh happily, stretching between them, and just take a moment to appreciate the glow I feel.

Of course, stretching brings out a few intimate areas that are sore this morning, but that just makes me smile. A few aches and some tiredness after a night of incredible sex are completely worth it.

Although it isn't just the sex that has me grinning right now. Even without that part, yesterday was one of the best days of my life.

"Looks like the snow has stopped."

Ryder's voice is rough with sleep.

"You're awake," I whisper, keeping my voice down so I don't disturb Tristan. Then I realize what he just said and sigh, looking out the window to confirm. "I suppose it was too much to hope for another snow day."

He chuckles, the arm he has around me tightening as he nuzzles my temple. "I'm sure there's still plenty of snow. It's just not falling anymore."

"You know what I mean."

His smile softens in a way I'm not used to seeing from him. "I do, love."

Tristan starts to stir behind me, and that's when I realize that sometime during the night, Beckett joined us in bed too. Just to sleep.

Well, it makes sense. He could have slept on the couch, but he's a big man and while the couch is comfortable, it's not *that* big. But I'd still like to think it's more than that.

I prop myself up on one elbow. "Good morning," I whisper to him.

He frowns. "We need to get moving and get on the road."

I laugh, shaking my head. "I don't think it's going anywhere."

He grunts, then rolls off the bed, grabs his phone, and pads toward the bathroom, giving me a view I *thoroughly* enjoy, since his ass is a work of art and it seems he slept in just his boxers.

He pauses in the bathroom door, looking up from his phone. "It says the roads have been cleared, and there's no more snow forecast for the next several days. We should be able to make good time."

"We should also be able to *have* a good time, don't you think?" I tease him. "While you're checking the route, be sure to drop a pin in on any good attractions."

He sighs, but I think I see his lips twitch before he turns away to go into the bathroom.

"He's not a morning person, is he?" I ask.

"He just needs to get laid," Ryder says with a smirk.

I laugh, and he cups my cheek and swoops in for a kiss.

I shove his chest, laughing harder as I dodge it, and accidentally wake up Tristan.

"No kissing until I brush my teeth. Morning breath!"

"I don't think he cares," Tristan rumbles, tipping my face around and giving me a sleepy smile. "I know I don't."

"But—" I start.

He doesn't give me a chance to finish before he's kissing me, and I guess I don't actually care all that much, either.

"Good morning, freckles," he murmurs once he lets me go.

Then he gives me a little push back in Ryder's direction. "Now why don't you make it a good one for Ryder too."

I give in, and Ryder smiles against my lips as he gives me a sweet kiss, then a dirtier one. They pass me back and forth for a few moments while the sound of the shower turns on, but as soon as Beckett finishes, I sit up.

"Dibs!"

"Were we not holding your attention?" Ryder asks, chuckling at my enthusiasm.

"Hey, I grew up with siblings! I learned a few things about sharing a bathroom."

Tristan grabs my wrist as I try to scramble out of bed, tugging me back for a moment.

"Do me a favor?" He runs his finger over the bridge of my nose. "These are gorgeous. Don't hide them with makeup today."

My freckles?

My heart skips a beat. I've been covering them up with foundation for most of my life, and I can still remember the way my mother would grab my chin and inspect my face every time I came inside from an outdoor activity, tutting under her breath about how I was ruining my skin by gaining new "blotches."

But the memory of her constant criticism and the disappointment on her face is wiped away by the expression on Tristan's.

"Okay," I whisper, surprising myself.

He grins, then twists around to grab his glasses from the nightstand, slips them on, and pulls me in for a last kiss.

"Gorgeous," he repeats. He pats my butt when I get out of bed before calling after me, "But save some hot water for us!"

I'm tempted to just invite him into the shower with me, but Beckett is probably right. We should really get on the road.

I get in the shower, tipping my face up and letting the warm water wash away a little of my disappointment. Part of me would have been happy to stay here the entire time. To skip out on Christmas with my family, and just spend the entire winter holiday exploring more kink with these three men.

"A girl can dream," I murmur to myself, sighing softly. Then my practical side kicks in, and I finish up quickly, applying light makeup before I get dressed, but leaving off the foundation like Tristan requested.

When I finish in the bathroom, the guys' personal belongings are already gone from the suite's bedroom, so I reluctantly organize my own things, repacking my suitcase. Even if the storm was still raging or the roads were completely blocked, stealing a few more days in this fantasy world with the three of them wouldn't actually satisfy the longing they've awakened in me.

But anything else isn't really feasible.

I've gotten to know each of them even better since leaving L.A., and while it might have made me start falling for them a little harder than I should, it's also confirmed what I've always known. I just can't really see how anything like what we're doing together on this trip could ever last beyond it, when we're all back in our normal lives.

"But I *can* quit pining for what isn't possible, and enjoy it as much as I can while it lasts," I remind myself softly, carefully folding the last item I have to add to my suitcase.

I run my fingers over the silky camisole as I place it in its spot, the glow I felt upon waking dimming a little as another wave of tiredness hits me.

I laugh softly, shaking my head. "See? If this were a long-term thing, that kind of sex would obviously wear me out too much," I murmur to myself under my breath, determined to see the glass as half full and not waste any of this magical time by being disappointed just because it won't last.

Tristan pops his head through the bedroom door. "What was that?"

I grin at him. "Nothing. Just talking to myself. It's a bad habit."

He saunters over, then takes the suitcase from my hands and kisses the tip of my nose. "Good."

I laugh. "Good?"

"If you were too perfect, I'd be in big trouble."

He keeps flirting with me as we check out and load up the

SUV, and even though I do feel a bit worn out, the glow is back. Even Beckett's grouchiness feels endearing.

He huffs out a breath when I claim the back seat with him, his body stiffening up. If he wanted space, though, he could take it. When he doesn't, I lean against him to rest my head on his shoulder and I find myself smiling with a deep contentment I rarely feel.

Ryder gets behind the wheel, and as he and Tristan talk about the route ahead and pull away from the hotel, I look outside at the wintery landscape, trying to soak it all in. The sexual adventures I've already had with these three have been amazing, but the quiet comfort in moments like this is something I'll miss too.

I nod off for a bit, lulled by the gentle hum of the engine and Beckett's warmth beside me. When I come to, Ryder and Tristan are deep in conversation about some band they both like.

"...and that's why their second album was clearly superior," Tristan is saying, gesturing emphatically.

Ryder scoffs. "You're out of your mind. The first album had way more raw energy."

I stretch, careful not to elbow Beckett. "What'd I miss?"

"Nothing important," Beckett grunts, his eyes still fixed on the snowy landscape rushing past us.

It's got nothing on the cold waves coming off him, though. He may have allowed me to sleep against his body, but it feels like his emotions are locked away behind a wall of pure ice.

I roll my eyes, but can't help the fond smile that tugs at my lips. Grumpy Beckett is kind of adorable, not that I'd ever tell him that. Still, it gives me a slight pang in my chest since we have so little time left before we go our separate ways again.

Not that an agreement to explore kinks gives me the right to more of him, but it already feels like I've been getting closer to him —to all three of them—than I have to anyone in a long time. Maybe ever.

Greedily, I want more of that.

I just wish he wanted it too.

218

"How you feeling, love?" Ryder asks, catching my eye in the rearview mirror. "You conked out pretty hard there."

I wave off his concern, even as I notice the lingering heaviness in my limbs. "I'm fine. Just catching up on beauty sleep."

Tristan turns in his seat, giving me a once-over that makes my cheeks heat. "Trust me, you don't need it."

Before I can respond, Ryder lets out a bark of laughter. "Oh man, remember that time we took the train to New York to try and sneak into that concert, but you passed out just as hard on the ride down?"

Tristan groans. "Don't remind me. We were so close to getting in..."

"Until genius over here," Ryder jerks his thumb at Beckett, "decided to pick a fight with the bouncer."

I turn to Beckett, eyebrows raised. "You didn't."

He shrugs, face and body language still completely closed off, and for a moment, I think that's all I'm going to get.

"Oh, trust me, he very, very much did," Ryder responds, laughing.

Beckett grunts. Then, the barest hint of a smirk playing at his lips, he mutters, "The guy was being an asshole."

"Yeah, and your dad was even more of an asshole when he had to come bail us out," Tristan scoffs, his tone light but his eyes watchful.

The shift in Beckett's demeanor is immediate. His jaw clenches, his entire body going completely rigid beside me.

"Shit, sorry, man," Ryder says quickly. "We shouldn't have brought that up. Your old man is dead to all of us."

I look between them, sensing the tension. "What happened?"

There's a moment of silence before Beckett speaks, his voice low and controlled. "My father didn't approve of... well, anything I did. Not unless it was exactly what *he* told me to do."

"Maybe because he's a judgmental asshole," Tristan mutters, pushing his glasses back into place and getting another low grunt from Beckett.

"But sneaking down to NYC to see a concert? You must have just been kids, right?"

In fact, I think Caleb might have been with them. This sounds vaguely familiar.

Beckett's jaw ticks for a moment, then he gives a short, sharp nod. "Yeah. That night was just one of many disappointments I handed him before it all started to chafe too damn much. It's why I cut him out of my life."

The bitterness in his tone makes my heart ache. I rest my hand on his arm, squeezing gently. "That really sucks. I'm sorry he was so hard on you."

Beckett pulls away slightly, his walls slamming back up. "You don't have to pretend to understand," he mutters, looking back out the window.

Looking away from *me*.

Something inside me snaps. Maybe it's the lingering fatigue I'm still feeling, or the rollercoaster of emotions from the past few days, but suddenly I'm done tiptoeing around his prickliness.

Grumpily endearing or not, I don't deserve his coldness, and while I'm not sure if it will last or where it's coming from, I'm suddenly fed up with putting up with things I don't deserve.

"Okay, you know what? You're being a dick." I turn to face him fully. "Maybe I don't know exactly what you went through, but don't act like I can't possibly understand what it's like to feel like you're never good enough for your parents. I've spent my entire life feeling like mine are never going to be satisfied with anything I do, that there's no chance I'll ever meet the golden standards set by my brother and sister. You're not alone, Beckett, so quit trying to hog the mantle of suffering under shitty parents all to yourself."

He turns to stare at me as the words tumble out of me, admitting things out loud that I usually shy away from stating quite so baldly. But his face? It's still completely blank, the stubborn, infuriating man choosing to remain closed off instead of admitting that we just might actually understand each other in a way not everyone can.

It sends my frustration skyrocketing.

"You think you're the only one who's felt worn down by impossible standards? Who's felt like the odd one out in their own family? News flash, Beckett—you're not."

The car goes silent other than my heaving breath. I can feel Ryder and Tristan exchanging glances in the front seat, but I keep my eyes locked on Beckett's. His expression is still unreadable, but there's finally a flicker of something in his eyes—surprise, maybe even a grudging respect.

It's not enough to cool me down, but I'm surprisingly not embarrassed by my outburst. It feels *good* to say what I actually think, and—much like the sex we've been having—it also feels freeing.

Ryder clears his throat. "So, uh, there's a rest stop coming up. Anyone need a break?"

"Yes," I say, suddenly desperate for some air. "Please."

I fan myself with my hand. I may not feel embarrassed emotionally, but apparently my body didn't get the memo. I feel like I'm burning up.

As we pull into the parking lot, I unbuckle my seat belt, ready to bolt as soon as we stop. But Beckett's hand on my arm stops me.

"Lana," he says, his voice low enough that only I can hear. "Look, I didn't mean to—"

I shake my head, cutting him off. I appreciate it, I do, but I need to get out of the SUV and get some fresh air. "It's fine. I just... I need a minute, okay?"

He nods, releasing me. As I climb out of the SUV, I catch a glimpse of his face. He's still closed off, still guarded, but there's something new there now too.

I hope it's a crack in his armor. He may have irritated the hell out of me just now, but I care about him far more than I should. I want to know him better, to be someone he can open up to about the complicated-sounding relationship he has with his father. And I want him to understand—no, to *want* to understand me too.

But I don't have the energy to analyze whatever it is I think I see behind his forest-green eyes. Not until I can manage to cool off the intense emotions still boiling under my skin.

I take a deep breath of crisp winter air, trying to shake the lingering heaviness of fatigue in my limbs. As much as I enjoyed sleeping in the same bed with all the guys, it clearly didn't allow me to get as rested as a full night's sleep should have left me feeling.

I move a little farther from the SUV, the cold air hitting my flushed skin like a slap. My legs feel shaky from the lingering frustration, but I figure what I really need is to walk some of it off.

I'm about to head toward the restrooms when Beckett's voice stops me.

"Lana, wait," he calls, his tone gruff but with an undercurrent of something I can't quite place. "You can't just say all that and walk away."

I whirl around, my temper flaring again, as if the heat under my skin wants to boil over. "Oh, I can't? That's rich coming from you, Mr. I-don't-want-to-talk-about-it."

He runs a hand through his hair, clearly agitated. "It's not that simple."

I stare at him, hating how he's keeping me at arm's length even now.

"It can be."

He shakes his head. "You don't understand—"

"Because you won't let me!" I shove at his chest, surprising both of us with the force of it. "You keep pushing me away, and I'm sick of it!"

I turn on my heel, feeling more emotional than I can explain. More than the situation probably warrants, if I'm being honest with myself, since it's just a temporary agreement we all made.

I head to the bathroom, ignoring him when he calls out again, needing to put some distance between us before I say something I can't take back. But as I take a step, the world suddenly tilts sideways.

My vision blurs, dark spots dancing at the edges. I try to call out, to reach for something to steady myself, but my body isn't responding.

The last thing I hear is Beckett calling my name again, his voice tinged with panic.

Then everything goes black.

23

BECKETT

My heart fucking stops. One second, Lana's standing there, fire in her eyes as she rips me a new one. The next, she's crumpling to the ground, her face going slack.

I'm at her side in an instant, shocked to see how steady my hands are as I check for a pulse when everything inside me feels like it's shaking.

"Fuck," I breathe out in relief.

Her pulse is there, so weak and thready that a completely unreasonable part of me is convinced if I take my fingers away it will disappear, but at least it's fucking present.

"Tristan! Ryder!" I bellow without taking my eyes off her far-too-pale face. "Call 911! Now!"

I hear them scrambling, Tristan cursing and Ryder's voice rising in intensity as he gets a dispatcher on the line, but I tune it out, focusing everything I've got on Lana.

She was getting flushed and overheated a second ago, something I figured was due to us arguing. But now, her skin is clammy and her breathing is shallow.

What the *fuck* just happened?

"Jesus," Tristan says tightly, kneeling down on the pavement next to me. "What—"

"I don't know," I bite out, one hand cradling her head while I keep the fingers of my other hand pressed firmly against her wrist, monitoring her pulse.

I can feel the tension radiating off Tristan and know him well enough to guess that he's biting his tongue to keep from lashing out with another slew of questions none of us have answers to. When Ryder joins us a moment later, we're both treated to a steady stream of creative cursing as he hovers over Lana across from me.

We've all got a little first aid training. It's smart for anyone, obviously, but doubly so when you're a Dom who's asking submissives to put themselves in your hands. And with the three of us running Radiance, it just makes sense.

But I can tell the guys feel exactly like I do right now—that the training we've got is completely insufficient, since none of us have a clue why Lana is on the ground, pale and unconscious, instead of lighting up every damn thing she touches, like she should be.

"This is my fucking fault," I mutter, the stab of guilt so intense it almost guts me.

"No," Tristan says firmly.

Ryder shakes his head. "Something is going on here."

I fucking know that, and I'm not so self-centered that I can't see the problem here is something medical.

Or that my friends are trying to bolster my spirits by reminding me of that.

I'm not wrong, though. Whatever the fuck this is, it's *also* my fault. Whatever took her down, getting her all worked up the way I did had to have aggravated whatever's caused this.

The ambulance arrives, and while logically I'm aware that it's only been a few minutes since Ryder placed the call, it takes everything in me not to tear into them for leaving her lying here on the ground for so long. As it is, I bark out answers to the EMTs' questions in a less-than-cordial manner, my heart hammering in my chest.

"Sir, we need to load her up," one of them finally says, trying to nudge me aside.

I growl, not wanting to let go.

Tristan's hand lands on my shoulder. "Come on. Let them work. We'll follow in the car."

"Like hell," I snarl, my eyes never leaving Lana's face. "I'm riding with her."

"Are you family, sir?" one of the EMTs asks.

I don't know what he sees on my face when I look up at him, but it makes him take a step back.

Ryder clears his throat. "He's family."

"Fine," the EMT finally says after a moment of tense silence. "But give us some room to work."

Tristan tugs me far enough away for the guy to get in there and strap Lana to a stretcher, then keeps a hold of my arm for a moment longer as they move her into the ambulance.

"Ryder and I will be right behind you," he murmurs. "Keep an eye on our girl, but remember to let them do their jobs too."

I give a curt nod, then shake him off and climb into the ambulance. I know he's right, but it still kills me to be even a little bit separated from her while she's so vulnerable.

The doors slam shut, and we're moving. And although the EMTs seem competent and professional, I don't think I manage to actually breathe until, about halfway to the hospital, Lana's eyelids finally flutter.

I lean in close, my heart in my throat.

"There you are, little menace," I murmur, taking her hand in mine. "You're okay. We're getting you to the hospital."

Her eyes focus on me for a moment, confusion clouding them. "Beck...?" she whispers.

"That's right. I'm right here," I assure her, squeezing her hand. "I'm not going anywhere. Still plenty of time for you to finish telling me off."

Fuck. I'm trying to lighten things up, but I'm no fucking Ryder, and the joke falls flat.

Maybe because it's really not one. She wasn't wrong for calling me out like that, and it will kill me if we're not able to finish that conversation so I can admit that to her.

I'm honestly not even sure she's really hearing me, though. She looks dazed as she blinks up at me. Then, when she finally wets her lips and tries to say something else, her eyes roll back before she can manage it.

Then she's out again.

"What happened?" I bark at one of the EMTs.

"That's what we're going to find out," he says, more compassion in his voice than I deserve right now.

I keep ahold of her hand since neither of them tell me I can't, but make room as the man I shouted at adjusts something on her IV.

I clench my jaw, feeling utterly fucking useless as they keep fussing over her for the rest of the ride.

She doesn't wake up again, and when we finally arrive at the hospital—beating Ryder and Tristan there—I stay with her as long as they'll let me. But eventually, a nurse stops me with a hand on my chest.

"Sir, you need to wait out here," she says firmly. "We'll update you as soon as we can."

My stomach twists, nausea rising as I watch them wheel Lana away and disappear behind a set of swinging doors.

I fucking hate this. Hate feeling helpless, hate not knowing what's wrong with her.

Hate that she's hurting in the first place.

I'm too keyed up to take any of the chairs in the waiting room, and I'm not sure how much time passes before Tristan and Ryder finally burst through the emergency room doors to find me pacing in front of the doors they took Lana through.

It can't have been *that* long, but with no word on Lana, it feels like forever.

They spot me and rush over.

"How is she?" Tristan demands, his usual calm demeanor cracking.

"Any news?" Ryder adds, his voice tight.

I run a hand through my hair, exhaling heavily. "She woke up for a bit in the ambulance. Seemed to recognize me, at least. That's gotta be a good sign, right?"

"Sure," Ryder says, putting a comforting hand on my shoulder as Tristan nods, concern still lingering in his eyes.

I get it. It matches the knot in my gut that won't fucking go away.

"We should sit," Tristan says.

Ryder keeps that hand on me and guides me toward a row of chairs, but all I manage is a few distracted grunts as the two of them murmur in low tones to each other.

I can't stop replaying the words Lana and I exchanged in my head. I refuse to let the harsh words I spat at her—words I didn't think through before saying and definitely didn't mean the way she took them—be the last ones she hears from me. That's totally unacceptable.

My hands clench into fists. "If something happens to her..."

"It won't."

My head snaps up at Tristan's raspy tone. I didn't even realize I said it out loud.

"She's going to be fine," he goes on, his eyes holding mine like he's challenging me to disagree. "Nothing's going to *happen* to her."

My teeth grind together. "Something already did happen."

"Yeah, and doctors are going to fucking fix it," Ryder whisper-shouts. "That's why we're fucking here!"

Under other circumstances, I almost would have smiled at the way they're both in my face right now. And it does help to know they're just as worked up about this as I am.

But it doesn't relieve any of the guilt.

No matter how much I want to believe that they're both right, the truth is, we just don't fucking know yet. And if they're not, and the last thing Lana heard from me was that bullshit I was spewing, I'll never forgive myself.

Finally, a doctor approaches us. "Family of Lana Reeves?"

We all stand, and to her credit, she doesn't question our claim.

I step forward. "How is she?"

The doctor gives us a reassuring smile. "Ms. Reeves is doing fine now. She's conscious and alert—"

"Then why the fuck did she collapse?" Ryder interrupts.

The doctor raises an eyebrow, and Ryder grimaces.

"Sorry."

"No apology necessary. I understand how frightening it can be, but it seems she just got a bit dehydrated. Would you like to come back and see her?"

Relief floods through me at her reassuring tone, even though I still don't get how something like dehydration could have hit her so hard. That shit can get sorted out later, though. Right now, taking the doctor up on her offer is the only thing that matters.

She leads the three of us to Lana's room, and my chest tightens when I see her. She's awake, but I'm not sure I agree with the doctor's assessment of her being "fine."

She's still too damn pale for my liking.

The doctor clears her throat, glancing at us. "If the three of you can wait in the hall for a moment, I need to discuss some medical matters with Ms. Reeves."

"They can stay." Lana's voice is soft but firm.

The doctor gives her an understanding smile. "Whatever you're comfortable with. Now that you're feeling more alert, I'd like to go over your health history."

Lana's breath hitches, a flare of panic lighting in her eyes that has me taking a step toward her. Then she sighs as she nods to the doctor.

"That's fine. Um, what do you need to know?"

They review a few basic health facts before the doctor says, "... and you were recently diagnosed with lupus, correct?"

My spine snaps straight, and on either side of me, Ryder and Tristan go tense as well.

Lana is sick?

"Yeah," Lana confirms with a shaky exhale, not meeting our eyes as she answers the doctor. "About a month ago."

"And have you been following the recommended lifestyle adjustments to manage your condition?"

Lana bites her lip, looking guilty. "Not... not really. I've been trying to not let it get in the way. To not, um, let it change me."

The doctor frowns at her. "Flare ups like you experienced

today are going to 'get in the way' much more severely than the life-style modifications I'm sure your regular doctor recommended."

"No, I know," Lana says, looking down as she twists the thin blanket covering her between her fingers. "I'll do better."

"Good." The doctor pats her hand with a sympathetic smile, then rattles off some information about these "lifestyle changes" she mentioned. One part of my brain methodically catalogues them all for future reference, while the rest of my mind gets stuck in a serious what-the-fuck loop.

Does she actually have lupus?

How could Caleb not have told us?

Fuck, why didn't *she* tell us?

Tristan and Ryder look equally shocked, and I can't wrap my head around how this shit can be true without any of us knowing about it.

"Let me get that steroid shot ordered up for you," the doctor finally says to Lana as she's wrapping up. "Then you should be free to go."

Lana nods, still not meeting our eyes, and when the doctor leaves the room, the silence is heavy.

"Lana?" I finally rasp.

She looks up, worrying her lower lip between her teeth, and she's still pale.

Pale and shaky.

I feel like I've been punched in the gut.

I've heard of lupus, but don't fucking know enough about it. As in, I know almost nothing.

But I do know that I can't stand the idea of her hurting like this.

"You knew about this, love?" Ryder asks her before I can find my voice.

Lana nods, then clears her throat and lifts her chin. "Yeah. But I... I haven't told anyone yet. Except you guys, now."

Her gaze flicks to me, and it hits me right in the chest when her eyes instantly soften. She looks so goddamn vulnerable.

"Please don't be mad at me about it," she says quietly, her voice

230

barely above a whisper. "I know I should have said something, but..."

"Fucking hell, Lana," I growl, hating that she thinks I would be angry with her right now.

She flinches at my tone, and I mutter another curse before striding over to her bed and doing what I should have done in the first place and getting my damn emotions under control.

I take her hand in both of mine, stroking my thumbs over the petal-soft skin as I lean down to rest my forehead against hers.

"I'm not mad," I murmur, my voice rough with emotion. "I was just so fucking worried about you. I'm sorry I got you so worked up. You were right. I was being a dick. Forgive me?"

The smile she gives me unknits something in my chest. "I can do that."

I stay there for a moment, breathing her in, wanting to kiss her so fucking badly it makes my chest ache. But finally, one of the guys clears their throat, and I straighten up and step back. Not enough to force me to drop her hand, but just enough to let Tristan and Ryder reassure themselves that she really is okay now.

They immediately move closer, all of us gathering around her bed as they each murmur sweet things to her.

Tristan's the one who finally asks what we're all wondering.

"Why didn't you tell us?"

Lana takes a shaky breath. "I was just scared, I guess. Not about you guys knowing the truth, but about what it means for my life, you know? Focusing on everything I'll have to change and give up... it just feels overwhelming."

I frown. I'll have to look into this shit a little deeper, but from what I heard the doctor rattle off—stress management techniques, following a balanced diet, monitoring symptoms, and some other basic health practices—it didn't sound like it would require her to give up the things I know matter to her.

But overwhelmed... well, even second hand, I can relate to that.

"You aren't going to be giving up shit," Ryder says, scowling.

"Ryder," Tristan murmurs.

Ryder sighs, scrubbing a hand over his face. "Sorry. I just mean, there's got to be workarounds, right?"

"I don't mean things like giving up chocolate," Lana says with a tremulous smile, reaching for him with the hand I'm not holding and squeezing his. "It's more about giving up the hope of, I don't know, meeting everyone's expectations of me?"

"What expectations?" Tristan asks, frowning.

"Oh, you know," she says, too flippantly to hide the fact that she means it. "Just being perfect at all times." Then she lets out another shaky breath and whispers, "I just... I didn't know *how* to tell people. Not when it meant admitting that I couldn't be—"

"Be what? Perfect? That's bullshit."

The words leave my mouth before I can stop them.

Lana blinks up at me. "What?"

And again, my mouth doesn't stop to ask permission. "You're already perfect."

Lana's eyes go wide, and my heart thunders in my chest. But I can't look away, can't take the words back.

And I don't want to.

24

LANA

As EFFICIENT AS the hospital's discharge process is, I start to worry as they walk me through the release paperwork.

"I was brought here in an ambulance?"

"That's right, love."

Ryder has his hand wrapped securely around the back of my neck, giving me a sense of stability, and with Tristan and Beckett on either side of me, I feel far more calm than I would have on my own.

But still...

"I've got pretty good insurance through work, but I'm not sure if it covers things out of state." I look up, glancing between the three of them. "Do you think it might?"

I'm not sure why I'm asking them. Maybe I hope they'll know since they own a business.

Or maybe I just want some reassurance.

"It might," Tristan says.

"It had fucking better," Ryder adds.

Beckett scowls, looking so grumpy as he crosses his big arms over his chest and glares at the paperwork I just signed that it warms my heart. "If it doesn't, we'll take care of it."

"What?"

"You heard him," Ryder says, giving me a comforting squeeze.

"And you also heard the doc say something about keeping your stress level down, right? So don't worry about that, love. We've got you."

I want to argue. They're talking about paying bills for me that they have no business feeling responsible for.

But it's just... nice. Really nice. So I keep quiet and decide that's a battle for another day, if necessary.

"How much time have we lost?" I joke once we finally leave the hospital and get back to the SUV.

"They didn't hold you long," Tristan murmurs as Ryder gets behind the wheel and Beckett helps me into the back seat as if I'm made of glass.

"I'm glad," I say. "That should let us get to the next town before dark, right?"

"No." Beckett shakes his head, the hand he's got resting on my knee tightening a bit.

"What?" I ask as Ryder pulls out of the parking lot, turning away from the highway.

He catches my eye in the rearview mirror. "Change of plans. We're not driving anymore today. We're going to find a hotel and rest up for the night."

"But—"

"No buts," Beckett cuts me off firmly.

"Fine," I agree with a little huff, turning my head away from him to hide the smile I can't quite stifle.

Just this morning, a part of me was actively wishing that the four of us could just keep driving. Not to get to New Hampshire faster, but just to stay on the road. Maybe even to skip ever arriving at my parents' place altogether.

Letting the lupus get the best of me isn't what I had in mind when I imagined getting more time with these guys, nor was having my condition exposed to them part of my secret fantasies, but surprisingly, I don't hate that that's where we're at.

I lean my temple against the cool glass of the passenger window, watching my breath fog it up for a moment before I straighten up again.

Beckett frowns at me. "Hang on a minute."

He twists around and digs into his bag, rummaging around before pulling out... the scarf. The one I've watched his big, tattooed hands work on during quiet moments of our trip.

"Should have done this before I let you step out of the hospital," he murmurs, wrapping it around my neck, his calloused fingers brushing against my skin.

I reach up to feel the yarn. "It's so soft and cozy."

"Good."

"Thank you," I whisper.

A smile spreads across his face, unlike any I've seen from him before. It's not his usual smirk or the occasional tight-lipped, guarded one he sometimes gives. This is a slow, private thing. A tiny slice of sun breaking through his typical storm clouds, and it makes my heart feel wrapped in something just as impossibly soft as the scarf he made.

It doesn't take Ryder long to navigate to a surprisingly upscale hotel, and my stomach flutters when I realize that Tristan booked a big suite online for all of us to share as we were driving over.

The first time we shared a room, it was an accident. But this time, they're deliberately choosing it, making the choice to stay with me, and I love that.

Although I could probably do with a little less hovering.

The minute we enter the suite, Tristan starts fussing with the thermostat, muttering about optimal temperatures. Ryder raids the mini-fridge, insisting I need to keep my blood sugar up and talking about running back out to stock up on food. And Beckett... well, Beckett just looms nearby, his presence both comforting and slightly overwhelming.

"Guys," I say, trying to keep the fond exasperation out of my voice, "I'm fine. Really."

"Are you sure you don't need anything?" Tristan asks, adjusting his glasses.

"She needs food," Ryder says, sounding almost as grumpy as Beckett usually is.

I laugh, holding up my hands. "I really don't right now. Honestly, I'm not hungry, but thank you."

I can tell he's going to argue or suggest something else, and although I appreciate how they've taken news of my lupus in stride, having their focus on me like this is starting to make me feel a little too self-conscious.

"I think I'm just going to take a bath," I blurt, needing a brief escape. They're being impossibly sweet.

But also a bit much.

They exchange glances, a silent conversation passing between them that I can't quite decipher. Finally, Tristan nods. "Alright, freckles. But if you need anything—"

"I'll yell," I promise, already heading for the bathroom.

As I'm about to close the door, I catch Ryder's grin. "Better not lock the door, in case you *do* need us."

My stomach flutters, and some of my self-consciousness eases with the confirmation that they're not just concerned about my health right now.

They still want me.

Once inside the bathroom, I start running the water, testing the temperature until it's just right. As steam begins to fill the room, I reach for my phone to put on some music, but pause when I see a notification.

It's a text from Mom.

Of course it is. We're already behind schedule.

My stomach clenches reflexively as my finger hovers over the screen. The preview text doesn't give away much, but it's all too easy to imagine any variety of my failings she might be messaging me to harp on.

But then I think about the doctor's words. About taking care of myself. About managing stress.

And I hear Beckett's voice, telling me I'm already perfect.

I take a deep breath. Then another.

I'm really not perfect. I mean, who is? But I do need to limit my stress right now, and that means not subjecting myself to whatever backhanded criticism my mother just sent.

I set the phone aside without opening the message. Whatever she has to say, it can wait.

Once the tub is full, I slip into the bath, the hot water enveloping me like a cocoon.

I lean back, close my eyes, let the soft music I chose wash over me, and just let myself enjoy it for a while. The tension from my mother's text is forgotten, and the lingering anxiety from the hospital stay slowly fades away too.

Out there are three men who, for reasons I can't quite fathom, seem to genuinely care about me. Who booked a suite just to be near me. Who look at me like I'm... special. Worth the effort. Perfect.

I push that word away again. It makes me feel cherished and anxious in equal measure, given my history of striving to please. And right now, I'm choosing not to let any outside thoughts intrude on this moment.

I'm choosing peace, even if just for a moment.

I'm choosing myself for once.

I must drift away for a bit, because the sound of a soft knock at the door has me startling back to awareness.

Tristan pushes the door open. "Just wanted to check on you."

"Have I been in here too long?"

He smiles, his eyes warm as they meet mine. "No such thing. Not if you're enjoying it."

"I really am."

"Then stay," he says softly, crossing the room and kneeling beside the tub. He rolls up his sleeves, then dips his fingers into the water. "Still warm enough?"

"It could be warmer."

He grins. "Let's fix that then." He turns on the faucet, and water swirls around my legs, feeling decadent. "Nice?"

"Very nice."

"Mmm," he hums in agreement, his eyes roaming over me. "You didn't put your hair up."

I reach up. The ends are all wet. "I should have."

"No," he says, capturing my hand and bringing it to his mouth. He kisses my fingers. "Would you let me wash it?"

My breath catches. "I... sure."

He leaves me for a moment, then comes back with the cherry-blossom scented shampoo from my travel case.

"I fucking love this scent," he murmurs as he pops the top open. Then he grins at me again. "But it smells even better on you."

My breath catches in my throat, the warm intimacy of the moment almost undoing me. It's not really sexual, but it's very, very *sensual*.

As his fingers start working through my hair, I melt into his touch. Letting him care for me like this is addictive, and he does it like it's the most natural thing in the world. Spoiling me without asking for anything in return.

No one has ever done this for me before, and I have to close my eyes when they start to sting with unbidden tears.

"Okay?" he asks softly, long fingers caressing my scalp.

"Perfect," I murmur, because it is... even though the contrast between this moment and everything I've ever come to expect from a relationship hits me hard.

Not that this is a *relationship*, of course. But it's still already better in every way than the one I had with Wade.

My ex-fiancé never did anything like this for me. I doubt he would have even considered it. He certainly wouldn't have *offered*. And while I don't miss being with him in the slightest, thinking about that sends a wave of sadness through me.

Wade was never abusive or cruel, but he also wasn't... kind.

And I put up with that for way too long. I never even realized how low I'd set the bar with him. How little I expected.

"Are you sure you're okay?" Tristan murmurs, his fingers massaging my scalp in such a soothing, mesmerizing rhythm that makes it easy to answer yes to that.

"I really am." I reach up and capture one of his hands, bringing it down and kissing his palm, soap and all. "Thank you," I whisper, staring into his eyes.

He's taken off his glasses, probably so they won't fog up in here, and in this lighting, his eyes look more blue than gray.

And the expression in them makes my heart flutter.

"My pleasure." He pauses for a moment, then adds, "You really scared us today."

I laugh softly. "Yeah, sorry about that. I scared myself too. And poor Beckett."

"You weren't wrong for laying into him like that."

"No, I wasn't," I agree. "But I still could have been a little more understanding."

"Hmm."

I splash him a little. "Hmm? What does that mean?"

He grins, then goes back to the slow, sensual head massage. "It means I'm glad you and Beck patched things up earlier."

I think back to the tenderness in Beckett's eyes as he wrapped the scarf around me.

"Me too," I admit softly, feeling like something has shifted between us that I have no words for.

Tristan is quiet for a moment. Then, almost like he can read my mind, he says, "You know, Beckett's always been a bit emotionally closed off. It's not just you."

I can tell he's hesitant to talk about his friend, but I can't help my curiosity.

"Why is he like that? Do you think it's because of the way his family life was?"

"Yeah." Tristan's exhale has a world of compassion in it. "Shit got so fucked up with his dad while we were all growing up. What you heard earlier was just the tip of the iceberg, and I know he didn't even share all of it with us. But it definitely shut him down. I think... I think it's his way of just making sure he doesn't get hurt again."

"That makes sense."

And it also makes my heart hurt for him.

Tristan nods. "I'm pretty sure it's why he doesn't want to have kids. I mean, who would, when their only example of a parent-child relationship is completely shitty, right? I know I'd appreciate having Grandma Meg no matter what, but in contrast to that..."

He shakes his head, and I twist around to face him, cupping his jaw.

"I'm glad you had her. You deserved someone to love you like that."

He stares at me hard for a second, then leans in and presses a sweet, simple kiss to my mouth before turning me back around so he can get back to my hair.

"Thank you. I wish everyone had that."

"Yeah," I murmur, my throat a little tight.

Tristan chuckles. "You know, Ryder would give me a ton of shit for psychoanalyzing them like this—fuck, they both would—but I think he avoids serious relationships for the same reason."

"Really?" I ask.

Tristan's probably right that the guys wouldn't be thrilled to hear how clearly he sees through them, but I'm greedy for all of it.

"Mmm." He hums in confirmation. "You heard what he said the other night. His parents basically abandoned him, and other than us—me, Beckett, and Caleb—he just doesn't let anyone in."

My heart clenches, but I nod.

I get it. I do.

"Because if he did, they might leave him too."

"Pretty sure that's what he thinks, yeah," Tristan agrees. "Or maybe not even consciously, you know? But getting close to someone probably feels like risking being abandoned all over again."

Before I can stop myself, I ask, "What about you? Have you dated anyone seriously recently?"

I'm veering into dangerous territory and I know it. This isn't any of my business, and unlike speculating about the two men who aren't in here right now, opening up this conversation with Tristan directly almost feels like too much of a confession about my own deepest desires.

It takes him so long to answer that I almost think he won't, but his hands never stop moving over my head, massaging my scalp, dragging in a slow, drugging rhythm through my hair that keeps any anxiety at bay.

"No, I haven't. Not really," he finally says quietly. "Grandma Meg always had plenty of advice about finding love, and I guess I took it to heart. She told me not to settle. To look for someone who made the world better, *my* world better, just by being in it. Someone who would light me up every time I see her. And since I hadn't really found anyone who did that..."

Our eyes lock as his voice fades away, and for a moment, the air between us feels charged. Then the intensity of the moment is broken by a crash from the other room, followed by Ryder's muffled cursing and faint, rumbling laughter from Beckett.

Tristan sighs, a fond exasperation in his voice. "For fuck's sake. I'd better go check on the children out there."

I laugh, waving him off. "Go, go. Make sure they haven't destroyed anything."

As he leaves, I sink back into the water, my head full of everything he just shared. Given the ways in which Beckett and Ryder have already opened up to me, Tristan's theories on those two feel spot on, and my heart aches for both of them.

But it's Tristan's words about his own relationship status that keep replaying in my head. About how he wasn't dating anyone seriously because he hadn't found anyone who met Grandma Meg's criteria.

Hadn't met anyone.

Past tense.

My heart races, and I close my eyes and sink all the way under the warm water, trying to tell myself not to read too much into it.

It could have been just a slip of the tongue.

It could have meant anything, or nothing at all.

But with my hair softly swirling around my face and the lingering sensation of his touch fanning the flame of hope deep inside my heart, I can't quite squash the tiny voice inside reminding me that there's a third option too.

It could have meant... *something.*

25

LANA

I'M MORE relaxed than I can remember being in ages when I finally emerge from the bathroom wrapped in a fluffy robe, my hair still damp. I don't actually realize I'm hungry until the scent of food hits me, though.

I smile as my stomach growls, quickly changing into soft lounging clothes before heading out to join the guys in the front room of the suite.

"Perfect timing." Ryder grins, gesturing to a truly impressive spread they've laid out. "Beckett insisted on getting you some actual food, not just room service. We found a place that claims to specialize in comfort food."

"And delivers," Tristan adds, leaning against the back of the couch with a takeout container in one hand and a fork in the other. He gives me a sheepish look, raising the fork. "Just taste testing."

I laugh softly, my heart doing a little flip. "It all looks delicious."

And Beckett was the one who insisted. For me.

"Thank you," I murmur as he finishes arranging the rest of the steaming containers on the table, buffet style. "You didn't have to do that."

Beckett grunts, not meeting my eyes. "You need real nutrients, not overpriced hotel crap."

I smile at his gruff concern.

"Why don't you get comfortable on the couch," Ryder suggests. "I'll make you a plate, and we can eat there."

They're treating me a bit like I'm made of glass, and although I don't want my diagnosis of lupus to change anything, the truth is, it has. And right now, it feels good to be pampered a little.

"Okay," I agree, settling into the soft cushions. "Does this mean another Christmas movie marathon?"

"Whatever you want," Tristan agrees, settling down next to me as Ryder follows through on his promise and brings me a plate.

Beckett takes the seat on the other side of me, and they fire up *It's a Wonderful Life* while we eat.

Halfway through the movie, Beckett surprises me by silently pulling out his knitting supplies, and I can't stop myself from reaching out to stroke the soft yarn he's using. It's the dark green of a winter forest, the same green as his eyes, and the sight of his thick, tattooed fingers manipulating the thin needles so gracefully is almost mesmerizing.

He adds a couple of inches to what seems to be another scarf, then looks up at me with an almost imperceptible smile.

"Want to learn?"

I nod eagerly, feeling a little thrill as Beckett shifts closer, his warmth radiating against my side. I really am interested, but more than that, it feels like an olive branch. Like he's opening up to me, even if it's not with words.

He hands me a spare set of needles and a ball of soft, cream-colored yarn.

"You ever tried this before?"

I shake my head.

"Okay," he rumbles, his deep voice oddly soothing. "First, you need to learn to cast on. Watch me."

He creates a neat row of loops on his needle, then nods toward the supplies he handed me.

"Give it a try."

My first attempt is clumsy, the yarn tangling around my fingers.

"Oh, shoot." I laugh at myself as I hold up the disaster. "How did you make it look so easy?"

Beckett grunts, but there's a hint of amusement in his eyes. "Everyone starts somewhere. Here, let me help."

His hands envelop mine, guiding my movements and sending a rush of butterflies cascading through my stomach.

Ryder chuckles, getting to his feet as Beckett demonstrates the technique again. "Hot chocolate?"

"I've created a monster," I tease him.

He grins. "I'll take that as a yes."

"It's always a yes," I murmur, most of my attention on copying the movements Beckett showed me.

"That's it," he says once I've finally made it through a complete row. "I knew you could do it."

His praise sends a wave of warmth through me. As Beckett continues his patient instruction, being sweeter than I ever would have guessed he could be in his own reserved way, the atmosphere between all four of us is relaxed and cozy.

It's a low-key sort of fun that has nothing whatsoever to do with keeping up the kind of appearances that are so important to my family. With the four of us chatting and laughing as one of my favorite movies plays softly in the background, I'm struck by how comfortable this all feels. How right.

My hands may still be clumsy with the needles, but here, nestled between these three men, I feel like I'm exactly where I'm supposed to be... and it would be everything I want right now if a small part of me didn't also feel that the night, one of the very few I have with them, is also being wasted.

I sigh. I don't mean to. But even though I'm enjoying this time with them, I also feel a twinge of disappointment.

"Everything okay there, freckles?" Tristan asks.

I hesitate for just a second before replying, but then nod.

I love hanging out with them like this. Getting to know them more deeply has only made me care for them more, which makes it feels selfish to admit that I feel like I'm missing out right now.

We agreed to a road trip full of kinky exploration, of pushing boundaries and indulging desires, but ever since leaving the hospital, none of them have made any moves to touch me beyond the most innocent of contact. Even the intimacy I felt with Tristan in the bath was more about comfort than sex.

But I hold my tongue, because I know what happened earlier scared them, and I really do appreciate the overwhelming sense from all three of just how much they care for me.

I only make it through three inches of my own scarf—three incredibly clumsy-looking inches—by the time I start yawning, and I don't complain at all when the guys insist we all head to bed.

Especially since they mean, once again, all of us in the same bed.

This time, Beckett insists on being next to me, radiating a protectiveness that I really don't hate, even if the three of them being so careful with me all night has left me feeling a bit broken and untouchable.

But sleeping between Ryder and Beckett, with Tristan in bed with us too? I will never complain about that.

"Good night, love," Ryder says softly, giving me the world's most platonic peck on the lips as Tristan kills the lights.

"Good night," I reply as Beckett drapes an arm over me, pulling me back against him.

"You good?" he murmurs, his voice a low rumble that I feel more than hear and his breath warm on my neck.

I nod, snuggling back against him. "I really am. Thanks for being such a great teacher."

He makes a soft sound of acknowledgment, his arm tightening slightly.

Warmth blooms in my chest again, my eyelids getting heavy. But as I drift off, I can't quite shake the feeling of disappointment from earlier.

Our time on this trip is limited, and as wholesome and cozy as the evening was, what I really want is for these three to teach me other things.

While we still have time.

THE NEXT MORNING, the tiny kernel of disappointment I went to sleep with starts to grow. I fight it, because they're still being ridiculously sweet—making sure I eat enough before we leave, asking how I rested, insisting on carrying all the bags when we check out and head to the SUV again. But once we finally get on the road, the easy banter from previous days is absent.

As we settle into the drive, silence falls over the car and lasts through the full day of driving. The men rotate behind the wheel each time we stop, and whenever they're not driving, they're each absorbed in their phones.

Not that they're ignoring me, exactly. They respond if I speak up, but the easy banter is gone.

After getting yet another distracted response when I point out some of the holiday decorations we're passing, I give up. Glancing around at the three of them, that sense of loss I started to feel last night hits me hard. Our time together is almost over.

All three of them woke up in the typical male state, but none of them suggested doing anything about their morning hard ons, and none of them have touched me all day today, either.

I pull out my sketchbook, my pencil moving restlessly across the page as I try to quell the growing unease in my chest. But my mind starts to wander, doubt creeping in like an unwelcome shadow.

Are they losing interest now that they know the truth about my illness? I've spent my whole life trying to be the perfect daughter, the ideal girlfriend, always put-together and pleasing until I finally decided to live on my own terms. And they seemed to like that version of me. The real one. The one I'm still discovering for myself.

But now they've seen me vulnerable, sickly.

And they don't seem interested in this version of me at all. Well, not sexually. They still care. In fact, every time we stop, their attentiveness is almost overwhelming.

"Lana, drink some water."

"Are you hungry? We should get you something to eat."

"Don't push yourself. I've got that."

And I appreciate it, I do. But I'm feeling so much better now, which only highlights how carefully they're treating me. Like I'm fragile. Breakable.

As we pull into yet another rest stop, Ryder hands me a bottle of water with a gentle smile. "Here, love. Stay hydrated."

I take it, forcing a smile. "Thanks. You guys don't have to keep fussing over me, though."

Tristan looks up from his phone, pushing his glasses up. "We're just looking out for you."

"I know, and I appreciate it, but..." I trail off, not sure how to express the jumble of emotions swirling inside me.

Beckett grunts from the driver's seat. "But nothing. We're not taking any chances."

"Thanks," I say with a tight smile as we pull back onto the highway.

Ryder and Tristan both immediately get distracted by their phones again, Beckett apparently lost in thought, and it doesn't get much better when we finally stop for the night.

The hotel is another nice one, but as we settle into our room, a small suite consisting of a single bedroom, bathroom, and a sitting area with a loveseat, low coffee table, and a few plush chairs, the now familiar routine of unpacking and ordering dinner feels almost stifling given the short, distracted answers they give to anything I bring up. It's like they're both hyper aware of me and also completely distracted. Each of them hovers a bit in his own way, treating me with kid gloves, but I can feel my frustration building with each passing moment.

Finally, as we're gathered around the low coffee table, Beckett and I on the loveseat and Tristan and Ryder across from us, finishing up our meal, I can't take it anymore.

"Okay, enough!" I burst out, setting my plate down with more force than necessary.

They all freeze, exchanging glances.

"I thought you liked orange chicken," Tristan says cautiously. "If you want to switch for the Moo Shu pork—"

I wave him off. "Why haven't any of you touched me since I collapsed?"

Tristan blinks at me, adjusting his glasses, while Beckett and Ryder both stare.

"We... have," Ryder says after a moment. "We literally all slept together last night. But we're definitely not going to push you, especially after that."

"Is that it, then?" I ask , trying and failing not to let my voice tremble. "Is our agreement over just because I'm sick? Do you... do you not want me anymore? None of you?"

The shock on their faces would be almost comical if I wasn't so disappointed.

Tristan is the first one to speak. "That's not it at all," he says, his voice soft.

Ryder nods, leaning forward in the seat he took on the other side of the low coffee table our food is set out on. "We just want to be careful."

"It's not about not wanting you," Beckett says gruffly. "But we're not going to go in blind and trigger a bad reaction. No Dom would be okay with that."

"No decent person would," Ryder adds, his eyes flashing with a ferocity that belies his usual laid-back demeanor.

I chew on my lip for a moment, frustration and relief warring inside me. "Thank you," I finally say, "But I'm not made of glass, you know. If you guys really do still want me, I won't break."

"We know that," Beckett says, turning toward me to tug my lip out from between my teeth. He keeps a grip on my chin, staring at me intensely. "But none of us have any real knowledge about lupus. Or we didn't. We've been researching it all day."

I blink, caught off guard. "Researching?"

He nods. "We need to know what can trigger flare-ups and how to help when one happens. There's no way we're going to let you get to the point of rushing to the emergency room again. Not if we can help it. But that's why we need to understand what kind of support you might need."

I look between them, stunned. All day, I thought they were pulling away, losing interest.

But instead...

"You've spent the day doing all of that... for me?" I whisper, my chest tight with emotion.

I don't wait for an answer. I can see by the earnest looks on their faces that it's true.

Before I can overthink it, I launch myself at Beckett.

"Thank you," I murmur against his lips before pressing mine against his.

He stiffens for a moment, clearly surprised, but then his arms come around me and he's kissing me back. No, he's doing more than that. He's taking control of the kiss, pulling me closer and manhandling me onto his lap, leaving no room between us at all.

"Fuck, Lana," he groans, adjusting the angle of my head.

Then he dips down to claim my mouth again, the end-of-day scruff on his jaw scratching my skin lightly.

I cling to him, melting against him. He kisses me just as hard and forcefully as he does everything else, and it's everything I need to quash the last of my doubts.

He tightens his arms around me, and I moan, giving myself over completely. If I'm honest with myself, I'm already starting to fall—for all three of them.

It's not smart, but I can't help it. All I can do right now is enjoy it.

Every last minute of it that I can get.

26

LANA

As Beckett owns my mouth, my body tingles with awareness, the air around us growing heated and thick with anticipation.

Tristan and Ryder are watching, their gazes caressing me almost like a physical force.

Beckett slides one hand under the heavy fall of my hair, gripping the back of my head as his other hand lands on my ass, silently encouraging me to grind against him.

I do, and when I hear someone groan—Tristan or Ryder, or maybe both of them—my nipples tighten, heat pooling between my legs as Beckett's cock thickens under me.

But then he pulls back, his large hand still holding my head firmly in place so I can't chase his mouth.

An embarrassingly disappointed sound escapes me. I'm not ready to stop. But almost like he can read my mind, he gives me a slow, sexy smile and puts those fears to rest before they can take hold, the deep timbre to his voice sending shivers through me.

"I'm not done with you, but we can't go any further until I know what you're willing to do."

"Anything," I burst out, letting my arousal speak for more. "More."

He grins, a quick flash that doesn't dim the intensity of his gaze at all.

"There will definitely be more," he growls, his voice pure Dom. "But 'anything' isn't a good enough answer. I need to know specifics. What you want to explore. What your limits are. Be good and tell me, Lana. Spell it out."

I shudder, his insistence just driving my need higher. I've done plenty of research to feed my interest in kink, and I know that communication is a huge part of it. That, and consent. But somehow, just reading about those things didn't prepare me for the real thing.

But the rush of going from feeling unwanted all day to *this* is overwhelming, and my mind blanks out as I struggle to find the words.

I lick my lips. "You decide. Please? I just..."

Beckett's eyes flare with heat, his cock pulsing beneath me. "I am a Dominant to my core, little menace. I will absolutely decide—once I know your limits."

"Thank you," I breathe out.

His lips tilt up with the hint of a smile. "You still need to talk to me first, sweetheart. I can only make those decisions after I'm clear on what your wants and needs are. Being a Dominant means that once you give me control, I will take it. I'll make the decisions, set the rules, and create the scene. But that power exchange can only exist within the boundaries we agree on. That's the only way I can truly *be* a Dom, one who takes responsibility for respecting your limits and ensures your safety while we play."

I nod. It sounds familiar. But I just want him to touch me again.

Still, I try to focus.

"Power exchange? Um, so you're asking me to submit to you, right?"

His hands remain firm, but his eyes soften. "Your submission, if you choose to give it to me, is a gift. And yes, I would love to receive that gift from you. I just need you to remember that it's a gift that you can take away at any time. I'll take charge, but you're the one ultimately in control here."

"You mean my safe words."

He smiles at me, and the hand he's got on my ass starts a slow, leisurely rub that sends tingles straight to my core and feels a hell of a lot like praise.

"Good girl. Your safe words are a part of it, yes. But like I said, so is me understanding the kinks you're interested in, and what your limits are. Because I will never violate those."

I would never doubt it. Not with him. But it still does something to me to hear it, making me even more eager as he reaffirms just how safe it is to let go with him.

He stops massaging my ass and scalp and tightens both hands, holding me in place. "Tell me, which kinks would you like to explore tonight?"

My mind blanks, sparks dancing over my skin. "I... I don't know. I mean, I'm not trying to avoid the question, I just... I can't think. What do *you* like?"

His gaze sharpens. "Total control."

My clit throbs. "Yes."

He releases my scalp, loosely circling my throat with his hand instead. "Choking."

I moan, leaning into the slight pressure.

He tightens his hand, not enough to restrict my breathing, but enough that I feel owned.

"I like edging needy submissives. Spanking them. Degrading them. I like obedience, and respect, and leaving my marks on what's mine."

My breath hitches in my throat. "Marks?" I whisper.

He holds me in place, hand around my throat, and holds my gaze as he squeezes my ass, forcing me to squirm on top of his cock.

"That's right, little menace. I want to see you covered in my handprints and bruises and cum. I want free use of your holes, however I want, for however long I want. I want your pleasure to belong to me, to grant or deny as I see fit. And I want you on your knees tonight, worshiping my cock until I'm satisfied."

"Yes," I whisper, my clit throbbing. I grind down on him. "Yes, *please*."

He tightens his hand like it's a collar.

"What are you saying yes to?" he asks. "I need you to be clear."

"All of it." A little voice of sanity works its way through the haze of my arousal, reminding me not to bite off more than I can chew, so I add, "At least, I think so. I'm not sure if I'd like a lot of pain. I don't think it's a limit. Um, not a hard limit. Is that what it's called?"

He smiles at me. "Yes."

"Maybe a soft one? Something to try, but... but I don't know if I'll enjoy it or not."

"Good girl. Thank you for telling me. Anything else?"

"No. I mean, yes. Yes to trying everything you said. *Please*. I just want to..."

I'm not sure what to say. Submit? Belong to him? Know what it feels like to be owned by someone who makes me feel cherished?

Beckett starts rubbing my ass again. "You want to be mine."

"Yes."

He frowns, his hand going still for a moment, then wipes the expression from his face as he adds, "For tonight."

"Yes."

"And I think we all know that you enjoy a little exhibitionism," he says with a tiny quirk of his lips. "But just so I know I have your full consent—"

"And because it's hot as fuck," Ryder murmurs, as if he already knows where Beckett is going with this.

Beckett smirks. "And because it's hot as fuck," he repeats in that deep voice that's pure sex. "You'd like to do a scene with me in front of these two, isn't that right? You want Tristan and Ryder to see you on your knees for me? To watch as I make you choke on my cock?"

A full body shudder goes through me, my panties flooding as he says it.

"I... I think you're right." I flush with a combination of embarrassment and excitement. "Exhibitionism *is* one of my kinks. So, yes. I want, um, I want Tristan and Ryder to watch us."

Tristan groans, and Ryder mutters a low, "Fuck."

I can hear both of them shuffling a little, the soft rustle of cloth as if one or both of them is adjusting themselves, but I can't look away from Beckett, the intensity of his gaze pinning me in place just as firmly as his grip on me does.

"Then let's begin," he says with a slow, heated smile.

"Okay," I breathe out.

"Call me 'sir' until the scene is over."

I nod, another shiver going through me. "Okay."

He raises a single eyebrow, his grip tightening me again. "Okay... *sir*."

"Oh! Sorry. I mean, yes! Yes, sir. Okay, sir."

Something heats up inside me with the use of the honorific, awakening a yearning I didn't know I had. I've tried so hard to be good, to be perfect all my life, but always felt like I fell short of it. Like I was a disappointment.

But not here. Not with him.

Beckett is telling me exactly what to do, and all I have to do to be perfect—at least, perfect for him right here and now in this scene—is to do it. It's both freeing and wonderful, and the thrill that rushes through me when he praises me for obeying him is so heady that it's almost addicting.

"Good girl. I know you can remember to address me properly. Now show me how well you can obey me." He releases his hold on me and moves me off his lap, setting me on my feet. "Take your clothes off."

I'm wearing a soft sweater and yoga pants, comfortable clothes from traveling all day but not anything particularly sexy. But the split second of disappointment I feel about that is gone in an instant, burned away by the heat of Beckett's gaze.

He's not concerned with what I'm wearing. He told me to be good for him. To obey. To undress.

I grab the hem of my sweater, lifting it quickly.

"Slower," Beckett says firmly, making my clit throb and my nipples pebble.

I pause, my sweater half off and goosebumps raising on my skin despite the warm temperature in our room. "Yes, sir."

"Good girl."

Those two words again, and this time they hit me so hard I actually sway a little.

Beckett reaches out to steady me, his fingers caressing my hip and then gripping it tight, like a reminder that we both agreed he's in charge right now.

"Go on. You know what to do."

I do, and he sits back in his seat, powerful legs spread wide as he watches me slowly finish taking my sweater off through hooded eyes.

A rush of pleasure hits me as his gaze flares with heat and the weight of Tristan's and Ryder's attention burns into me from behind. My clothes may have been chosen for comfort, but the bra and panties I have beneath are sheer and lacy, giving me a boost of confidence.

I reach back, undoing the clasp on my bra.

"No," Beckett says firmly. "Pants first. I want to see if my pretty little slut chose a matching set."

The word hits me like a shot of adrenaline, lighting me up inside in a way I never would have expected. Maybe it's because I know degradation is one of his kinks, something he's getting off on. Or maybe it's because I'm discovering it's one of mine too, unlocking the freedom to be completely shameless in my submission.

I hook my thumbs in the waistband of my yoga pants, slowly pushing them down to just below the curve of my ass, letting him see exactly what he asked for. That the pale blue panties are sheer enough to see my trimmed bush through, just like he can see the darker pink of my areolas around my pebbled nipples through the matching bra.

"Like this, sir?" I ask breathlessly.

His eyes, darkened with lust, sweep over me. "Yes. Fuck, look at you. Lush and sexy, and all mine. Isn't that right?"

A shiver runs through me at the growl in his tone, the praise making me glow. "Yes, sir."

I start to push my pants the rest of the way down, but he stops me again.

"Turn around. Let me see my new toy from every angle."

I turn, slowly, my skin flushing at the feeling of being so exposed and the illicit thrill of the way he's objectifying me. They've all seen me naked before, but this feels different, somehow. Even more intimate and raw than being completely bare.

Maybe because I'm being watched right now, not touched or used or fucked. Just... watched.

Beckett's toy, which he's sharing—to an extent—with his friends.

"Fucking hell, you're beautiful," Tristan says softly once I've done a full circuit and am facing Beckett again.

Ryder makes a low, appreciative sound in the back of his throat, his eyes raking over me, but both of them have a certain reserve to them that makes it clear they're only voyeurs at the moment. That this is Beckett's scene. That I'm here for nothing more than their viewing pleasure, a literal object of desire.

A shiver goes through me, liquid heat pooling between my legs. It is degrading, and I'm not sure if I could put into words why it feels so good to be objectified by this. I just know that it does, and that probably a huge part of that is because it's them.

"May I continue getting undressed, sir?"

"Yes." Beckett's gaze is locked on mine, a muscle in his jaw jumping. But his voice is steady as he gives me his next command. "Finish removing your pants."

I do it, the way he keeps control of me with his eyes alone leaving no room for self-consciousness or awkwardness as I step out of them.

"Good girl. Now the rest."

I take my time. Unsnapping my bra. Sliding it off. Slowly lowering my panties, then stepping out of them. The usually mundane actions feel anything but casual with Beckett's eyes burning into me. The familiar brush of my own fingers against my skin as I remove each item sends ripples of fire through me, as if it's his touch, not mine.

Then my breath hitches, and I have to squeeze my thighs together tightly as a wave of excitement tightens my core, making my clit throb and my pussy flood with wet heat, because it is his touch. I'm his right now, so my body belongs to him. My hands belong to him. My fingers. And using them to remove my clothes is just carrying out his will for me.

"Sir," I pant, trembling as I stand before him.

He lets his heated gaze roam over me, leisurely and sure. Then he reaches for a throw pillow from the couch, and drops it on the floor between his spread feet.

"Kneel."

He leans back like a king, knees wide and arms loosely spread on either side of him, my place clear.

"Yes, sir," I breathe, falling to my knees eagerly.

His answering smile is slow and heated. "So eager. We haven't even started, and already you're desperate for me. You really are a hungry little slut tonight, aren't you?" His eyes drop to my mouth. "You're lucky I've got something to fill one of your empty holes."

The filthy words make me clench, my nipples hard and my clit pulsing, and he hasn't even touched me yet.

I don't know how he manages to turn me on like this, to leave me wanting and aching with words alone, but it's almost overwhelming.

"Yes, sir. Thank you, sir."

His eyes flick down. "Show me."

My heart thumps, the room suddenly seeming much warmer. "Show you, sir?"

His lips quirk. "Show me what you're going to do to earn this." He grabs the growing bulge in his pants, squeezing it suggestively, then releases and rests his hand on my head. "Kiss it."

I reach for the snap on his jeans, and his fingers dig into my hair and tug sharply. "No."

I shudder, gasping as my eyes water and I jerk my gaze up to his. "S-S-Sir?"

"I said kiss it. I didn't say you'd earned the right to touch it or see it yet."

I swallow. "Y-yes, sir. Sorry, sir."

He holds my gaze for a moment, then smiles. "You're forgiven. I know you want to be a good girl. Now put your mouth on me."

"Yes, sir," I pant, my cheeks heating and my skin prickling with anticipation as he uses his grip on my hair to tug me forward.

I lean in, pressing my lips against the front of his pants, then opening them wide and licking his fabric-covered cock through his jeans as I nuzzle him.

I can't feel the double-row of his Jacob's ladder piercings at this angle, but his cock is thick and swollen under the denim. Not fully hard yet, but getting there.

I open wider, mouthing him hungrily, then moan when I feel it grow and stiffen under my attention, a rush of accomplishment feeding into my instinct for submission.

"Fuck," Beckett growls, holding me in place. "That's a good start. Keep going. If you get me hard enough, I'll let you taste it."

I lick and nuzzle, breathing him in, the flavor of him saturating the fabric and the feel of the rough material against my lips somehow making everything seem dirtier. Filthier. Just as degrading as he promised.

And it turns me on like crazy.

By the time he finally tugs my head back and orders me to pull him out, his cock is a throbbing beast and I'm so wet my thighs slide together.

I unbutton his pants and carefully lower his zipper, my breath hitching when the head of his cock, swollen and a dark, angry red, pops free. I whimper, my mouth literally watering. But when I move toward it, he tugs my hair again.

"Who's in charge?" he demands, his tone leaving no question as to what the right answer is.

"You are, sir," I say, giving it to him eagerly.

Heat flares in his eyes. "Good girl. Remember that. Your hot little mouth is my hole to fuck tonight, but that only happens when I say so. You suck when I say you suck. You lick if I tell you to. You swallow when I'm ready. Do you understand?"

I nod, panting. "Yes, sir. I understand."

"Color?"

"Green."

The smile he gifts me is almost feral as he pushes my head down to his cock. "Then suck."

I'm vaguely aware of the low curses and murmurs of appreciation from Tristan and Ryder behind me, and I'm moaning before Beckett's wet cockhead even touches my lips. But all of that, even my own arousal, is nothing more than background noise.

The heady thrill of existing to be used by him is almost overwhelming, and everything else fades away, my attention completely on pleasing my sir.

Beckett groans as my lips close around him, and his fingers tighten in my hair.

"That's it. Suck my cock, my filthy little slut. This is what you were made for. You've never looked more beautiful than with your lips stretched wide, your mouth being used so perfectly."

The words are like a forbidden fruit I didn't know I was allowed to enjoy, their flavor bursting over my tongue like the musky salt of his pre-cum does.

I love this side of him. I love that he's finally willing to share it with me. That he's letting me in and creating this private, heated space for the two of us to exist in.

Beckett has always been intense, but for the first time since I've known him, it feels like every single ounce of his strong, gruff energy is completely focused on me and me alone. And nothing has ever made me feel more wanted, or sexier, in my life.

"Good girl," he grits out. "Fuck, you take direction well. Keep going, just like that. Use your tongue."

His cock slides deeper into my mouth, and I moan at the salty taste of pre-cum as his piercings slide back and forth over my tongue.

He holds my head steady, using my mouth instead of letting me bob over his shaft and making it crystal clear which one of us is in control here. It's... *perfect.*

I get lost in the rhythm, my own arousal rising like an unstoppable tide inside me as he pushes deeper and deeper with each thrust, forcing my lips to stretch and my cheeks to ache, saliva pooling in my mouth and dripping down my chin as I stare up at him.

Then he suddenly pulls me off his cock completely, wrapping his free hand around the base of his shaft in a tight, punishing grip and tugging my hair sharply, forcing my eyes back to his.

"You've been wanting this for a while, haven't you, little menace?"

"Yes, sir," I whisper, my voice feeling raw.

His eyes burn into mine with a fierce intensity. "You wanted to put your mouth on me the other night. You wanted to taste me then. You wanted me to use this pretty mouth of yours."

He means the night I sucked Tristan's and Ryder's cocks. When all three of them agreed to explore this with me.

But Beckett held back. He jerked himself off, but didn't touch me. Didn't let me taste him.

"Yes. I wanted it. I wanted your cock that night, sir. I've wanted it—"

I close my mouth quickly, my cheeks flushing. I was about to say that I've wanted it for years, but that seems like too much.

This is just a scene, nothing more. He wants communication, but not all of my truths need to be shared.

27

LANA

Beckett and I lock eyes, his flaring with that intense fire he usually keeps banked so deeply inside him.

I can see that he wants to know more. He wants to hear what I stopped myself from saying after confessing how badly I want his cock. But he doesn't push for more than I want to give, and when he accepts my silence and moves on, I sink even deeper into my submission.

It's easy to do with him, because I trust him.

He keeps a tight hold of my hair, slowly stroking himself in front of my face. "You've earned this tonight."

"Yes, sir," I whisper. "Thank you, sir."

"How much of it can you take?"

I lick my lips, my nipples tingling and my clit throbbing like it's alive. "As much as you decide I deserve."

Approval flashes across his face, but he tugs my hair sharply, reminding me of what I forgot.

"Sir."

He smiles. "Good girl. And you're right, I'll decide. But tell me, do you want to choke on it?"

"Yes, sir."

He guides the head back to my lips and rubs it across them,

back and forth, while he stares at me. "You're saying you want to gag for me? That you can take as much as I give you?"

"Yes," I pant. "Yes, sir. Please, sir."

"Put your hands on my thighs."

I do it, my heart pounding as I stare up at him. My hair tickles my bare back, reaching almost down to the top of my ass, and I'm suddenly intensely aware of how I must look from behind, to the men who are watching Beckett use me.

Knees spread, pussy wet, back arched.

And now this. His to use and abuse, my throat his toy.

Begging for it.

"I'm going to fuck your throat," Beckett promises. "You won't be able to breathe, but keep your eyes on me and I'll make sure you get enough air when you need it."

"Okay." I tremble, licking my lips. "I mean, yes, sir."

"If you need me to stop, you'll use your safe word by tapping my leg twice."

"Yes, sir."

"Show me."

I blink, feeling dazed and turned on and so eager for him to overwhelm me, use me, let me be good for him, that I'm lost.

Beckett wraps a hand around my throat again, pressing under my chin with his thumb to force my head up, then pinning me in place with his eyes. "Show me how you'll tap my leg if you need me to stop, Lana. You won't be able to speak. You won't be able to say 'red.' Not with my cock choking you. Now be good and let me know you can follow directions."

I whimper, and the sound is barely out of my throat before Beckett has pulled his hand back, his grip on my hair tightening. "Fucking do it."

His dominance has my head spinning, and I'm suddenly so wet, so close to coming even though I've had no stimulation other than his words, that I can't think.

"I-I-I..."

He pulls my hair sharply. "You can. Tap my thigh. Now. Two taps mean stop."

The intense sting against my scalp clears my head, making me moan, and I finally give him what he's asked me to, tapping his thigh twice.

"Good girl. What does that mean?"

"Stop. Red. Um, that I need to breathe."

He smiles at me. "Good. And what color are you now?"

I blink up at him. "Green."

He doesn't ask again, just tells me to open, then his thick, swollen head is pushing past my lips and the smooth steel nubs of his piercings are sliding over my tongue and nudging the back of my throat. He goes so deep this time that I instinctively swallow around him, and the way he groans as my tongue spasms against his shaft sends a rush of pleasure through me.

I did that. I'm making him feel good. I'm not just his to use, I'm pleasing him.

"Suck," he says sharply, the command sending another burst of arousal through me.

I do, and Beckett curses, his voice low and throbbing, and pushes even deeper.

"That's it. Fuck, your mouth is like a dream. So perfect. I could keep you on your knees like this all fucking day. But right now, I need more."

He pulls out, leaving me gasping, then slides back in again, forcing my mouth open wide and my lips to stretch around him as he drives deep again.

"Tap my thigh if you need a break," he growls when I shudder.

I blink up at him, my eyes watering, and relax my hands on his thighs, telling him in every way I can that a break is the last thing I need.

I want more of this. More of *him*.

Beckett gets the message. My pulse pounds as he does it again, his grip on my hair tightening as he thrusts in and out, deeper and deeper, fucking my face just like he promised he would.

"That's a good girl," he growls. "So fucking hot and tight, you're going to make me come. Now take a breath and hold it. I need to feel your throat milk me."

My chest is already heaving, my breasts heavy and nipples tight. But when he pulls out and tells me to take a deep breath, the anticipation ratchets up another notch, making my skin prickle and my pussy clench with excitement.

Beckett doesn't wait. As soon as I draw some air in, he shoves back inside me, his piercings sliding into my throat as his cock forces it to open for him, his grip on my hair holding my head perfectly in place.

I moan, my throat vibrating around his shaft and my head starting to get light and floaty as he holds me in place, his cock buried deep and his balls pressing against my chin, grinding against my face.

My eyes flutter closed, my whole existence narrowing down to the taste and feel of him.

"Fuck," he grunts. "Your *mouth*."

He grinds against my face again, his shaft swelling against my tongue and choking me exactly the way he promised he would, and then he's cursing, grip tightening and thick thighs turning to rock under my hands.

And then he's gone, pulling out so fast that I'm left gasping, whining at the loss.

He was about to come. I know he was.

And I want it.

Like he said, I *earned* it.

"Jesus fucking Christ," he growls, his fingers locked like a ring around the base of his shaft. "You really are hungry for it, aren't you, baby? Did that get you wet?"

"Yes," I rasp, completely shameless, my voice wrecked by his hard use. "Yes, sir."

"Show me."

I blink up at him, panting. I need more direction.

"Touch yourself," he instructs. "Slip your fingers inside."

I do it, sliding my fingers over my slick folds and moaning as I rub my clit, tugging on the ring there to heighten my pleasure.

Beckett grabs my wrist, holding it still. "I didn't say you could come. I said slide those fingers into that sweet pussy and show me how wet you are. Fuck yourself with them like the filthy girl you are. Get them good and slick, then show me what sucking my cock did to you."

I'm breathing heavily, his words pushing me higher, making my skin burn and my nipples ache and the pressure build inside me.

"Do it," he orders, releasing my wrist.

"Yes, sir," I breathe out, trembling. I press all four of my fingers together, longing for the thickness of his cock, and obey him.

"That's it. Just like that. Dirty fucking girl, aren't you? Show me how much you like getting on your knees for me."

I moan, fucking myself as he keeps talking, keeps praising and degrading me, keeps pushing me higher and higher until I'm not sure I can obey his order not to come.

"Fucking hell," he growls as I shudder, clenching around my own hand. "I can smell how turned on you are from here. Show me those fingers. Good girl. Now lick them for me. Tell me if it's as sweet as it looks."

I obey, then moan and arch my back, unable to help the way I writhe as I suck my own fingers, pushing my other hand between my legs and grinding against it as the salty sweetness of him mingles with the taste of my own desire on my tongue.

I've never been so turned on in my life, and I need to... I need...

"Please," I moan, fingering myself frantically, "Please, sir. Let me come."

Beckett grabs my hair again. "No."

My core clenches tight, the denial somehow even hotter than if he'd told me to push myself over the edge.

He tips my chin up. "Do you want me to fuck you, dirty girl? Do you want me to fill that slick little hole with my cock? Do you want your pussy stuffed the way I stuffed your throat? Do you want to feel my piercings inside you?"

"Oh fuck. Yes. Please. *Please*, sir."

He stands abruptly, pulling me to my feet. "On the bed."

It's too far. I want to whine again. Want to beg him to fuck me right here, right now.

But I'm not in charge, and neither of us want me to be.

Beckett strips off the rest of his clothes, making my mouth water, then turns me in the right direction.

My legs tremble as the heat from Tristan's and Ryder's gazes sears right through me. Then Beckett gives my ass a firm swat to motivate me to move, and they both follow us to the bedroom.

"Hands and knees," Beckett orders once I reach the bed, massaging my ass with both his hands as I shamelessly spread my knees wide and present myself for him. "I'm going to spank you now. Color?"

"Green," I whisper. "Green, sir."

"Good girl. I want to see this luscious ass bright red and covered with my marks."

"Yes! Yes, please," I pant, my arms trembling as I hold myself up. Earlier, I wasn't sure if I wanted pain, and I'm still not sure it will hurt—that anything even could when I'm this turned on.

But I am sure I want it.

I'm desperate for it.

And Beckett delivers.

He starts off slowly, letting me adjust and warming me up, but he doesn't linger. He doesn't give me the chance to doubt or second guess, or for reality to intrude. All that exists is the sharp sting of each swat. The heat that blooms every time his hand connects with my ass. The pain that steals all my attention, making every nerve ending sing until I can't tell where pleasure starts and pain begins.

"Sir," I gasp. "Please..."

Beckett chuckles darkly and rubs my throbbing ass. "You look so good in red. Did you need something, little menace?"

I moan, my head hanging low. I'm trembling. I'm not sure I can talk.

"It looks like she needs a good fucking," Ryder murmurs, sending a shudder through me.

"Yes. Yes, please."

"You can do better than that," Beckett says firmly. "What do you want?"

"You. Your cock. Please."

"And where do you want it, my dirty little slut? Back in your mouth?"

I'm shaking, my clit pulsing with the need to come. But I want to be good for him, so if that's what he wants...

"Okay," I whisper.

Beckett spanks me again, quick and sharp, and I yelp, another shudder of pleasure going through me.

"What. Do. You. Want?" he demands.

"Fuck, look how wet she is," Tristan mutters. "Do you really have to ask?"

"Yes. If she wants to be fucked, she needs to say so."

"Yes!" I finally blurt. "I do. I want it. Please, sir."

"You want my cock inside you?"

"Yes!"

"In your hot little pussy?"

"Oh god. Yes. Please, Beckett. Please, sir," I beg shamelessly, desperate for him. "Fuck me. Use me. I need it. I need your cock. I want to be a good slut for you. I want... I want you to get me filthy and leave me dripping with your cum. Tell me how to earn it. Please, please, I'll do anything. Please, just give me your cock."

"Holy shit," Ryder groans.

"Jesus fucking Christ," Tristan rasps.

Beckett lets out a low curse, then presses the head of his pierced cock against my soaked entrance, rubbing it back and forth and making me practically sob with need.

"You want my cum inside you, dirty girl?" he growls, leaning over my back and fondling my breast as he tortures me. "You don't want me to suit up, just go in raw and fuck you bare? You want to know how that feels? How filthy I can make those sweet thighs of yours once my cum is spilling out of you and sliding down them, after I'm done with you?"

I cry out, the words ratcheting my arousal even higher.

"Is that a yes?"

"Yes," I whisper, shaking.

"Color?"

"G-g-green. Green, sir."

He bites the back of my neck, a deep growl rumbling in his chest. "Good girl. Then take what you asked for."

I half expect him to slam into me, but instead, he grabs my hips and pushes inside one slow inch at a time.

"Oh god," I breathe when the first set of piercings enter me, a wave of heat and pleasure radiating out from where he's penetrating me and leaving me shuddering. "I can feel them."

"That's it, dirty girl. All for you. Count them for me."

"Yes, sir."

He pulls out, and I whine. Then he spanks me hard, and I shudder, my arousal turning into a raging wildfire within me.

"I said count," he growls before slowly pushing back in.

"One," I hiss as soon as I feel the extra stimulation from the first two metal balls on his Jacob's ladder again. "Yes, sir. One."

"Good girl. Do you remember how many there are?"

I've seen his cock. Touched it. Played with them with my tongue. But my mind is so fuzzy with want right now that it takes me a minute to actually remember.

"Eight?"

He gives me another slow thrust, rewarding me for answering him properly. "That's right. Keep going."

"Two," I moan when I feel the next set. Then, on a gasp, "Three."

I already know his cock is large, both thick and long, but feeling it inside me, knowing we're not even halfway there yet, is something else. I've never felt so full.

I also never realized Beckett would be the kind of man to torture me like this, entering me in a long, slow glide as I finish counting them off that leaves me trembling and panting by the time he finally bottoms out.

"Eight," I repeat once we get there, my thighs shaking and my pussy so wet that the sound of him entering me is almost obscene.

"Good girl," Beckett rasps, his grip on my hips tightening. "Now hold on. This is where I fuck my new favorite cocksleeve."

The objectification just does it for me, and I'm too turned on, too lost in the fuzzy delights of subspace, to worry about why or judge myself for it. But Beckett is done going slow. He pulls back until just the thick head of his cock is inside me, then slams back in so hard that I would have flown forward on the bed if he didn't have a rock-solid grip on me.

I cry out, pleasure spiking through me as he gives me exactly what I need, driving in and out of me with no mercy once he gets started; fucking me so hard that all I can do is grip the bedspread and hold on, his piercings sending spikes of pleasure through me with every thrust.

"Yes, yes, yes," I chant, gasping and shuddering as he turns me into a mindless vessel for his pleasure. "More."

"You fucking love this. You really are a slut for my pierced cock."

"*Yes*."

"You know I got them for the same reason you got yours." His big, rough fingers bite into my hips as he leans down over my back, the change in angle driving his piercings against my G-spot and making me cry out all over again. "These piercings? They're for *your* pleasure, baby. So say thank you. Tell me how much you appreciate it."

"Thank you," I gasp out. "Thank you, sir. Fuck, please don't stop. Please don't ever stop."

"Good girl," he grunts, fucking me even harder.

My body is like a live wire, my core tight and coiled and so close to release that I can taste it. But every time he calls me his "good girl," he owns me even more, and no matter how quickly the pleasure builds as he fucks into me, I can't—*won't*—let myself go until he gives me permission.

But that doesn't mean I won't beg for it.

I have to. He's got me teetering right on the edge, fucking me so perfectly it's almost like an out-of-body experience, and I don't think I can take anymore no matter how good I want to be for him right now.

"Please," I gasp out. "Beckett. sir. I... I can't... I need..."

"You need what I give you," Beckett growls, reaching around

and rubbing my clit with one hand and using the other to wrap around my throat. "And you'll wait until I tell you."

"Yes," I moan. "Yes, sir."

He pulls me up and against him, my back to his front, my knees spread wide and still on the bed, and the way he holds me upright makes the new position feel almost as if he's riding me.

"That's it," he mutters in my ear. "You're my little fuck toy tonight, and your only job is to feel it. Take it. Enjoy it. Let me hear how much you love taking my cock."

His words push me even higher, and his hand moves between my legs, fingers sliding down and playing with my clit, then tugging on the little ring there as his cock pumps into me again and again, until I really can't hold on anymore.

And like he can read my body perfectly, Beckett has mercy on me, and finally gives his permission.

"Come, dirty girl," he snarls in my ear, his cock hitting a new angle inside me. "Come on my cock, right the fuck now."

LANA

Beckett's command to come is all it takes to send me over the edge, and when he slams inside me again, I choke out a cry as my orgasm tears through me, hard and fast and blinding.

"Fucking hell," he mutters, his voice raspy as he fucks me through it. "That's it. Let me feel you squeeze my cock. Give me fucking everything, you dirty, beautiful little thing."

I am. The waves of pleasure have me shaking, and as I clench around his cock, my body goes liquid, boneless, and completely his.

"Fuck," he growls, his hips stuttering against my ass as his rhythm finally falters. "*Fuck*, Lana."

My pussy flutters around his shaft, and he curses again as he curls his body around me, his thick cock pulsing inside as he comes.

Warmth spreads through me as he fills me with his cum, just the way he promised. Then he's kissing me, wrapping one hand around my waist and using the other to tilt my head back so he can take my mouth.

"You did so fucking well," he murmurs as I moan into the kiss, his stubble scratching my sensitive skin.

"Thank you, sir," I gasp once he lets me up for air.

He rumbles an approving sound against the corner of my lips, then trails his mouth across my jaw, kissing his way down my neck and finally burying his face in my hair. Our breaths sync up for a moment, his softening cock still buried in my pussy.

After a moment, he slowly pulls out, his cock giving one last pulse inside me before he fully withdraws.

I make a small sound of dismay without meaning to, hating to lose the feeling of fullness and the connection I feel with him right now, and he turns me around in his arms, something both fierce and tender in his gaze.

"You okay?"

I nod, then remember his command to address him properly during the scene. I'm not sure if it's over yet, but the need to submit, to show him respect as my Dom, still thrums in my blood.

But before I can give him a *yes, sir*, he smooths my hair back from my sweaty forehead, leans in, and kisses me again.

"Do you want more, baby?" he asks when he pulls back, his thumb brushing my swollen bottom lip as he pulls away.

"More?" My body starts humming with anticipation, even though I'm floating on the high of the first orgasm. "What do you mean?"

"I want to watch you take my friends now."

My breath catches, that low hum flaring up into arousal again.

Beckett's eyes darken, and he takes my face in his hands, gazing at me intently. "I want Tristan and Ryder to fuck you, but only if you can take it."

"Yes," I breathe out, the weight of the other men's stares setting me on fire.

"Are you sure?" Beckett asks, giving me a searching look as holds me in place so I can't look away.

"Yes," I repeat. "I want it. I want *them*. I want all of you."

He nods, approval flashing in his eyes. "Good. But you *will* tell me if that changes. If you're not feeling up to it, if you're dizzy, or weak, or sore, I need to know. This only works when you're transparent and honest about your needs, but also about any limitations. Promise me, little menace."

His dominance makes me shiver, but it's the concern in his eyes that truly gets to me. He's taking charge but leaving me in control, just like he promised. Not deciding for me what I can or can't take, but respecting that even in my submission, I'm an equal part of this scene.

I lean into Beckett's hands, nodding. "I promise. I'll tell you if I need a break or need to stop. I'll use my safe word if I have to. But I want this. I want all three of you tonight. Just tell me what to do."

"Fucking hell, you really are amazing," he says, the approval burrowing deep into my heart.

He pulls me roughly against him one last time, kissing me with a possessive dominance that has me melting into him. Then he moves away, leaving me flushed and panting on the bed, and Ryder comes to take his place.

Ryder's eyes drop to my pussy, and I bite my lip as he looms over me, suddenly hit with the worry that seeing me dripping with his best friend's cum will be a turn off.

"Look at you," he mutters, dispelling that worry almost as fast as it forms. "So fucking hot."

He pushes my thighs apart, his gaze fixed on me as his thick cock slides through my folds, spreading Beckett's release and mixing it with my own arousal.

"Fucking love this thing," he groans as his cockhead teases my clit, bumping against my piercing.

I gasp, clutching his biceps as I arch against him. "I'm pretty sure it loves you too."

He meets my eyes, chuckling, then drops his focus back down to watch what he's doing to me.

"Need to be inside you, love." He reaches down and tugs on the little ring, sending an electric jolt through my body. Then he guides his tip to my entrance, but doesn't push in yet. "Just look at you, all pink and swollen and so fucking wet for us. None of us had any idea how filthy you were."

My breath catches at the dirty praise. "I'm not sure I knew, either."

He grins, piercing me with his gaze again, and I love the heat in his eyes as he looks at me. "Well, I like it."

"Me too." I bite my lip for a moment, but Ryder isn't the same kind of Dominant Beckett is, and my submission to him feels more playful, so I go with it. "You know what else I'd like?"

He leans in, tugging my hair until my head drops back and nipping at my throat.

"I think I do," he murmurs against my sensitive skin. "But tell me. I want to hear it."

"I'd like you to fuck me, just like Beckett wants."

He groans, and my breath hitches. But instead of pushing into me, he grinds his cock against my clit again as he grabs my hips, holding me against him, then flips us both on the bed, landing on his back with me on top of him.

"Ryder."

I laugh, and he grins up at me. He kneads my ass, his playful smile turning into something hotter.

"Ride me, love."

I blink, a flutter of uncertainty breaking through my haze of arousal. I've always been self-conscious about being on top during sex, and the idea of putting myself on display like that makes me hesitate.

But Ryder doesn't let me wallow in that old, familiar anxiety or get lost in self-doubt. He rolls his hips, the move making his cock slide over my clit again. I whimper, and he grips my hips tightly.

"Get on my dick."

It's not a request, it's an order. It's demanding and authoritative this time, and it's exactly what I need.

I rise up to position myself, and Ryder uses his grip on my hips to guide me above his cock.

"That's it," he mutters as I grip his shaft and line him up. "Take me at your own pace."

Beckett's cum leaks from my pussy onto my fingers, making Ryder's thick length slick and sloppy. It's the filthiest thing I've ever done, and by the look in his eyes as he watches me slowly sink down, he loves it as much as I do.

"Christ, you're gorgeous," he grits out, his muscles standing out in stark relief as he holds himself still and lets me set the pace.

My stomach flutters at his words, and I gasp once I fully settle on his hips, rocking a little as I get used to the feeling of overwhelming fullness. They've all fucked me now, but this is different. I'm not sure if it's the angle, or the control I have in this position, or the feeling of being exposed in a way I've never been comfortable with during sex before.

Wade hated the idea of me being on top, and I haven't had enough partners to really experiment like this before.

But I think I like it.

The bed dips next to me, and I gasp, my eyes flying open even though I don't remember closing them.

Ryder's fingers dig into my hips, his gaze burning into me while he waits for me to move, but now Tristan is on the bed too. He's kneeling next to Ryder, watching with his eyes half-lidded and his fist wrapped around his cock.

"Keep going," Tristan murmurs when he catches me looking. "Let us watch. Let us see you."

"You heard him," Beckett says from where he stands at the foot of the bed. "Fuck yourself on Ryder's cock."

My heart pounds. With their eyes all locked on me, I suddenly don't feel self-conscious anymore. All I feel is powerful and sexy and desired.

Ryder growls as I rock my hips again, his abs contracting as his cock pulses inside my pussy.

"That's it. Now lift up, love. Tighten that pussy around me and drag it up my cock."

I do, and it feels incredible.

"Lean back a little. Brace your hands on my thighs."

I obey, and his cock pulses again, nudging my G-spot as I slide back down his shaft.

"Oh fuck," I whimper, repeating the motion. I know I could come this way if I kept going, but my arms start to shake. "I... I can't."

Ryder's fingers dig into my hips as he urges me upright again. "Do whatever feels good."

"I want... I want to make *you* feel good," I pant.

275

Tristan chuckles, still working his cock. "You are. Just look at him."

I do, and the expression on Ryder's face makes me feel like a goddess. It's almost too much, so I let my head fall forward, my hair brushing his chest as I brace myself on his firm pecs and look down at where we're joined instead.

I lift my hips up, watching his cock slide out of me as I rise. Both his shaft and my thighs glisten with my arousal and Beckett's cum, and the sight is so raw and sexy that I lose whatever inhibitions I still have. I impale myself on him again, rocking back and forth as I chase my pleasure.

"Oh, fuck yes," Ryder groans as I start truly riding him. "That's so fucking good, love. Take what you need."

He slides his hands up and cups my breasts, flicking my nipples and sending a bolt of pure fire down to my core.

I moan, my rhythm faltering as I instinctively lean into his touch and grind my clit against him. "Oh god, yes."

"Tug that little ring in your clit," Beckett growls.

I obey without thinking, then cry out, my inner muscles clenching around Ryder's cock at the sharp burst of pleasure.

"Keep going," Beckett directs me, voice directly behind me. "Keep touching yourself while you ride him. I fucking love the way your ass shakes while you're bouncing on his cock."

Instead of embarrassment, the idea of him watching me like this almost sends me over the edge.

"*Please*," I beg when my thighs start to burn, not sure what I'm asking for as I frantically rub my fingers over my clit.

But Ryder must know. He bends his knees, planting his feet on the mattress and grabbing my ass. Then he thrusts up into me so hard that I scream.

"That's it, dirty girl," Beckett says as Ryder does it again. "Tell him how you like it. Tell us exactly what you need."

My breasts sway as I lean over Ryder again, meeting every one of his hip thrusts with my own. The angle is incredible, my clit grinding against his pubic bone and his cock sliding so deeply inside me that I swear I can feel him in the pit of my stomach.

"Harder," I gasp, shameless and greedy. "God, I want it harder. Faster. More."

"Then take it."

Beckett's hand lands on the back of my neck, anchoring me in place as I do what he commanded. I fuck Ryder with total abandon as the molten core of pleasure inside me coils tighter and tighter, until I'm so close to coming that white light tinges the edges of my vision.

"Yes, yes, yes," I chant, flinging my head back and grinding down on him as I teeter on the peak.

"Jesus fuck," Tristan groans, his voice raspy.

Ryder stares up at me with a smoldering gaze. "He's gonna fucking lose it before I do, just from watching you."

I drag my eyes away from his and meet Tristan's gaze, and when Beckett tightens his grip on the back of my neck and leans over my back, forcing me forward again, my breath catches.

"It's all for you, little menace," Beckett growls in my ear. "Your pussy is gonna be flooded with Ryder's cum any second now, and you're feeding one of Tristan's kinks too. And do you know why we all fucking love watching you so much?"

I moan, my whole body shuddering as the tightly coiled pressure inside me finally snaps.

"Because nothing is fucking hotter than your pleasure," Beckett finishes as the orgasm rushes through me.

"Jesus," Ryder gasps, his voice choked. "Your pussy... holy fuck."

His fingers bite into my hips as I cry out and clench around him, and then his own climax hits and his cock starts jerking inside me. He drags me down against his chest as he comes, capturing my mouth with his and kissing me hard.

I'm so lost in the pleasure that I don't even realize Tristan has moved around behind me until Ryder releases me to catch his breath. But as soon as he does, Tristan yanks me off Ryder's shaft, pulling my hips up so I'm straddling Ryder on all fours, and drives his own cock into my cum-soaked pussy.

"Oh god," I gasp, as he fucks me hard and fast.

I've never known Tristan to lose control before. But he is now. He's clearly at his breaking point, and the fact that it's for *me* is like a drug I can't get enough of.

"Look what you do to him," Beckett rumbles as if he can read my mind, stroking my cheek and tilting my head to the side. "Do you have any idea how good you look when you're being fucked like this?"

I moan, and Ryder runs his big hand down the middle of my chest, between my breasts, and lower, stopping right before he reaches my clit and dragging his finger back up the same path as Tristan slams into me, over and over.

I'm surrounded by them. Possessed by all three of them. And when Tristan finally gives in and comes inside me with a rough, raw groan, another orgasm slams through my body, making it feel like we're all connected on a level I've never felt with anyone else.

When his cock stops twitching, Tristan gathers up my hair and moves it aside to place a soft, warm kiss on the back of my neck, then slowly pulls out.

A warm trickle of cum follows, the mingled release of all three of them dribbling down my thighs. I collapse on top of Ryder with a sigh, Tristan's weight still on top of me, sandwiching me between them.

Tristan places one more tender kiss on the back of my neck, then helps to gently peel me off Ryder with a soft laugh. We carefully untangle our limbs, and the feel of their fingers drifting over my hair and shoulders makes my heart stutter as we separate.

Then Tristan cups my cheek, his thumb brushing my bottom lip. "You okay there, freckles?"

I nod breathlessly. "I'm perfect."

"I couldn't agree more." His voice is warm and a little rough, and he leans down to press a soft kiss to my lips.

He eases himself off the bed, but when I go to follow, Ryder chuckles and tugs me back so I'm curled against his chest.

"Not so fast. Let us take care of you a little."

I'm not sure when Beckett stepped away from the bed, but he's suddenly right there, a warm, steaming cloth in his hands as he starts cleaning me up.

"You don't have to—" I say, only to be shushed by all three of them.

"Of course we do," Beckett rumbles. "Aftercare is essential." He pauses, then adds gruffly, "It's also a fucking privilege."

"Aftercare?"

Tristan leans down to press a chaste kiss to my temple as I snuggle deeper into Ryder's embrace. One of his hands settles on my hip while the other stays wrapped around the nape of my neck.

"That's right. An intense scene like that floods your body with endorphins. It's important to ease out of it with proper care, both physically and emotionally."

My throat tightens, emotions swelling inside me. "Thank you."

Ryder tips my head back, kissing me before giving me a lazy, satisfied smile. "Like Beckett said, it's a privilege."

"I like it," I admit, feeling sleepy and sated as I smile back at him.

It's the understatement of the century, but I feel so good I don't even have it in me to worry about getting too attached right now.

"Let's get ready for bed," Tristan murmurs, helping me to my feet.

I nod, loving the domesticity of it as the four of us do just that.

But just as we're all starting to settle in, all three of the men's phones ping at the same time.

Beckett reaches his phone first.

"The club," he grunts after thumbing his notifications open.

The other two are already reading their messages, and both of them nod. None of the men seem tense about it, though, so whatever's happening with Radiance, it can't be a bad thing.

"Is everything okay?" I ask, giving into my own curiosity when none of them volunteer any more information.

There's a moment of hesitation between the three of them as they all exchange glances, then Ryder answers me.

"Just an update, love. We've been working toward expanding the business."

My stomach zings with excitement for them, and I grin. "Really? That's great! Radiance is already so successful. I'm thrilled to hear that you're going to be able to grow it, though! What are your plans?"

He smiles at me. "We're still trying to finalize that, but we definitely want to focus on another destination city. New York is in the running, but so are New Orleans and Miami. Each one has a very different energy, so we're taking our time with the market research to make sure the new club will be a good fit for us."

My brows shoot up. "Oh. You're opening a second club?"

When he said expansion, I was thinking along the lines of adding in theme nights, or partnering with other businesses around Los Angeles.

"It's time," Tristan says, rubbing a hand up and down my back, almost absent-mindedly. "We've got great staff in place, and as soon as we can get Beckett to admit that they don't need micro-managing..."

He trails off with a smirk at Beckett, who rolls his eyes.

"I know they're capable," he says a little gruffly. "There's no way we'd even be at this stage if I didn't think Radiance would be in good hands once we move to the new city."

"You're... you're all going to move to whichever city you open the new club in?" I ask, my stomach dropping.

They've been in L.A. the whole time I've lived there, and if I'm brutally honest with myself, it's part of the reason I moved across the country in the first place.

It just never occurred to me that they'd leave the city.

My question makes Tristan snort, and Ryder shoots Beckett another teasing look as he answers me.

"There's no way we'd trust anyone else to oversee the early stages of the new place."

Right. Of course they'd want to be involved in a hands-on way with every part of such an important step in their business.

I swallow down the lump in my throat, hiding my sadness at the realization that I'm going to have to give up more than just this temporary arrangement with them soon. I'll have to give up being involved in their lives at all, once they move so far away.

Because the one thing the three cities they mentioned have in common is that they're all incredibly far away from L.A.

But this isn't about me, so I don't share any of that. I'm proud of what they've managed to build, and even though we're all tired, I can sense their excitement as they talk about the next step for their business.

"You'll have to keep me posted," I say, forcing a smile. "I can't wait to hear about what you do with the new place. I'm excited for you!"

The three of them set their phones down, then crawl into the big bed we're all sharing tonight.

"Thanks, love," Ryder murmurs, kissing me and pulling me close.

Surrounded by all three of them,

I push aside thoughts of the future and just bask in their presence as we all fall asleep.

29

RYDER

THE NEXT DAY, I lean back against the leather seat, my fingers absently combing through Lana's hair as she sleeps with her head on my lap. The steady hum of the engine and the rhythmic click of Beckett's knitting needles from the front passenger seat create a soothing backdrop to the peaceful moment.

I can't help the smile that tugs at my lips as I gaze down at her. We definitely wore her out last night, but it was worth every second. Still, I'm glad we all insisted she take it easy today. She put up a bit of a fight about skipping her driving shift, but Beckett shut that down pretty quickly.

After all, she made a promise to us to take better care of herself, and to let *us* take care of her for the remainder of the road trip, so that she doesn't get another flare up of her lupus.

I frown for a moment, my hand going still. All the research we did the other day on this disease has left me feeling overly protective of her, and I'm not used to it.

Not because I think Lana isn't capable of taking care of herself now that she's no longer hiding from her diagnosis, because she's hands down one of the most capable people I know.

The part that has me feeling a little thrown is just how much I want to take on some of that burden with her.

A small huff of air escapes me, and Tristan's eyes meet mine in the rearview mirror.

"Is she okay?"

I grin at him, a little of my unease with my newfound feelings easing when I see that same protective instinct reflected back at me from him.

"Yeah. Just resting."

"Good," he says, his eyes crinkling at the corners as he smiles and then turns his attention back to the road. "She needs it."

I chuckle and go back to stroking her hair, a flicker of arousal filling me as I recall how Beckett finally got her to agree to skip her driving shifts today.

He's a clever bastard who knows exactly which buttons to push, and he did it by pointing out that if she rested up during the day, she'd have plenty of energy to let us fuck her the way she deserves when we finally stop for the night.

She gave in quickly after that, and I'd be lying if I said my cock isn't already twitching with interest as I look forward to it.

But now isn't the time, so I shake off those thoughts and try to distract myself with something else.

"What're you working on there?" I ask Beckett over the quiet clicking of his needles. "Another scarf?"

"Hat," he grunts, not looking up from his work.

I study the rich, warm colors of the yarn he's chosen, then grin. "Bet it'll look great with Lana's hair."

Beckett's hands falter for just a second, and I know I've hit the nail on the head. He doesn't say anything, but he doesn't need to. I can read the big guy like a book after all these years, and if I'm not mistaken, there's the faintest hint of pink on his cheeks.

Tristan glances over at him while he drives, snorting softly.

Yup. I'm definitely not the only one in this car who's at risk of catching feelings here.

Not that those feelings can go anywhere, but it's still nice to know we're all affected by her.

She sighs softly, shifting in her sleep, and my chest tightens with an unfamiliar warmth as I look down at her.

If she wasn't Caleb's little sister, or if we'd come together under different circumstances, I wonder if...

"Ryder, do you need a pit stop?"

I look up, jolted out of my thoughts as Tristan points to a sign listing the amenities in the upcoming town.

"I'm good," I tell him, reeling a little as I realize how wistfully I was starting to imagine a different kind of future with Lana. One where we didn't go back to business as usual at the end of this trip.

I don't even know what it is that I'm wishing for, exactly. I've never wanted a serious relationship before. I've always kept things casual for a reason. But now, the idea of letting this—letting *her*—go makes my chest tight.

It's confusing as hell, and when I spot another sign up ahead, I jump on the chance to focus on something simpler. Something guaranteed to make Lana smile.

"Forget pit stops," I say, pointing to the sign. "That's the place we looked up, right?"

Tristan glances at it. "Oh, right. Good catch."

"Exit coming up in about a mile. Don't miss it."

Tristan rolls his eyes at me, already signaling. "Yeah, yeah, I just said I see it. Are you going to wake her up?"

I don't have to. As he pulls off the highway, Lana stirs in my lap.

She blinks up at me, sleepy-eyed and slightly rumpled, and it's the most adorable thing I've ever seen.

"Are we there?" she mumbles, rubbing her eyes. "Did I really sleep that long?"

I chuckle, smoothing her hair back from her face. "Nah, love. It's still mid-afternoon. We're just making an unplanned stop."

That gets her attention. She sits up, curiosity brightening her blue eyes. "Unplanned stop? What for?"

I exchange a quick glance with the guys in the front seat, then smirk at Lana. "You'll see."

She looks between the three of us, her lower lip jutting out in an adorable pout. "Oh, come on! You can't just say that and not tell me."

Tristan chuckles. "Watch us."

I lean in close, nipping at her ear because I can't help teasing her a little. "Just remember, good things come to those who wait."

She shivers, and I have to bite back a groan. Fuck, the things this girl does to me without even trying.

"Fine," she huffs. "But it'd better be worth the suspense."

By the time we finally arrive at our destination, I can practically feel Lana vibrating with curiosity next to me. As Tristan guides the car into a parking spot in front of the enormous warehouse, the curiosity on her face turns to confusion.

It looks a bit like a winter wonderland with ice sculptures all around, festive lights, and tasteful greenery, but there's nothing to immediately identify why we're here.

"Is it... a holiday craft fair?" she guesses as we all get out of the vehicle and start walking toward the warehouse.

Before any of us can answer her, we get close enough to catch sight of the posters advertising the exhibition inside, and she gasps, coming to a stop.

"Nope. Not a craft fair," Beckett says, watching her as realization dawns on her face.

"Holy shit," Lana breathes. "Emilia Rossetti? Are you guys serious right now?"

I grin. I'd never even heard of the woman Lana identified as her favorite artist before she shared some of her work with us the other day, so it felt like fate when a quick internet search showed that this special installation of her work was directly on our journey.

"Surprise, love," I whisper, wrapping my arms around her from behind and pressing a kiss to her temple.

She whirls to face me, her expression a mix of shock and pure joy. "You guys remembered?"

"It's no giant ball of string, but—"

She flings her arms around me. "Thank you!"

Beckett watches us with a rare smile softening his features, and as soon as Lana releases me, she launches herself at him, throwing her arms around his neck. "Thank you, thank you, thank you!"

Her excitement is contagious, and as she proceeds to hug

Tristan and then drag us all inside the warehouse, it hits me just how much I fucking love making her this happy.

I can't say it's *better* than the sex, but I'd be lying if I said it wasn't just as good.

We make our way inside the warehouse, and I have to admit, the setup is pretty impressive. The cavernous space is filled with a mix of paintings in what I'm already starting to recognize as the artist's signature style, as well as sculptures, mixed-media pieces, and other decorative touches that all seem to have the sole purpose of highlighting her work. And interspersed among them all are the same towering ice sculptures on display outside the warehouse, catching and refracting the light in mesmerizing ways.

Lana's eyes go wide with wonder. "This is... it's incredible."

As we start to make our way through the exhibition, Lana eagerly explains the significance of each piece we come across.

I try to pay attention, I really do.

But I'm finding it hard to focus on anything but her.

The way her eyes light up as she talks about the symbolism in a particular painting. The graceful sweep of her hand as she gestures toward an intricate ice sculpture and points out the way it complements the artist's work. The soft curve of her lips as she smiles up at me when she catches me staring.

"You're not even looking at the art, are you?" she teases.

I grin, unabashed. "Can't help it if the view right in front of me is better than anything on these walls."

"I second that," Tristan says, adjusting his glasses with a grin as Beckett grunts in agreement.

Lana blushes at our words, and I have to fight the urge to haul her into my arms and kiss her.

"Come on!" She laughs, tugging us toward the next piece before I give in to the impulse.

We end up spending most of the afternoon at the exhibition, and Lana's enthusiasm never wavers. By the time we leave, the sun is already starting to dip low on the horizon, painting the sky in brilliant oranges and pinks.

None of us are particularly tired despite the hours spent

wandering through the installation, so we could probably make it a good distance farther before stopping for the night. But instead of getting back on the road, we decide to explore the quaint little town we've stumbled upon.

Snow crunches under our boots as we make our way down a picturesque street lined with shops, their windows glowing warmly in the fading light.

Suddenly, Lana stops short, her eyes fixed on something in one of the shop windows. I watch as her face lights up for a moment, then dims just as quickly.

"What's up, love?" I ask, following her gaze.

She shakes her head, a wistful smile on her face. "Oh, it's nothing. I just... I liked that dress, but it's not really my style."

I study the dress in question—a slinky, form-fitting number that would hug every curve of her body. Then I look back at Lana, seeing the conflict in her eyes.

I get it. I know all about the expectations of wealthy parents, the constant pressure to fit in and be "appropriate." Which, for someone as naturally curvy as Lana, definitely doesn't include flaunting her assets the way I'm pretty sure that dress would.

But fuck that. The dress is gorgeous, and so is she.

I grab her hand and pull her into the shop. Tristan and Beckett follow, exchanging knowing looks. We're clearly all on the same page about this, just like we so often are when it comes to running our business together.

We find the dress and call over a salesperson.

"Tell her your size," Beckett says, letting some of his inner Dominant through.

It works, because even though Lana's cheeks pink up a little, she turns to whisper quietly to the salesperson, then takes the dress into the fitting room without any further protest.

When she emerges a few minutes later, looking unsure and vulnerable, I swear my heart stops for a second.

"Holy shit," Tristan breathes beside me.

Beckett just nods, his eyes dark with appreciation.

"You look fucking incredible," I finally manage to tell her, my voice rougher than I intended.

She blushes, already shaking her head. "It's a little much, don't you think?"

"No."

"But—"

"It suits you," I say before she can come up with some other excuse.

"Really?"

She looks up at all three of us, searching our faces like she's trying to suss out whether we're just showering her with empty compliments or actually mean it.

"Really," Tristan says, holding her gaze.

"It was fucking made for you," Beckett agrees.

I grin at her. "There's no way you're walking out of here without that dress, love." I hold up a hand when she starts to protest again. "I'm buying it for you."

She bites her lip as she runs her hands over the material. "I can't really wear something like this, can I?"

I grin, stepping closer to her. "Well, since it's coming with us, if you don't, I guess I'll have to."

That startles a laugh out of her, and she looks up at me with a bright smile that hits me right in the chest. After a lifetime spent avoiding attachments—at least, other than to my three best friends —it feels strange to think that making someone else happy can feel so fucking fulfilling.

It's not long before Tristan and Beckett get in on the action, insisting on buying her clothes too. I don't know if they're feeling things for her as strongly as I am right now, but they clearly love the shy way she glows with each compliment just as much as I do.

It makes spoiling her all too easy. None of us can resist her joyfully authentic responses when she actually tries on clothes— clothes that *we* suggest—that highlight her true beauty so well.

"You guys are spoiling me," Lana protests weakly as we pile more clothes into her arms, helping her pick out clothes we can tell she really likes instead of just things she feels like she *should* wear.

"You deserve it," Tristan insists.

She ducks her head, but not before I see that dimple in her cheek as her grin breaks free. "I'm just not used to this."

"Then I guess you'd better get used to it," Beckett rumbles, a hint of a smile on his face as he tips her face back up, his eyes caressing her in a way that seems more intimate than a kiss. "Think you can do that?"

She laughs instead of answering, but hearing him tease her like that really does make me think we might all be feeling things we weren't prepared for.

It should freak me the fuck out, but for some reason, it doesn't. And when Lana leans into me once we're finally checking out, a teasing glint in her eye as she says, "I bet you do this for all the girls, huh? Whisk them away on road trips, buy them pretty things…"

For once in my life, I don't even consider joking back. I just look down at her, brushing the backs of my finger down her satiny cheek as I smile at her, and tell her the truth.

"Nope. Just you."

Three words that should spell trouble and send me running as fast as I can in the other direction, but I've never meant anything more in my life.

And I don't want to run anywhere at all.

30

LANA

THE MEN INSIST on carrying the truly ridiculous number of bags we leave with, and as we step out of the shop, crisp winter air nips at my cheeks and a giddy level of happiness fills me to bursting.

I pull the scarf Beckett made for me tighter around my neck as I take in the picturesque town. The street is bustling with holiday shoppers, but my eyes are immediately drawn to something that makes my heart skip a beat.

"Oh my god," I gasp, grabbing Ryder's arm. "Look!"

A beautiful old-fashioned sleigh is parked at the end of the street, two magnificent horses hitched to it. It looks like something straight out of a Christmas card, and I can't contain my excitement.

Ryder follows my gaze and rolls his eyes, even though I can tell he's fighting off a smile. "Seriously?"

"Oh, come on," I plead, giving him my best puppy-dog eyes. "It'll be fun!"

Tristan chuckles, adjusting his glasses. "I'm with Lana on this one. When was the last time any of us went on a sleigh ride?"

"Never," Beckett grunts, his lips twitching into a half smile. "Could be interesting."

Ryder looks between the three of us, his expression a mix of exasperation and fondness. "You're all ganging up on me now?"

"Don't be such a grinch," Tristan teases. "Live a little."

I hold my breath, watching Ryder's face. For a moment, I think he might actually refuse, but then his shoulders slump in mock defeat. "Fine. But if this turns into some kind of cheesy singalong, I'm jumping out."

Grinning triumphantly, I grab his hand and practically drag him toward the sleigh before he can change his mind. The others follow, laughing at my enthusiasm.

We all pile in, and I end up nestled between Ryder and Beckett, with Tristan across from us. As we set off, the rhythmic clip-clop of the horses' hooves and the jingling of bells fills the air. The town looks like a winter wonderland, strings of twinkling lights crisscrossing the streets and wreaths adorning every lamppost.

I can't stop smiling, drinking in every detail. The cold air on my face, the warmth of the men beside me, the festive atmosphere—it's all intoxicating. When I glance over at Ryder, my breath catches in my throat. Despite all his protests, he's smiling, his eyes soft as he takes in our surroundings.

"Well, well," I tease gently, nudging him with my elbow. "Look who's finally starting to understand the appeal of my favorite holiday."

"Maybe I am," he admits in a low voice, turning his head so that his lips brush my ear. "I didn't realize until now that Christmas could involve some of the hottest sex of my life, developing a new appreciation for hot chocolate, and..." He pauses, chuckling. "The joy of taking a few unexpected detours."

I flush, my heart doing a little flip. He thinks our encounters have been some of the hottest sex of his life?

I know that being with the three of them has been amazing for *me*, but since he's so much more experienced, both sexually and with kink in general, it's hard to believe he feels the same way.

But the truth in his eyes is unmistakable. He means it.

Heat races through me, and I have to fight the urge to climb onto his lap right here in the sleigh. Or, even more embarrassing, confess how much it means to me to hear him say that.

Instead, I try to deflect the intensity of my emotions by teasing him about one of our "detours."

"Admit it, Christmas just won't feel complete for you anymore without a few roadside attractions."

He grins at me, and Tristan joins in on the teasing, asking, "Are we talking about that dinosaur thing we stopped at?"

I sniff haughtily, trying to make them laugh. "Thing? I think you mean *art*."

It works, and as we continue our ride through the twinkling, snow-covered streets, the laughter keeps flowing as we recount some of the adventures we've already had on this trip.

I can't help but marvel at how much has changed in such a short time.

A week ago, I never would have imagined being here, snuggled between three men I've crushed on for half my life, feeling more cherished and desired than I ever have before. And for once, instead of trying to remind myself that it's only temporary, with the Christmas lights sparkling off the snow around us and the sound of sleigh bells in the air, I just let myself enjoy it.

Once the sleigh returns us to our starting point, we disembark and wander through the festive streets.

"Do I smell... pretzels?" Tristan asks as we pass a vendor selling them fresh out of the oven.

The vendor grins at us. "Best ones you'll find in the north east!"

The scent really is too tempting to resist, and we each get one, savoring the salty-sweet taste as we continue our stroll.

It's not long before I catch the guys exchanging glances, though.

"What is it?" I ask, rubbing my icy cold nose.

Tristan tugs my hand away and taps the tip of my nose, smiling at me. "Maybe we should head back to the hotel. We don't want to overdo it."

By "we," I'm pretty sure he means me, and I'm about to argue, mostly out of habit, when I notice the concern in their eyes. I did promise not to push it, so instead, I nod.

"Good girl," Beckett murmurs. But then he cuts a glance at

Ryder, a teasing smirk appearing on his face. "But since Ryder is such a fan of hot chocolate now, maybe we can head back to the car by way of that cafe over there."

I laugh, loving this glimpse at a slightly more playful side of him. And loving even more that, no matter how he plays it off, I know he's suggesting we grab the warm treat because of me.

"If we must," Ryder says with an exaggerated eye roll, playing along. And soon, we're all holding steaming cups of rich, creamy hot chocolate.

The warmth seeps through my gloves, and I inhale the sweet scent with a contented sigh as we make our way back to the SUV and all pile in.

I'm practically buzzing with happiness as I settle into the back-seat next to Beckett, cradling my hot chocolate in both hands.

Ryder takes the driver's seat this time, and as we head to a nearby hotel, I carefully remove the lid on my cup to reveal a mountain of whipped cream.

"I can't believe you didn't get any whipped cream on yours," I tease Beckett as he sips from his own cup, watching me.

"It looks like they gave you enough for the both of us," he shoots back, lifting a brow.

I laugh, but he's right. I tip my head forward to breathe in the sweet scent, then dart my tongue out to lick the whipped cream.

Beckett's already dark green eyes darken even more, until they're the color of a forest at night.

"Careful," he rumbles, his voice low. "You might find yourself in trouble if you keep that up, little menace."

A thrill runs through me. I honestly wasn't trying to tease him. Not like that. But the heat in his gaze makes me feel bold.

I maintain eye contact as I slowly, deliberately swipe another dollop of whipped cream from my drink, this time on my finger, then bring it to my lips.

I lick it. Then I suck my whole finger into my mouth, making sure to do it exactly the way I would if I were on my knees for him again.

Beckett's eyes narrow, the tension between us crackling. "What did I just say about trouble?"

I slowly slide my finger out of my mouth, then rub the pad of it back and forth over my lower lip as my pulse speeds up.

"I don't remember. You might have to remind me."

"Remind you? I think you mean I might have to fuck the brat out of you," he growls.

I shiver, my mind going blank when he slides a hand between my legs.

"I fucking love these gorgeous thighs of yours. As soft as silk, and thick enough to take a pounding."

I instinctively tighten them around his hand. Not to block him, but to keep him touching me.

Beckett smiles, a dangerous, wicked look. "You know why I didn't get any whipped cream?" His thick fingers brush against me, the heat of his touch burning right through the thin layers of cloth separating us. "Because I'd rather taste this. I'd like to live with my head between these pillowy thighs of yours, feasting on you all night long."

My breath stutters, my arousal already making my panties grow damp. But I can't resist teasing him a little bit more.

I take another sip of my hot chocolate, letting some of the whipped cream stick to my upper lip, and then meet Beckett's eyes as I part my legs, giving him full access as I slowly lick it off.

He curses under his breath. "Ryder, take the long route."

"But we're almost to the hotel," Ryder starts to say, before glancing back at us in the rearview mirror. "Oh," he adds with a smirk. "Gotcha."

"I need to teach our girl a lesson," Beckett growls, his fingers curling against me.

A thrill shoots through me that goes beyond the pleasure of feeling his touch. My head knows he's only claiming me that way in the heat of the moment, but my heart stutters anyway, loving the way he called me *theirs*.

"Color?" he asks, his eyes burning into me.

"Green, sir."

The honorific slips out so naturally I don't even have to think about it.

"Good girl," he murmurs, taking the paper cup out of my hands and then handing both his and mine to Tristan in the front seat. Then he leans over me and releases my seat belt. "Take your shoes off."

It's not a request. It's a command.

"Yes, sir."

I bend over to slip my boots off, then let him help me wiggle out of my pants, leaving me in just my sweater and a tiny lace thong.

"On my lap, little menace. Now."

I scramble to obey him, my heart racing and my body flushed with excitement.

I've never done anything like this before. Ryder turned off the highway a little while ago, choosing dark, winding back roads where the night wraps around the SUV like a blanket. The houses here are set back from the road with big sections of land between them, and only the occasional car passes us as Ryder navigates carefully along the route.

Beckett's big hands slide up the backs of my thighs, helping me spread my legs wide as I straddle him, then guiding me down on top of the thick ridge of his clothed cock.

"You're hard," I breathe out, rocking against him.

He moves his hands to my ass, tightening his grip in a silent reminder that he's in charge right now.

"You said you wanted some cream, dirty girl," he says with a wicked smile. "Be careful what you ask for."

Before I can answer, he kisses me possessively. His tongue slides between my lips as his big hands knead my ass, slipping under my thong to pull me even closer.

"Fuck." Ryder groans. "You're making it hard as hell to focus up here, putting on a show like that back there."

"Just don't run us off the road," Tristan murmurs. "I'm

suddenly feeling very motivated to make it back to the hotel in one piece."

My pussy clenches at the promise in his words, and I can't help grinding against Beckett as he claims my mouth. His cock is rock hard, and the pressure against my clit feels too good for me to stay still.

He pulls his hands out from my thong and swats my ass, loosely wrapping his other hand around my throat as he pushes me back enough to look in my eyes. "Are you trying to get on the naughty list?"

"No, sir," I answer breathlessly.

Ryder laughs. "You sure you don't want to rethink that answer, love?"

"Even nice girls are allowed on the naughty list this time of year," Tristan teases, making me flush.

Beckett reaches between us, keeping one hand around my throat as he slowly lowers his zipper. "Do you know what you get when you land on the naughty list?"

I shake my head, then lift up when he directs me to.

He pulls out his cock. "They get fucked, baby. They have to sit on my lap and tell me what they really want. But you already did that, didn't you?"

He slips his free hand inside my thong again, sliding his fingers through my folds, then pulling aside the lace as my thighs start to tremble.

"You want some cream, but you're gonna have to work for it. Put me inside you, then sit down on my lap."

Every time any one of these men touch me, I discover new levels of arousal. But this? Staring into Beckett's unblinking gaze as I sink down onto his cock is the most sensual moment of my life. It feels both forbidden and private, reckless and safe to be doing this surrounded by nothing but the night.

"Fuck," Beckett hisses, his hand tightening on my neck as I fully seat myself on his lap. "That's it, you naughty little thing. Take all of it. Earn your place on Santa's list."

His filthy praise combined with the teasing role play and the stretch of his thick, pierced cock inside me is too much. I let my eyes flutter closed, savoring the pleasure—but they immediately snap back open when headlights wash over us. Another car is coming over the rise behind us, illuminating the interior of our SUV.

I gasp, my heart pounding as a surge of adrenaline at the thought of being caught like this floods me. I'm honestly not sure whether I'm thrilled or terrified by the idea, but then Beckett draws my attention back to him by rocking his hips up.

"Eyes here."

"Yes, sir."

He's in charge. These three men will never let anything happen that pushes my boundaries further than I can handle. I'm safe to explore everything I've ever fantasized with them, and this moment is no different.

Beckett releases my throat, both hands going to my ass and holding me in place as Ryder throws the blinker on and turns onto a dark side road, allowing the other set of headlights to disappear into the darkness.

Then Beckett starts fucking me.

I may be on top, but this is completely different from Ryder telling me to ride him back at the last hotel. I'm not even close to being in charge right now. Beckett is in total control, driving up into me as he uses his hands on my ass to move me on and off of him, forcing me to take every single inch of his cock and lighting up nerves I didn't even know I had with his Jacob's ladder.

"Your pussy is so fucking greedy, little menace," he grunts out. "So hungry for cock, so tight and wet. You're soaking. I can feel you dripping down my balls, you naughty little thing. Is this what you wanted?"

I moan, letting my head drop back, only for Beckett to grip my chin and force me to meet his eyes again.

"I asked you a question."

"Yes, sir," I gasp, trying to keep eye contact. But my eyes flutter closed when he slams into me hard enough to make the springs of the seat groan. "I... I wanted this. You. I want you to... to fuck me just like this. Fuck the sass out of me."

"Touch that pretty clit of yours," he growls, driving up into me like a man possessed, over and over. "Tug that ring and give me a show, baby. I want you to come all over my cock before we make it back to the hotel."

"Yes," I gasp. "Yes, sir. I... I..."

I'm so keyed up, so close to tumbling over the edge into an abyss of pure pleasure, that for a moment, I can't make sense of the jarring ringtone that suddenly blares from my phone.

It sounds again, and Beckett glances down at where I left it on the seat next to us.

"Wade," he grunts, reading off the screen.

I tense up at the sound of my ex's name—hearing it now, while I'm impaled on another man's cock and moments away from an earth-shattering orgasm, is almost surreal.

"I'm sorry. Ignore it," I gasp. "It... it will stop in a second."

Beckett's hands tighten, and he maneuvers my hips in a slow, rolling motion that makes his piercings rub against my g-spot.

My eyes roll back in my head, my thighs starting to shake as that fucking ringtone I set for Wade months ago keeps blaring out from the seat next to us.

"I don't like to ignore things, little menace," Beckett tells me with an almost feral grin. "Answer it."

"What?" I whisper, my eyes flaring wide.

He holds my gaze. "I said, answer your phone."

He's pure Dom, his authority rolling over me and making me shudder. I could use my safe word. I know that.

But I don't want to.

"Yes, sir," I whisper, keeping my eyes locked with his as I blindly reach out next to me, feeling around for my phone.

Beckett smiles as I swipe to answer and bring it to my ear. He adjusts me on his lap, holding me in place instead of driving up into me, and starts playing with my clit piercing while I do as I've been told.

"Wade?" I answer breathlessly, stifling a moan as Beckett pinches my clit, tugging gently on the little ring.

"Lana." Wade's crisp voice comes through. "I'm returning your call."

I bite my lip, then have to bite back another moan as Beckett continues teasing my clit, rolling the pad of his finger over it. He's making it impossible to concentrate.

"My call? I didn't—*ahhhh*."

Beckett gives me a wicked smile while Wade's impatient huff sounds in my ear.

"I have a missed call from you. One which you clearly forgot to disconnect after it went to my voicemail."

It sounds like he's talking about an accidental butt dial. I'm sure of it when he goes on.

"I could hear you laughing and talking with... someone. Several someones, actually. Who were you with?"

"Today?" I ask, the snap in his tone barely registering thanks to the way Beckett's cock pulses inside me as he watches me struggle.

"Yes, today," Wade says, annoyance clear in his voice.

"Oh. Um..."

I can't think. Beckett has stopped playing with my clit and started slowly raising and lowering me on his cock again, lifting my ass in his big hands and then guiding me back down with agonizing precision as Wade's voice drones in my ear.

My whole body feels hot, my toes curling as the pleasure begins to build again.

"Lana," Wade snaps. "Who did I hear you talking to when you left that message earlier?"

Even though the call isn't on speaker, Beckett and I are close enough that I can tell he hears my ex-fiancé's part of the conversation too.

"Answer the man, dirty girl," he murmurs, so low the phone doesn't pick up his words.

My stomach flips.

"Friends," I blurt, then suck in a sharp, audible breath when I feel another set of hands on me.

It's Tristan. It must be. He reaches back from the front seat and pulls my panties aside even more, fingering my ass while Beckett starts playing with my clit ring again.

I press my lips tight together, so focused on restraining my sounds of pleasure that I can barely concentrate on what Wade is saying.

"I suppose it's a good thing you're enjoying your vacation," my ex says stiffly. "I know the Christmas season is your favorite."

"How, um, oh god, how do you know I'm on... on vacation?"

Beckett's thrusts up hard, the tendons in his neck standing out as he starts increasing the pace again, pushing me right back to the peak as he stares into my eyes.

"Is everything alright, Lana?" Wade asks.

"Yes," I choke out, my voice high and thready. "It's... it's perfect."

"I've missed you," Wade says abruptly. "Hearing your laugh on that voicemail... well, it made me think that maybe we should reconsider this separation."

I'm going to come. Beckett has given up all pretense of teasing me and is back to fucking me with a single-minded intensity that wipes out all my higher reasoning.

Wade keeps talking, but I honestly have no idea about what. My orgasm is building, relentless and undeniable, and I know I can't hold it off much longer.

"Wade," I pant, cutting off whatever he's saying. "I've... I've gotta go."

I slap at the red "end call" button and toss my phone aside, not caring where it lands as the wave of pleasure that's been building inside me hits its peak.

I cry out, shaking with the force of it, but Beckett doesn't stop fucking me.

"Do that again," he demands. "Wade didn't get to hear you come, little menace. This time, I want you to scream so loud he hears it all the way back in California."

He wraps an arm around my waist, holding me to him as he drives into me over and over. I can feel every piercing of his Jacob's

Ladder sliding in and out of me, the friction only adding to the fire consuming me.

"Give it to me," he growls, his breath coming in harsh pants. "Give me one more, then I'm gonna fill that greedy pussy with my cum."

My whole body shudders, his filthy words sending me over the edge again.

"That's it," he groans, his hips stuttering as his cock jerks and pulses inside me. "Fucking perfect."

He slumps back against the seat, bringing me with him, and I'm still floating in a haze of pleasure as I collapse against him, utterly boneless.

He runs a hand down my hair, his touch gentle in the aftermath. "Tell us what that worthless prick wanted."

I know he heard most of it, but I repeat it all, wanting to share this—just like everything else—with Tristan and Ryder too.

"He said he missed me," I admit, wrinkling my nose. He claimed he wanted to rethink our 'separation' and what's best for our future."

As the fog of pleasure starts to clear and I fully process Wade's words, it hits me in a rush just how over him I really am. I don't even feel like the same person he dumped. I'm not even sure I recognize that person now that I've had a taste of being who I really want to be.

I straighten up abruptly, Beckett's softening cock still buried inside me, and snatch my phone up again.

"What are you doing, baby?"

I show him, turning the screen so he can see as I pull up Wade's contact and move to delete it, then change my mind and hit "block" instead.

I don't just want my shitty ex out of my phone. I want him out of my life entirely. I don't need him anymore, and I sure as hell don't want him to call me again.

Something blazes in Beckett's eyes, and he grips my hair without saying a word, then kisses me hard.

I melt into him. Not submitting this time, but meeting him as an equal. Kissing him the way I want to—because he makes me feel more like myself, more seen and authentic and real, than I ever thought was possible.

And because he makes me feel so many other things too.

I know it's impossible for this thing that's growing between us to last, but that doesn't mean I don't wish things could be different.

I wish I could keep him.

I wish I could keep all three of them.

31

LANA

I BLINK AWAKE the next morning, soft light filtering through the curtains. As I stretch, I notice that the bed is empty beside me, and when I glance over at the clock, I realize that I've slept in later than usual.

Guilt washes over me as I hurry out of bed, throwing on some clothes. The guys are probably already packing up so we can get back on the road, and here I am, still lounging around.

As I step out of the bedroom into the suite's living room area, Tristan looks up from his tablet. A soft smile spreads across his face as he adjusts his glasses.

"Good morning, sleepyhead."

"I'm so sorry—" I start, but he cuts me off, crossing the room and pulling me in for a gentle kiss.

"Don't apologize," he murmurs against my lips. "None of us mind. We want to take care of you, freckles."

I pull back slightly, searching his face. "But I slept so late."

He shrugs easily. "Then you needed it."

"I mean, who doesn't like sleeping in? But with you guys all already up and handling the packing..."

Tristan shakes his head, his blue-gray eyes serious behind his glasses. "There's a difference between enjoying a lazy morning and respecting your body when you require a little more rest. From what we read about lupus, there are always going to be times you need extra sleep because of the fatigue. Of course we're going to accommodate that."

I flinch a little at the mention of my illness. Being so open about it, even if it's just with the three of them, is still new to me. I've had a lot more practice denying my diagnosis than trying to accommodate it the way Tristan is.

"I know," I admit, chewing on my lip for a moment. Then I sigh. "But that doesn't mean I want to be seen as, I don't know, the weak link here?"

He cocks his head to the side. "You're not. I know I speak for Ryder and Beckett when I say it doesn't change how we see you. It's just a part of you, like any other part." He tugs on my lower lip, dragging out from between my teeth as he grins. "And believe me, we like *all* parts of you."

My stomach swoops. "You do?"

"Of course we do," he says, tucking a strand of hair behind my ear. "You know, when I was recovering from my accident, my grandmother took care of me. She had to do so much, and I don't just mean physically. I was useless for a while, but she never made me feel bad for it."

"You were just a kid," I remind him softly, my heart clenching at the thought of a young Tristan going through such trauma. "You were in pain, and probably in shock from losing your mother. You were what, eight? Nine?"

"What matters is how it felt to have someone give me that kind of unconditional acceptance. And believe me, I'll never make you feel bad for needing to take care of yourself."

The ache in my chest intensifies. I know about his accident, of course. I know he lost his mother. But hearing him talk about it gives me a whole new appreciation for how resilient he is.

And how wonderful his grandmother is too.

I cup his face, my fingers playing over the scars there.

He smiles at me, leaning into the touch instead of pulling away like I've seen him do so many times before when it comes to downplaying his scars.

"Thank you," I whisper, burying my face against his chest.

"No thanks even necessary," he murmurs as his arms wrap around me.

He holds me close, and I breathe in his comforting scent of amber and spice, struck by how safe I feel in his arms.

Ryder and Beckett enter the room a moment later, talking quietly to each other. Beckett's eyes immediately zero in on me with their signature burning intensity, and Ryder is wearing a mischievous grin.

"What's up?" I ask as Tristan and I separate.

Beckett crosses his arms, a hint of a smile playing at his lips. "We've got an early Christmas present for you."

"You guys didn't need to do that."

"We wanted to," Ryder says, his grin widening. "Especially since this trip will be over soon."

A pang of sadness hits me at the reminder that we're almost to New Hampshire now, but I push it aside.

"Well, that really is sweet of you," I say, a little flustered. "But I hope you know I wasn't expecting anything. Whatever it is, you can just wait and give it to me at my parents' house."

It's silly, I know, because they're not just going to disappear from my life when they finally drop me off there. But still, I like the idea that they'd have a reason to make sure to see me again while we're all in New Hampshire.

But Tristan smirks, sharing a glance with the other men that proves he's in on this surprise too.

"Trust me, freckles. Not this gift. We wouldn't let you open it in front of them even if you wanted to."

"Besides, this is something we most definitely want you to enjoy now," Ryder adds.

"With us," Beckett rumbles.

"What do you mean?" I ask, wondering what kind of gift they could have gotten me that they wouldn't want me to open in front of my parents. "Oh," I breathe as they all give me heated looks.

Beckett steps closer, his green eyes meeting mine. "Safe words still apply, of course."

I've never received a gift that might require a safe word, and now I'm *very* curious what they got me. "Okay." I lick my lips. "What is it?"

Ryder brings a small gift box out from behind his back, festively wrapped in gold Christmas paper. "Open it and find out."

"Does this mean I made it onto the nice list after all?" I joke as I take it from him.

Beckett chuckles low. "I guess that depends on whether you like your gift or not."

I tug on the bow, anticipation building in my chest. But when I finally open the box, I'm a bit stumped.

"What is it?" I repeat, looking up at the three of them.

Ryder lifts the pretty gold... thing out of the box. It's tapered on one end, maybe the length of my palm, with a gorgeous red jewel on the other flared end.

It definitely fits with a Christmas theme.

"It's a butt plug, love," he tells me. "For you to wear."

His wicked smile makes my stomach flip over, and I can't deny I'm intrigued. But...

"Will it fit?" I ask, blushing.

"It will," Tristan says from behind me, lifting my hair away from my neck and leaning down to kiss me there. "And it will also stretch you a bit."

I shiver at the implication, thinking of the way he played with my ass while Beckett fucked me in the SUV last night.

It felt good, and I'd be lying if I said I haven't wondered if I could take a cock back there.

One of *their* cocks.

"We want you to wear it today," Beckett says. "Are you willing?"

"All day?"

He nods, and although my stomach flutters, I'm already nodding.

"Yes," I whisper. "What do I need to do?"

His eyes flare with heat. "Turn around. Bend over the back of the couch."

Tristan guides me over to the couch and Beckett produces a small, clear bottle from somewhere as Ryder works my sleep shorts down, then trails the plug over the back of my panties, teasing me through the thin silk.

"We wanted a pretty one for you," he murmurs. "My vote was diamond, but Beckett thought the red was more festive, and now I think he was right. It's going to look gorgeous against your creamy skin."

I shiver as he backs away, slipping my panties down.

Beckett takes his place behind me as Ryder comes around to cup my face and kiss me. I moan into his mouth as I feel Beckett's thick fingers, slick with lubrication, spread my cheeks and circle my asshole, teasing it with a light touch.

Ryder smiles against my lips, then kisses his way down to my neck, nibbling the skin there as Beckett slips one finger inside me. The foreign feel of it sends sparks of sensation shooting through me.

"Relax," Beckett rumbles. "Why don't you help her with that, Tristan?"

Ryder's mouth drops lower, and he and Tristan both play with my breasts, sucking and teasing me as Beckett keeps fingering my ass, touching sensitive nerves I didn't even know I had back there.

Then one of them starts working my clit, and I lose all track of whose hands are where. I only know that they're turning me on. I feel worshiped, almost dizzy with the intensity of their attention. The more they touch me, the faster my body reacts, as if it's already becoming trained to respond to them with earth-shattering orgasms.

"I need... I need to come," I gasp. *"Please."*

Ryder tips my face up, lifting a brow. "No."

I shudder, then gasp when Beckett pulls his finger out and replaces it with something hard and cool. I didn't even realize Ryder had handed him the plug.

Beckett places a firm hand on my lower back, anchoring me. Tristan tugs on my clit piercing, whispering, "Breathe. That's it. Now bear down and let it in."

I do, crying out softly as Beckett pushes the plug into my ass. The stretch as my body accepts it has me craving more in a strange way.

"Please," I repeat, my body instinctively clenching around the intrusion as Beckett gets it fully seated. He taps the jewel on the end, sending a fresh shock of sensation through me.

Then all three men step back, leaving me gasping.

"Fucking beautiful," Beckett comments from behind me. The other two murmur agreement, then they tell me to stand up.

My knees feel weak, but I do it. Ryder helps me pull my clothes back into place, his hands lingering and caressing me the whole time.

"You're really not going to make me come?" I whine. My whole body feels like a live wire, every touch from the three of them a zap of electricity.

But Beckett just grins, stepping in close and gripping my jaw, tilting my head back to meet his eyes. "We're really not. And you're not allowed to take care of it yourself either. Do you understand, little menace?"

My breath hitches, my ass clenching around the plug as I nod.

"I understand."

"Sir."

I moan softly at the reminder. "I understand, sir."

"Good." He kisses me, quick and hard. "Because if you come before we give you permission, there *will* be consequences."

"Okay," I agree quickly, more than happy to suffer through the ache between my legs, because I already know I'll like whatever the reward will be. "Thank you, sir."

"God, you are such a fucking temptation," he mutters, his eyes dropping to my mouth again. But instead of another kiss, he turns me toward the bedroom and swats my butt, sending another zing of unexpected pleasure from the plug to my core. "Go shower, but remember to be good."

There's literally no way I can forget. I've never worn anything like this before, and my awareness of the plug as we get ready to leave the hotel is distracting, to say the least.

By the time we pile into the SUV, I can't stop squirming. The men take full advantage of my arousal to tease me as we drive, making it impossible for my body to calm down, edging me to the max.

The entire day is torture, with every hour seeming to drag on forever. But somehow, despite the filthy promises they each whisper to me as we fly down the highway and the teasing touches that slowly ramp my arousal up to an almost maddening level, I manage to hold back from begging.

"You sure you're going to make it?" Tristan asks toward the end of the day, brushing my hair back and nipping at my ear as I hold back a whimper.

I nod, although I'm not sure if it's true.

Will I make it? They've kept me at a medium level of arousal for so many hours that my entire body feels flushed, and I know it wouldn't take much to push myself over the edge

Just one touch. Just a little pressure in the right place. Just—

"Where are we going?" I ask, dragging my mind away from how much I want to come when I notice that Beckett, who's driving now, is exiting the freeway.

There are still a few hours of driving time according to the route we planned, but I'm not complaining.

Ryder turns around from the front passenger seat, smirking. "That depends on you, love. But if you want to go, we thought we'd take you to a kink club that some friends of ours own near here."

I gasp, both shocked and thrilled, especially after the way Beckett essentially kicked me out of Radiance.

"Really? You mean it?"

"Does that mean you're interested?" Tristan teases me.

I laugh, playfully smacking his chest. "Yes!"

"In that case..." Beckett turns into the parking lot of a nice-looking hotel. "Let's drop our stuff off and find you something sexy to wear. But Lana?"

"Yes?"

He arches a brow. "Keep the plug in, and do *not* make yourself come."

I already agreed to that, but it's easier said than done after a full day of edging. But I manage to hold on to my resolve as I slip into the sleek dress they bought me, then step out of the bathroom to show it off.

All three men stop and stare, and I smooth my hands down my curves. "Is it okay?"

"Wow," Tristan breathes, his eyes roaming over me appreciatively.

Ryder lets out a low whistle, while Beckett just nods, his eyes dark.

"So, you said it's a kink club, right?" I ask as we finally head out. "Um, which means an actual sex club?"

"That's right," Ryder answers me as we pull up outside. "Last chance to back out."

"Absolutely not," I say emphatically.

This is everything I've been wanting, everything I imagined when I first showed up at Radiance.

No, it's better, because this time, I'm with *them*.

All three of the men flank me as we approach the entrance, and I feel a giddy mix of excitement and nerves bubbling up inside me.

Beckett must sense it because he leans in close, his breath warm against my ear.

"Color?" he murmurs, his hand coming to rest on my lower back possessively.

"Green," I say with no hesitation.

He smiles. "Good. And remember, we've got you. There will be a lot going on, and you can explore anything that interests you, but while we're here, you're *ours*."

Tristan makes a sound of agreement as Ryder adds, "We're not sharing you with anyone but each other."

As we step inside the club, my heart flutters with anticipation.

For this one night at least, it sounds like I'm truly going to get everything I could ever want.

32

LANA

Stepping into Eclipse, the sex club they've taken me to, reminds me a lot of my single trip to Radiance. The layout is a little different and the color scheme leans more toward industrial—all matte blacks and distressed steel versus the deep reds and dark leather of Radiance—but the energy is the same.

I love it.

The three men follow through on their promise to stick close to me, giving off possessive, protective vibes as they lead me deeper into the club.

The front of the place is sedate, with tables and quiet seating areas, but farther in, music thrums through the air, a deep bass vibrating through my body that feels as sensual as the sights I'm seeing.

With Tristan, Ryder, and Beckett like a moving fortress around me, the hint of shyness I feel can't stop me from looking around with hungry eyes. I don't know where I'd start if I were here on my own. It's everything I've been fascinated by, fantasies I haven't even fully acknowledged yet, laid out in front of me.

It's intoxicating.

"This way," Ryder murmurs, his hand brushing my lower back as they guide me along a dimly lit corridor.

The walls are a montage of dark, shadowy figures, the black

steel railing cool under my palm as we descend a short flight of stairs. My heart pounds in my chest, a thrilling rush as we delve farther into the underground playground.

The men point out the various stations to me—the spanking bench, cages, and St. Andrew's cross—and my cheeks flame at the sheer audacity of it all. I don't think I'm ready for any of that, but being immersed in it, especially after the full day of edging, is spiking my arousal to the point that I'm almost panting.

And all three of them clearly know it.

My eyes widen as we pass an open room where a woman is pinned to the wall by a man, his hand tightening around her throat as she writhes. My breath catches at the raw, primal energy between them, and a heady rush coils low in my belly as my steps slow.

"We're going to play in private," Beckett whispers, leaning down as he threads his fingers through mine. "But if you see anything you want to stop and enjoy along the way, just say so."

I nod, then shake my head, looking up at him in a silent plea that he seems to intuitively understand. I'm curious about all of it, and I love that they seem to have truly taken my interest in learning about kink to heart. That they're willing to help me not just explore, but explain and enjoy all the sensuality a place like this has to offer.

But right now, I need *them*.

Beckett smiles, then nudges me forward. A little farther along the hallway, they usher me into a private room, and my eyes widen at the sight that greets me.

The space is outfitted with things I've only read about, some of which intrigue me and some that I'm not sure I'll ever want to explore. There are clean, leather-covered surfaces at different heights—I'm not sure whether to call them beds, benches, or something else, but they're clearly there to accommodate all sorts of different positions —and around the edges of the room are a variety of toys and implements displayed almost reverently. Whips, chains, cuffs, and other things I don't know the names of hang from wall hooks, and sleek, polished wood drawers line the walls, no doubt filled with other equipment.

"This place is incredible." My breath catches as I take it all in, my body tingling with anticipation.

Beckett squeezes my hand, his thumb brushing over my knuckles as he guides me farther in. "We wanted to give you a taste of everything. See what piques your interest."

My gaze falls on a collection of nipple clamps, and my clit throbs. Blindfolds hang next to them, and I imagine the sense of surrender that would come with not being able to see or anticipate what the men might do to me.

"And these..." Beckett's voice drops to a husky murmur as he opens a drawer to reveal an array of floggers. "Are for sensation play. Feeling brave, little menace?"

"Maybe." I bite my lip, my heart hammering. "I think so."

Beckett steps toward the nearest wall, trailing his fingers along the display of toys. "Some people are into pain. We can explore that, if you're interested. But for now, I want to show you things that will give you pleasure."

I swallow, my eyes tracing the outline of a sleek, black paddle. "That... I mean, I'm interested in learning. All of it."

His smile is slow and sexy as he turns to face me. "Good."

Ryder takes my other hand, and with Beckett leading the way, the three of them guide me through the room.

"Anything you see here can be used on any part of the body," Beckett continues. "It's all about sensation."

My gaze falls on a collection of delicate crops, the tails made of thin strips of leather. I imagine the sting they'd deliver, a sharp bite that would light up my senses. Nearby hangs a length of chain, the metal glinting in the soft lighting.

"And over here..." Beckett leads me to another display. "We have the ropes. There are different types, each with its own unique feel. Tristan's the one to tell you about these, though."

"And the one to use them," Ryder adds with a sexy smirk as I take in the array of ropes, all neatly coiled and waiting.

Tristan picks up a length of soft rope, running it through his fingers. "This is jute. It's soft and flexible, perfect for shibari." He smirks at me, his eyes burning. "One of my favorite ways to play."

My heart pounds as I imagine him binding me with those ropes, my body on display for their pleasure. Being tied up, unable to move, is something I've fantasized about but never admitted aloud.

It's too much. My mind is racing in overdrive, and I can't decide where to start.

"You choose," I whisper to all of them as my pussy throbs, my ass clenching around the plug. "I'll... I'll safe word if anything is too much, but please. I just want to *feel*."

"We can do that, love," Ryder murmurs, his fingers trailing over my lower back.

"We will *happily* do that," Beckett rumbles as Tristan gives me a piercing, enigmatic smile.

And then they're on me, surrounding me, their mouths claiming mine, their hands mapping my body with eager possession. I'm breathless and overwhelmed, in the best possible way. My senses are alive, every nerve ending singing as they strip me of my clothes, their mouths and hands everywhere.

I gasp as a hand slips between my thighs, already so keyed up from wearing the butt plug all day.

"Please," I whisper, not sure who I'm begging, but not caring. I'm theirs, and I need them to finish what they started.

"Not yet, baby," Beckett murmurs roughly. "We're just getting started."

Their mouths move over me, hands teasing, stroking, until I'm a quivering mess, pleasure coiled tight and ready to snap.

Beckett's mouth finds my neck, his teeth nipping at my pulse point as his hands roam lower, delving between my legs.

"So fucking wet already," Ryder growls as he takes in the sight of me, my breasts heaving, nipples tight.

Tristan presses against me from behind, reaching around to pinch them.

"Beckett," he says, his deep voice sending a shiver down my

spine as the two of them exchange some sort of silent communication.

"Yes," Beckett says, and before I can answer what it is they've just agreed on, Ryder captures my mouth in a searing kiss, his tongue tangling with mine as his hands map my body, flames licking across my skin where he touches.

I'm lost in it, my eyes closed and my breath ragged, when suddenly Tristan's fingers are gone. He moves away from behind me, and a cool, silken cloth slips over my eyes.

They're blindfolding me.

"Color?" Beckett asks.

"Green," I whisper.

A moment later, cool metal touches my skin, trailing along my ribs and over my stomach. I suck in a breath, every nerve ending alight. I have no idea what it is, but the sensory deprivation makes even that light touch feel electric.

Then they drag the metal implement up to my breasts, and twin points of pressure on my nipples have me biting back a moan as something cool and shifting drags between them.

Nipple clamps, attached by a delicate chain.

I saw them in a drawer before they blindfolded me.

It's not painful, but the pressure is intense, sending a bolt of sensation straight to my core. My breath comes in short gasps as the clamps are tightened more, making my knees shake.

"That's it, baby," Ryder murmurs, his lips brushing my ear, sending shivers down my spine. "Let yourself feel it all."

"You look fucking incredible like this," Beckett says, close enough to tell me that he's the one who's attached them.

"I feel... I..."

I'm left gasping, not sure how to put it into words. *Good* doesn't seem like a big enough word, and even *incredible* doesn't cover the overwhelming sensations rolling through me.

"You're doing so well." Beckett's warm praise washes over me. "And we're just getting started. We want to show you just how much your body can take."

"Yes," I gasp. "Yes, please."

They lead me over to one of the leather covered benches, bending me over it and directing me to spread my legs.

"Oh fuck," someone mutters.

Tristan, I think. But maybe Ryder.

I'm starting to feel like my head is floating. So turned on that I'm lightheaded, but also disoriented in a sensual way by the blindfold and the inescapable sensation of the clamps. The only thing I *can* do is obey their softly murmured commands... and *feel*.

Someone spreads my legs wider, groaning softly, then taps the jeweled plug I'm wearing.

I moan, a shudder going through me. A moment later, a soft, almost soothing waterfall of touch caresses my ass.

"This is a flogger," Beckett says from behind me, dragging the tails through my crease and teasing my inner thighs with them. "I'm going to need you to count as I use it on you. Can you do that for me, baby?"

"Yes," I promise. "Yes, sir."

"Good girl. Let's begin."

As the flogger's tails trail over my skin once more, I suck in a breath, tingles sparking where it makes contact. Then the first strike lands across my ass.

"One," I breathe, the sensation like stinging bees.

"Beautiful," Beckett praises, the flogger falling again in another sharp snap that makes me gasp.

"Two," I manage, feeling my knees weaken as the sting blooms.

Another strike, this time lower, the tails landing with a thwack against my sensitive inner thighs.

"Three."

The heat that follows the sting works its way into my core, fanning the flames of the arousal inside me until it feels like I'm about to be consumed.

"You're doing so well, love," Ryder encourages, his warm breath against my ear as he nuzzles my neck.

The next strike lands on my ass, closer to the plug, and a jolt of sensation shoots straight to my core. I cry out, my body arching. "Four!"

The final strike lands, and I cry out again, my body vibrating with sensation. "Five! Oh god. Please. Please, sir. I need to come."

I writhe against the smooth leather, and the feeling of my clamped nipples dragging across its surface drives me crazy.

"Not yet," Beckett says, making me sob. "I think you can do five more."

"No," I whisper, even as a part of me yearns for it.

Not for more flogging, necessarily, but for pleasing him. For pushing myself because he wants me to. For earning more praise and discovering how much I can really take.

And since "no" isn't my safe word, Beckett gives me all of that, coaxing me to count out five more, making me lose myself in the rhythm of the flogger, my body on fire, pleasure and pain blending into an overwhelming mix that has me hovering right on the edge of release so that I'm not even sure if I am counting anymore.

Not until he finally stops.

"That's it," he murmurs, his voice a deep rumble of approval as he runs a hand over my ass, my thighs, between my legs.

"Fucking incredible," I hear Ryder say over the sound of my breath, coming in short gasps as I just exist in a sea of sensation.

I'm floating, pleasure coiling so tightly that I can barely breathe. My body is on fire, sensation thrumming through every nerve ending as I hover right on the edge of release.

And then Beckett taps on the plug, his voice a commanding rumble. "Do not come, little menace. Not until you have permission."

But it's too late.

At his words, I shatter, pleasure bursting through me in a rush. I cry out, my body shaking as I'm overwhelmed by the most intense orgasm I've ever experienced.

"Oh, you dirty little thing," Beckett growls, chuckling. "You know better."

My breathless, shuddering response is lost in the waves of pleasure still rolling through me. My body feels boneless as they reposition me, lifting me up and supporting me as they remove the blindfold.

The return of my sight is like a shock of bright light, and I blink as I find them all gazing down at me with raw desire in their eyes.

Beckett gives me a slow, wicked smile. "You've been a very bad girl, coming without permission."

"I'm sorry, sir."

I'm not sorry. Not in the slightest. I'm trembling with excitement at the dark promise in his eyes.

"For that..." he murmurs, stroking a hand down the center of my chest, all the way to my pussy where he hooks a finger into my clit piercing. "I'm going to have to fuck you."

I shudder, my body clenching around the butt plug as the pleasure still coursing through my blood spikes.

"Yes. Yes, please."

He tugs my piercing gently, using it as a tether to lead me to the lowest, widest leather bench, one the size of a bed. Then he seats himself on it and slides his hand between my legs to play with the plug as I stand before him. "I'm going to fuck you while this is still inside you."

My pussy clenches with involuntary excitement. I already feel so full, I can't imagine how intense it will be to have him inside me too.

But I want it.

"Green," I whisper, making Beckett's eyes flare.

He draws his hand back, dragging it through my wet folds. Then he licks my arousal off his fingers.

Tristan and Ryder stand like twin sentinels on either side of me as Beckett reclines on the leather bench and frees his cock.

All three men are bare chested now, having stripped down to just the form-fitting pants they each wore to the club, and the clear bulges of Tristan's and Ryder's cocks makes my mouth water.

I want to touch them. I want them to touch *me*. I want everything with these men.

But right now, all those wants are eclipsed by one: obeying my Dom.

"Straddle me," Beckett orders, his thick, tattooed fingers playing over his Jacob's ladder piercing as he slowly strokes his cock, watching me like a king who doesn't question for a moment that he'll be obeyed.

And I do. I scramble to obey, eagerly settling myself over him, our eyes locked together and the plug shifting inside of me as I get into position.

His hands immediately grasp my hips, guiding me down onto his shaft. With a slow, torturous slide, he fills me, and just like I suspected, with the plug already taking up space inside me, it's so intense it has my eyes rolling back.

"That's it, baby," he rumbles, his thumbs stroking my hips. "Take it all. Fuck, you feel even tighter like this."

I whimper, shuddering on top of him. "So full," I whisper, overwhelmed by it.

But they really have awoken something greedy and carnal in me, because all I want is more. And Beckett gives it to me. He grips my hips tighter, guiding my movements as I rock against him.

"You're doing so well," he praises, his eyes shining with a combination of pride and raw lust as he starts to fuck me. "Your pussy feels like fucking heaven. Are you going to give me another one?"

"Another... another orgasm?"

It's inevitable. I'm already racing in that direction as he moves me on top of him.

"That's right," Beckett says, his eyes piercing me just as deeply as his shaft does. "You came without my permission. Now you'll need to come on my command."

"Yes, sir."

He thrusts up, making me cry out, my clit throbbing and my ass clenching around the plug.

"If you can take this," Beckett growls, doing it again, "you can take two cocks."

His words are like a lit match inside me, heating my blood into a firestorm. I have no idea if it's just dirty talk or a promise. If it's something I could really do, or if it would be too much. But I do know that the thought of being filled by two of them at once is both thrilling and terrifying.

And that if Beckett tells me I can, I believe him.

He chuckles, tugging gently on the chain of my nipple clamps. "You like that idea, don't you, baby?"

I nod frantically, beyond words as the sensation builds. I move against him, finding a rhythm that has sparks of pleasure shooting through me.

"That's it. You'll need to keep fucking yourself on my cock, open yourself up so you're ready for that second one. Get your pussy nice and primed for another release. Fuck, you're perfect," he growls, his hands sliding up to cup my breasts, thumbing the clamps.

I moan, the sensation of his Jacob's ladder piercing brushing against my sensitive walls competing with the sharp zing from the clamps and the heating sensitivity as he rubs his hands over my well-flogged ass and thighs, until I'm swimming in so many layers of pleasure that all I can do is let my body follows its instincts.

And my instincts are to do exactly what my Dom is telling me to.

I brace my hands on his wide chest, my fingers pale against the thick black tattoos that cover his dusky skin, and chase my pleasure as I bounce on his cock with an urgency I've never felt before.

I need everything he's promising. I need to *come.*

Tristan and Ryder move closer, their eyes burning as they watch me ride Beckett. They reach out, trailing their hands over my skin, stoking the flames of my arousal even higher.

"Jesus, you're so beautiful like this," Tristan murmurs, his fingers brushing my hair back where it clings to my face. "Your pleasure is fucking gorgeous."

Ryder's hands skim lower, gripping my ass, helping me move against Beckett and lighting up the reddened skin there.

"You're doing so fucking well, love. Take it all. Take what you need."

"What she needs is another cock," Beckett growls, palming my ass and spreading my cheeks apart. "You volunteering, Ryder?"

"Fuck yeah," he says, the bed dipping as he comes up behind me, pushing me down until I'm flattened on Beckett's chest.

I moan, his cock pushing against my g-spot as my clit grinds against his hard body. Then my breath catches, the pressure of the plug beginning to ease.

Ryder's taking it out, working it free from my body with gentle, relentless tugs that light up the nerve endings in that sensitive spot.

I whine when it comes out, not liking the sudden emptiness. At first, it was almost too much, but now I crave the missing fullness.

Beckett tangles his hand in my hair, cupping the back of my head and pulling me down to kiss me as his cock jerks in my pussy.

I moan, giving myself to him completely, and a moment later, I feel Ryder tracing the sensitive rim of my back hole.

His fingers are slick with lube, and he groans when he slips one inside me. "Look how well you take me, love. Did you like being plugged?"

I can't answer. Beckett's groaning into my mouth, holding me against him as he keeps his other hand on my ass, holding me open for Ryder to play with.

Then Ryder's fingers disappear, and his cock presses against me, entering me in a way no man ever has before.

"Oh god," I gasp, arching my back as that wonderful fullness returns and then some, pushing my body to its limits.

"You can do this," Tristan murmurs as he guides me to lean back and adjust the angle, letting Ryder in.

I start to shake, the feeling overwhelming as Beckett's thick cock seems to swell inside me as Ryder's enters me from behind.

It's too much.

But it's also not. It's *perfect*.

"So fucking tight," Beckett groans, his hands fisting in my hair as my body takes both of their cocks, just like he promised I could.

He holds himself still, every muscle in his body as tense as a rock, while Ryder works his way in with short, shallow strokes.

Each one goes deeper. Each one pushes me higher. And when he's finally fully seated, the heat of his body making the reddened skin Beckett worked over with the flogger flare with sensation, he groans, reaching around to cup my breasts as he pants against the side of my neck.

"Fucking incredible," he grits out from behind me, his cock throbbing in my tight channel. "Nothing has ever felt as good as being inside you, love. Fucking *nothing*."

"Damn right," Beckett growls.

They begin to move in tandem, building a rhythm that has me crying out, my body trembling with the intensity of it.

"That's it, baby," Ryder encourages, his arms wrapping around me, one hand tweaking my clit piercing. "Let yourself feel it."

The pressure builds, their cocks stroking something deep and primal inside me. Their hands are everywhere, tugging my nipple clamps, playing with my piercing, their mouths on my neck, my shoulders, my breasts.

I've never felt so completely owned, so free to just get lost in the pleasure, and I can't hold back my escalating cries when my body starts to shake as I near the peak. I'm beyond words, beyond rational thought, reduced to a being of pure sensation as they drive me higher, working me over their cocks until I finally shatter, sobbing with the force of my release.

It sweeps through me, a tidal wave of sensation that leaves me trembling and boneless between them as they keep fucking me through it.

"Oh fuck," Ryder groans from behind me. "You're milking me so fucking well. Gonna pull everything out of me at this rate, love. Is that what you want? You want it all? You want to be dripping with our cum before you walk out of here?"

"Yes," I gasp.

"Then give us another one first," Beckett demands. "I want to feel this perfect pussy of yours squeeze my cock again. Come on, dirty girl. Show me how good you can be. I know you've got one more in you. Give it to us. One more now."

I want to say I can't, but they're relentless, their thrusts becoming more urgent and their grips on my body fiercer. Their grunts and curses fill the room, animalistic sounds that fuel the flames of my arousal once more, and before I know it, I'm tumbling over the edge again, my desperate cries joining theirs as they follow, spilling themselves inside me with a final few thrusts.

"Perfect," Ryder murmurs, pulling out of me slowly and then guiding me upright, my thighs wet with their releases and still spread wide around Beckett's hips.

He tugs gently on the chain of the nipple clamps.

"Ryder's right. You were perfect, baby," he praises, his eyes shining with pride and desire. "You did so fucking well."

"Thank you, sir," I whisper.

He releases the clamps, leaning up to kiss each nipple tenderly as an indescribable sensation rushes through me at their removal.

Beckett runs his hands down my body, his softening cock giving one last pulse as he pins me with a wicked look. "But you don't think we're done yet, do you?"

He cups my chin, then turns my head so that I'm facing Tristan.

Tristan's eyes are heated behind his glasses, his gaze trailing over my body with a look of such hunger that the flames these men have just sated instantly flare to life again.

He's as still and contained as he always is, but his cock is visibly throbbing behind his pants, his body flushed and his nostrils flaring with every breath.

I shiver, equal parts excitement and anticipation coursing through me. As blissful as the afterglow of being fucked by Ryder and Beckett is, I do need more. I need Tristan too.

And when he finally drags his eyes back up my body to meet my gaze, I know I'm going to get everything I could ever want from him, even though I've got no idea what he has planned.

"It's my turn now," he says, his voice low and full of promise as he smiles at me. "Color?"

"Green," I whisper.

33

TRISTAN

Lana is a vision, freshly fucked and gorgeous, with her hair falling across her face as she blinks up at me.

Her lips are swollen from Beckett's and Ryder's kisses, tempting me to slide my aching cock between them. I'm so turned on after watching my friends fuck her that I'm aching with it.

I'm not sure I've ever seen anything as perfect as the way she surrendered herself to them. The three of us have shared before, and it's always a rush to do scenes with a willing submissive together.

But it's never been like this.

With Lana, it's not just about the sex. It's not even strictly about kink, although helping her explore her interests is an unbelievable rush. But the trust with which she hands herself over to us goes far deeper than any of that.

Ryder rolls to his feet, helping Beckett lift her out from between them, and I pull her straight into my arms, cupping her face in my hands and kissing her deeply.

Her mouth is hungry on mine, tasting of sin and sex, and I can't get enough. She's always gorgeous, but messy like this, covered in my two best friends' cum with her skin gleaming and hair mussed from the pleasure they've all shared makes her fucking breathtaking.

When we finally part, breathless, Lana asks, "How do you want me?"

"Bound. Restrained. Beautiful."

She blushes, her eyes darting to the ropes Beckett pointed out earlier. "In those?"

"That's right, freckles. I want to tie you up."

"Shibari," she breathes out, reminding me that when the subject of the Japanese art of rope bondage came up between all of us in the car once, she looked intrigued.

But then the excitement on her face fades, replaced by a flicker of nervous uncertainty.

"Nothing happens that you don't want here," I remind her.

"No, I do," she says quickly. "I'd like to try. It's just that I've never done it before, and..."

Her cheeks flush pink.

"And?" I prompt her.

She looks away. "I—I've seen some videos, but I'm not the typical size for it, am I?"

I turn her face back toward me. "There is no typical. Kink is for everyone. And you? Your body is perfect for this."

"Is it?" she whispers.

"Yes," I answer, my voice husky as I trail my fingers along her curves. "You'll look stunning with rope wound around you right here... and here... and here. Shibari is more than kink. More than bondage. It's art, and your body is my canvas. But you will always be the one in control, I promise, sweetheart. You can stop everything at any time with a single word."

Her breath hitches at my words, and she swallows hard, her eyes glowing with a mix of vulnerability and trust that guts me.

"Okay," she whispers, her voice shaking slightly. "And if I don't want to stop? If I want you to push me a little?"

I smile, my heart surging in my chest. "Then you've already given me that word."

Green.

Fuck. She couldn't be any more perfect if she tried.

Beckett and Ryder move around the room, cleaning themselves up a little but never taking their eyes off her as I lead Lana over to the piece of equipment I want. Everything in here is versatile, and while this one tends to be referred to as a spanking bench most often and I have no intention of spanking her, it's perfect for the position I want her in.

Because once I have her in my ropes, I'm going to need to fuck her, and the image of having her bent over and bound while I slide into her hot, cum-slick pussy makes my cock pulse inside my pants, hard enough to make me groan.

"Spread your legs around it. That's right. Just like that." I guide her, her curves soft and lush under my hands as I help her straddle the bench, then push her flat against its wide surface.

She folds over it like a dream, turning her head to the side and resting her cheek against it with a sigh.

I take a moment to make sure she's truly comfortable before reaching for the ropes, admiring the picture her flushed skin makes against the black leather.

"Fucking gorgeous" Beckett murmurs, as if he's reading my mind.

I select a long length of forest-green rope. Then, with a little smirk, grab a second length. This one a deep, ruby red.

Ryder chuckles. "How festive."

Lana's eyes have drifted closed, her body relaxed and trusting. But at Ryder's words, she opens them and, when she sees the holiday colors I've chosen, bites her lip, smiling.

"Ready?" I ask, brushing her hair back from her face.

"Yes." She licks her lips, drawing my gaze to the plump, kiss-swollen flesh. "I want it. I want to know what it's like."

Her eagerness spurs me on. Her submission is a gift, and the need to push her, to see how much she'll take, somehow meshes perfectly with my desire to protect her.

I drag the soft rope over her spine, my cock throbbing at the shiver that goes through her. Then I lift her arms, bringing them together behind her back.

A tremor runs through her, a soft sigh escaping her lips.

"Alright?" I check in.

"Yes," she whispers, her eyes drifting closed as I start to wind the rope around her.

Ryder and Beckett are totally silent, clearly as caught up in watching her reactions as I am as I slowly tug her arms further behind her, stretching her body out beautifully.

She moans softly, and I tie off the first knot just under her elbows, then start to weave the ropes in a more intricate pattern. One that will put her into a state of complete vulnerability.

"How does this feel?"

"Secure." She inhales deeply, tension visibly flowing out of her body as her chest expands with her breath, straining against the ropes for a moment. "Restrained. Good."

I can tell she's not trying to break free of them, just testing their limits.

"Good," I praise her. "That's it. Just feel."

Her eyes flutter shut, her features softening as I carefully wind more of the rope—the red one—down her forearms, sliding my fingers beneath it and testing as I go to ensure that it's tight enough to bind but not so tight that it puts her circulation at risk.

"Fuck, that looks incredible," Ryder murmurs.

"Mmm," Beckett agrees, his gaze intent upon her. "Fucking beautiful."

I work slowly, methodically, wanting to take care with her but also enjoying the process itself. I've always found shibari to be both arousing and meditative, putting me into a headspace where I'm completely focused on the submissive giving me their trust. And fuck, the way Lana takes to it is like no one I've ever played with before.

She's a natural.

I reach her palms, tying an intricate, beautiful pattern around her wrists and between her fingers, then tie off another knot, fully securing her hands behind her back.

Lana whimpers, her body trembling. I can see her pulse fluttering in her throat, the rapid beat mirroring the thrum of her blood in her veins, the flush staining her cheeks as she tests the ropes again, then practically melts against the spanking bench when she realizes her arms are fully restrained.

This is one of the many reasons I love shibari. The security it gives a sub, the ability to reassure them without any words being spoken that they are completely free to let themselves go, is utterly addictive.

"Green," Lana murmurs as I reach for the next rope.

I grin. I have no idea if she's confirming that she's willing and receptive to this, or just making an observation, since I've grabbed the forest-green colored rope for her legs. But either way, the slightly dreamy quality in her voice tells me she's quickly falling into subspace.

I crouch down and start to bind her ankles to the base of the bench, winding the ropes in another intricate pattern as I work my way up her legs, one that will keep her spread wide and available for use.

I'm always careful when I do this. The safety of any sub who puts their trust in me is always my first priority. But with Lana, it feels so much deeper than that. I'm not just careful; I'm driven by an almost primal need to take care of her and ensure that it's an experience she enjoys.

Her breath starts to quicken as I continue, and she starts squirming a little and subtly rocking her hips against the bench. Her body is still relaxed and pliant, but her growing arousal is obvious too.

And it starts to test my control.

Rope work always turns me on. Any submissive willing to put herself in my hands does. But Lana is something more. I'm not just sharing something I love with her. I'm discovering that she was made for it.

"Fuck, love," Ryder murmurs as I finally reach her thigh and tie off the rope, then start in on her other side. "Tristan's wrapping you up like a Christmas gift for us."

He leans back against the wall, lazily fisting his cock as his eyes rake over my work, and Beckett grunts his agreement.

"That's exactly what you are," I tell her as I finish her other leg and tie off the final knot, securing her to the bench. "A gift. I wish you could see yourself. Next time, we'll have to make sure we take pictures for you."

She moans, the red flush from the flogger making her lush thighs and ass call to me even more now that they're framed by the elaborate knot work I've completed.

"Too much?" I check, stroking my hand down her thigh, tracing the line of the rope. Testing it. Toying with it.

"No." She shakes her head, her lips parted as she breathes heavily. "Just—a lot. But in a good way. The *best* way."

"You're taking it so well," I praise her. "But nothing pinches? Nothing feels too tight?"

"No," she whispers, squirming again. "It feels perfect."

"Comfortable?" Beckett chimes in, watching her attentively.

She laughs softly. "Um, I'm not sure if I'd call it that, no."

"Does anything tingle?" I double check.

She squirms against the bench again, biting her lip. "*Yes.*"

"Fuck," Beckett grunts.

I chuckle, my own cock throbbing in response to her need. "Not your pussy, freckles. I'll get to that soon. But I mean your limbs, any area I've restrained. Does anything feel numb?"

"No, nothing like that," she pants as I walk around the entire spanking bench, trailing my fingers over her gorgeous body as I check the ropes again. "I just feel... exposed," she goes on, her words becoming slower, more relaxed. Almost dreamy. "My shoulders aren't used to this. But I think I like the way I have to just accept that. I can't move, I can't do anything but take it, and that's almost a relief. Does that make any sense at all?"

"Yes," I reassure her, meeting my friends' eyes. "Perfect sense."

I know we all understand what she's struggling to put into words. Submission isn't necessarily about comfort. Quite often, it's the opposite. And part of the beauty of that gift is the pleasure a sub takes in choosing to be *un*comfortable.

I circle back around behind her, my cock aching as I step between her spread thighs and drag my fingers through the cum dripping down her soft flesh.

"You're so beautiful," I murmur, cupping her pussy. My touch elicits a soft whimper, and a shudder ripples through her body. "And so utterly filthy. Do you feel well-used now that you've taken two loads... or do you still need more cock?"

She whimpers, her voice breaking. "Please. Yes."

"Yes, what?"

"Yes, sir. I do. I feel... I feel used, but I still need more."

"Good girl."

I push two fingers inside her, my cock jerking with excitement at the way she clenches around them. She really has been well-used. Her tight pussy is warm, wet, and welcoming, and it takes all my restraint to drag things out instead of just sliding right into her slick heat and losing myself there.

"Fuck," Beckett growls, his jaw set tight, his nostrils flaring. "How does it feel inside her, Tristan?"

"So fucking good."

I twist my fingers as I answer, and her walls squeeze around them. She's drenched, the scent of her arousal thick in the air, but no matter how desperate I am to bury my cock inside her, I want her desperate too.

"Tell me what you need." I crook my fingers, brushing her g-spot. "Do you need *this*?"

"Yes," she hisses, a tremble coursing through her. "God, yes."

"Say it. Beg for it."

"You," she gasps. "I need you."

"You need me to... what?"

"To fuck me," she sobs. "To fill me up. I'm so empty. *Please*, Tristan."

I smile, a fierce wave of satisfaction rolling through me as I pull my fingers out, wiping them on her plush ass.

"Not yet."

She gasps, twisting her torso around to look at me. "What?"

I pull out a final length of rope, then gently push her body flat again.

"And that right there is why. I want you completely restrained before I fuck you. I don't want you to have anything to do but accept my cock, to let me fuck you until you're sobbing for release and realize that the only way it will come is with your total submission."

She makes a beautiful sound of desperation, but doesn't use her safe word, so that's a yes.

I slowly start winding the final length of rope around her body, binding her shoulders to the bench and weaving it into a final, beautiful pattern over her torso and back.

Ryder and Beckett move closer, murmuring filthy promises and words of praise as they touch and tease her softly while I finish fully securing her.

By the time I'm done and standing behind her again, fingering that hot, wet pussy while finally freeing my cock from my pants, she's a desperate, gasping mess.

Completely immobilized.

Completely turned on.

And loving it. Needing it. Needing *me*.

"Color?" I murmur, guiding my cock to her pussy and rubbing it through her slick slit while I wait for her answer.

"Green," she whispers. "Green, *please.*"

"Fuck," Beckett says, his voice strained as he strokes her hair. "So beautiful. You're doing so fucking well, baby."

"Yes," Ryder murmurs, tracing the intricate pattern of ropes across her upper back. "We're so proud of you. Look at you, all trussed up and spread wide. Begging for more cock like you just can't get enough."

She makes a mewling sound of pure need, straining to arch her back, push against my cock, move in any way at all... and completely unable to do so.

And it finally snaps my control.

I grip her hips and push into her, groaning at the feel of her hot, tight walls closing around me. I can feel her quivering, shaking as she adjusts to the sudden fullness, but I know she wants to be overwhelmed, and I want to overwhelm her, so I don't stop.

I'm not even sure I fucking can.

I thrust deep, bottoming out and grinding into her lush, welcoming body with a curse.

"Yes," she pants. "Oh god, fuck me. Please keep fucking me."

I drive into her, over and over, loving the way she looks like this, bound in my ropes and spread out like an offering. But what I love even more is the way she moans and pleads for me to keep going, the way her pussy clenches around my shaft, the way her breath comes in ragged gasps and her body writhes, desperate to move, to take, to get more of what I'm giving her.

I love having her at my mercy, and knowing I'm giving her exactly what she needs.

I slide my hand between her thighs, finding her clit, and she screams.

"That's it," I groan, fucking her hard. "Let me hear how good it feels. Show me what a good girl you are. Beg for my cum. Beg me to fill you up too, just like Ryder and Beckett did."

"Yes, please," she pants, her body trembling as I drive into it, over and over, my own arousal racing so fast toward release that it's making me a little crazy. "I need it."

"Then come," I demand. "Come on my cock, freckles. Let me feel it. Milk the cum right out of me. Right the fuck now."

"Oh, god," she gasps, and then her body seizes up, her pussy clamping down on my shaft as a wail escapes her, her release rocking her so hard that it almost takes me with her.

It feels fucking incredible, like her body really is trying to pull my cum out and force me to empty my balls inside her. And I'm desperate to do it. I want nothing more than to know she's full of all three of us as I empty myself inside her.

But there's something I want even more than all that.

I want to give Lana everything.

I push in to the hilt, grinding against her as I knead her ass. I tug on the ropes around her wrists, leaning down to press hot, open-mouthed kisses against her glistening back as I force myself to hold on to my control.

"Tristan," she whimpers.

"Right here. Now turn your head. Do you see that wall?"

She obeys me slowly, panting as her body continues to clench around my cock with the aftershocks of her orgasm.

"Yes," she breathes.

"Do you know why there's nothing there?"

No shelves attached to it. No toys hanging from it. Nothing to impede the view.

"N-N-No," she stutters.

Beckett mutters a low, *fuck*, and Ryder groans.

This isn't the first time we've played at Eclipse, and they know exactly where I'm going with this.

"We're not alone in this club," I remind Lana, palming her ass. "Is exhibitionism a kink you're interested in exploring?"

She hesitates for a moment, then nods.

Ryder groans again, sounding almost wrecked.

It's a kink I know he particularly enjoys. I've always been more into watching others than being watched myself, and I know that, on some level, it has a lot to do with my scars. But Lana makes me want things I never have before, and she's not the only one open to exploring new things right now.

"I like it when the three of you watch me," Lana whispers.

"We know you do, love," Ryder says, "but we've got the option to turn that opaque wall right there into a window too. A flip of the switch, and it will become transparent. Then everyone in the club will be able to see in here."

"They'd see how fucking beautiful you look in Tristan's ropes," Beckett growls. "You'd be showing everyone how fucking lucky we are. They'd get to see you bound and submissive, spread out and fucked hard."

Lana's breath becomes ragged with excitement, and Ryder curses softly under his breath as he moves closer, circling her like a predator.

"Do you want that?" I ask, hooking my fingers in the ropes I wove around her body and pulling her back against me as my cock throbs inside her.

She whimpers a little, squirming in her restraints as she stares at the opaque viewing wall with wide eyes, as if she's picturing everything she just heard.

"Do you want other people to see how gorgeous you look like this?" I press her as her skin heats with another flush of arousal. "Do you want to show off how well you take our cocks? Just say the word, and we can show everyone out there who you really are. We'll show them that you're made for this. Made to be fucked. Made to be worshiped. Made to offer up your submission and fly high with pleasure."

A gorgeous shudder wracks her body, and her pussy squeezes my shaft in a rolling wave that leaves me groaning.

She's so responsive that it's almost intoxicating, but I need an answer. A verbal one. I need to hear her say it. But even before I do, her body is already answering for her, telling me without words everything I need to know.

And exactly what I was hoping to hear.

Tristan's cock throbs inside my pussy, and even though I've just come, I want more of it. I want him to go hard. I want him to make me come again.

And I think I want him to do it while the entire club watches.

Having sex in front of strangers isn't something I ever thought I'd be into, but with every word the three of them said about what it would be like to let other people see me, my arousal spiked even higher.

No one here will recognize me. I feel safe, and the blissful security of the ropes Tristan bound me in is only one small part of that. But more than that, I realize that I want to share this moment publicly. I love the idea of people seeing these three amazing men fuck me.

Somehow, it feels like that will take it beyond just fucking. Beyond kink, even. It will help imprint this moment like a photograph and make it feel even more real. It will turn it into something that can never be taken away from me. Something I can come back to, again and again, even after it's over.

"What do you say, little menace?" Beckett asks, his eyes burning into me and his cock hard again.

My mouth waters as I stare at it, but he asked me a question, so

I drag my eyes up to meet his and get a heated smile that makes me moan.

Ryder is looking at me just as intensely, the burning need in his eyes lighting me up inside, and the way Tristan is filling me up, gripping my hips and grinding against me, makes it hard to think.

But I don't really have to. He said it earlier, all I have to feel.

And right now, I feel sexy. Desirable. Bold.

All my self-consciousness is gone. Tristan said my body was perfect for his ropes, and I feel that too. I'm exactly where I want to be, and so turned on that there's absolutely no room left for doubt or shyness.

I lick my lips, then submit completely to my true desires.

"Yes," I whisper. "I want everyone to see this. Open it."

Tristan groans behind me, pulling out and sliding into me so slowly it's almost torture. Torture of the very best kind.

"So fucking hot," Beckett grunts as Ryder does something to the wall that turns it clear, just like they said.

The change is so abrupt that I gasp, reality hitting me like a jolt of adrenaline as our privacy disappears and I see the mass of kinky club goers just on the other side of the wall.

And then a few of them start to notice the change, turning more fully to face us. Looking at us. Looking at *me*.

"Oh fuck, love, look at them watching you," Ryder says with a low groan. "So fucking hot."

Tristan makes a hot, hungry sound of agreement as he slips his fingers under some of the ropes for leverage and starts to fuck me harder.

"Oh god," I gasp, even more aware of how completely restrained I am. I can't escape this. I can't do anything but take it.

Take it and let them all watch.

It's the most amazing thing I've ever felt, as if I haven't just submitted to these men, but I've surrendered all my inhibitions too.

A tall man covered in tattoos pulls his submissive in front of him, her back to his chest as they both watch me. He reaches around her, pinching her nipples through the thin black lace halter top she's wearing. The Dom next to them pushes a woman dressed in nothing but a pair of heels down to her knees and feeds her his dick, his gaze locked on me.

"Look what you're fucking doing to them," Beckett growls. "They want you, little menace, but they can't have you. You belong to us. Look at them watching you. Every fucking one of them is jealous of Tristan right now. Every man out there is imagining sliding into that sweet, wet pussy of yours. Wondering what you taste like. What it feels like to have your soft lips wrapped around his cock. Imagining those gorgeous fucking eyes of yours staring up at him while you moan with his cum sliding down your throat. You're a goddamn fantasy, you dirty little menace. But tonight, you're all ours."

I moan, his wonderfully filthy words doing things to me that ramp every sensation up even higher.

"Oh fuck, you like that, don't you, love?" Ryder groans.

"Yes," I gasp as Tristan's thrusts quicken, the sound of our bodies slapping together loud in the otherwise quiet room.

Ryder and Beckett stroke themselves as they watch us, and I'm shocked by how turned on the knowledge of their pleasure makes me. Theirs, and everyone out there who's watching. The weight of all those strangers' gazes on me is like a thousand caresses to my inflamed skin. It's a sensual freedom I've never known before, and it has me feeling completely uninhibited, almost like I'm flying.

"How does it feel?" Ryder's eyes burn into me. "How does it feel to be so fucking wanted?"

Pleasure ripples through me, like the slow build of another orgasm, even though I'm not sure I actually have another one in me.

"It feels—God, it's incredible," I pant.

"Fuck yeah, you are," Beckett says, his voice a guttural rumble.

"How many of those people out there do you think are getting off right now?" Ryder asks, his voice rough, his hand stroking his cock with slow, steady pulls. "How many are touching themselves while they watch you getting fucked?"

I shiver, the thought pushing me closer to the edge, until I'm not sure if this is an orgasm or something even more intense.

"Fuck, you feel so good," Tristan groans, his fingers digging into my hips as my back tries to arch, forcing me against the ropes.

"Show them how incredible you look when you come," Beckett demands. "Come all over Tristan's cock while they all watch from out there, wishing it was them."

"Oh god," I moan. "I... I don't think I can."

"You can," Ryder insists as Tristan slams into me again, almost making me believe it.

"Help her," Tristan rasps. "Touch her. Get her there."

Ryder's grin is wicked as he comes closer, his hand going to my face as he leans down to kiss me. Then he gives the ropes binding my torso to the bench a single tug, and they fall away.

"Quick-release knot," he says when I gasp, my back arching.

Ryder instantly takes advantage, sliding his hands under me to toy with my nipples.

"Oh god," I gasp. They're still sensitive from the clamps, and pleasure races down to my core as he pinches and tugs, rolling them between his fingers while Tristan keeps fucking me.

"That's it," Beckett rumbles, running his hand down my side and squeezing my ass. "Take it all, baby. Take him so fucking deep. Take him like everyone out there is dreaming of with you. Do you know how fucking jealous they are right now?"

Tristan pulls me upright, my knees resting on padded supports at the base of the bench and my arms still bound behind me as he holds me there and fucks into me hard.

"They can dream of it," he grunts, "but that's as far as it goes. Dreaming and looking. No one else fucks you. No one else touches you. Only us."

"You heard him," Beckett growls, his thick fingers playing over my clit. "Now say it."

"Only... only you. Only the three of you."

"Good girl," Beckett says, giving my clit piercing a tug as Tristan hits my g-spot.

I cry out, overwhelmed, and Ryder swings a leg over the bench so he's facing me, then grabs my face and kisses me again, swallowing my moans as his tongue teases mine.

I'm surrounded by them, and the possessive way they're handling me is pushing me toward the edge even faster.

"Oh, god," I whimper when Ryder breaks the kiss and lifts my breasts in his hands, sucking one of my nipples into his mouth while he teases the other with his fingers.

It's too much. As Beckett keeps stroking my clit and Tristan keeps fucking me, the sound becomes a high-pitched, keening wail, and the pleasure suddenly explodes into an orgasm that feels like a genuine out of body experience.

Subspace, a distant part of my mind whispers as my head falls back on Tristan's shoulder, wave after wave of pleasure rolling through me, each one taking me higher, until I'm floating in a sea of bliss that goes on and on and on.

Tristan swears, his hands tightening on my body and his hips stuttering as if he's finally losing his control. Then he's coming too, his cock pulsing and his body shuddering against mine as his release floods into me, filling me up, just the way he promised he would.

I genuinely don't know how long I float. I've brushed against the edge of subspace since starting to explore kink with these three, but I've never let go as completely like that before. I've never felt anything like it.

I finally start to come down from it as they carefully untie me, each one of them kissing me gently, touching and soothing me, as they hold me and pass me between them.

"Drink, baby," Beckett rumbles gently, holding a water bottle to my lips.

I do, the cool liquid soothing my throat.

"That's it," Ryder murmurs. "You did so well, love."

"Mmm," I hum, not sure I can find words just yet.

Tristan runs his hands over me, firmly and tenderly, almost as if he's examining each of my limbs. Then I realize that's exactly what he's doing, rubbing the faint marks his ropes left, turning and lifting each part of me to get a good look, checking me over protectively.

They all are, and I'm so overwhelmed by their care that tears prickle at my eyes.

"Hey," Ryder says, cupping my face and searching my eyes. "You good?"

I smile as I blink them away. "I'm fine. Perfect."

He gives me a soft smile, then kisses my forehead. "That's exactly what you are."

Once Tristan is finally satisfied, they settle around me, cuddling against me as they continue to feed me light snacks and encourage me to finish the water. I'm so unbelievably relaxed that it takes me a while to notice that the observation wall is opaque again.

Beckett catches me looking.

"Aftercare should always be private," he murmurs, his big hands stroking me in a way that's sensual and comforting without being sexual. "This part is just for us."

I sigh, leaning my head against his chest. "I'm glad."

His hand slows for a moment. "How do you feel about the scene?"

"I never knew I'd enjoy all of that," I tell him honestly. "Pain isn't something I could see the appeal of before, but the flogger took me right out of my head."

"It was fucking beautiful to see," he says. "All of it."

I bite my lip, still floating in a sea of endorphins as the various ways they pushed me replay in my head. Then I nod.

"God, yes. I never knew I'd enjoy the line between pleasure and pain like that, or be able to, um, to take two of you."

Ryder grins. "Fuck, that was hot. I'm so proud of you for letting us push you like that."

"It was amazing. But it was also a lot, being restrained was perfect after that. It made me feel..."

I stumble over my words, not finding the right ones. It made me feel so much.

"Secure," I finally settle on. "And god, it heightened everything."

Tristan turns my head toward him, and kisses me deeply, pulling back to rest his forehead against mine. "Thank you for trusting me with that."

"Thank you for knowing how much I needed it." I bite my lip, then glance toward the opaque wall. "It feels like you guys know some of my needs before I do."

Beckett rumbles a laugh, then kisses my neck, his lips trailing down my spine as he hugs me from behind. "Now, that's a fucking compliment."

My cheeks heat. "It's just the truth."

"You were so fucking sexy, love," Ryder murmurs. "You always are, but that was amazing."

It really was, and a twinge hits me as I look around the room. "Do we need to leave the club now that we're, um, done in here?"

I'm not up for more sex, but I don't want the night to be over.

"No," Beckett reassures me, settling me more firmly against him as he lounges back on the wide bed-like platform.

Somewhere, they even rustled up a few soft blankets, and it's cozy and... well, perfect.

"We're in no rush," Tristan murmurs, giving me a fond look.

Ryder pulls me in for another kiss, and it's almost scary how happy I am. The way they're touching me isn't going to lead to anything else, and as much as I love all the sex, I might even love this part more.

It's one of the last thoughts I have as I drift off to sleep, so deeply relaxed and satisfied that I don't even try to fight it.

My body feels more relaxed than I can ever remember after a scene like this. Not just sexually sated, but something deeper that I'm not willing to look at. Instead, I carefully disentangle myself from the others and get to my feet.

The room is quiet except for the soft breathing of the others. Lana is still fast asleep, looking soft and flushed and just as tempting in sleep as she does awake. Ryder and Tristan have both dozed off on either side of her, and it's far too tempting to pull her back into my arms, close my eyes, and stay a little longer.

Tempting, but dangerous. I was not fucking prepared for this.

I scrub a hand over my face, then turn away to grab my clothes. I've kept my feelings for Lana locked away for years, buried so deep I thought they'd never see the light of day.

No matter how good the sex is—and it's fucking phenomenal— it's not the time to unearth those feelings now.

Or ever.

I get dressed as quietly as I can, then slip out of the room, wondering if I should have stuck to my initial plan when Tristan first proposed this arrangement. I was determined not to let her touch me even after we all agreed to help her explore her kinks. I instinctively knew that if I broke, if I really got into this with her, there was a chance I would never recover from it.

But I did break, and while I'm not sure I was wrong about it wrecking me, what's done is done now. And I wouldn't give up these past few days for anything.

Still, right now, I need to clear my head.

The hallway outside the private room that our friend Dustin, Eclipse's owner, gave us for the night has mostly emptied out now, and I head toward the main area, hoping to find him.

"Looking for something I can help you with, sir?"

A curvy sub wearing a bracelet that tells me she came to play smiles at me as I pause near the St. Andrew's cross in the main play area, scanning the dimly lit area for the familiar face of my friend.

"I'm good," I tell her absently, finally catching sight of Dustin.

I grin at the sight of him. We've been friends for years, and the guy is even more heavily tattooed and pierced than I am.

He's also one of the main people who first encouraged me, Tristan, and Ryder to open Radiance—encouragement that he followed up with a lot of practical advice.

He's always been a good sounding board, and as I approach him, he takes one look at me and gets a knowing smirk on his face.

Fuck. He knows me too well, and I've got no doubt at all that he realizes some of the shit I'm currently so off kilter about after that incredible scene.

Then again, I guess that's why I sought him out.

"Well, well. Look who finally emerged," he says with a grin, nodding toward an empty barstool near the tall table he's leaning against. "I was hoping I'd get a chance to say hello."

"You know I wouldn't show up without doing that," I tell him, clapping his back when he pulls me in for a hug.

I slide onto the barstool he indicated and ask about his wife.

Dustin's eyes go warm. "Carolyn is great. She'll be sad she missed you."

"You'll have to tell her hello from all three of us."

"You know it, brother."

He turns to a passing server, flicking his fingers toward us, and a moment later, she comes over and slides a pitcher of water and a couple of glasses onto the table.

"I could use something stronger," I grunt, making him laugh as he pours and passes me a glass.

We both know alcohol and consent don't mix. It's why neither one of our clubs allows it, not on any night that play is allowed.

I take the water, though, and he raises his own glass in a mock toast, smirking. "I heard you drew a crowd. Don't tell me that wasn't a good time."

"It was a fucking great time," I say with a grin that feels a little feral.

My mind may still be reeling from all the feelings I can't seem to shove back down tonight, but Lana consenting to putting on that hot-as-fuck show of exhibitionism is something I'll never forget.

"Thanks for letting us have the room for the night," I add. "You know I owe you one now."

Dustin waves me off. "Don't mention it. That's what friends are for."

"That just means that you're gonna have to bring Carolyn out to L.A. one of these days so we can host the two of you at Radiance."

"She'd fucking love to get out to the coast like that," he says, "but not gonna lie, what I'm really interested in is checking out the new place you three are planning to open up. How's that coming along?"

"On track," I tell him, ignoring the twinge I get at the thought of what it will mean.

Not that I'm not fucking excited about it, because I am. It's a smart business move, and as proud as I am of Radiance, I'd be lying if I said I'm not itching to take some of what we learned from running the place and take things to the next level with our second location.

But fuck, it means moving out of Los Angeles.

Which means moving away from Lana.

I shut that train of thought down fast, and Dustin and I fall into some comfortable shop talk about the differences between the scene here versus out west, operating our clubs, and general management shit.

But after a while, the wily fucker steers the conversation back around to this surprise visit we dropped on him.

"So, the girl you brought in..."

He lets his words trail off, and I treat him to a dead-eyed stare that doesn't throw him off at all.

"What's her name again?" he asks with a shit-eating grin.

"Lana," I grunt. "Lana Reeves."

"Was it her first time in a kink club?"

My mind flashes back to the shock that ran through me that night she walked into Radiance, but that doesn't count since nothing happened.

"Yeah, pretty much. It's something she's, uh, been wanting to explore, so we thought we'd give her a treat since we were in the area."

He smirks. "A treat? Is that what we're calling it now."

I flip him off, then glance back toward the hallway I left when I catch the swing of long, wavy brunette hair out of the corner of my eye.

It's not Lana, but when I turn back, Dustin is looking at me curiously. "She means something to you."

"Of course she does. You remember Caleb, yeah? Plays for the NHL? She's his little sister. We grew up with her."

"Hm."

I raise an eyebrow. "What the fuck does 'hm' mean?"

He grins. "I've seen you play with subs before. I've seen all three of you scene with temporary partners over the years. But this was different, wasn't it?"

Fuck yeah, it was. Admitting it out loud feels like I'd be unleashing a shit show I'm not prepared for, though, so I just give him a hard stare that I know from experience would keep any submissive in this place quiet, and hold my tongue.

Too bad Dustin isn't a fucking submissive.

"She must be special," he pushes, that shit-eating grin back in place. "The way the three of you walked in with her. Hell, what I saw when you opened up the room..."

"What about it?"

"She means something to you," he says, dropping the shit stirring act and laying it out there plain and simple.

And fuck, hearing it like that makes my heart twist.

"Yeah." I clear my throat. "To all three of us."

Dustin waits a beat, then leans in. "But...?"

I let out a heavy sigh, running a hand through my hair. "But it's too fucking complicated, man. She's Caleb's sister, for one thing. No way would he be pleased to know what went on here tonight."

"Good thing he's not here then."

I glare at him, but the understanding look on his face makes me drop it. The truth is, I do need to unload this shit, and while my usual go-to for anything deep like this would be one of the men down the hall, I'm not going to bring it up with them when I can tell we're all struggling with something similar.

They're too close to it, but Dustin isn't.

"Even if that wasn't the case, she's settled in L.A. We haven't finalized the city for the new club, but we're down to three contenders and are just a few months away from making the move."

Dustin nods, but stays quiet as I drain the water glass, then pour another, really fucking wishing it was whiskey right now.

"Plus, she wants kids," I say, slamming the empty glass down on the table a little too hard. "I don't. Never have, and that's a fucking understatement. I'd be a shit father. Besides, what would it even look like? All four of us in a relationship?" I snort, shaking my head. "Fucking, doing a few scenes, sharing a bed, that's one thing. One very fucking temporary thing. But anything beyond that would get..."

I shake my head, a heavy weight settling on my chest.

Fuck, spilling all of that just worked me deeper into a funk, and that's a goddamn travesty after the incredible high from the scene we just shared with Lana.

Dustin leans forward. "It would get what, Beck? If you tried to make it not so interesting, things would get... interesting?"

I narrow my eyes at him. "Complicated."

346

The fucker *hmms* at me again, nodding as he holds my stare with an almost-smile on his face.

"What?" I demand.

Dustin just shrugs, that knowing look still in his eyes that kind of makes me want to punch him.

And also kind of makes me hope he has some amazing insight I've missed.

"Remember when I first met Carolyn?"

"'Course I do. Fuck, that demo you two did together was hot."

He strokes his chin, a predatory gleam appearing in his eyes. "Everything with that woman is hot." Then he shakes it off, focusing on me again. "Too hot, I figured at the time. Convinced myself that trying to take that combustible chemistry between us out into the real world was a fucking recipe for disaster. Hell, there were a dozen reasons why we wouldn't work. Our schedules alone made it fucking impossible, what with me primarily needing to work nights."

I frown, not sure where he's going with this. "You two are solid though, yeah?"

A look comes over his face that makes my heart clench again. "Oh, fuck yeah. She's my forever."

I knew that. Hell, anyone who's ever seen them together knows that.

"I'm happy for you, man."

He grins at me. "And I'm happy I pulled my head out of my ass. Once I did, it turned out, none of those reasons I talked myself around in the beginning ended up being as insurmountable as I first thought. Not once I got clear on my priorities."

"Priorities?"

He gives me a look like I'm an idiot. "My priority is Carolyn. Full fucking stop."

I don't know what to do with that. I get what he's saying when it comes to him and Carolyn. Like I said, I remember when they met. But this thing with Lana isn't the same situation at all.

Not that I can find the words to explain why—to him *or* to myself.

The silence stretches between us for a moment, then Dustin claps me on the shoulder and thankfully, changes the subject. After a few minutes, though, I start to get antsy.

"I should get back," I tell him, getting to my feet.

Dustin nods, reaching out to clasp my shoulder. "Take care, man. And remember, sometimes the things that seem impossible are the ones most worth fighting for."

I grunt in response, not trusting myself to speak. We say our goodbyes, and I head back toward the private room I left Lana and the guys in, my mind a whirlwind of conflicting thoughts and emotions.

When I slip back into the room, Tristan and Ryder are already stirring.

"Time to head out?" Ryder asks as Tristan cleans his glasses, then starts putting away the ropes.

I give him a look, an understanding passing between us without words. It's time to leave the club, yeah. And fuck, we're also almost to the end of this trip.

The guys get themselves ready, and I move to the bed where Lana's still sleeping peacefully. For a moment, I just look at her. She looks like a fucking dream, and my chest tightens at how beautiful she is like this.

Not that she isn't always, but tonight it's different. We staked a claim here, and temporary or not, it's gonna leave a mark on me.

She sighs in her sleep, her eyelids fluttering as she reaches for a warm body that's not next to her anymore.

I capture her hand and hold it in both of mine. "Come on, little menace. Time to wake up."

Her eyes open, still soft with sleep and a little out of focus. Then I squeeze her hand, and when she focuses on me, she smiles.

"Is it time to go?" she asks, her voice husky.

"Yeah," I say, brushing a strand of hair from her face. My fingers linger on her cheek for a second longer than necessary, and I'm tempted to kiss her.

But I'm also content with just this—the feel of her silky skin under my fingertips and the warm, trusting look she gives me that has my chest feeling tight again.

I clear my throat, then help her up, all three of us making a silent note of how worn out she still is. I'm not sure if it's the lupus or how hard we played, but Tristan, Ryder, and I are all in sync about the need to take a little extra care with her.

We help her get dressed, and when she tries to stifle a yawn as we head for the exit, I scoop her up into my arms, cradling her against my chest.

"Beckett!" She laughs, her eyes drowsy as she shakes her head. "You don't have to carry me."

Ryder snorts. "I'm pretty sure 'have to' isn't the right word for it, love."

"I want to," I admit, holding her gaze as Dustin's comment about priorities flashes through my mind.

A hint of a blush colors her cheeks, but after a second, she nods. "Well, okay. If you're sure."

"Sure? Trust me, little menace, there's nothing I want more than to have you in my arms right now."

It's the most honest I've ever been about emotional shit, and when she gives me a sweet, sleepy smile, resting her head on my shoulder and relaxing against me, I can't even regret it.

LANA

THE INSISTENT BUZZ of my phone drags me from the depths of sleep. By the time I'm fully conscious, the ringing has stopped, leaving me in disorienting silence. I blink, taking in the unfamiliar hotel room as memories of the night before, at Eclipse, flood back, making me smile.

At least, until I realize I'm all alone in the bed.

I sit up, running my hands over the sheets. They're cool, not a trace of body heat left on either side of me, so the guys have been up for a while.

A pang of disappointment hits me, and I silently curse myself— well, the lupus, at least—for robbing me of one last morning sandwiched between warm, muscular bodies. I'm tired of being so much more fatigued than normal.

But even worse is the thought that this *is* my new normal.

I sigh, then shake it off. It's our last day on the road, and I want to savor every moment, so I might as well not waste any more time wallowing in my thoughts. Besides, I *am* grateful that they let me sleep. It's just one more way they've gone out of their way to take care of me.

But we're close to my hometown now. We'll get in today for sure, since there's no convenient bad weather to hold us up at this point, so I'll have to tuck those feelings away like a treasured gift now. Whatever this is between us, and I don't just mean the amazing sexual side of it, it's about to be over.

Before I can wallow too deeply in that bittersweet thought, my phone starts buzzing again. Mom's name flashes on the screen, and I brace myself before answering.

"Lana! Finally," Mom says without any greeting. "Where are you? I can't believe you're still dilly dallying when you could have avoided all of this by booking a flight."

I grit my teeth, but don't say anything. She's never going to care about how much I hate the idea of ever getting on a plane again, and that makes it feel a lot like she just doesn't care about *me*.

It's something I haven't let myself think about quite so frankly before, but after spending all this time with three men who go out of their way to care for me, it's a lot harder to pretend that's not how it is.

"You were supposed to be here days ago!" Mom goes on, her voice shrill with stress, making me wince. "Are you ever going to make it?"

"Good morning to you too, Mom," I say, trying to keep my tone light to keep the peace. "And yes, we're close. We'll be getting in today, I promise."

She huffs, clearly not appeased. "It's practically Christmas Eve already! There's so much to do, and you're gallivanting across the country."

I bite back a sigh. I wish she was bringing up Christmas Eve because it was important to her to spend the holiday together as a family, and while that *is* important to her, it's for appearances sake. God forbid I miss the party she sets so much store in throwing every year.

"I know, I'm sorry," I tell her. "We got delayed by weather, but we're making good time now."

"Well, I suppose it's better late than never," she says with a huff. Then her tone takes on that particular lilt that always makes my stomach clench. "Though it's a shame you missed your sister's party last night."

And there it is.

"Vivian and Kyle really do host the most delightful gatherings," she gushes. "The Morgans were there, and the Turners as well! Even that charming news anchor from channel five!" The wistfulness in her voice is palpable. "It was such a lovely opportunity to connect with influential people in town. Your father and I had a wonderful time."

The unspoken comparison hangs heavy in the air. Vivian is their perfect daughter, hosting picture-perfect parties, rubbing shoulders with the kind of people my parents think matter thanks to marrying the son of the mayor, and fitting into the mold of everything that matters to them—a mold that's always fit me poorly, like a too-tight pair of uncomfortable jeans that pinch at the waist.

Actually, no. More like a mold that just *doesn't* fit me.

"Her party does sound nice," I manage, hating how inauthentic I feel when I automatically slip back into my lifelong habit of trying appease her. "I'm glad you enjoyed it."

"You could have enjoyed it too," Mom says with a snap to her voice. "Or at least considered how much trouble your sister went through to organize the party when you made your travel plans."

I bite my tongue to keep from pointing out that, knowing Vivian, I'm sure she hired a party planner and caterers and couldn't have cared less whether I attended or not.

Mom doesn't notice my silence as she launches into more details about the party, each word feeling like another tiny needle pricking my self-esteem.

I make small noises of interest until she finally winds down. She finally ends the call when I manage to interject something about needing to get ready so we can get back on the road. As soon as we hang up, I sigh.

I toss my phone aside and flop back onto the pillows, staring at the ceiling. The warm cocoon of contentment I woke up in has evaporated, replaced by an all-too-familiar weight of inadequacy. It's not just the end of my arrangement with Tristan, Ryder, and Beckett that's weighing on me now. Mom's call was a reminder that returning home also means returning to all the expectations that come with it.

The bedroom door bursts open, startling me out of my thoughts.

"What?" I gasp, scrambling upright.

Tristan, Ryder, and Beckett all file in, each wearing a bright red Santa hat. The sight is so unexpected and ridiculous that I burst into laughter, the tension in my shoulders evaporating.

"Where on earth did you get those?" I ask, shaking my head in amusement.

Ryder grins, adjusting his hat with a flourish. "We have our ways."

"What he means is, we have connections," Beckett deadpans, making Tristan snort.

I grin. "Well, so far, I like what these 'connections' are hooking you up with."

"We noticed that yesterday." Tristan's eyes gleam behind his glasses.

I blush but can't help smiling. "I enjoyed it."

His eyes soften. "I'm glad."

Ryder chuckles. "Is 'enjoying it' what we're calling all that sexy whining and begging you were doing on the road yesterday?"

He means when they were edging me to death, while I was wearing the butt plug. Which means...

"Wait. Did you buy those hats at a sex shop?" I burst out, half scandalized and half amused.

He waggles his brows. "A gentleman never reveals his secrets."

"Good thing none of us are gentlemen," Beckett mutters under his breath, his eyes heated as they roam over me.

I bite my lip. I couldn't agree more.

But that doesn't mean we have time to linger in bed this morning. Especially not with the three of them insisting I eat a proper breakfast and stay well-hydrated before we leave.

As much as I love the sex we've been having, I don't even mind. The care they're taking with me warms my heart in ways I wasn't prepared for, and by the time we hit the road, they're not the only ones in good spirits.

Once we're on the highway, a festive energy takes over the car.

We sing along—badly—to Christmas carols, swap embarrassing stories, and play ridiculous road trip games. Unlike the sexy edging from yesterday, it's innocent fun.

But it's also everything I could have hoped for on this last leg of our journey. I've gotten so much closer to all of them on this trip, and even if we can't continue the carnal side of our relationship, it feels like a reminder that this, at least, is something that doesn't have to go away.

Although the high-spirited banter is more than just a reminder. It's something they're doing on purpose, and I know it.

None of us want to dwell on the fact that in a few short hours, this magical bubble we've been living in will pop. I had enough wallowing in disappointment this morning, though. Right now, I want to soak up every last second of laughter, every casual touch, every inside joke before we have to part ways.

So much has changed in such a short period of time. These men used to be Caleb's friends, people I knew in passing. Sure, I had huge crushes on them for years, but never with any hope of anything coming of it.

But now I know the taste of Ryder's skin, the sound Tristan makes when he comes, the feeling of Beckett's arms around me. I know their hopes and fears, their quirks and passions, and they know so many of mine.

I've got no doubt that they'll stay in touch, but they'll also be moving out of L.A. soon. They'll be busy with their new club. They'll think of me fondly—or at least, I hope they will—but it won't be the same.

And I'm going to miss them so fucking much.

The realization crashes over me as we turn off the highway onto a quiet stretch of road. My parents' house is maybe thirty minutes away now, and suddenly, I can't breathe.

"Ryder," I say, my voice choked as I interrupt a funny story he's telling. "Stop the car."

He glances at me in the rearview mirror, concern etching his features. "You okay, love?"

"Please," I whisper. "Just... stop the car."

Without another word, he pulls over onto the shoulder. The second we're stopped, I'm fumbling with my seat belt. I stumble out of the car, gulping in deep breaths of the crisp winter air.

"Lana?" Tristan's voice is gentle as he approaches. "What's wrong?"

I turn to face them, all three now out of the car and watching me with worried expressions. My heart clenches.

"I'm okay," I say quickly, holding up a hand. "Physically, I mean. This isn't about my lupus. I just... I needed a moment."

They exchange glances, clearly unconvinced, but give me space. I take a deep breath, gathering my courage for what I need to say.

"This trip," I begin, my voice shaky. "It's meant so much to me. More than I can possibly express. I know the three of you agreed to help me explore kink, but I feel like it turned into so much more than that. I feel like I've found a part of myself I didn't even know was missing."

Dragging in a deep breath, I look at each of them in turn.

"I just needed to thank you for that before we end this. To thank you for seeing me, for pushing me, for... everything. It's honestly been one of the best Christmases of my life, and it's not even Christmas yet." I laugh a little self-consciously, biting my lip before I whisper, "I'll never forget it."

For a moment, nobody moves.

Then Ryder steps forward, cupping my face in his hands. His lips crash into mine, stealing my breath in a searing kiss.

When we part, his eyes are blazing. "You, Lana, are extraordinary," he murmurs. "Don't ever let anyone make you think otherwise. These past days with you have been... fuck, they've been incredible."

Before I can respond, Tristan is there, pulling me into his arms. His kiss is softer but no less intense, and when he pulls back and lifts my hand, deliberately pressing my palm against the scarred side of his face as he holds my gaze, my heart melts.

"It's meant a lot to me too," he says quietly, echoing my own words back. "Thank you, freckles."

My eyes sting at the nickname he's given me during this trip. Not just because it's a sign of how much closer we've gotten, but because of what it says about how he sees me.

Something I grew up hiding, thinking was a flaw, being *told* was a flaw, he finds beautiful.

I give him a soft smile, overwhelmed by emotion. And then Beckett is there, his strong arms enveloping me. His kiss is fierce, almost desperate.

"If this trip changed you," he rumbles against my lips, "it changed us too. It changed *me*. Don't ever doubt that."

We stand there for a long moment, his forehead resting against mine, sharing breaths. Part of me wants to beg them to keep going, to never stop. To ask if maybe, just maybe, we could find a way to make this work beyond our little bubble.

But the words stick in my throat.

What they each just said was so beautiful that I'll never forget it—but I'm also intensely aware of what they *didn't* say.

That they want more.

That they'll miss this the way I already do, with an ache deep in my chest and a choking tightness in my throat.

That they don't want it to end.

So, with a shaky breath and an even shakier smile, I finally step back. "Thank you for stopping. We should probably get going, though."

I tell myself it's a good thing none of them said any of those words, because even if they did want it, it's still not really possible. Not for the four of us together. Who does that? Not with them moving away from L.A. soon. Not with...

Well, not with a lot of things. But listing out all the roadblocks to what I'll never have anyway isn't helping me let them go, so I stop and just focus as much as I can on enjoying these last few moments with them.

Half an hour later, we pull up to my parents' house.

My stomach twists with a mix of emotions, and before I can decide if there are any last, private words I want to say to them while I still have a chance, the front door swings open, Caleb leading the way with a huge grin and my parents following him.

"Hey, you finally made it!" my brother exclaims as he reaches us, clapping Beckett on the back before moving to hug Tristan and Ryder in turn.

He turns to me last, ruffling my hair like he did when I was a kid before turning me in for a brief, tight hug. "Good to see you, sis."

I barely have time to respond before he's releasing me and turning back to the guys. "How was the drive?"

Reality comes crashing back with a vengeance as I watch them interact. These aren't just the men I've spent the last week falling for. They're Caleb's best friends. Whatever fantasy my heart might be holding on to about somehow making something work with them is blown to pieces by the reminder of just how complicated it would all be.

No matter how much I want Tristan, Ryder, and Beckett, I'd hate to drive a wedge between them and my brother.

"Lana," my father says gruffly, giving me a short nod which passes for a greeting. "Let's get your bags out of the boys' car so you don't hold them up. Which ones are yours?"

I point them out, then my mother pulls me away, looking me up and down with a critical eye.

"We're glad you finally made it, dear, but please tell me you've only let yourself go because of being on the road, and this isn't some new trend from being out in California."

"What?"

"You're not wearing any makeup," she says, reaching out to brush my cheek with a tut. "Your freckles are showing."

I flinch internally, feeling about two inches tall. But before I can muster a response, Tristan speaks up.

"If you ask me," he says, his voice firm, "those freckles are one of her best features. They bring out the sparkle in her eyes."

My mother blinks, clearly taken aback by being contradicted.

I don't think anyone else even heard, but the warmth blooming in my chest as we're all ushered inside does a lot to heal over the sting of my mother's constant criticism.

"Will you be staying to catch up with Caleb?" she asks the guys as we all enter the front room.

Before they can respond, my father speaks up. "We've only got one of the guest rooms free, Kate," he says to Mom with a frown. "I'm sure these boys don't want to all cram in there together."

Caleb snorts. "They don't give a shit about that."

"Language, Caleb," Mom says with no real bite to it.

He rolls his eyes, and Ryder smirks.

"We've got no problem sharing if you don't mind having us, Mrs. Reeves."

Even though he doesn't look my way, the memory of just how very much they did *not* mind sharing—either a single bed, or me— has my cheeks heating.

"You're always welcome here," Mom says to him. "Of course we'd love to have you."

"That's very kind of you." Tristan steps in smoothly. "We'd be happy to stay tonight. Thank you."

Caleb heads back outside with them to grab some of their luggage and my father disappears deeper into the house. Before Mom can start in on me again about who knows what, my sister Vivian sweeps in, her perfect hair and immaculate outfit making me feel even more disheveled.

My nephew Oliver trails behind her, and I can't believe how much he's grown since I last saw him in person. With his blond hair, gap-toothed smile, and bright hazel eyes, he's adorable.

"There you are!" Vivian exclaims when she sees me, air-kissing my cheek. "We were starting to wonder if you'd make it at all."

I force a smile. She really is our mother's daughter. "It's good to see you, Vivian."

The men come back inside, and Caleb immediately drops the bag he's carrying and scoops up Oliver, dangling him upside down as he laughs and squirms.

Then Oliver catches sight of the other three men, and his eyes widen a bit as Caleb sets him down. It's been a while since he's seen them, and since he's only five, he probably doesn't remember them all that well.

He looks between all three of them, his attention lingering on Beckett, who towers over everyone else in the room.

"Whoa," Oliver breathes. "You have so many pictures on you."

Beckett blinks, clearly caught off guard by the boy's fascination. He looks down at himself. "Uh, my tattoos?"

Vivian's mouth purses in disapproval, and I fight not to roll my eyes at her judgmental attitude.

Oliver scrambles down from Caleb's arms and cautiously approaches Beckett. "Can I see?"

"Oliver," Vivian says sharply.

"Chill, sis," Caleb laughs, rolling his eyes. "Beckett doesn't bite."

Technically, he does, a thought that has my face heating all over again. But those dirty thoughts are washed away by fond amusement as I watch Beckett shift awkwardly, clearly unsure how to handle this interest from a five-year-old. He clears his throat, then crouches down to Oliver's level.

"Sure, buddy. Uh, take a look."

Oliver steps closer, poking at the intricate designs on Beckett's hands and arms, and chattering at him in a stream of consciousness about other "pictures" he thinks would look good on Beckett.

"I could help color them in for you if you want," I hear him offer, blinking big hazel eyes up at Beckett. "You just got the outlines here."

"Uh," Beckett starts, glancing back down at the black linework like he has no idea what to say.

Luckily for him, Oliver moves right along, rambling about a million other things that tug at my heart to hear, just because they're so sweetly innocent.

Beckett is so clearly a bit out of his depth, but he's so patient with my nephew. It's a side of the burly, gruff man that I never expected to see, and I can't seem to draw my gaze away from the two of them.

After a moment, my mother's voice cuts through the chatter.

"Lana, dear, come help in the kitchen. We've got cookies to finish for tomorrow's party."

It's not a request—it's an order. But as she bustles me off toward the kitchen, I glance back at the guys with a twinge of longing. They're being led in the opposite direction by Caleb, Oliver tagging along and still chattering, and they don't look back.

Probably for the best. They're not mine, and what we had is over. I just need to accept that.

MOM DRAGS Vivian into the kitchen to finish up the cookies too. I tie on an apron and join my sister at the counter, and the scent of vanilla and cinnamon wraps around me like a comforting blanket, momentarily distracting me from the whirlwind of emotions I'm feeling.

"Where's Kyle?" I ask, realizing I haven't seen my brother-in-law yet.

Vivian doesn't look up from the cookie dough she's rolling out. "Oh, he had some work stuff to take care of today. You know how it is." There's something in her voice, a slight tightness that wasn't there before, but it's gone so quickly I wonder if I imagined it. "He'll be at the party tomorrow night, of course."

Mom bustles over, flour dusting her perfectly pressed slacks. "Kyle's been so busy lately," she says, pride evident in her voice. "He's really moving up in the firm. On track for partner, I hear. Isn't that right, Vivian?"

Vivian murmurs a quiet affirmative without looking up from the cookie dough, no doubt just as focused on getting that perfect as she is with everything else in her life.

I sigh softly, not liking my own bitter thoughts. My sister really does do everything right according to my parents, though, and her husband is no different. He's not just well-connected; he's also successful and ambitious in a field they approve of—law. In other words, he's the perfect husband for their perfect daughter.

"It's too bad Wade couldn't make it this year," Mom says out of the blue. "I was looking forward to having him at the party this year. There are definitely a few people on the guest list who I'm sure he'd appreciate an introduction to."

My stomach clenches as I freeze for a moment, my cookie cutter hovering over the dough. With everything that happened during the road trip, I sort of put the fact that I haven't told her about the breakup yet out of my mind.

I know I need to find a time to do it, but she's almost as enamored of Wade as she is of Kyle, and I'm just not up to having that conversation right now. Not with my emotions still reeling, and not in front of Vivian, either.

Thankfully, Mom was just getting in another subtle dig at me, not looking for actual answers on Wade's absence. So when I make a non-committal sound and refocus on the cookies, she happily rolls right into other topics.

"How are things going with your job, Lana?" she asks. "Your father was just talking to Richard the other day, but he didn't mention anything about that promotion you were hoping for."

Richard Sanders isn't just my boss, he's one of my father's friends. Saying I'm hoping for a promotion is a bit of a stretch, though. My parents are the ones always pushing me to move up in the company.

"It's going fine, Mom," I tell her, knowing full well she won't be interested in hearing how unfulfilling and stifling I find the job.

"Fine?" she repeats, her lips tightening for a moment. "Honestly, Lana, I thought you'd be further along by now. Your father pulled a lot of strings to get you that position, you know."

I bite my lip, fighting back the urge to remind her that I never asked for his help. That the job was thrust upon me, a "favor" Dad did to me that I never asked for and am constantly reminded of.

"Did you use orange zest in this dough?" I ask in an attempt to change the subject.

"Lemon," Mom says. "The flavor pairs better with the frosting."

Vivian's lips tilt up in what could almost pass for a smile. "The citrus is a nice touch. Remember those orange-cranberry cookies we used to make? Those were always my favorite."

Mom tilts her head. "Oh, I do. Why haven't I made those recently? They really were divine."

"Maybe we could do a few batches this year?" I suggest, feeling a spark of hope for a moment of genuine connection.

Mom tuts, shaking her head. "There really isn't time. And really, we certainly don't need to add more carbs to the party menu, now do we?"

"But... it's Christmas."

"And there are plenty of festive foods that we can enjoy while still being mindful of our figures, hm?"

I glance at Vivian as my mother speaks, and to my surprise, I think I catch a subtle roll of her eyes.

"Is that why we're doing truffle mashed potatoes?" she asks.

I grin. "Oh god, those are delicious."

"Well, we do have a delightful recipe for a Brussels sprouts gratin that I think everyone will love on the menu," Mom says.

"Mmm, Brussels sprouts," Vivian says almost playfully.

Mom gives her a little tut, but smiles. "You like them."

Vivian starts sliding the cookie shapes onto a baking pan. "I like the butternut squash and sage risotto too."

"And your sweet potato casserole," I throw in. "Nothing tastes more like Christmas than that."

"Oh, we're not doing that this year," Mom says just as Caleb and the guys pass by the doorway.

Ryder tosses me a playful wink, but his smiles slips a little as he reads the disappointment on my face.

"No sweet potato casserole?" I repeat, hoping my voice doesn't sound as tight as it feels. I clear my throat. "It's my favorite."

"It will be good for you to try something new this year," Mom says dismissively as Caleb leads his friends into the living room. "I got the new recipe for the Brussels sprouts from Kyle's mother. She says he loves it, and if it's good enough for the mayor's table, it's good enough for ours."

"Of course," I murmur as Vivian turns away to slide the cookies into the oven. "I'm sure it'll be delicious."

I'm also sure I'm being ridiculous for feeling emotional about a simple dish, so I brush that aside as we move on to dinner preparations, throwing myself into chopping vegetables and stirring sauces until everything is ready and I can finally escape upstairs to my old bedroom to get myself ready for dinner.

As I pass the living room, I catch sight of Tristan, Ryder, and Beckett laughing with Caleb, their easy camaraderie evident. A familiar twinge of longing tugs at my heart, but I hurry past before they can see me. What we had is over, and Caleb would probably find it awkward if I tried to intrude on his time catching up with his friends.

I find my luggage waiting in the room I grew up in. It's been transformed into a generic guest room, something my parents did as soon as I moved out, but it's still where I stay each time I come back to visit.

The walls that once held my posters and dreams are now adorned with tasteful, impersonal art, all traces of my childhood erased, but I still find a bit of comfort just in being between these four walls. I wasn't always happy here, but it was still *my* space. A private sanctuary that I was free to dream in, even if I learned to keep those dreams to myself.

I open my suitcase, debating what to wear. My fingers linger on the soft fabric of the new clothes the guys bought me during our trip. Each piece feels like a tangible reminder of the woman I became on the road—bold, authentic, free. But as I glance at the prim dress hanging in the closet, clearly left by my mother as a not-so-subtle suggestion, I falter.

It will be easier if I don't rock the boat, so with a resigned sigh, I reach for the safer option. The one they'll approve of.

Freshly changed, I make my way back downstairs. As I near the bottom of the stairs, I hear Oliver's excited voice coming from the living room.

"And then the Millennium Falcon goes whoosh! It's got so many pieces, like a bazillion! Mom says it's too comp-uh-cated for me, but I really, really want it for Christmas. Do you think Santa will bring it?"

I peek around the corner to see Oliver, eyes shining with enthusiasm as he talks Beckett's ear off about what I have no doubt is a coveted Lego set.

I half expect to find Beckett looking a little shell-shocked and trying to escape, but to my surprise, he's crouched down to Oliver's level, nodding seriously as he listens.

"I'm not up on what Santa's planning, kid," Beckett rumbles, a hint of a smile softening his usually stern features. "But the toy sounds pretty cool."

"It is," Oliver gushes, beaming up at him. "If I get it, you can help me put it together if you want."

"I'm sure Caleb's friend doesn't have time to be playing with Legos," Vivian says, swooping in to collect her son and bustle him toward the dinner table. "Come along, Oliver. Best behavior now."

He grumbles, but follows directions as Beckett pushes himself to his feet, meeting my eyes for a moment. There's something sweet and tender there that takes the sting out of hearing my sister refer to him as *Caleb's* friend, and I find myself smiling back when his lips quirk up.

"You're not up on Santa's plans?" I tease him quietly, the image of the men in their silly, festive hats fresh in my mind. "That's not how it looked this morning."

He snorts, amusement glinting in his eyes.

"That was a one-time thing, little menace," he murmurs as we follow Vivian and Oliver to the table.

Caleb catches his attention as we take our seats, and I settle in as the conversation flows around me.

Then I notice something unexpected on the table. There, nestled between the turkey and the Brussels sprouts, is a dish of sweet potato casserole.

My brow furrows in confusion.

"I thought she didn't make it this year," I murmur, more to myself than anyone else.

Ryder, seated next to me, leans in close. "Sweet potato casserole? I heard it was missing from the line up earlier," he says casually. "Can't have that, though. It's a Christmas favorite."

"You like it too?"

He just smiles at me, and I remember his wink from earlier. He doesn't mean *a* Christmas favorite. He means it's one of *my* favorites.

"But... where did it come from?" I ask, a lump forming in my throat because I think I already know the answer.

"I ran out and picked it up," he says like it's nothing.

My stomach swoops. It's such a small gesture in the big scheme of things, but the thoughtfulness of it overwhelms me.

"Thank you."

"Anytime," he murmurs, reaching for the casserole dish and serving me some. "You *do* have to share, though."

I laugh as he adds some to his plate as well.

With so many of us around the table, there's no shortage of conversation, and before long it inevitably turns to Caleb's hockey career.

Dad leans forward, his eyes shining with pride. "So, son, tell us how the season's going. I hear you're on track for the playoffs?"

Caleb grins, his easy-going nature on full display. "Yeah, we're doing pretty well. Coach says if we keep this up, we've got a real shot at the cup this year."

"We're so proud of you," Mom beams, reaching over to pat Caleb's hand. "We always knew you'd do great things. They're lucky to have you."

Caleb shrugs. "It's a team sport, but we're definitely gelling nicely this season."

"Yeah, yeah, NHL superstar," Ryder drawls, a mischievous glint in his eye. "But can you still score on Tristan? I seem to remember him shutting you down pretty regularly back in the day."

Caleb grins easily. "Only reason I improved."

Tristan smiles, a glint in his eyes as he gives my brother a little shit. "Have you, though?"

"Hey, now!"

Beckett snorts. "It's a valid question, Caleb. I distinctly remember catching you face-planting on the ice the last time I had ESPN on. Is that the 'improvement' you're talking about?"

The table erupts in laughter, and I join in. It's nice to see this side of the guys, the easy friendship they've always shared with Caleb. For a moment, I let myself imagine being a part of that, not just as Caleb's little sister, but as... something more.

"Seems to me there's one way to find out," Ryder says, grinning widely as he looks at his friends. "Does that pond behind the old Miller place still freeze over at this time of year?"

"I've still got gear stored at Grandma Meg's," Tristan says, taking off his glasses and polishing them as he gives Caleb a playfully challenging look. "Unless you're not up to hitting the ice without all those heavy hitters backing you up."

"Oh, it's on," Caleb says gleefully. "And you know we can probably round up some more guys to make it a little more interesting."

They keep shit-talking while they plan out their potential pickup game, but as dinner winds down, Caleb leans back in his chair, turning his attention back onto me.

"What?" I ask as he grins at me silently.

He shrugs, still smiling. "You look good, sis. That west coast air must really agree with you."

"What?" I repeat, caught completely off guard.

He waves a hand toward me, as if he's taking in my whole appearance. "You look, I dunno, kind of radiant. Just more relaxed and happy than I've seen you in a while. Back me up here guys. Living out in L.A. is good for her, isn't it?"

I feel a flush creep over my cheeks as Tristan, Ryder, and Beckett all murmur agreement. The weight of their stares makes it clear that they know just as well as I do that it's not the California sun responsible for all that.

"Thanks," I murmur, even though I know he'd be having an

entirely different reaction if he actually knew what—or rather, who —was responsible for my newfound radiance.

"Oh, I don't know, Caleb," my mother puts in, her eyes narrowing a little as she gives me a critical look. "I think Lana looks a bit tired. Are you remembering your sunscreen out there, dear?" She tuts, shaking her head. "It's not just more freckles you need to worry about. I'm already seeing some fine lines around your eyes. It's never too early to consider Botox. Thirty will be here before you know it."

I blink, glancing at Vivian in some misbegotten quest for solidarity, given that she's the one actually over thirty. I'm only twenty-six, for fuck's sake. But my sister's skin is flawless, of course, and she's busy quietly admonishing Oliver for his manners, not paying attention to the way Mom is nitpicking my appearance.

Caleb's attention has also moved on, back to something about hockey, and I force a smile, used to these little jabs by now. "I'll keep that in mind, Mom."

Thankfully, dinner is just about done, and as we clear the table and start on cleanup, I feel the weight of the day settling on my shoulders.

Vivian gathers up a sleepy Oliver, making her exit with promises to see us all tomorrow for the party preparations. The rest of us migrate to the living room, settling in for some post-dinner conversation, but I can't quite shake the feeling of emotional heaviness, and find myself not participating so much as just existing on the periphery.

I'm hyper-aware of Tristan, Ryder, and Beckett's presence. They're so close, lounging on the couch and laughing with Caleb about old times, but feel impossibly far away. They aren't ignoring me. If anything, it almost feels like they're providing a buffer to my fatigue by keeping up the lively conversation. Still, I'd give anything for a moment alone with them even if I'm not sure what I'd say if I got it.

We already had our moment of closure earlier.

It doesn't matter anyway, since I don't get the chance, but later, lying in bed in the sterile-feeling guest room, I miss the comforting feel of three warm bodies around me.

I roll onto my side, hugging a pillow to my chest. It's a poor substitute for what I really want, but I suppose I'll get used to it.

I'll have to.

LANA

THE NEXT MORNING, insistent rapping on my door drags me from a fitful sleep. "Lana, time to get up!" Mom's voice chirps through the wood, far too chipper for... I squint at the bedside clock and groan as I realize it's barely seven o'clock.

"Coming," I call back, my voice still rough with sleep. As I drag myself out of bed, a familiar heaviness settles into my bones. The fatigue is hitting me hard today, but I can't tell Mom that. Not without bringing up my lupus diagnosis.

I can't keep it from my parents forever, but I know it will be just one more disappointment to them once I tell them the truth. One more way I've failed to be the child they truly wanted. And I just can't deal with that right now.

Instead, I paste on a smile, get myself ready for the day, then head downstairs, ready to be conscripted into party prep.

"There you are," Mom says as I enter the kitchen. "I was beginning to think you'd sleep the day away. Now, we need to get started on the hors d'oeuvres. The caterers are handling most of it, of course, but you know I like to add a personal touch."

"Uh huh," I answer, just to reassure her that I'm listening. I know she doesn't actually want or need my input.

Something she proves as we get to it, chattering away in a familiar litany of my siblings' accomplishments. Today's version includes an update on Vivian's latest charity project, praise for Caleb's recent game-winning goal, and more talk of Kyle working toward becoming a partner at his law firm, complete with a few subtle digs about my own failure to get a promotion yet.

I half tune it out, making small sounds of feigned interest just to satisfy her as I let my thoughts wander, fighting off the exhaustion I'm still feeling.

"Did you hear me, Lana?"

"Sorry, what?" I ask at her sharp tone, dropping a serving spoon with a clatter when she startles me out of my thoughts.

She sighs, giving it a pointed look until I pick it back up. "I said, it's a shame you couldn't have arrived earlier. There's still so much to do before the party."

I give her a tight smile. "Well, I'm here now. What else can I help with?"

She immediately starts rattling off a list, and just as I'm resigning myself to a day of thinly veiled criticism and exhausting tasks, salvation arrives in the form of three familiar figures sauntering into the kitchen.

"Morning, Mrs. Reeves," Ryder grins, charm oozing from every pore. "Hope we're not interrupting."

"Not at all," Mom smiles, clearly won over. "What can we do for you boys? Did you already get breakfast?"

Tristan steps forward, adjusting his glasses. "We did earlier, with Caleb. Thank you, ma'am. We were just about to head over to see my grandmother now."

"How is Margaret?" Mom asks, making me want to roll my eyes.

I've never heard a single person call Tristan's grandma by her full given name other than my mother.

"She's doing really well, thank you. But when she heard Lana was in town, she insisted we bring her along today for a visit. You don't mind if we steal her for a bit, do you?"

I hold my breath, hardly daring to hope for an escape.

Mom hesitates, glancing at the half-prepared appetizers. "Well,

I suppose we are mostly done here. If it's really that important to your grandmother..."

"It is," Tristan says firmly as I snort, quickly trying to hide it with a light cough. She's sure singing a different tune than she was a few minutes ago, though.

Luckily for me, appearances are everything to her, so she reluctantly agrees, and as we all head for the door, Caleb catches up with us.

"Mind if I tag along?" he asks with an easy grin, slinging his arm over Tristan's shoulders. "Been a while since I've seen Grandma Meg."

Tristan grins. "She'd love it."

We all pile into the car, and as we pull away from the house, I feel the tension in my shoulders start to ease. Maybe it's the company, maybe it's the brief reprieve from Mom's expectations, or more likely it's both, but suddenly, I feel like I can breathe again.

"Thanks for the rescue," I murmur to Tristan.

He gives me a soft smile that makes my heart flutter. "Anytime, freckles."

"Wait," I say as he takes a turn I wasn't expecting. "This isn't the way to your grandmother's house, is it?"

He laughs. "Nope. She's still over on Rockford Drive, but we've got to make a very important stop first."

"Where?" I ask, a little thrill of adventure going through me that reminds me of all the random, offbeat places we stopped on the road trip.

Tristan grins, then mimes zipping his lips, making me laugh. A few minutes later, we pull into the parking lot of a quirky thrift shop whose windows are dripping with gaudy holiday decorations.

"Um, here?"

Ryder leans forward from the backseat. "Tristan didn't tell you? Grandma Meg's house has a dress code this time of year."

I laugh. "What does that mean?"

"She insists on everyone wearing an ugly Christmas sweater," Tristan says as we all get out of the car. "It's a tradition. She says it keeps everyone from taking themselves too seriously."

I smile. "I love it."

Inside the store, we fan out, each on a mission to find the most outrageous sweater possible. The racks are a riot of garish colors, tinsel, and questionable design choices. I laugh as Ryder holds up a sweater with a 3D reindeer nose protruding from it.

"Oh, that's definitely a contender."

Ryder grins. "I don't know, I think Beckett might need this one. It will really complement his tough guy image."

Beckett grunts from the next aisle over. "I heard that."

As we continue to search and joke around, I find myself relaxing in a way I haven't since we arrived home. This easy camaraderie, the laughter, the shared looks of amusement—even with Caleb's presence keeping it all PG, it feels so natural. So *right*.

For a moment, I let myself imagine what it would be like if things were different. If the connection I forged with Tristan, Ryder, and Beckett on our road trip wasn't just a temporary thing. Could we still have moments like this, all of us together, if they were actually... mine?

Would Caleb's protective big brother instincts kick in the way we've all assumed, or would he see how happy they make me and give us his blessing?

I shake my head, trying to dislodge those thoughts before my heart gets any more invested than it already is. No matter how deep our connection was, the guys made it clear that they weren't looking for more. I need to let it go.

But as Tristan holds up a sweater covered in blinking lights for my approval, I remember how those hands felt on my skin. How his lips tasted. How he knows exactly how I like to be touched, how to make me fall apart.

How they all do.

"Earth to Lana." Caleb's voice breaks through my reverie. "What do you think? Is this the winner?"

He's modeling a sweater with a stuffed Santa stuck halfway down a chimney, the legs kicking comically.

I laugh, refocusing on the present moment. "Oh, definitely. Grandma Meg will love it."

As we make our way to the checkout, I catch Beckett giving me a long, inscrutable look. My heart flutters, and for a moment, I think he might say something. But then Ryder bumps into him, breaking the spell.

They tussle playfully for a moment, making Caleb put two fingers between his lips and whistle loudly, like he's a hockey referee trying to break up a fight.

We're all laughing again as we pile back into the car, now each wearing a truly hideous sweater. A short while later, Tristan pulls up in front of his grandmother's charming cottage-style house, its porch festooned with twinkling lights and garlands. Even the guest house in the back has a wreath on the door.

I gasp, making all four of them laugh.

"What?" I ask, blushing. "It's beautiful. You know I love holiday decorations."

There's a stark contrast between the warm, inviting atmosphere here and the pristine, almost sterile feel of my parents' home.

We all pile out of the car, and before we can even reach the porch, the front door flies open. Grandma Meg bursts out, arms wide. She's wearing a sweater that looks like a Christmas tree, complete with dangling ornaments, and she's got Baldwin, the adorably ugly little dog she adopted a few years ago, in her arms. Baldwin, of course, is also sporting a festive sweater, and wiggling so wildly it's a miracle she's able to keep hold of him.

It's adorable.

"My boys!" she exclaims, pulling each of them into a fierce hug. When she gets to me, her embrace is just as warm. "And Lana! Oh, it's so good to see you all."

As we step inside, the scent of cinnamon and freshly baked cookies envelops us. The house is a cozy jumble of mismatched furniture, colorful throw pillows, and walls covered in photos of smiling faces, the majority of them featuring the four men I'm with. It's the kind of place that immediately makes you feel at home.

"Alright, everyone get comfortable," Meg instructs, ushering us into the living room. "I want to hear everything that's been going on with you all."

We settle in, and Meg turns to Tristan. "Now, tell me how business is going?"

My eyes almost bug out of my head at the idea of this sweet woman asking him about a kink club, and for a moment, I almost wonder if she knows what "business" he's really in, or if he's somehow downplayed Radiance as being a regular nightclub.

I'm quickly corrected on that as I listen in on their chatter, and instead of being awkward, hearing her genuine interest gives me a strange feeling of warmth. She clearly accepts Tristan for who he is, and more than that, she's proud of the success he's created with his friends.

He's never had to hide anything from her, and it's bittersweet to see firsthand that that kind of familial love exists. And not just toward Tristan, either. She turns to Ryder and Beckett next, pride evident in her voice as she asks about their roles in the club and their planned expansion. There's no judgment, no comparisons—just genuine interest and support.

"And my favorite hockey star!" she gushes to Caleb after she's wrung all the details out of the other three men, her eyes lighting up.

"Did you hear that, Tristan?" Caleb teases him. "Her favorite hockey star."

"Yeah, yeah." He rolls his eyes, but his easy grin reassures me that he really has made his peace with the fact that his accident forced him to take a different path. "She just loves you because you give her something to bet on with her friends."

"What's this, now?" my brother asks, laughing.

Meg beams at him. "You know I watch all your games. Nearly gave me a heart attack with that last-minute goal in Toronto."

Caleb laughs. "Sorry about that, Grandma Meg. I'll try to score earlier next time."

"You'd better," she wags a finger at him playfully. "Mrs. Donovan from my knitting circle roots for the Maple Leafs on account of her having no taste—"

Tristan snickers. "I think you mean on account of her daughter being married to a Canadian."

She waves that off. "The point is, I've got a lot riding on you boys winning the next game."

"That's a lot of pressure," Caleb jokes. "How much are we talking here?"

"The bet isn't about money," Tristan butts in. "The stakes are a lot higher than that."

"Oh?"

He nods. "The winner bakes the weekly pies for her knitting circle."

"The winner?" Ryder asks, looking between them with confusion. "Don't you mean the loser has to do that?"

"Of course not," Meg scoffs. "The winner *gets* to. Every single one of those women think their recipe is the best. We have to take turns baking for our club each week, or else we'd all die of diabetes!"

"Oh, I see." Ryder grins. "You're not gonna let Grandma Meg down now, are you, Caleb?"

"Wouldn't dream of it," Caleb promises solemnly.

As I watch the easy interaction, the genuine affection flowing between Tristan's grandmother and everyone in the room, I feel a lump form in my throat. This is what the holidays—no, what *family* should feel like. Warm, supportive, filled with laughter and love.

I'm glad Tristan has that.

Well, I'm glad they all do, since Meg so clearly includes all of "her boys" in her heart.

As if she senses me thinking about her, she turns to me next, her kind eyes crinkling at the corners. "And Lana, dear. How are you doing? Did these boys treat you right on your trip?"

I flush, memories of exactly how 'right' they've been treating me flashing through my mind.

"They've been perfect gentlemen," I manage, ignoring Ryder's barely suppressed snort.

As far as I'm concerned, it's true... at least in spirit.

"Good." Meg nods decisively. "Because if they weren't, they'd have me to answer to."

Conversation flows easily, fueled by warmth and laughter that's a stark contrast to the stilted, performance-like interactions at my parents' house. At one point, I find myself drawn to one of the walls covered in photographs.

In one, a much younger Tristan is missing his two front teeth, grinning widely at the camera. In another, he's on ice skates, looking determined and focused. I'm so engrossed in the photos that I don't notice Grandma Meg approaching until she's right beside me.

"He was always such a serious little thing," she says softly, reaching out to touch one of the frames. "Even before... well, you know."

I nod, understanding the weight of what goes unsaid. The accident that made Tristan an orphan and left him scarred, both physically and emotionally.

"This one," Meg continues, pointing to a photo of Tristan holding up a trophy, "was taken just a few months after he came to live with me. His first hockey championship after the accident. I wasn't sure he'd ever want to play again, but that boy..." She shakes her head, admiration clear in her voice. "He's got a strength in him that never ceases to amaze me."

As I listen to Meg talk about Tristan, about his resilience and determination, I feel my heart swell with an emotion I'm not quite ready to name. "He was lucky to have you," I say, my voice thick with feeling.

Meg smiles, patting my hand. "Not just me, dear. He had your brother, of course, and Ryder and Beckett too. Those four have been thick as thieves since the day they met. And he had you too."

I blink, surprised. "Me?"

"Oh, yes." Meg nods. "I remember how you used to toddle after all the boys, determined to keep up. You were like a little ray of sunshine, always making Tristan smile even on his darkest days."

The lump in my throat grows, and I blink away the sting

behind my eyes. If Meg only knew how Tristan makes me feel now, how he lights me up from the inside...

"I... I should probably get back to the others," I manage, gesturing vaguely toward the living room. "Thank you for sharing these stories with me."

Meg gives me a curious look that makes me wonder if I've been as subtle as I hoped, but she doesn't press. Instead, she pats my cheek affectionately and lets it go as I rejoin my brother and the guys.

39

TRISTAN

THE AFTERNOON LIGHT is starting to fade as our visit winds down. Grandma Meg starts gathering the empty platters and plates, her movements as spry as ever despite her age. I push myself off the couch, ignoring the twinge in my left leg from sitting for so long.

"Let me help with that, Gram," I offer, already reaching for a stack of dishes.

She beams at me, her eyes crinkling at the corners. "Such a sweet boy. Always were."

We make our way to the kitchen, the sounds of laughter and conversation following us. I catch a glimpse of Lana on the floor, laughing as she tries to coax Meg's dog, Baldwin, into rolling over.

Since he's one of the hairless variety of Chinese Crested dogs—not counting the stringy fur around his face, tail, and paws, of course—Grandma Meg is always knitting him cute sweaters to wear. It feels like some kind of message from the universe that the ugly Christmas one she chose for him today just so happens to match Lana's so well.

"It's so wonderful to have you here, Tristan," my grandmother says as we start loading the dishwasher. "I've missed you."

I lean down to kiss her cheek, breathing in the familiar scent of cinnamon and vanilla that always clings to her. "Missed you too, Gram. More than you know."

We work in companionable silence for a few minutes, falling into the easy rhythm we've perfected over years of shared chores. But I can feel her eyes on me, studying me in that way she has that always makes me feel like she can see right through me.

When laughter sounds from the other room, we both turn to look just in time to catch sight of Baldwin working through his repertoire of tricks. The dog's yappy bark mingles with Lana's musical voice, and something in my chest tightens.

"That Lana," Grandma Meg says, her tone casual but her eyes sharp. "She's grown into quite a lovely young woman, hasn't she?"

I nearly drop the glass I'm holding. "Uh, yeah. I guess she has."

Meg hums thoughtfully. "And I couldn't help but notice how... close the four of you seemed on the drive up. You and Lana. And Ryder and Beckett too."

Heat creeps up the back of my neck. I video-called her a few times during the road trip, checking in on her the way I always do now that she's living all alone. And yes, a few of those times, the others popped onto the screen to say hello.

I just didn't stop to think how perceptive she always is.

"Gram, I—"

She holds up a hand, cutting me off. "I'm not judging, dear. I'm just... observing."

"Okay."

I believe her. She's never judged me and has always supported me wholeheartedly.

Then she grins. "Well, maybe not *just* observing. I'm curious too."

I swallow hard. I've never lied to her about anything important, and she knows me too well to believe it even if I tried. Still, I know she'll drop it completely if I want her to.

I *don't* want to, though. I don't even think I have it in me to deny what I'm feeling for Lana, and certainly not to my grandmother, who knows me better than almost anyone. "There was... something," I admit, doling out my words carefully. "During the

trip. Between all of us. It wasn't planned, or expected, it just...
happened."

Meg nods, her expression warm and compassionate. "And
now?"

"And now it's over." The words taste bitter on my tongue, but
they're still true. "We're back in the real world now, so whatever it
was we were doing can't continue, obviously."

Meg is quiet for a long moment, her hands stilling on the dish
she's drying.

"And why is that, sweetheart?" she finally asks.

I blink. "What?"

She puts the dish aside, dries her hands, and faces me fully, her
voice soft but firm. "Why can't it continue?"

The question hits me like a punch to the gut.

The answer is so obvious it goes without saying, isn't it? And
yet... I'm having trouble articulating it as I stand staring at her with
my mouth gaping open like a fish.

She smiles at me, patting my hand fondly even though her gaze
stays serious. "Tristan, honey. I've known you your whole life. I've
seen you go through more pain than anyone should ever have to
endure. And I've never seen you look at anyone the way you look at
that girl. That goes for the way your friends look at her too. And
that sweet girl? She looks at each one of you like you hung the
moon."

I swallow, my jaw working. "It's complicated, Gram."

"Life usually is," she says with a soft chuckle. "But that doesn't
mean it's not worth holding on to the things that make our hearts
sing."

Another burst of laughter drifts in from the living room. I can
pick out Lana's voice, bright and clear, mixed with the deeper tones
of Ryder, Beckett, and Caleb. The sound wakes up that deep ache
in my chest again, and I turn back to the sink, my hands shaking
slightly as I reach for another dish.

My grandmother's advice about life has usually been spot on,
but this time, I can't see it the way she does. And that hurts.

"What's really stopping you from pursuing this, sweetheart?" she asks gently.

I focus on the dish I'm rinsing. "I'm not sure there's really a 'this' to pursue. We all agreed it was temporary, Gram. Something to explore during the road trip, but that's it."

She snorts, shaking her head. "No, I asked what's *really* stopping you."

I fight off a smile despite myself. She always did call me out on my bullshit. But then I sigh, because this time, there truly are valid reasons.

"She's Caleb's sister, for one thing," I begin, the words tumbling out. "He'd never be okay with that. And the guys and I will be moving out of L.A. in a few months anyway. You know long distance things never work. And even if we could get past all that, I love Ryder and Beckett like brothers, but polyamory? I'm not even sure I'm cut out for a serious relationship, and I hear they're complicated enough with just two people involved. With four of us..."

I shake my head, that constriction in my chest getting tighter and tighter as I spell it all out.

But my grandmother's eyes never leave my face. When I finally run out of words, she reaches out and takes my hand.

"Tristan," she says softly, "I've known you your entire life. I've seen you grow, struggle, and overcome so much. And in all that time, I have never seen you look at anyone the way you look at Lana. *Never*."

I don't doubt for a second that it's true, but when I open my mouth to respond, she cuts me off with a little squeeze of my hand.

"You've always been good at hiding your feelings, but I know you too well, dear. The way your eyes follow her, the softness in your voice when you speak to her? It's all there, plain as day to me. And as for your list of reasons..."

She cocks her head, narrowing her eyes at me.

"Caleb is a wonderful man—but he's Lana's brother, not her keeper. What she chooses to do with her heart is ultimately none of his business, and I'd like to believe that he's mature enough to come to terms with that, regardless of any knee-jerk reaction he may or may not have. And long distance relationships? I most certainly do *not* know that they never work. What I do know is that *all* relationships take work, and the good ones often look like compromise on the outside, but from the inside..."

She shakes her head, smiling fully now.

"What?" I ask, my heart pounding.

"Well, from the inside, each relationship is as unique as the people who are involved in it. And if that's all four of you, then that is absolutely no one's business but your own, no matter how unconventional it is. And do you know what's almost as challenging as making a good relationship succeed?"

I shake my head.

Her smile softens. "Making a business succeed the way you and your friends have done with Radiance, my dear. Balancing each other's strengths and working through your differences to nurture something you all love."

She holds my gaze as if she's daring me not to see the parallel she's drawing, to argue again that I actually believe sharing something important—or some*one*—with Ryder and Beckett would ever become a problem between the three of us.

I swallow hard, because I can't argue that. It's just not true, and in my heart, I know it.

"I'll think about that, Gram. I promise."

She huffs a laugh, patting my cheek again before turning back to the dishes. "Do better than just thinking about it, sweetheart. You know I've never been one to tell you how to live your life, but you deserve to be happy. Don't let this go without figuring out which of those reasons you just listed are actually big enough to keep you apart."

Her words stick in my mind, and I find myself turning to look back into the living room as if needing visual proof of what I've been trying to convince myself I have to give up.

Lana is there, sandwiched between Ryder and Beckett on the couch, Baldwin on her lap and her head thrown back in laughter at something Caleb has said. The sight of her there, so perfectly at ease with the men who are as close to me as brothers, makes my heart swell.

I feel a gentle touch on my arm and turn back to find Meg watching me with a knowing smile. No words are needed; the understanding between us is as deep and unshakeable as always.

I cover her hand with mine, a silent thank you for her wisdom and unwavering support.

We finish up the dishes, and not long after, we take our leave, heading back to Lana's and Caleb's parents' place. During the drive back, Grandma Meg's words continue to echo in my mind, and I steal glances at Lana in the rearview mirror, the certainty growing in my chest getting stronger and stronger with each mile we pass.

My grandmother is right. I don't have all the answers to the obstacles I laid out. Hell, I don't have *any* of those answers. But I also don't want to let this go.

"Everything okay?" Ryder asks me as we trail after the group heading into Lana's parents' house.

"Yeah."

"You've been quiet."

I raise my eyebrows, and he laughs. I've always been the most reserved one in our friend group, but I get that he's saying something more. He can tell something's going on in my head. I'm just not ready to share it yet since I'm still figuring it out.

And maybe the truth is I want to share it with Lana first.

Ryder lets it go, and as soon as we walk in, Caleb is called away by his father to help him with some project in the garage, and Lana's mother is on hand as if she's been waiting for us, asking for help with a bit of furniture moving for her party.

Lana slips away, heading upstairs, and Ryder gives me a nudge in her direction, proving how perceptive he really is, before more loudly volunteering himself and Beckett for the furniture moving.

I give Ryder a nod of thanks, then follow her. My heart pounds as I take the stairs two at a time, catching up to her just as she reaches the landing.

I don't have a plan, I just have a sense of urgency that can't be denied now that I've pulled my head out of my ass.

"Tristan?" she asks, smiling at me with that adorable dimple peeking out and a light in her eyes that really does make my heart sing, just like Grandma Meg pointed out.

"I need to talk to you."

I pull her into her childhood bedroom, and her eyes go wide with surprise as I tug her against me, one arm wrapping around her waist while my other hand cups her cheek.

"Tristan?" she repeats breathlessly. "What are you doing?"

I take a deep breath, drinking in the sight of her as I experience a blinding moment of clarity.

The answer to which obstacles in front of us are big enough to keep us apart is: none of them. Not if there's a chance she wants this to work too.

I stare into her eyes, the blue of a summer sky—hopeful and light.

"I can't pretend this is over anymore, because it's not. Not for me."

Her breath catches in her throat as her eyes search mine. "What do you mean? It's not... it's not possible to keep it going, right? How can what we had on the road trip work beyond being just a temporary fling?"

Something relaxes inside my chest, and I smile, resting my forehead against hers as I let my thumb trace the curve of her cheek and dip into the sweet divot of her dimple.

She's not saying she doesn't want it. All her questions are laced with the same hope that sparks inside me too.

"I don't know exactly how we'll make it work," I tell her honestly. "I just know that we'll figure it out. Because I've never felt like this before, Lana. Never. And I'm not willing to give it up."

Her chin trembles, her eyes turning glassy. "But—"

"No buts." I cut her off with a finger over her soft lips, my voice dropping to a whisper as the words pour out of me like a dam breaking. "You've woken something in me I didn't even know was there. The way you look at me, the way you touch me... it's like you see all of me, scars and all, and you still want me. I've never had that before."

"Tristan," she whispers as she pulls my finger away from her mouth. "I—"

I shake my head, smiling at her. I'm not done.

"You're a light, Lana. You make me *feel* light, on the inside. You're radiant. Glowing. Hell, even your brother saw it today. But that radiance inside you spills out into everyone you touch, into *me*, and I'm not ready to let it go. I'm not ready to let *you* go."

A single tear breaks over her lashes, tumbling down her cheek.

I catch it, smiling down at her. "I've always been drawn to you, but the feelings that have grown between us during this trip are too big to stuff back inside and pretend to ignore now. Even if I could, I don't want to. I want... more."

"With me?"

"Yes."

That radiance I just told her about breaks through like the sun breaking through the clouds, lighting up my whole heart as she smiles at me.

"I want more too," she says breathlessly. "I—"

The soft click of the door interrupts her, and we both turn to see Ryder slip into the room. His eyes lock onto us, a mixture of determination and vulnerability in his gaze that I've rarely seen.

"Am I interrupting the party?" he jokes as Beckett follows him into the room.

"It looks like we're just on time," Beckett says gruffly, his eyes searching Lana's face before landing on me. Whatever he sees in my expression makes him smile, his shoulders relaxing. "And unless I'm way off base, we're all here for the same reason."

Lana brushes another tear from her cheek, giving them each a shaky smile. "I really hope that's true."

40

LANA

I HOLD my breath as I glance between Ryder and Beckett, waiting for them to speak.

Beckett steps forward first, his nostrils flaring as he drags in a breath. "I'm not done, little menace. I'm not ready to give you up."

"Same." Ryder nods firmly, coming to stand beside Beckett. "I don't know who the fuck I was trying to fool, saying that I ever could. You've gotten under my skin, and I don't think I'll ever get you out."

"But you... you don't do relationships," I stammer, my heart thundering.

He pulls me into his arms, his smile radiating the kind of pure heat that makes my knees weak. "You're right. I didn't. But when will you get it into that beautiful head of yours, love? You're my exception."

"To what?" I whisper.

His smile widens, and he tucks my hair behind my ear and then cups my cheek.

"To everything."

The words steal my breath, and my pulse flutters wildly in my throat. A small sound escapes me as he lowers his head, claiming my lips in a deep kiss.

And then there are two more sets of arms around me,

surrounding me. More hungry kisses follow as Tristan and Beckett step closer and overwhelm me in a blur of sensation.

There's no way I can doubt this is real. Not with the way all three of them are holding me like they'll never let go.

I melt into them, the fatigue I've been suffering from all but forgotten.

"You really mean it."

"Fuck yeah, we do," Beckett growls, his breath tickling my ear as he nuzzles my neck. "Let us show you. Let us make you feel what you do to us. Tell us you want it too, little menace."

"I do," I confess. "I want this too. I know it's barely been a day, but it's been torture not being able to touch any of you anymore. I haven't been able to stop thinking about the three of you, and about how it was during the trip. I wasn't ready for it to end. I... I want so much more."

Beckett tips my chin up and stares into my eyes, searching them for a long moment.

Whatever he sees on my face must satisfy him, because he crushes his mouth to mine, muttering, "Thank fuck."

My head is spinning, and the only thing keeping me grounded is their hands all over me. Then I'm backed up against the wall, held firmly in place by their bodies as Beckett captures my mouth again while Ryder moves to my neck, leaving Tristan to kiss trails of fire across my shoulder.

We've done far kinkier things than this together, but somehow, with emotions and desires all swirling inside me and the possessive, demanding way they're handling me, this moment feels hotter than any that have come before it.

It's as if they're afraid to let me go. As if they don't want to lose me again.

I know how they feel.

"Fuck, I love the sounds you make," Beckett murmurs, nipping at my earlobe. "I need you naked."

His fingers move to the hem of my sweater, and a moment later, I gasp against his lips as his calloused hands slide over my stomach, his thumbs skimming the undersides of my breasts.

Ryder turns my face to the side and captures my mouth, swallowing the sound down with a groan. "Not letting you go again, love."

"Ours," Tristan mutters, working my clothes off with single-minded focus. "That's the new deal. You're *ours* now."

"Can we... can we really do this?" My voice shakes slightly. "Can all three of you really share me?"

"Pretty sure we're doing it right now," Beckett rumbles, stepping back so he can pull the ugly sweater over my head, then unclasping my bra.

He thumbs my nipples, then pushes my breasts together and sucks them both into his mouth at once.

I arch against him, completely naked now, as someone else's hand slips between my legs.

It's so good I can barely think, but I need to know.

"Can you share me beyond just sex, I mean? Is that... is that what we're talking about?"

They all stop for a moment, three sets of eyes burning into mine.

"Yes," Beckett says firmly.

Tristan smiles. "We want everything."

"As long as you want it too, love, we absolutely can and will share you in every way possible," Ryder adds. "But only with each other, do you understand? This is a closed deal. You're ours, and we're yours. But no one else fucking touches you."

My breath hitches. It really is everything I've dreamed of.

"That's all I need," I whisper. "It's all I *want*. Just you three. Just us. I don't want anyone else."

"Good," Ryder says as Beckett's stern expression slowly spreads into a predatory smile.

"What he said."

"Fuck," Tristan groans, his voice hoarse. "I have to taste you again." He doesn't wait for a response, dropping to his knees in front of me. "I've missed your taste so damn much."

Ryder claims my mouth again, and Beckett groans, kneading my breasts and rolling my nipples between his fingers. Tristan's hands slide behind my thighs, pulling my legs wider and lifting me a little, until I'm supported by all three men as they rest my back against the wall.

"Oh fuck," I breathe. "Oh god, I—"

My words cut off in a whispered scream, which is muffled by Ryder's tongue as he plunges it back into my mouth.

"Quiet, freckles," Tristan murmurs, hitching one of my legs over his shoulder. "You can do that, can't you?"

I shake my head, panting, and he gives me a devilish smile and tugs on my clit piercing with his teeth.

"Oh fuck," I hiss. "Oh shit. Oh god, please, Tristan."

"You heard him," Beckett rumbles in my ear. "You're gonna have to stay quiet. Do you need some help with that, dirty girl?"

"Y-yes," I gasp.

He swallows my next sound with a kiss, while Ryder whispers filthy praise in my ear.

Tristan drives his tongue into me, and my hips buck helplessly against him until someone's hands hold me still. I have no idea whose. Their touch is everywhere, surrounding me, overwhelming me, and the sensation overload is so incredible, especially after thinking I'd never have this again, that I'm already barreling toward the edge.

"You're so fucking delicious," Tristan mutters as he feasts on me. "I've been starving for you."

My head is spinning. It's so good, and so much, that his words undo me. Sounds spill from my throat that I've got no chance in hell of containing, a mix of whimpers and moans as he laps at me with hungry flicks of his tongue.

"Oh god," I pant. "I can't... I'm gonna—"

"Do it," Beckett orders, fisting my hair and tilting my head back. "Come for us."

I cry out softly as pleasure rocks through me on his command, rocking against Tristan's face as he groans and works me through it. He digs his fingers into my hips to hold me steady, drawing out every last drop of pleasure until I finally slump against the wall, breathless.

"Fucking hell," he pants, looking up at me with hooded eyes. "I'm never gonna get enough of that."

"But it's my turn, now," Ryder says, turning me around and bending me over the edge of the bed.

I'm still riding the high from Tristan's talented tongue, but I bite my lip in anticipation. Ryder's fingers trace the curve of my ass, teasing me, and I whimper.

"You like that, don't you?" He leans in until I can feel his teeth graze the sensitive skin of my ass cheek. "You want me to eat you out like this? Ass up and on display for me?"

I nod, unable to form coherent words.

"Good. Because I can't fucking wait."

His mouth is on me before I can even react, his tongue tracing the length of my slit from behind. I bite my lip to muffle the moan that threatens to escape, but it's no use. The sensation is too much, too intense, and I can't hold back.

Someone's hands run through my hair. More hands hold me down against the bed as I writhe on Ryder's tongue.

"Shhh. Quiet now."

"Be good, little menace."

Ryder's hands grip my hips tighter, holding me in place as he devours me. His tongue is relentless, teasing and probing me deep as he gropes my ass, lifting my hips until I'm practically riding his face.

"I could do this all fucking night," Ryder mutters, rubbing his face back and forth, the hint of rough stubble on his jaw sending bolts of electricity through my thighs. Then he rubs a finger through my slick folds, drenching it with my arousal before lapping at my pussy again and circling his finger around my sensitive asshole.

I hiss out a breath, and he groans, pressing his fingertip inside. A jolt of pleasure rocks through me, and I push back against him, desperate to come again as I whimper and rock against his face.

"Fuck, you're so wet," he groans, his voice muffled. "I can't get enough of you."

I can feel myself getting closer to the peak, pressure building inside me, and I whimper, trying to muffle the sounds.

Beckett's low, sexy chuckle washes over me, his big hand holding my head down against the mattress. "Careful, little menace. We're not alone in the house. You want your family to hear this?"

"She did like being watched," Tristan murmurs, a dangerous, teasing lilt to his voice. "Maybe she wants an audience again."

I whine as my stomach flutters at his words, a burst of adrenaline shooting through me.

"Is that why you're so loud, dirty girl? You want to be caught? Or is it just that Ryder's mouth is that good?"

"No! I mean, yes!" I whisper, shaking my head. "I'm... I'm close. Please."

"Come for me," Ryder growls. "Let me fucking taste it."

With his fingers buried in my ass, he spears his tongue back into my pussy, and I lose it. Pleasure floods through me as another climax hits, and I bite down on the blankets, stifling my noises as I ride the wave.

His tongue fucks me through it, drawing out every last second of bliss until I collapse on the bed, boneless and spent.

"I don't think so," Beckett rumbles, hauling me up to my feet before wrapping an arm around me and pulling my back against his chest. "We're not fucking done with you. I need some too."

"I'm yours," I breathe, my body feeling like it's floating as he grinds his cock against my back, kissing my neck and fingering my pussy.

"Damn fucking right, you're ours," he says, his other hand sliding up to my breasts for a moment before he turns me around to face him.

I expect him to kiss me—but instead, he slides his hands around to the backs of my thighs and lifts me off my feet, making me yelp quietly as I clutch at him for balance.

Then he tosses me back onto the mattress, gazing down at me with blazing eyes.

"Beckett," I whisper. "What are you—"

"You asked us a question," he says, stepping closer. "And I'm gonna give you an answer. I'm gonna prove how much I love sharing you. Are you going to be good for me?"

I feel like I'm falling apart, unraveling from the two orgasms these men have already given me. We've gone so far past good I don't even know if the word applies.

But I still *want* to be good.

"Yes," I promise, licking my lips. "But... I'm not actually sure I can stay quiet."

"Goddamn. You really are a little menace."

Gripping my ankles, he drags me to the edge of the bed in a quick motion. Then he dives in, his tongue flicking and teasing my sensitive flesh with a ferocious intensity that makes me feel like he's starving for me.

"Oh god," I pant, fighting to keep quiet as I dig my fingers into the sheets. "Oh god, I can't..."

"You fucking can," he mutters. "You fucking will."

His hands tighten around my thighs, holding me open for him as he devours me. I can't even remember how to breathe.

And then the bed dips on either side of me, Tristan and Ryder gathering close.

"So perfect," Tristan murmurs, brushing hair out of my face and kissing me softly. "You're so fucking perfect. Look at you, all spread out and on display for us."

"Fucking beautiful," Ryder mutters, leaning down to drag his tongue down my throat, over my collarbone, down to my breasts.

Then he sucks one of my nipples into his mouth as Beckett groans into my pussy, fingering me while sucking on my clit, and I almost scream.

Tristan swallows the sound down, his mouth tasting of my arousal. I can already feel myself building toward another orgasm, my body writhing beneath the three of them as Beckett takes me apart with his mouth.

"Give me another one," he orders, his voice hoarse. "I need to taste your pleasure. I want to fucking drown in it. Come for me, little menace."

I whine, bucking against his face. I'm so close, but I need something...

"That's it," Ryder murmurs. "God, I love how responsive you are. Give Beckett what he wants, love."

Beckett growls his agreement, and the vibrations push me over the edge.

The orgasm he demanded crashes through me, and I throw my head back, letting out a sound that's quickly muffled by Tristan's kiss.

My back arches off the bed, my whole body shuddering as I thrash against the sheets, riding out wave after wave of bliss.

"Fucking hell," one of them mutters as I come down from the high.

I drag my eyes open, and Tristan helps me sit up.

The men surround me, all three of their cocks are hard and straining behind their pants, and I don't even try to stop myself from reaching for the closest one.

Ryder.

He captures my hand before I touch him, placing a kiss on my palm as he shakes his head at me. "We don't have time for that, love."

I blink, my brain trying to come back online.

He smirks when he sees my confusion. "Did you forget where we are?"

"Oh god. My parents' house."

Where they're still downstairs preparing for the party tonight.

"You were loud enough on your own," Tristan teases me, a gleam in his eyes. "We'd definitely get caught if we fucked you the way we want to right now."

"But—"

He shakes his head, stopping my argument with a finger to my lips. "But we'll make it up to you tonight. Promise."

Ryder nods, and Beckett gives me a smile that makes my stomach flip.

"We'll be back in this room after everyone's asleep, little

394

menace. Leave the door unlocked, and we'll make sure to take care of you."

I nod, my heart racing at the thought.

Ryder leans in to plant a kiss against my forehead, then gently cups my face. "You should rest. At least take a nap before the party tonight."

The moment he says it, I can feel fatigue pulling on me again. But the reality is that here in my parents' house, I have obligations.

I shake my head. "I can't. My mother will be expecting me to finish helping with preparations."

"No," Beckett says, crossing his arms over his chest.

I blink at him. "But—"

Tristan smiles at me. "We'll cover for you, freckles. Your mom won't even notice you're gone. I promise."

"And *you* promised you'd take better care of yourself," Beckett reminds me, a fondly stern look on his face.

"If you're sure…"

"We've got this handled," Ryder says, grinning. "But Beckett's right. You need to rest up. We're not fucking around with the lupus anymore, right?"

"Right," I murmur, my heart swelling at their insistence. It really is about more than sex with them. They care about me. *All* of me.

I've never felt so cherished, so protected, and without thinking, I reach up and pull Ryder into a soft kiss. When I break away, I turn to Tristan, pressing my lips to his. Then finally, I kiss Beckett, pouring all my gratitude and affection into it.

"Thank you," I murmur before the three of them slip out of my room, each giving me a final lingering look before disappearing through the door.

As it clicks shut behind them, I find myself staring at the space they just occupied, a light feeling of happiness filling my chest, even as fatigue tugs at me.

I sink back onto the bed, closing my eyes. I still don't know exactly how a relationship with all four of us will work, but I know I want it.

And even better, they want it too.

41

LANA

I WAKE from my nap feeling refreshed, a smile playing on my lips that I can't quite contain. The memory of three sets of hands on my skin, the taste of their kisses, and the whispered promises of more to come—it all feels like a dream.

But it's real. *We're* real.

With a contented sigh, I drag myself out of bed and into the shower. As the hot water cascades over me, I actually start to look forward to my parents' Christmas Eve party. Normally, it feels like a performative obligation, but I do love the holiday, and I just feel hopeful about everything now.

Standing in front of the mirror, wrapped in a fluffy towel, I eye the dress I'd originally planned to wear. It's nice enough, I suppose. Demure. Parent-approved. Exactly what's expected of me and chosen specifically to meet my parents' standards.

But I'm not that girl anymore.

Instead, I reach for the garment bag tucked in the back of the closet. Inside is a dress I picked up during our road trip, encouraged by Ryder's wolfish grin and Beckett's approving nod. It's a deep emerald green that makes my eyes pop and hugs my curves in all the right places. The neckline is just low enough to be enticing without being scandalous, and the hemline hits mid-thigh, showing off my legs.

As I slip it on, I feel a surge of confidence. This is me. The real me. The one Tristan, Ryder, and Beckett fell for.

I take a deep breath and head downstairs, the click of my heels on the hardwood announcing my arrival before I'm even visible.

I can already hear the low hum of conversation and the quiet clink of glasses over the tasteful Christmas music my mother has playing. As always, the decorations are worthy of a magazine spread, and I know I'll find all of the city's most influential people mingling below.

My parents have been throwing this Christmas Eve party ever since I was a little girl, and they always make sure the guest list is a who's who of everyone they might want to network with.

As I descend the staircase, I see my parents first. Their eyes widen, and I can practically feel the waves of disapproval rolling off them. Mom's lips purse, while Dad's brow furrows in that way that always made me feel two inches tall as a child.

I'd be lying if I said it didn't still make my stomach clench a bit, but then I catch sight of the three men who've changed everything for me.

Tristan is mid-conversation with Caleb, but he stops mid-sentence when he sees me, his eyes darkening with unmistakable heat. Ryder, leaning casually against the wall, straightens up, a slow smile spreading across his face that makes my insides flutter. And even Beckett, ever the stoic one, can't quite hide the way his gaze rakes over me, his jaw clenching in that way I now know means he's fighting for control.

Their reactions, subtle as they are, bolster my confidence. I lift my chin, meeting my mother's disapproving stare with a serene smile.

"Is everything alright, Mom?" I ask innocently when she comes forward to meet me at the bottom of the stairs.

She clears her throat. "Lana, dear, don't you think that dress is a bit... much for your figure?"

I shrug, the movement causing the fabric to shimmer in the light. "I think it's perfect for a Christmas party. Festive, don't you think?"

Before she can argue further, the doorbell chimes, announcing the arrival of more guests. Dad shoots me one last disapproving look before plastering on his host smile and moving to answer the door.

As I move farther into the room, Ryder sidles up next to me, his voice low as he murmurs, "You look absolutely stunning, love."

A blush creeps up my neck. "Thank you. I'm glad you approve."

"Oh, I more than approve. In fact, I'm already planning out all the ways I want to get you out of that dress later."

My clit throbs, and I have to resist the urge to kiss him in front of everyone. Instead, I offer him a coy smile. "Patience is a virtue, you know."

He grins wickedly. "And virtues are overrated."

I shiver at the promise in his eyes, but as the party gets into full swing, I find myself swept away from my men in a whirlwind of greetings and small talk. Old family friends exclaim over the effort my mother put into the party, ask politely about my life in L.A., and not-so-subtly brag about their own successes.

I paste on a smile and nod along. I'm used to it, and regardless of the slightly critical looks my mother keeps shooting me, I know how to play my part and represent my family at these kinds of events.

Still, I'm acutely aware of Tristan, Ryder, and Beckett's presence. No matter where I am in the room, it's like I can feel their strength grounding me.

When I spot Vivian arriving with her family, I use it as an excuse to gracefully remove myself from a conversation with one of my father's friends and head over to greet her.

Vivian looks impeccable as always, and her husband Kyle looks as polished as ever in his tailored suit. Oliver is adorable in a miniature version of his father's outfit, and he takes in the array of Christmas lights with avid interest.

"Vivian! Kyle," I greet them, leaning in to air-kiss my sister's cheek. "You all look wonderful."

Oliver tugs on my dress. "Is Beckett here, Auntie Lana?"

I laugh, and as soon as I point him in the right direction, he lets out an excited whoop and darts off into the crowd.

Kyle's lips pinch. "Vivian, did you forget to speak to him about manners?"

I roll my eyes since he's not looking at me. Sure, Oliver's excitement was a little loud, but he's a child, and it's Christmas.

Vivian gives him a bland smile, plucking two champagne flutes off a passing server's tray and handing one to her husband. "Isn't that Brent Tennyson from First National Bank over there?"

Kyle turns to look, his spine straightening, and mumbles something about needing to talk to the man, leaving me alone with Vivian.

An awkward silence settles between us, and I scramble to fill it.

"Oliver's getting so big," I say, smiling. "He's absolutely adorable in that suit."

Vivian nods, her lips curving into an almost-smile that doesn't quite reach her eyes. "He is. Thank you."

I take a deep breath, deciding to make a real effort. "You have such a beautiful family, Viv. Truly. I'm really happy for you."

Her eyes flick in the direction Kyle went for a moment, her placid expression and perfect smile never faltering.

"Thank you," she repeats, her tone cool.

There's another moment of silence before she takes a sip of her drink, and my heart sinks a little at her disinterest in... well, in truly being sisters. We've always had a bit of a strained relationship, but if I could, I'd love to have a real connection with her. She's family.

I take a sip of mine too, searching for something else to say. Before I can, she empties her champagne flute and grabs another one when a server walks past.

I blink when she empties half of that one in one go too. "Vivian, is everything okay?"

She seems to catch herself, glancing down at her drink and then smoothing her features into a neutral expression. "Of course. Why wouldn't it be? If you'll excuse me, I should go mingle."

Before I can respond, she's gone. I sigh, reaching for a glass of champagne for myself, and turn back to the party.

I scan the room for Ryder, Tristan, or Beckett, and spot Beckett with his arm slung around Oliver's shoulders. He's crouching down, talking to him with a smile on his face, and my heart melts at the sight. But before I can head in their direction, a woman who serves on the board of one of the nonprofits my mother is active with pulls me into conversation, and I'm once again swept up into small talk.

"Lana," my mother says, coming to find me after a bit and pulling me away to murmur quiet instructions. "Please go into the kitchen and ask the caterers about the dessert trays. They should be out by now. Your father and I need to attend to our guests, and we can't be seen to be neglecting them."

"Of course."

I take care of that quickly, startling when I turn around to leave the kitchen and find Ryder leaning against the counter, out of the way of the staff, smiling at me.

"Sneaking off?" he asks with a grin.

I couldn't stop my smile if I tried. "Not very well, since you've found me," I tease him. "What are you doing in here?"

His eyes roam over me appreciatively. "I've been watching you all night. Can't seem to take my eyes off you."

"You did pick out the dress," I remind him, smoothing my hands over it.

Ryder grins, taking a step closer but still maintaining a respectable distance. "Trust me, love. You look incredible in it, but it's not the dress that's got my attention."

I want him to come closer. I want him to touch me. I want to sink into his arms, then find Tristan and Beckett and actually enjoy this party, the amazing food, the beautiful holiday decor.

But even if I chose to wear what I wanted instead of something my parents' would approve of, I'm still very aware that my purpose at this party is to keep up appearances for them.

When Ryder's hot gaze softens into something more tender, I know he understands.

"How are you holding up?" he asks.

"The nap was refreshing," I assure him. "I really do feel good."

"Oh, believe me, I know," he says, heat flaring in his eyes.

"I meant energy-wise."

I laugh as I speak, realizing that for all my good intentions about keeping my distance, I've drifted closer to him.

"Good." He smiles down at me, still keeping his hands to himself. Then he leans a little closer, lowering his voice a bit. "I do have another question, though."

I raise an eyebrow. "Oh?"

"Naughty or nice list tonight?"

I squirm, remembering the men's promise to come to my room later.

One of the caterers drops a tray behind us, making me jump, and Ryder chuckles, pulling me closer to clear the walkway.

"I need an answer, love," he whispers in my ear. "I need to know if you want us to fuck you like a good girl or a bad girl later."

A tiny whimper spills from my lips, heat pooling low in my belly.

"Ryder," I breathe, glancing behind me nervously.

We're not alone in here. The kitchen is bustling with activity, and even though his voice is quiet, I can't help feeling like everyone knows what he's saying.

"Naughty list," I whisper, so low it's barely audible. "Fuck me like the bad girl I am."

"Noted." He smirks and , steps back to a more socially acceptable distance, his gaze so full of heat that it's a wonder the kitchen doesn't catch on fire. "Ready to rejoin the party?"

"You're horrible," I hiss, although I'm not mad about it at all. All three of these men are masters at edging... and I love it.

"I see where you get your love of Christmas," Ryder murmurs as he leads me back out of the kitchen.

At first, I'm not sure what he means. I do love Christmas, but this party, and the way my family celebrates the holiday, has never felt like it includes the things I love about it.

But if I take my focus off the room full of inflated egos and look at it through the lens Ryder just gave me—my own love of the holiday—I'm struck by the warmth and coziness of the atmosphere.

The room is bathed in the soft glow of twinkling lights, garlands draped elegantly over every available surface. The enormous Christmas tree in the corner sparkles with gorgeous ornaments, and the air is rich with the scent of cinnamon and pine.

Christmas music plays softly enough to add to the ambiance without overpowering conversation, and all of it is punctuated by the occasional burst of laughter or the clink of glasses.

I smile. Despite the constant undercurrent of tension with my parents and their thinly veiled disapproval tonight, I feel my spirits lift as Ryder's comment reminds me of what's important.

"Christmas always has been my favorite time of year," I say, smiling up at him as the festive environment wraps around us like a warm blanket.

But then my mother bustles up again to check with me on the caterers, and Ryder rejoins his friends when she pulls me away to introduce me to a few more people. As we walk, she starts whispering to me, a non-stop stream of instructions of what she wants me to say to whoever it is she's about to introduce me to.

I get that she wants me to impress her guests so that I reflect well on her, but I'm hoping we can have a moment of actual connection instead.

"Mom, you've really outdone yourself this year," I compliment her, interrupting her mid-sentence.

She stops, glancing at me. "With the party?"

"Yeah." I smile at her. "It's really lovely."

"Of course it is. Didn't I tell you I used that new designer Beatrice recommended?"

I sigh quietly as she goes off about the coup of scoring this particular up-and-coming designer's services, letting my attention wander.

Tristan, Ryder, and Beckett are all chatting with Caleb near the fireplace, Oliver still trailing after Beckett like an eager little puppy. My heart thuds at the sight of them, and as soon as I can politely do it, I murmur an excuse and leave Mom talking with a local businessman and his wife so I can join them.

I've just grabbed a fresh glass of champagne and started to

make my way over to my men when the sound of a familiar voice stops me in my tracks.

It sounds an awful lot like my ex-fiancé, but since Wade is very much my *ex* now, and also back in L.A., it can't be.

But when I turn around, it is.

I stand frozen in shock as my parents swoop in, their faces alight with excitement.

"Wade!" Mom exclaims, air-kissing his cheeks. "What a wonderful surprise!"

Dad claps him on the back, beaming. "We didn't think you'd make it this year, son."

Wade flashes that perfect smile again, the one that used to make my heart race but now just makes my skin crawl. "I wasn't sure I could, to be honest. But I hated the thought of Lana being here alone."

He searches the room, and when his eyes land on me, they gleam with something I can't quite read as his smile widens.

"I moved some meetings around, caught a last-minute flight," he tells my parents. "I couldn't miss your annual Christmas party, could I?"

My parents are practically glowing with approval, and I feel my cheeks burning with a mix of embarrassment, anger, and shock.

"Lana," my mother calls out, looking around until she finds me and then gesturing me over excitedly. "Look who's here!"

I don't move. I'm completely frozen. But Wade doesn't seem to have that problem, and when he crosses the room and takes my hands, I'm too stunned to react.

What does he think he's doing? How dare he show up here, acting like nothing has changed? And why on earth is he lying to my parents and making it sound like we're still together?

Before I can voice any of these thoughts or yank my hands away from him, Wade tugs me closer, a smug glint in his eyes.

Then he kisses me.

42

LANA

My mind reels with shock, and I push Wade away from me with a gasp, my hand flying to my lips.

At least, I try to push him away. His smile never wavers, and he keeps a tight grip on my arm that locks me in next to his side.

"What are you *doing?*" I hiss quietly, barely able to comprehend the reality of his presence at my parents' Christmas party.

Instead of answering me, Wade turns toward the room at large, his voice cutting through the din of the party.

"Everyone, if I could have your attention please!" He flashes the million-dollar smile that used to make my heart flutter, but now it just makes my stomach churn. "For those of you who don't know, I'm Wade Bradshaw, and Lana just asked me what I'm doing here."

Friendly chuckles surround us. He's playing to the crowd, knowing damn well that just about everyone here thinks he's my still boyfriend—although none of them have any idea that he proposed to me and then dumped me.

"Lana has been more than understanding about my work obligations," he goes on. "But I couldn't bear to miss this party, because we have a big announcement to make, and I can't think of a better time or place to share our good news."

Ice spreads through my veins as I stare up at him in shock. We did have a plan to make an announcement together at this party, but that was before he dumped me. So there's no way he—

"Lana and I are engaged!" he announces exuberantly, snatching a glass of champagne from a nearby waiter and lifting it high.

Someone tries to shove another one into my hand as the room erupts in cheers and congratulations, but I'm frozen in place and it almost drops to the floor.

I don't even notice if the waiter saves it or not over the heavy thumping of my heartbeat. Adrenaline surges through me, but I still can't move. I feel like I've been dropped into an alternate reality as my parents rush forward, my mother's eyes brimming with tears.

"Oh, sweetheart! This is wonderful news!"

"I couldn't be happier, son," my father adds, clapping Wade on the back. "We've been hoping for this day."

My parents' joy is like a splash of ice water, but instead of freezing me in place this time, it finally snaps me out of my stupor.

"What are you doing?" I repeat to Wade, louder this time.

He wraps an arm around me, pulling me close against his side. His smile never drops as he leans in, speaking low enough that only I can hear.

"I know we hit a rough patch, baby, but hearing your voicemail the other day? It reminded me why I fell in love with you in the first place."

I blink. "What?"

"You sounded so happy, so carefree," he murmurs. "It reminded me of why I loved you, and what a good partnership we'll make now that you've come out of your slump."

I stiffen in his embrace, my mind racing. Then it hits me—the accidental call I made to him on our road trip. The butt dial where he heard a recording of me laughing with Tristan, Ryder, and Beckett.

"My slump?" I ask, narrowing my eyes.

He brushes my cheek, then tucks a stray piece of hair behind my ear. "You have to admit you'd stopped being any fun before our unfortunate break, but I'm willing to move on from that. It's why I'm here, just like we originally planned."

He beams at me again, like he actually expects me to accept that as a compliment and just fall right in line with his pompous, unasked for grand gesture.

I pull back slightly, meeting his gaze. There's not a shred of doubt in his eyes, no sign that he's stopped to consider my feelings or wonder why on earth I was in a "slump" in the first place.

He's right that I sounded carefree and happy the day I accidentally called him. It was because of the three men I've fallen for.

"Smile, Lana," Wade says softly, but with a hint of bite in the words. "Your parents are taking pictures."

The shock I'm in suddenly gives way to a kind of fury I've never felt before. Wade doesn't want me. He doesn't even know me. He just wants the version of me that will look good on his arm, and he honestly thinks he can just waltz back into my life, pick back up where we left off, and pretend the breakup never happened.

Judging by the smug look on his face, he thinks I'll be grateful for it.

A flash goes off nearby, and Wade leans in as if he's going to kiss me again.

I jerk away, my chest tight.

"What the hell, Wade?" I snap, backing away from him. The room falls silent, all eyes on us.

He reaches for me, his smile turning strained. "Come on now, baby, I'm sorry for showing up late, but the important thing is that I'm here now."

I knock his hands away and straighten my spine, meeting his gaze head-on.

"No, the important thing is that you're full of shit."

"Lana!" my mother gasps.

"Don't make a scene," Wade says tightly, finally lowering his voice a little. "You're embarrassing your parents."

He's wrong. I'm pissing my parents off. *He's* the one who looks embarrassed. And while in the past, either one of those things would have made me instinctively shrink down to appease every-one, right now, I just don't care.

The old Lana might very well have gone along with this farce, just to make other people happy.

But the woman I am now sure as hell won't.

"You want to talk about making a scene?" I ask, holding his gaze as I raise my voice. "What do you call showing up uninvited and announcing an engagement that doesn't exist?"

Gasps and murmurs ripple through the crowd. Wade's face flushes, his composure slipping. "Lana, please—"

"No," I cut him off, my voice clear and strong. "I'm not marrying you, Wade. We broke up, remember? You dumped me. You told me, and I quote, chubby girls aren't *wife material*."

"Lana," my mother hisses again, her gaze darting around the room as twin spots of color bloom on her cheeks. "Keep your voice down."

"No," I tell her simply. "My ex-fiancé just told everyone here a lie. Don't you think he's the one you should be chastising right now, Mom?"

"I'm sure it's just a misunderstanding," she says tightly. "Isn't that right, Wade?"

"Of course it is, Mrs. Reeves," Wade says, a muscle starting to tick in his jaw as he glances around the room. "I even brought Lana something special for Christmas—"

His hand goes toward his pocket, but I've had enough. I take another step back, holding up a hand to stop him. I'm done shrinking myself to fit others' expectations or going along with their plans for me.

"I don't want anything from you, Wade. I don't want *you* anymore. We're over."

The room goes dead silent other than my mother's quiet gasp, so even though Wade lowers his voice again, his words carry to everyone.

"Lana," he hisses. "You're overreacting. Let's just talk about this privately."

I huff a laugh, shaking my head. "We don't have anything to talk about."

The charming facade crumbles, replaced by a look of anger and wounded pride. "You can't be fucking serious."

He takes a step toward me—but one step is all he gets before three large figures materialize in front of me, forming a protective barrier between me and Wade.

Tristan, Ryder, and Beckett stand shoulder to shoulder, their stances resolute.

"Oh, she's definitely fucking serious," Beckett growls, his voice low and dangerous.

Tristan's voice is calmer, but no less firm. "You heard Lana. It's over."

Ryder glares at him. "And since you weren't invited in the first place, that means it's time for you to go."

Wade's eyes widen. "Who the hell are you?"

The men don't answer him, but I can see the wheels turning in Wade's head, connecting the dots.

My ex's face contorts with a mixture of disgust and fury as his eyes zero in on me past Beckett's shoulder. "These are the guys I heard you on the phone with, aren't they? The ones you were traveling with?"

"Don't talk to her," Beckett bites out, shifting his bulk to block Wade's view of me. "Don't think about her. Don't even fucking breathe in her direction. She's made it clear she doesn't want to see you, and I believe Ryder just told you to get the fuck out, so I strongly suggest you do that. Now."

I move to Beckett's side, putting a hand on his arm and feeling the tautness of his muscles.

I love the way they're standing up for me, but I want to stand beside them right now.

"He's right, Wade. It's time for you to go."

Wade's eyes drop to my hand on Beckett's arm.

"So this is why you don't want to get back together," he sneers. "You've been fucking one of them, haven't you? Is that what this is really about? Which one was it? This guy?"

He makes a rude gesture toward Beckett, and Beckett's muscles flex under my hand.

Ryder lets out a dark chuckle.

"*One* of us?" He arches a brow, his tone filled with amusement but his eyes hard. "Oh, buddy. You should really have more imagination than that."

Wade's jaw drops, his face flushing an angry red as the implication of Ryder's words sinks in.

"Lana," my father grits out between clenched teeth, his voice carrying over the low buzz of titillated gossip springing up around the room as my parents' guests watch the drama unfolding here.

"Lana?" I repeat incredulously, turning to my father. "Don't you mean Wade? The man who showed up, lied to you, and is currently causing a scene at your party?"

My father's eyes spark with anger, but Caleb steps up next to him and says something under his breath, stopping whatever reply Dad was about to make.

Caleb doesn't look any happier than my parents do, but I don't have the bandwidth to deal with my family right now. Not when the men I... I care for are in a tense standoff with my ex, the tension in the air like a powder keg.

"Please leave, Wade," I repeat, squeezing Beckett's arm as I turn my back on my family.

"Are you going to let this guy talk about you like that?" Wade sputters instead, jabbing a finger at Ryder.

Ryder crosses his arms over his chest and gives Wade a cold smile.

"Just... go," I whisper.

"I'm not going anywhere." Wade's eyes narrow, zeroing in on my left hand. "Where the hell is your engagement ring? I gave you a three-carat diamond!"

"Oh, that little thing?" Tristan says before I can answer, his dry tone laced with steel. "Guess it must have fallen off while she was busy screaming our names."

Wade's eyes bug out as he looks between the four of us in disbelief. Then, as the room falls silent again—everyone clearly reading into that exactly what Tristan meant—Wade's face turns a shade of purple I've never seen before.

"You're not taking me back because you're fucking three men at the same time?" he snarls, all pretense gone. "Are you fucking serious right now?"

"She told you to get the fuck out," Beckett says in a low, deadly voice, his muscles bunching under my hand. "Last warning."

Wade ignores him, his eyes raking over my body as his lip curls in disdain. "I see you've put on even more weight since I dumped you. Hell, everyone can see it in that dress. Is that because you're eating for four now, Lana, or do you just need the extra cushion now that you've decided you'd rather have a gang bang than be in a respectable relationship?"

Beckett growls, shaking my hand off his arm, then slams his fist into Wade's jaw.

43

LANA

I GASP, pressing my hand to my mouth as Beckett's punch sends Wade reeling sideways. The room erupts into chaos—a blur of motion and screaming as my parents' guests scramble backward, clearing the space around us.

I can hear my mother shouting something at me, but it doesn't even register over the sound of my pounding heart.

Tristan and Ryder rush forward, grabbing Beckett and holding him back before he can go after Wade again. The expression on their faces make it crystal clear they're only doing it to protect him from doing something that could land him in jail.

"Are you planning on being smart or are you planning on being hurt," Ryder snaps at Wade when he finally finds his feet and turns back toward Beckett instead of toward the door.

Wade answers with an inarticulate sound of rage and lunges at Beckett, fists flying.

Beckett breaks free from his friends' hold just long enough to land another punch that sends blood spraying from Wade's nose. When Wade tries to retaliate, Ryder intercepts him, catching Wade's flailing arm and twisting until Wade yelps and goes down on one knee.

"Get out," he snaps.

But Wade doesn't listen. He fights his way back up to his feet, and Beckett lunges at him again, turning it into an all-out brawl.

"Oh my god," I gasp

I rush forward as the fight careens toward the entrance hall. I can tell Tristan and Ryder are doing their best to push Wade toward the door while simultaneously keeping Beckett from murdering him, but the white-hot rage on Beckett's face makes me doubt they'll be able to manage that.

Glass shatters—a stray elbow taking out a side table—as Beckett struggles against Tristan and Ryder, his eyes fixed on Wade with laser-like intensity.

"Be smart," I hear Tristan mutter as he hauls him back, but then Wade surges forward, his face twisted with fury, and Beckett breaks loose again.

My stomach drops as Wade lets loose a vicious right hook aimed at Beckett's jaw, but Tristan and Ryder drag Beckett out of range before it connects.

Wade loses his balance, careening into the front door. For a moment, he just stands there, breathing heavily, his eyes wild. Then he lurches forward with a snarl, like he just doesn't know when to quit, and the three men move in perfect sync, picking him up and literally throwing him out of the house.

I race for the door as they follow Wade out, watching as they physically drag him down my parents' driveway. I'm vaguely aware that I'm not the only one crowding into the doorway watching, but I don't care. My heart is hammering in my chest, every ounce of my attention focused on Tristan, Ryder, and Beckett.

"Stay the fuck away from her," Beckett snarls once they finally release Wade at the end of the driveway, giving him a shove that sends him stumbling.

Wade staggers, and for a moment, I think he might be dumb enough to actually keep fighting.

He eyes Tristan and Ryder, sizing them up as they eye him back, never taking their focus off him. It almost looks like he's thinking of taking them on too, but then his eyes flick toward Beckett and he pales.

I bite my lip, my heart in my throat. But luckily the reality of the situation seems to hit Wade all at once, and after muttering what sounds like a few choice curse words, he goes from a raging bull to a sniveling weasel, turning and limping off down the street.

The men watch until he finally reaches a corner and disappears from sight, then they turn back to me.

I release a breath I didn't know I was holding, realizing in a rush how quiet it's gotten behind me. The festive atmosphere has evaporated, replaced by a thick, uncomfortable tension.

I'm guessing we've officially ruined my parents' party, but I can't think about that yet. Not until I make sure my men are okay.

Ryder smirks as they head back toward me as if he can read my mind, and the intense way all three of them watch me as they approach has my pulse starting to race for a different reason.

"Excuse me," someone says, dragging my attention away from them for a moment.

An older couple I vaguely recognize needs me to step to the side since I'm blocking the doorway. As soon as I do, they scurry past me, and I can hear the rustle of coats and the murmur of hastily made excuses from behind me as the other party guests scramble to leave too.

My stomach twists as the reality of what just happened crashes over me. It all unfolded so quickly that I haven't really had a chance for everything to sink in.

I'm still reeling, both from Wade's arrogant audacity in showing up here the way he did, and from the way the guys jumped to my defense. But the one inescapable fact that starts to crowd out all the rest is that the truth about our relationship—the one we've only just officially started and which I know my parents will never approve of—has now been laid bare for everyone to see.

I know I want to be with Tristan, Ryder, and Beckett, but since I never thought it was possible, I also never thought through how I'd present such a thing to my family. Now I have no choice, and I have no idea what's going to happen once my parents' house clears out and it's time to face the music.

When the men finally reach me, they each take a moment to

touch me. Beckett gives the back of my neck a reassuring squeeze, Tristan strokes my hair, and Ryder pulls me close and kisses my temple.

Then, like a living shield, they move with me inside the house, their presence both comforting and anxiety-inducing as the last of the party guests leave.

My family has gathered in the foyer shoulder to shoulder. I doubt they mean to block the entrance into the house, but it couldn't be more obvious that they're on one side of an invisible line, and the guys and I are on the other.

Vivian and Caleb both have shocked expressions on their faces, staring at me like they've never seen me before, but my parents are a different story. Unmistakable anger radiates off both of them, hitting me like a palpable wave.

I have no idea what to say. The silence stretches, taut and uncomfortable, between all of us.

"What the *hell* was that, Lana?" my father finally bursts out. "How could you humiliate us like this? Do you know how many important people just saw that vulgar display you just subjected us all to?"

I flinch at his tone, but before I can respond, he continues, his anger building with each word.

"Do you have any idea how much work your mother put into this party? The planning, the preparation—all ruined because you couldn't keep your... your promiscuous indiscretions private?"

He's practically spitting. I've never seen him so outraged.

I swallow hard. "Dad, I—"

"No!" he cuts me off, his face flushed with anger. "I don't want to hear your excuses. This behavior is completely unacceptable. You've embarrassed this entire family in front of all our friends and colleagues. And Wade! What the hell was all that? I don't know what happened between you two, but he was clearly here to forgive you and make things right—"

Something inside me snaps.

"Forgive me?" I shout, the volume of my voice powered by

years of pent-up frustration over never being seen as anything but a disappointment, no matter how much I've tried.

My father gapes at me for a moment, and I take a deep breath, steadying myself, then go on.

"I have spent my entire life trying to make you happy." I look between my mother and father. "Every decision, every choice I made, including dating Wade in the first place, was all about living up to your expectations. And you know what? It was never enough. Not for either of you."

My mother scoffs, looking away, while color rises in my father's cheeks as a muscle starts to tick in his jaw.

My voice breaks slightly, but I push on. "No matter what I did, no matter how hard I tried, I've always fallen short of being who you want me to be. And all it did when I tried was keep me living a life that was suffocating me. It was fake. Wrong. At least, wrong for *me*." I swallow. "I was living *your* version of my life, not my own."

I don't see any sign that I'm getting through to either one of them, both of their faces stuck in all too familiar matching expressions of disapproval. But then I feel Tristan's hand slip into mine, giving me a reassuring squeeze, and the way all three of my men surround me gives me the strength to continue.

I straighten my spine and take a deep breath, centering myself as I look straight into my father's eyes, then my mother's.

"I'm done doing that. I'm done living by your standards. Done hiding who I really am. Done pretending and twisting myself into knots just to please you."

"Lana." My mother's lips are pursed, her voice tight as her eyes flick to the men and then back to me. "If you were... compromised during the road trip—"

"Oh my god," I burst out. "Seriously, Mom? Did you even hear anything I just said?"

"What I heard, what *all my guests* heard, is you announcing your promiscuity to the man who gave you a three-carat engagement ring!"

Beckett growls as all three of them move closer, but I put a hand on his chest before he can jump to my defense again.

"Yes, I've slept with Tristan, Ryder, and Beckett," I say, holding my mother's gaze. "But it has nothing to do with Wade. I just want to be with them. All of them."

My father sputters. "You can't—"

"I can," I cut him off. "I *am*, and I'm done pretending otherwise. The four of us are in a relationship now, and I *like* who I am when I'm with them. For the first time in my life, I feel like I can truly be myself. Because you know what? They like who I am with them too. Not some idealized version of who I should be, but who I *actually* am."

I can see the shock and disbelief on my parents' faces, but for once, it doesn't make me feel small. With Tristan, Ryder, and Beckett's silent support radiating into me, my chest feels lighter than it's ever been in this house.

For the first time in my life, I've spoken my truth without fear or hesitation, and riding the wave of my newfound courage, I take a deep breath and continue, "There's something else you should know. I've been diagnosed with lupus recently."

All four of my family members freeze for a moment, and then my father's jaw tightens. "Is this something you caught from... *them*?"

"Jesus, Dad," Caleb whispers harshly. "That's not what it is."

I shake my head, my voice trembling slightly. "It's not an STD. It's a... a condition. It's triggered by some combination of environmental and genetic factors, they think."

"Genetic?" Mom shakes her head, looking stunned. "But we didn't give it to you!"

"And that's exactly why I tried to hide it from you," I tell her tightly. "Because I knew you'd judge me for it. I felt guilty for an illness I have no control over, all because I've spent my whole life trying to meet your impossible standards. And I'm done feeling less than because of it.

"No, you know what? I'm more than done. I'm mad about it! I'm angry that you keep treating me this way, even now."

My voice cracks, but I don't let that stop me.

"Why isn't your first question whether or not I'm okay? I just

417

told you I'm sick, and Dad, you imply that it's my own fault, and then you, Mom, sneer about how it's... what, beneath a Reeves to be imperfect? Well guess what, I'm *not* perfect, but I'm happier being my real, imperfect self than I ever was trying to live up to who *you* wanted me to be."

For once, neither one of my parents has a stinging retort. They both stand there looking stunned by my tirade, blinking in shock for a moment. But when my father opens his mouth to speak, I can tell by the expression on his face that nothing I said actually got through to him.

It almost makes me feel defeated, but then Tristan steps forward, his voice calm but hard.

"With all due respect, Mr. Reeves, I'd think carefully about whatever you're about to say before you throw away something you can't get back."

"And what would that be?" my father says, his tone suspicious.

"Your daughter."

My father blinks, and before he can say anything in response, Ryder jumps in.

"All these years, you had the chance to really know her, and you made her hide her light. You dismissed her talent, pushed her toward your own dreams instead of hers, and made her feel like your love was conditional. You've missed out on seeing how truly wonderful Lana is because you refused to fucking *look*."

My mother's mouth tightens at the profanity, but Ryder stares her down, standing like a solid oak tree behind me.

"Lupus is something your daughter is going to be living with now, so you might want to spend a little more time researching it if you actually give a shit about her well-being. But as a courtesy, I'll clue you in."

His unyielding tone has an edge I've never heard before, and it's enough to shut my parents up as he goes on.

"Lana gets tired a little more easily now. She's got to take care to manage her stress. To avoid triggering foods. Stay hydrated. Monitor her symptoms at all times and adjust her lifestyle accordingly. Despite that, she's been pushing through this entire trip. A little *too* hard sometimes."

His lips quirk up, and his eyes drop to me for a moment before he looks back at my parents.

"But never complaining, always letting her inner radiance light up the room even when the fatigue hits her. Putting others first—especially her family, despite the fact that I've yet to see any one of you do the same for her."

Caleb flinches a little, but I stop watching my family as the men keep talking, my attention riveted to the three of them instead.

"She's brilliant and creative," Tristan says. "Have you even seen her artwork? It's incredible."

"What's really fucking incredible is her laugh," Ryder says, holding my gaze. "It's like that one Christmas song, you know, with the tidings of joy and shit."

"That's not Christmas, that's just Lana," Beckett rumbles. "She brings a little magic to everything she touches."

"Like roadside attractions." Ryder smirks, but his eyes are soft as he looks at me. It's almost as if they're not telling my parents off anymore, they're speaking directly to me. Publicly confessing feelings that make my heart race and my eyes sting with unshed tears.

"She's adventurous."

"Brave."

"Full of determination and passion."

"She's beautiful," Tristan adds quietly. "The fire in her eyes when she stands up for what she believes in, when she sees herself the way we do, is..."

"It's everything," Beckett finishes, his gaze finding mine and making the rest of the room fall away.

Then Caleb clears his throat, and I remember we're not alone.

"Mom, Dad," I start, a lump growing in my throat as they silently stare back at me.

The tension in the room is palpable, thick enough to cut with a knife, and I sigh, shaking my head.

I tried, and they either can't hear me or don't care. Anything more is going to have to come from them.

"Get your stuff," Tristan says, resting his hand on my lower back. "We'll go to Grandma Meg's."

"No, I'll get it," Beckett interjects, glancing at Tristan and Ryder. "Take Lana outside. I'll meet you out there."

He stalks past my parents, heading for the stairs, and Tristan and Ryder flank me, guiding me out of the house without any goodbyes.

A moment later, Beckett is back, my suitcase in hand, and we leave.

44

RYDER

My heart is pounding as we leave Lana's parents' house, adrenaline coursing through my veins and my emotions a total mess. I keep my arm wrapped tightly around her as we quickly walk to the SUV, partly to support her, but also because focusing on her helps me keep all those wild emotions in check.

I didn't expect things to blow up like that. None of us did. But dealing with the aftermath will have to wait for later. Right now, she's the only thing that matters.

As we pile into the SUV, with Tristan taking the wheel and Beckett joining Lana and me in the back, I can feel the tension radiating off all of us like it's a living force. I'm definitely not the only one on edge from all that bullshit, and we're barely out of the driveway when Lana's composure starts to crumble.

A sob escapes her, and I pull her closer, letting her bury her face in my chest. Beckett's jaw hardens, and I'm sure he's currently wishing he hadn't let us stop him from pounding the shit out of Wade.

He puts a hand on her back and he rubs slow, soothing circles there as I stroke her hair.

"S-S-Sorry," she stutters out, clutching my shirt.

"It's okay, love," I murmur. "Let it out."

"We've got you," Beckett adds.

She drags in one more shuddering breath before the floodgates open, all the pent-up emotions she's been holding back for who knows how long pouring out as she cries.

I catch Tristan looking back at us in the rearview mirror, his eyes tight and worried, but I give him a subtle shake of my head. It fucking guts me to have her so torn up, but at the same time, this release is probably exactly what she needs right now.

It's a good thing, even if it stokes my rage at everyone who helped contribute to it.

Finally, her sobs start to fade, and I clear my throat.

"We owe you an apology," I start, knowing for sure I speak for all of us. "We shouldn't have blurted out the fact that we were fucking like that without talking to you first."

"We got carried away," Tristan adds from the front seat, his eyes meeting mine in the rearview mirror again. "It wasn't our place to out our relationship in front of your family."

"No." Lana's voice is hoarse but fierce as she lifts her head. "Don't apologize. None of you. It's not your fault."

Beckett grunts, and she twists to face him, covering his mouth with her hand before he can argue the point.

"I said no."

He stares at her, then captures her wrist, kisses the fingers she's got pressed to his lips, and pulls her hand down to hold it over his heart.

"Thank you," Lana whispers, drawing in a shuddering breath and wiping at her eyes with her free hand.

Then she straightens her spine and looks between the three of us with a determination blazing in her eyes.

"You were standing up for me," she says softly. "And even though things... escalated, I don't blame you for any of it. If anyone is to blame, it's Wade for thinking he could just show up and take me back like that, like I'd be grateful after the way he treated me."

My blood starts to boil at the reminder, and Beckett growls under his breath. But we both hold our tongues, because Lana's not done.

"It's my parents' fault too," she goes on, her voice hardening.

"They've made me feel like I had to keep my whole life a secret, everything that actually mattered to me, just to earn their love. And when things went sideways tonight, they didn't check to see what *I* wanted. They didn't... didn't check on me at all."

I tighten my arm around her as I remember the way her voice cracked when she called them out on their reaction to hearing about her lupus, a surge of protectiveness washing over me.

I can see Beckett's hand clenching around hers as he has his own reaction to that, and Tristan's knuckles go white on the steering wheel at the same time.

A feeling of bone-deep solidarity hits me, and I'm suddenly struck by how fucking *right* it is, after a whole fucking lifetime of avoiding getting trapped in a serious relationship, to be in one now.

Not just any relationship, and not just with Lana, but a relationship *with my friends* with Lana.

There's no one on this earth I trust to have my back more than the men in this car, and now that extends to protecting her too. And I'm not saying I wouldn't want her if they didn't, because nothing could make me not want to be with Lana. Ever. But sharing her with Tristan and Beckett?

It's not just perfect; it's whatever word there is for something that's even better than that.

She looks between us again, a little smile hovering on her plush lips. "But you three?" she says softly. "I'm not mad at any of you for what you said back there. I don't know what it would have taken for me to come clean to my family about our relationship, but no matter how it came about, I'm glad that it happened.

"I don't want to hide how I feel about being with you. All of us together like this may not be what people expect, but I'm not ashamed of it. You three are... well, you're the best thing that's ever happened to me."

"Fuck," Beckett says softly, almost reverently.

Her words hit me like a punch to the gut too, and I pull her closer, leaning in and pressing a gentle kiss to her forehead.

"Ditto," I whisper.

Lana sighs, still subdued but more relaxed, and a few minutes later, we pull up to Tristan's grandma's house.

She's expecting us since Tristan texted her on the way to fill her in, so it's no surprise to see her already waiting for us on the porch. And as soon as we pile out of the car, she immediately heads toward Lana, tugging her right out of my arms and enveloping her in a massive hug.

"Oh, sweetheart," Meg says, her voice warm and comforting. "You poor thing. Come here."

Lana melts into the embrace, and I can see her shoulders start to shake again. But this time, it feels different. Like she's releasing the last of her pent-up emotions in a safe space. Getting something she needs, something more parental, that the guys and I can't offer her.

"Thank you," Lana whispers, her voice muffled against Meg's shoulder.

Meg pulls back, cupping Lana's face in her hands. "You don't need to thank me, dear. Now, let's get you all inside and warm."

We follow her into her cozy living room, settling onto various chairs and sofas. As soon as we do, Baldwin races into the room wearing another one of those tiny knitted sweaters Meg is always making for him.

His claws skitter on the floor for a moment, and with a shrill yap, he makes a beeline for Lana.

"Oh, hey, you," she says, her face lighting up.

The ugly little fucker yaps at her again, then hops up onto her lap, curling up there like he thinks he owns it. He gazes up at her with big, soulful eyes that I've gotta admit are pretty cute.

"Very festive," Lana says, stroking the hot pink and neon green Christmas sweater he's wearing.

"Baldwin just loves the holidays," Meg says, making me snort since we all know *she's* the one who chooses his daily sweaters.

Tristan meets my eyes, holding back a fond smile, but Meg and Lana carry on talking about the dog like they don't notice, Lana's body relaxing more and more as she pets the little guy.

"Did Tristan tell you why, um, why we're here?" Lana asks Meg after a minute.

Meg pats her knee, her expression warm. "A little bit. I don't need any details you don't want to share, though. You're always welcome here."

Lana looks down at Baldwin. "I think I'd like to share them, if you don't mind. I feel a little... raw right now."

"And sometimes talking helps," Meg says with a nod.

Lana smiles at her, brushing away a tear that wells up in her eye, then starts to recount all the shit we just went through again, getting it off her chest. As she fills Meg in on what happened, I marvel at the easy acceptance radiating from Tristan's grandma. There's no judgment in her eyes, just concern and love.

Seeing that kind of support does something to me. I think it does something to Lana too, because as she winds down, a change comes over her.

"I'm proud of you." Meg pulls her close, making Baldwin grumble and scramble off Lana's lap as they hug.

"Thank you," Lana says, her tears drying up as Meg lets her go, replaced by a fierce determination that lights up her eyes. She sits up straighter, her chin lifted slightly, and I can practically see the weight of her parents' expectations falling away from her shoulders as she takes a deep breath and exhales.

"And I'm... I'm done," she says, her voice steady and strong. "I'm done trying to please them, done living my life by their rules."

She said it before. Hell, she said it straight to their faces. But something about the conviction in her voice right now feels like it just sinks into my soul.

Our relationship coming to light like that may have been rough, but I don't doubt for a second that she meant it when she said she doesn't regret it. Seeing her come into her own like this is sexy as hell, and it has my chest tightening up with a mixture of pride and admiration. Watching her find this inner strength, this resolve to stand up for herself and what she wants, is fucking incredible.

It's inspirational.

My relationship with my own parents is so messed up that I

know it's beyond redemption, and I've grappled with that—with their indifference and neglect—for years. The pain of growing up in a house full of wealth but devoid of warmth, raised by a revolving door of nannies while my parents lived their lives as if I was just an afterthought, has left scars inside me just as deep and permanent as the ones Tristan wears on his skin.

The shit Lana has gone through with her own parents is a different flavor, but the same damn recipe. They never outright neglected her, and they were there for her in some ways, but they did neglect the most important thing. Her heart.

"What?" she asks, catching my eye and blushing the sexiest fucking shade of pink I've ever seen. "You're smiling at me like..."

"Like you're incredible? That's because you are."

Her dimple pops out as she grins, and Meg gives me a fond look as she rises to her feet.

"And on that note, let me get us all something to snack on."

Tristan hops up, offering to help her, but before either one of them can make a move toward the kitchen, the doorbell rings.

We all freeze, exchanging glances.

"Grandma?" Tristan says. "Are you expecting someone else?"

"Expecting? No. But I'll never turn away carolers," she says as Baldwin goes zipping toward the door, yapping away.

It's not carolers, though. It's Caleb.

Lana's body stiffens with tension as Meg leads him into the living room, giving him a welcoming pat on the shoulder as she urges him to join us.

As soon as he takes a seat, Meg scoops up Baldwin and heads into the kitchen, no doubt to prepare the snacks she mentioned.

"Caleb," Lana whispers, her spine still straight but her voice quivering.

"Lana," he replies, his face a storm of emotions as he stares back at her.

I'm immediately on edge. Which fucking sucks, because this is *Caleb*. I'm definitely not alone in that, though. Tristan and Beckett straighten up too, all of us instinctively moving closer to Lana.

"Just a heads up," I say, my voice low. "You're gonna want to think about whatever's about to come out of your mouth next. Your sister's been through enough tonight."

Tristan backs me up, his usually gentle demeanor hardening. "If you're here to give her a hard time—"

"I'm not," Caleb cuts him off, his gaze still fixed on Lana. Then he glances at each of us, his eyes narrowing a little. "I just... I need to understand what's going on."

"We may be friends—" Beckett starts.

"Exactly," Caleb snaps before he can get any further. "You're my friends, so what the actual fuck?"

"Language, boys," Meg calls out from the kitchen.

Caleb's mouth works open and closed for a moment with no sound coming out, then he sighs, scrubbing a hand over his face.

"Why didn't you tell me?" he asks Lana, his voice tight with hurt. "About any of it? The lupus. *Jesus*, Lana. Lupus? How long have you known? And... and *this*." He waves a hand, taking in all four of us. "I'm your big brother."

"I know," she says quietly.

"So why am I just hearing about everything tonight? Like *that*."

She runs a hand down her face. "I mean, in my defense, it's not how I was planning on telling you."

"*Were* you planning on telling me?"

She sighs, chewing on her lower lip for a second, and it takes everything I have not to butt into this conversation. We need to have our own talk with Caleb, but right now, this is between Lana and her brother.

Her eyes get glassy again, but no tears fall as she lifts her chin. "I don't know. I think so. But honestly, Caleb, it's not all about you. My lupus diagnosis is new, and I'm still coming to terms with it. And me and the guys? That's also new."

Caleb grits his teeth, then huffs out a breath. "I mean, I'd hope so." He eyes all three of us. "How new are we talking? Is this why you all offered to drive across the country with her?"

I roll my eyes as Tristan snorts and Beckett huffs out a breath, shaking his head.

Lana laughs. "I wish." She bites her lip again. "I... really care about them."

"All of them," Caleb says flatly, not making it a question.

She gets that fierce, sexy fire in her eyes as she stares him down. "Yeah, Caleb. All of them. This is what makes me happy. *They* make me happy. And they are your friends, so I'd think you of all people would understand what amazing people they are."

He holds her stare for a second, then slumps back in his seat, looking at the ceiling. "Fuck."

Meg bustles back into the room with a tray of Christmas cookies and drinks. "I'll pretend I didn't hear that."

"Sorry, Grandma Meg," Caleb mutters sheepishly. Then he looks back at Lana. "And you're right. I do understand that these three guys... aren't horrible."

Beckett chuckles, and when Caleb's hand twitches in his direction, I'd put money on Grandma Meg's presence being the only reason he doesn't flip Beckett off.

Which means our friendship is still okay.

At least, mostly.

Which is fair. I get that this shit caught him off guard, but I can see that he's trying his best not to be a dick about it. He just has to wrap his head around it.

"I don't want my relationship with the guys to affect your friendship," Lana tells Caleb firmly. "But if it does, that's *your* choice. Not mine, and not theirs. They mean everything to me, and I love you, Caleb, but I'm not giving them up."

Caleb blinks at her for a moment, then smiles. "Well, damn. Who are you, and what have you done with my little sister?"

She laughs, shaking her head and rolling her eyes. Then Caleb's smile fades, and he leans forward, placing a hand on her arm.

"Actually, I shouldn't joke about this. I feel like I didn't really know about a lot of what you've been going through recently, and I'm sorry about that. I really am. I want to be someone you feel like you *can* tell this stuff to."

"Thank you," she says, squeezing his hand back tight.

"Although I'm not gonna lie, I may... need a minute to wrap my head around all of this."

She smiles. "Okay."

He looks over at me, then Beckett and Tristan. "I'm pretty sure I remember telling you guys that not one of you should make a move on her, but fuck—uh, sorry, Grandma Meg—but seriously, I wasn't trying to imply that all *three* of you should do it instead."

Tristan snickers, and Beckett's resting-fuck-off face relaxes into something close to a smile.

"Who says it was us that made the move?" I joke, making Caleb groan and hold up a hand.

"TMI, man. I said I need a minute. I didn't say I need you to tell me all the details."

"None of us need those," Meg says with a snort. "But what we do need are snickerdoodles."

Baldwin barks excitedly, and she taps him lightly on the nose.

"I didn't mean you, mister."

That gets a laugh out of all of us, breaking the tension, and somehow we roll into talking about the season Caleb's team is having, and then Lana shares a few stories from our road trip. Baldwin manages to con Beckett into feeding him a thumbprint-sized bite of cookie, which brings Meg's wrath down on the man and cracks me the fuck up.

There's still some tension with Caleb through all of it. Not everything is cool between us about what we're doing with Lana, but it feels like we'll get there. Still, it's a much more pleasant evening than I would have predicted a few hours ago.

When Caleb gets up to leave, Meg touches his arm and stops him for a second. "Why don't you come back tomorrow to celebrate Christmas with us?"

He hesitates for a moment, then nods. "Yeah, okay. I'd really like that."

"Me too," Lana murmurs, catching his eye.

They smile at each other, putting some warmth in my chest. Then he leaves.

45
LANA

As Caleb leaves, a mix of emotions swirls inside me. I'm exhausted, every nerve ending raw from the day's events, but there's also a sense of relief washing over me. It's as if a festering wound has finally been lanced, allowing the poison to drain away. I feel lighter, somehow, despite the weight of everything that's happened.

Grandma Meg's warm voice breaks through my thoughts. "You must be worn out, dears. It's been quite a day. Why don't you use the guesthouse for the night? There's plenty of room for all of you to share the space."

I blink, a blush stealing over my cheeks. But there's no judgment in her voice, no raised eyebrows or pointed looks. Just simple, straightforward hospitality.

She really does accept the four of us being together.

"That would be wonderful, thank you," I manage, my voice thick with emotion.

Meg steps forward, enveloping me in another hug. "You're welcome here anytime, dear. All of you."

As we pull apart, I feel a nudge at my legs. When I look down, Baldwin stares back up at me with those soulful eyes, his tail wagging furiously, like a little pom pom.

"I think someone wants to say goodnight," Meg chuckles.

430

I kneel down, scratching behind Baldwin's ears as he leans into my touch. "Goodnight, little guy," I murmur, feeling a surge of affection for this quirky, sweater-wearing pup.

With final hugs and thank-yous to Grandma Meg, the men and I make our way out to the guest house. The cool night air feels refreshing against my skin, and I take a deep breath, letting it cleanse some of the day's tension from my body.

"This is cozy," I say as soon as we step inside the guesthouse.

Tristan grins. "I thought you'd like it. There's not much to it, but I think it will do just fine."

He's right. It's not huge, but it's warm and inviting. Just a small sitting room, a tiny kitchen, a closed door that I'm guessing leads to a bathroom, and an open door with what seems to be the guesthouse's only bedroom.

And inside it, all the proof I need that Meg really does accept our relationship.

I laugh. "There's only one bed."

"Feeling a little déjà vu?" Ryder teases me, his strong arms wrapping around me from behind. His familiar cinnamon and bergamot scent envelops me as he pulls me close. Within moments, Tristan and Beckett join in, creating a cocoon of warmth and safety around me.

"I'm definitely feeling something," I murmur, melting into their embrace.

The tension I've been carrying all day drains right out of me. The hug isn't sexual, but it's perfect. Their touch grounds me, reminding me of what truly matters.

It wasn't just because of them that I found the courage to stand up to my parents—that was something I've needed to do for myself for a long time, and I know I deserve credit for finding the strength to finally confront them. But there's no doubt in my mind that these three men have helped me find that strength.

They've shown me who I can be when I'm not holding back, when I'm true to myself, and that means everything to me.

"What do you need right now, Lana?" Beckett's deep voice rumbles softly against my ear.

They've all been so attentive, so concerned and caring. And in light of the day we've just had, I'm pretty sure this is Beckett's not-so-subtle way of checking in on my energy levels.

But for once, I'm not feeling fatigued. Maybe a little tired, sure, but sleep isn't really what I want right now. And it's definitely not what I need.

I pull back a little so I can look at them, and all three men immediately loosen their holds.

"I need you to fuck me. All of you."

Time feels suspended for a moment, the private bubble we're in, tucked away in this guesthouse, seeming to shrink around us. The air hums with electricity.

And then Beckett growls, his voice low and husky. "We can do that. We can do anything you need, little menace."

I let out a slow, shuddering breath. "I want..."

He kisses me before I can put it into words, but I don't have to. Not with these three.

Beckett's lips are demanding, his kiss pushing me toward the bed. Tristan and Ryder are right there with us, their hands reaching, pulling, tugging at my clothes as they undress me.

"Look at you, freckles," Tristan murmurs, his breath hot against my neck as he nuzzles the curve of my shoulder. "So fucking beautiful."

A thrill tumbles down my spine. Then Ryder's fingers dance along my sides, feather-light touches that make me squirm.

"Ticklish, love?" he teases, his lips brushing my ear as he nibbles on the lobe. "Or are you wiggling around for some other reason?"

"Let's find out," Beckett says, dragging his mouth away from mine to suck and bite gently at the sensitive spot where my neck meets my shoulder.

I gasp, my back arching, and he chuckles, low and dark as Tristan cups my breasts, his thumbs rubbing slow circles over my nipples until they pucker and tighten.

Then he dips his head and sucks on them.

They're worshiping me, revering every inch of my body like it's sacred, and it's both wonderful and maddening, liquid heat pooling between my legs as they push me higher and higher.

"Oh fuck. *Please.*"

Beckett slides his hands down to my hips, pulling me against the bulge in his pants. "Is this what you need?"

"We're going to make you feel so fucking good." Ryder's voice is hot and breathless against my skin. "You look so damn perfect when you're hungry for cock, but you'd look even better spread out on the bed for us."

My breath catches at the possessive edge in his voice, then their hands are guiding me down and spreading me out, just as Ryder said.

"Don't move," Beckett orders as all three men strip down to skin.

Then the bed dips, and they're surrounding me again, Beckett's hand between my legs.

"So fucking wet already," he says approvingly, tugging on my piercing as his fingers slip inside me. "You like being on display like this, don't you? You like knowing we're all thinking about how much we want to fuck you. How fucking sexy you are, begging for our cocks like the hungry slut you are."

My heart is racing, a hot, electric current running through my veins, and when Beckett slides his fingers free and licks them clean, I moan.

He's right that I'm hungry for it. I need their cocks inside me like I need air. And if Beckett wants me to beg, I'm more than happy to. I'll do anything for these three men.

"Please," I breathe. "I'm yours. All of you. Please. I want it. I need it. Fuck me like you promised."

"Like we promised?" Ryder grins down at me, hot and wicked. "Because I remember someone asking to be fucked like a bad, bad girl tonight. Is that what you want?"

My thighs clench involuntarily, a rush of heat sweeping through me. I remember too.

"Yes," I gasp, my voice cracking.

"Say it," Beckett rasps, his hand sliding down to wrap around his cock, those thick fingers playing up and down the row of piercings in his length.

I can't tear my gaze away. My pussy throbs, aching for him, and my fingers twitch, desperate to touch him too.

"Yes," I repeat. "Please. I'm your bad girl, and I need you to fuck me. All of you. Fuck me like I'm filthy."

"Fuck, you're perfect," Ryder groans, dipping down to kiss me hard.

Beckett groans, pushing my legs apart and lifting them to his shoulders, then fitting his cock against my entrance and driving in to the hilt in one hard thrust.

I almost cry out, but Ryder swallows the sound quickly before letting Tristan take over where he left off.

Someone's hands are on my breasts.

Someone else tugs on my piercing.

And Beckett fucks me like I really am on the naughty list, thrusting hard and fast right out of the gate, with no slow, sensual build up. Giving me exactly what I need, claiming me with an intensity that leaves me breathless.

I cry out, overwhelmed and already racing toward an orgasm.

"More," I beg. "Harder. Faster."

"You'll get what I fucking give you," he growls as his hips snap forward, driving deeper, his strength on full display as he powers into me.

My head falls back, my spine arching, a primitive, helpless sound tearing from my throat. I scrabble for purchase on the sheets, unable to do more than hold on as Beckett pistons between my legs, using my body for his pleasure.

"Fuck, I need some of that," Ryder grunts, fisting his cock next to me as Tristan drags his mouth from one of my nipples to the next, sucking and biting, marking my skin like he owns it.

I'm right on the edge, but for once, they're keeping me there. Not pushing me over into a sobbing, quivering mess of pleasure, but edging me almost as badly as the day they made me wear the butt plug.

"Ryder," Beckett grunts, pulling out of me abruptly. "Get some of this."

Ryder's cock immediately takes his place, slamming into me and fucking me with a punishing rhythm that makes my eyes roll back in my head.

"Fuck, your pussy feels amazing," he says, pushing me legs up until they're folded in half, my knees at my shoulders while he drives into me. "It was made to take our cocks."

His thrusts are brutal, and I whimper, my pussy clenching, a new wave of wetness flooding me as my core tightens into a fist-sized ball of need. I'm close. So close...

Then he pulls out.

My whine of protest turns into a moan when Tristan immediately takes his place, pushing inside me, thick and relentless, his pace a little slower but so deep I'm shuddering.

"That's right," he says, his voice a low purr. "Let me feel it. Give yourself over to us. You belong to us now, don't you?"

"Yesss," I hiss, the word ending on a strangled cry as he pushes deeper.

"Good girl. So fucking tight. I want to stay buried in you all night."

"Yes," I pant, trying to move, needing him to go faster, harder. Needing more.

But he just holds my legs tight, pressing them down to keep me still, his gaze dark and hungry.

"I want to, but you need something else, don't you? You need to know you're owned by all of us."

He pulls out, and Beckett picks me up like I weigh nothing, setting me back down on his cock.

My pussy pulses, a shiver of lust racing up my spine as he impales me. He's leaning against the headboard now, and he doesn't ask me to ride him. He palms my ass in both hands, slams his hips up to drive his thick cock even deeper, and makes me.

I scream, clutching his arms, and he does it again. And again. Fucking me so hard the entire bed is shaking.

"You're ours," he snarls, his gaze locking onto mine. "All of you. Forever. Mine. Ryder's. Tristan's. Ours. Tell us."

"Yes," I choke. "Oh god, I'm going to... I'm going to..."

"Not yet," Beckett says with a wicked smile, lifting me off his cock and passing me back to Ryder.

I lose count of how many times they pass me back and forth, edging me until I'm sobbing.

It's perfect. I feel cherished and used and adored. Like a goddess. Like a whore. It's a heady combination, and it makes me feel more connected to them than ever before. I needed this so much.

But it's not *everything* I need.

I'm upright, on my knees, Ryder's mouth on mine and his fingers on my clit as Tristan fucks me from behind, but I need more.

"Closer," I beg when Ryder drags his lips down my throat. "Need you."

He groans, and this time, when Tristan pumps into me, it pushes me flush against his body, his hard cock sliding through my slick slit and bumping my piercing.

"Yes! Fuck me. Please, Ryder. Need your cock."

Tristan slams into me again, kissing the back of my neck, then starts to pull out.

I reach behind me and grab for his hip. "No! Don't go. Keep fucking me. I need you in me too. I need both of you."

"Oh, fuck," Ryder groans. "That's a lot, baby. You want Tristan to pull out and take your ass so I can have your pussy?"

"No," I pant. "I want you both in the same hole. Share me. Take me."

Ryder's chest vibrates, a low, primal growl emanating from him.

Tristan sucks in a sharp breath, and his cock throbs inside me. "Are you sure?"

I nod frantically. "Please."

He and Ryder share a look, and then his arms wrap around me, sliding down to my waist. He lifts me slightly, and Ryder shifts, grabbing the base of his cock and guiding it lower—not to my clit this time, but to my entrance, which is already stretched around Tristan's shaft.

He pushes his tip in, and my eyes widen, my lips parting. Tristan throbs inside me, his fingers digging into my hips as Ryder slowly starts working his way in too.

It burns. It's overwhelming. It's perfect. Especially with Beckett's hot gaze burning into me as he watches them fill me, inch by inch, slowly fisting his cock.

"Oh god," I breathe, the sensation stealing the breath from my lungs as I let my head fall back on Tristan's shoulder and pant through the sensation.

Ryder's grip on my waist tightens, holding me still. "Fucking incredible," he grits out. "Can you take more?"

"All of it. Ryder, give me all of you!"

He pushes forward, and a sob escapes my throat as I feel my body stretch, opening up, taking him and Tristan both.

"Holy shit, you're amazing," Tristan pants. "You're doing so good, freckles. So fucking perfect."

I'm pinned between their bodies, full of cock, and it's not enough.

"Fuck me," I plead. "Need more."

They oblige, slowly rocking against me, the two of them finding a rhythm that's somehow not quite fast enough and perfect at the same time. It's intense and amazing, and like nothing I've ever experienced before.

"Don't stop," I beg, the words pouring out of me. "Oh fuck, don't stop. Don't ever stop."

"Fuck, Lana. You're gonna make me come," Tristan groans, turning my head and kissing me.

The bed dips next to us, and when Tristan releases my mouth, panting against the back of my neck Beckett takes my chin in his hand and tilts my head toward him.

"Kiss me," I whisper.

He does, hard and fast, but then pulls back, the heat in his eyes almost undoing me.

"I want to see your face," he murmurs. "You have no fucking idea how incredible you look taking two cocks."

"I want three."

He freezes, the heat I thought I saw in his gaze before flaring into an inferno.

"What?"

"I need you, Beckett. I need you too."

"Fuck," Ryder groans, his cock throbbing inside me. "What are you saying, love?"

"I want all of you at once."

"How?"

"Jesus."

"Fucking anything," Beckett promises in that low, rumbling growl that always gets me. "Where do you want me?"

His hot gaze has me pinned in place just as thoroughly as Tristan's and Ryder's cocks do, and I couldn't look away if I tried. "I want you in my pussy, Beckett. I want all three of you at the same time."

46

LANA

THREE COCKS. I don't know if I can take it, but I want it. And the way that Beckett's eyes widen, the heat flashing through his gaze hot enough to incinerate me, tells me he does too.

And he's not the only one.

"Oh fuck," Tristan breathes into my ear, the two cocks already inside me both swelling even larger.

Ryder's grip on my hip tightens, his chest rumbling with a groan of approval, and a shudder of need goes through me.

"Please," I add when Beckett doesn't move.

"It'll be a lot to take. Are you sure?"

I can see how turned on he is, but it's the note of caution, his unshakeable concern for me, that has emotions rushing into my chest.

I nod. "I know, but I want it. I trust you."

He stares at me hard, searching my face, and I let him see everything. How much I want this, all of this, and so much more. That I want to give them everything and take everything in return.

My heart is so damn full it's overflowing, and I know without a doubt that this is where I'm meant to be, right here, right now.

Then, like a rubber band snapping, he moves. Lunging for me and taking my mouth in such a primal form of ownership that it steals the air from my lungs.

He kisses me, hard and hot, his tongue stroking against mine and demanding everything I have to give. His hand slips between our bodies, his thick fingers circling my clit as all three men work together to drive me wild.

Their hands are everywhere, three hot mouths on mine, lips trailing down my throat, kneading my breasts, pinching my nipples. My moans fill the room, Tristan kissing a path along my jaw as Ryder's teeth nip at my throat.

"Oh god, yes," I pant, completely owned by them.

Beckett finally tears his mouth away from me with a groan, pulling back and raking his gaze over me as he licks his lips. "Fuck, you're beautiful. If we're doing this, we need to do it right."

He gives Ryder and Tristan a look, something silent passing between them, and both men slowly ease out of my pussy, the sudden emptiness making me gasp.

"Please," I whisper, almost shaking with the need to be filled again.

"We've got you, little menace," Beckett rumbles, pulling me against him and stuffing his fingers into my pussy like he can sense my need.

He doesn't fuck me with them, just holds them there, keeping me full as he directs the action.

"Tristan, grab the lube. Ryder, lie on your back." Beckett nods toward the center of the bed, and as Tristan grabs the lube, Ryder obliges, laying himself out like a calendar model. With one hand folded under his head and the other hand lazily stroking his hard cock, his eyes drill into me with an intensity that makes me feel more wanted than I've ever felt before.

"Are you ready for her?" Beckett asks.

"Fuck, yes." Ryder nods.

Tristan comes to stand next to us, his hand stroking gently over my hair, and Beckett pulls his fingers free, shifting to the side.

"Climb on top of him," he orders, and I immediately move, crawling toward Ryder. "That's it, dirty girl. Lie on top. No, baby, on your back."

My pulse jumps as I settle myself on top of Ryder, my head resting on his shoulder, the hard length of his cock slipping upward through my thighs. I feel utterly exposed, and for a second, I tense up, wondering if he really wants my weight on him like this.

Then he skims his hands up my sides, fondling my breasts as he shifts beneath me, angling his hips and pushing his cock against the lips of my pussy, and I realize that he can handle me. He wants me here just as badly as I want to be here. Each one of these men love everything about my body, and that's exactly why I want to share it with all of them.

No, to be *owned* by all of them.

"Can't fucking wait to be back inside you," Ryder mutters as he starts to push into me. "Oh fuck. That's it. So fucking good. You feel like heaven. Never want to be anywhere else but right here buried inside your hot pussy."

My breath catches in my throat, a new rush of wetness coating his shaft as he presses deeper, and Beckett's voice breaks through my pleasure haze.

"Hands on her hips, Ryder. Hold her steady for Tristan."

I look up, finding Beckett's eyes, and the raw, animalistic desire I see there makes my pussy clench, tightening around Ryder.

"Fuck," he curses, his fingers digging into my skin, but his hips remain still, like he's waiting for a signal.

I can't form words, the need inside me clawing to the surface and stripping away any ability to speak. But I don't need to say anything. Not with these men.

Beckett reads me like a book, and his voice is hoarse when he speaks.

"Now, Tristan. She's ready."

Tristan coats his cock with lube, then crawls onto the bed with us. The mattress dips as he kneels between our legs, his knees pressed into the backs of my thighs as he hikes my legs up. Ryder's cock pulses inside me, and his hold on my hips tightens even more.

"Do it," Beckett growls, kneeling next to us and stroking his thick length.

With a groan, Tristan fits his cockhead against my entrance, staring down at where we're connected with a heated reverence in his eyes that makes my chest ache. Then he pushes in, stretching me around him, his cock above Ryder's as he slowly works his way back inside me.

My head falls back against Ryder's shoulder, my lips parted in a silent scream as he sinks deeper. The angle is different than when they were both inside me before, and it's overwhelming.

"Too much?" Tristan's voice is tight with restraint.

"No," I manage, my voice ragged and barely audible. "Give me all of you."

He pushes in another inch, his breathing as ragged as mine, and then Ryder shifts, and a long, drawn-out moan leaves my lips as I'm suddenly filled with both of them.

"Oh god," I whimper, the feeling almost too much.

Tristan's hips jerk forward, shoving his cock the rest of the way home. "Fuck," he grits out. "You're so tight like this. I can feel Ryder's cock pulsing right against mine."

Ryder groans, and then they're fucking me, moving my body as if it's their own personal toy, using their strength and their cocks to send me soaring, pushing me closer and closer to the edge.

It would be so easy to tip over it and come on their cocks, but I want more. I want everything.

"Please, Beckett," I manage, looking over to where he's kneeling next to us, his eyes blazing as he fucks his fist like he's about to die.

I reach for him, sweaty and breathless, and he makes a feral sound of pure possession as he swoops down to kiss me. Then he straightens up, exchanging a look with Tristan.

Tristan leans back, holding himself still, as Beckett slicks his cock with lube and then straddles my hips.

"You're a fucking dream," he mutters, his eyes roaming over my body as his thick thighs bulge with strength, holding him between me and Tristan. "You ready for this, little menace?"

"I need it," I whisper, the most honest thing I've ever said.

Ryder and Tristan both hold themselves completely still as

Beckett strokes his leaking cockhead over my clit, sending a wave of heat to my core that almost drowns me.

Then he fits the blunt tip just above Tristan's cock, sliding it through my slick arousal to press against the lips of my pussy.

He feels impossibly big. Even bigger than usual.

He rubs his cockhead up and down, coating it with my wetness, and then starts to push inside, working his way into me with short, shallow movements that send shockwaves through my body.

It's almost more than I can take, the stretch so intense it blots out everything else, consuming me. Tears prick the backs of my eyes, and I throw my head back against Ryder's shoulder, panting as an equally intense pleasure starts to roll through my body, wave after wave of it with every inch Beckett gains.

"That's it. Fucking look at you, love. We've got you," Ryder mutters, his big hands still holding my hips steady as his muscles tense and contract under me, telling me without words that this is just as intense for him—for all of them—as it is for me.

"Oh fuck," Tristan whispers, a shudder going through him that I feel in my core. "Fuck, fuck, fuck, Jesus, fuck."

"Lana," Beckett growls, the low, deep sound reverberating through all three of them. "You fucking belong to us. You're taking me so damn well. I'm halfway there."

I'm shaking, trembling so hard that it feels like I'm falling apart. But these men won't let me. They're here, holding me together. Holding me open. Making me theirs.

"Take it," Beckett grits out. "Take all of me, dirty girl."

The pressure builds and builds as he gets deeper, and I gasp, the breath stolen from my lungs when he finally slides all the way home, his body rubbing against my clit as he settles against me with a groan.

Then they start to fuck me, instinctively finding a slow, coordinated rhythm that has their three cocks sliding in and out of me in a series of small movements that sets off a chain reaction I can't stop.

My core tightens into a fist-sized knot of need, and a strangled cry leaves my lips. "Oh god, I'm coming. Oh fuck. Fuck, fuck, fuck, yes. Yes! I'm... I'm..."

My whole body goes taut, the world falling away around me as I break apart. They're still moving, their cocks pushing into me, stretching me, claiming me. But the pleasure is so intense that it almost hurts.

And it's still not enough.

Beckett leans down, his eyes flashing, and captures my mouth in a brutal kiss, the motion driving his cock even deeper.

"Another," he demands, my pussy still rippling with after-shocks around their cocks.

He bites my bottom lip, and my moan turns into a ragged cry as Ryder and Tristan start to move, their cocks sliding against each other inside me, stretching and filling me to capacity.

"Fuck," Beckett groans, his grip on my chin tightening as he holds me still. "I can feel it. Every time they fuck you, I can feel them moving inside you."

"Please," I moan, the pressure building inside me again.

"Fuck, I'm close," Ryder grits out. "If you want this sweet pussy of yours to be filled with our cum, you're going to have to do what Beckett told you to and give us another first. Show us how much you want this. Show us how much you can take."

As Ryder speaks, Beckett lets go of my chin and adjusts his position, his thighs tensing as he balances above me and slowly presses into me with the strength of his legs alone.

"Yes!" I cry out, the word almost unintelligible.

"Come," he demands, his voice a low growl. "Now."

His hand snakes down between us, fingers brushing over my clit as he tugs on my piercing, and with no further warning, I hurtle over the edge.

I scream, my body seizing, every muscle locking down as my vision tunnels, the pleasure so intense that it's almost pain. I've never come like this before, like it transforms my whole body into a quivering vehicle of pleasure.

I hear their voices, but they sound far away. Like they're under-water. Then Beckett's hand closes over my throat, his big palm covering the sides of my neck, and everything snaps into crystal clear focus.

"Look at me. I want your eyes right here as we fill you. Beg for our cum, little menace. Tell us you want it."

"I do," I whisper. "Please."

He groans, and just like that, all three of them go off, one after the other. Their cocks swell and pulse inside my pussy as they pump me full of their cum, the feeling so incredible that it sends me into another orgasm.

The world falls away, the pleasure drowning me, and I'm only vaguely aware of their sweet, filthy words and powerful hands on me as they ease their way out of me, disentangling us and then shifting me to lie on the mattress.

"Let me see," Beckett rumbles, a hot look of possession in his eyes as he moves my body like it's a doll.

He spreads my legs, groaning as he watches their combined cum drip down my thighs.

He scoops it up, using his thick fingers to stuff it back in my pussy. "This is where it belongs, little menace. I want you to have it all."

"Fuck," Tristan breathes. "I love knowing we're still inside you."

"Our dirty, perfect girl," Ryder mutters, nuzzling the back of my neck.

Beckett kisses me, soft and sweet and possessive, his fingers buried inside me like he's determined to keep every drop inside me for as long as he can. "Good girl."

I smile, a bone-deep satisfaction spreading through me as the three men shift to cradle me, their bodies warm and protective as they kiss and caress me.

Eventually, they clean me up, insisting I drink some water and eat a few bites of the snacks Meg sent with us.

My body feels utterly used, and it's incredible. Like my brain is completely quiet and at peace, the emotional chaos of the last twenty-four hours silenced, replaced by a soul-deep certainty that these men are truly mine, and I'm theirs.

Not just now, but forever.

I look up at the attentive way they surround me, feelings pulsing through my chest.

"I love you," I whisper, the words coming out before I can stop them.

As soon as I say it, I feel a flutter of panic. "I know it might be too soon to say that, but it doesn't feel too soon. I've known you all for so long, seen what amazing men you are. After everything we've shared... I just... I love you. All three of you."

I bite my lip, suddenly unsure, but then Beckett's hand gently tilts my chin up.

"I love you too," he rumbles, his green eyes intense. "You've broken down walls I didn't even know I had. You're the perfect counterpart to me, Lana. The softness to my hardness, the light to my darkness. I didn't even know my life was missing anything before, but now I know that it was you all along."

There's no way I can doubt his sincerity, the depth of his emotion taking my breath away.

"Thank you," I whisper.

His full lips tilt up in a tender smile. "You don't ever need to thank me for loving you. It's my privilege. You're the best thing that's ever happened to me."

I blink back tears as Ryder's palm caresses my arm before he laces our fingers together and lifts my hand to his mouth.

"You don't know how long I've waited for someone like you. Hell, I didn't even know I was waiting. I was convinced I didn't need anyone besides my best friends. They were the only ones I trusted enough to get close to. But this?" He moves our joined hands to his chest, right over his heart. "I've spent my whole life running from this feeling, convinced I'd never want it. But loving you turned out to be as easy as breathing, and just as fucking necessary for my survival. I love you, Lana Reeves, and that's never gonna change."

My heart swells, his words making me feel cherished. Wanted.

"I feel the same." Tristan's voice is quiet. "My grandmother always told me to wait for someone who makes the world brighter just by being in it. Someone who lights me up every time I see her. That's always been you. It just took me a while to believe it was something we could actually have. But now that you're ours, I won't ever give you up."

My eyes well up with tears, and he brushes one away, smiling at me tenderly.

"I love you, freckles. And I always will."

Their declarations mean everything to me, their sweet words almost sounding too good to be true. And as much as I want them to be, I can't help biting my lip as I worry that maybe, in the after-glow of the amazing sex we just had, they're looking at me through glasses that are a little too rosy.

"Always is a long time," I force myself to say. "What about my lupus? There might be days when I'm not... fun to be around. When I'm tired or in pain. That's not going to go away."

Tristan cups my face gently. "We want all of you. The good days and the bad."

"Your illness doesn't change how we feel," Ryder adds, his voice firm.

Beckett nods, his eyes intense. "We're in this for the long haul. Whatever comes. Don't ever doubt that you're perfect for us, just the way you are. We wouldn't change a fucking thing."

Their words wash over me, soothing my fears as warmth spreads through my chest, bringing with it a sense of complete acceptance I've never known before.

"Thank you," I whisper. "You are... everything to me."

"I couldn't have said it any better, love," Ryder says tenderly, giving me a soft, sweet kiss that Tristan and Beckett quickly repeat before cleaning me up and preparing us all for bed.

"I could really get used to this," I say once the lights are out and I'm surrounded by their warmth and strength, all of us together under a fluffy down comforter subtly scented with pine.

"You're going to have to," Tristan murmurs, his arm draped over my waist.

Ryder's hand rests on my hip, and Beckett's fingers interlace with mine, as if all of them need to stay connected just as much as I do.

As their steady breathing lulls me toward sleep, I smile in the darkness, my heart so full I'm surprised my chest has room for it.

It's not where I expected to be the night before Christmas. It's so much better. Whatever Christmas day brings tomorrow, it's already the best one I've ever had. Because I've already been given every Christmas wish I ever could have asked for.

47

LANA

I wake slowly, cocooned in warmth and the comforting weight of three hard bodies pressed against mine. As my eyes flutter open, I'm greeted by the soft morning light filtering through the curtains of Grandma Meg's guest house. A quick glance out the window reveals a world transformed—a fresh blanket of snow covers everything, turning the landscape into a winter wonderland.

We're having a white Christmas.

I can't help but smile. This is exactly how I want to wake up every Christmas morning for the rest of my life.

"Merry Christmas," I whisper, my voice still scratchy from last night as the men start to stir next to me.

Tristan presses a soft kiss to my shoulder. "Merry Christmas, freckles."

Ryder's arm tightens around my waist as he mumbles a sleepy, "Merry Christmas, love."

Beckett's eyes are still closed, a small smile playing on his lips. "Merry Christmas," he echoes. "Did Santa leave us any presents?"

My mouth falls open. "Did you just make a joke?"

He chuckles without answering, but then I remember something and grin.

"Hang on a second." I carefully extricate myself from the

tangle of limbs, then pad across the room, crossing my fingers that I'll find what I'm looking for in one of their bags.

I do—the Santa hats they surprised me with on our road trip are tucked into the side pocket of Ryder's duffle bag, and a fluttery feeling of joy hits me as I pull them out. Fuck, I really do love Christmas.

Turning back to the bed, I'm struck by the sight of my three men, all sleep-rumpled and naked. They're more than just sexy, though. They're all incredibly good sports, letting me put a Santa hat on each of them for the low price of a single, filthy kiss.

"Are we gonna have to wear these all day?" Ryder asks when I step back to admire the view.

"That depends," I tease him. "Just how happy do you want to make me?"

I fan myself, playing it up, but I'm not exaggerating. The image of them like this—all naked except for those ridiculous hats—is one I want to burn into my memory forever. Sexy and silly and all mine.

Ryder's grin is positively wicked. "I think you already know the answer to that."

Tristan smirks. "And I think someone might have a Santa kink."

Beckett just raises an eyebrow, and I laugh, feeling light and happy.

"What can I say? I must have been a very good girl this year to get such wonderful presents."

"Oh, I don't know about that," Ryder teases, reaching for me and snagging my wrist. "I seem to remember you being on the naughty list last night."

As Ryder tugs me back onto the bed, I shiver at the memory of how very thoroughly they took care of that.

"Is Tristan right?" he whispers, deftly rolling me under him, face down on the bed with his hard, warm body pinning me to the mattress. "Do you have a Santa kink, love?"

"I... I think I have a *you* kink."

"I can work with that," he says, his chuckle warm and wicked as he grinds his cock against me, groping my curves.

I spread my legs in an instinctive response, and he groans, low and deep, as he pushes my hair aside to kiss the back of my neck. "Fuck, I can't get enough. One of these days, I'm going to get you under me like this while you're still sleeping. Just spread your thighs and sink right in. Fuck you while you're still half-dreaming and let you wake up impaled on my cock and already coming."

"Oh, god," I whimper.

His grip on my waist tightens, and I feel his cock thicken and harden against my ass. "Is that what you want, love? Are you gonna be a good girl and let me do that? Let us have you whenever we want, however we want?" His voice lowers, his breath ghosting across my ear and making me shiver. "Let me fuck you in your sleep?"

"Yes. Fuck, yes. Please."

He rolls off me, grinning as he sits up and pulls me into his lap. "Good."

"What?" I smack his chest playfully. "You're seriously going to say all that, do all that, and then... and then..."

"Not fuck you?"

I try to glare at him, but when he taps my cheek right where I know my dimple is, I know I've failed miserably.

"I love you," he says. "And it's Christmas morning. I will absolutely fuck you, but since there's no way we'd let you out of bed if we got started with that right now, and none of us want to make you miss Christmas..."

God help me, I'm tempted though.

But I'm also incredibly touched. I know the holiday isn't his favorite, but he knows for sure that it's mine.

"Thank you," I say, running my fingers over the rough stubble on his cheeks and leaning in for a chaste kiss. "I really do love you."

"My turn," Beckett rumbles, tugging me off Ryder's lap and pulling me onto his.

He wraps a hand around my throat, tipping my head back so he can kiss me. Then he lifts me up and sets me on the ground, rising from the bed in one fluid movement.

"Wha—?" I ask, feeling a little dazed and a whole lot turned on.

He gives me that wicked grin I love so much, blatantly adjusting his hard cock. "Ryder is right. We'll keep you busy in here all day if we don't exercise a little self-control."

I pout. I can't help it. And instead of his usual resting hard-ass Dom face, Beckett laughs.

Tristan grabs his glasses off the nightstand and fits them on his face, then pulls me close and smiles against my lips as he kisses me. "For the record, I second all of that, freckles, but I also know Grandma Meg has probably been up and cooking for at least an hour. How about we head into the main house and exchange gifts?"

"I'd love that."

"I want this Christmas to be everything you've dreamed of, even though..." He hesitates, his playful expression turning a little more serious. "I know you were expecting to be with your family today."

"I was," I agree softly.

"Are you okay?"

I pause, considering my answer. The confrontation yesterday was intense, but it was also a relief, and I decide not to let myself feel bad about it. Sometimes, family is more than blood. It's the people who choose you. Who put you first. Who prove that they care.

The people I'm with today.

I smile up at Tristan, nodding. "Yeah, I am. This trip definitely hasn't gone the way I expected, but I feel like I'm exactly where I'm supposed to be."

He pulls me into a hug. "Damn right you are."

Beckett nods, stepping closer. "We've got you, little menace. Always."

"But about being exactly where you're supposed to be..." Ryder grins, adjusting his Santa hat and pulling a wrapped gift out of his duffle bag. "We should get a move on. I swear I can smell bacon cooking in the main house."

Tristan laughs. "Pretty sure that's wishful thinking."

Ryder looks stricken. "No bacon?"

Beckett throws his toiletries bag at him. "No way in hell you'd be able to smell it from here, so hurry up and get dressed so we can go find out."

His words are punctuated by his stomach rumbling, and we all hurry to shower and get dressed, laughing and joking as we leave the guesthouse.

Outside, it's a real-life winter wonderland.

"Oh my god." My hands fly to my cheeks as the brisk air hits them, and I turn in a circle, taking in the pristine snow that blankets the ground.

"It's beautiful," Tristan agrees, but when I glance at him, he's not looking at the snowscape.

He's looking at me.

My heart stutters in my chest—and then I stifle a laugh as I see Ryder stealthily packing up a snowball behind him.

"Watch out!" I blurt, warning Tristan just in time for him to turn and take the snowball right in the chest.

"Oh, it's fucking *on*," Tristan declares, dropping to his knees and packing a snowball of his own.

Before he can get it ready, another snowball smacks him in the shoulder. He turns and narrows his eyes at Beckett.

"Seriously?"

Beckett shrugs. "What? You weren't paying attention."

Tristan makes a grab for Beckett, but the massive man just laughs, ducking out of the way and sending a snowball whizzing through the air, aimed right at me.

I let out a squeak. "Hey! I thought you loved me!"

Ryder laughs, tackling me into a snowbank. "You know what they say, all is fair in love and war."

And with that, he grabs a handful of snow and almost manages to cram it down the front of my coat.

"Oh, you are in so much trouble," I growl as I roll away, leaping to my feet and grabbing my own handful of snow.

The three men look at each other.

Then they run.

I give chase, laughing my head off and pelting them with snowballs, then shrieking as they turn on me, catching me and tossing me up into the air before catching me.

"Uncle! Uncle!" I cry.

They're laughing too, their arms around me, their breath steaming, and their faces flushed with exertion. They're the sexiest men I've ever seen, and they're all mine.

"Damn," Ryder murmurs. "Maybe we should head back to the guest house."

I smack his chest, wiggling free. "No. I was promised bacon and presents and Christmas."

He groans. "So fucking greedy."

My cheeks flush, the heat in his eyes telling me that—just like I am—he's remembering all the other times they've accused me of being their greedy, dirty girl.

He pushes my hair back from my face and kisses me, our breath fogging the air, then the four of us all head into the main house.

The minute we walk in, the sounds and smells of Grandma Meg cooking breakfast waft over us. Baldwin races toward us, yapping excitedly as if to point out that yes, there is in fact the scent of bacon in the air.

I scoop him up. "Merry Christmas, you little fashionista."

Meg has him dressed in yet another ugly Christmas sweater today, one that makes him look like the world's cutest ugly little elf, complete with tiny bells around his ankles.

Grandma Meg walks out of the kitchen, drying her hands on a Christmas-themed dish towel.

She grins, taking in our snow-covered state. "I see you kids started the festivities early. Come on in before you catch your death. I'll see about getting something to warm you back up."

True to her word, as soon as we've shed our wet outer layers, Meg joins us in the living room, bringing with her a tray that smells like Christmas. She hands each of us a steaming mug of what turns out to be spiked eggnog.

"This should take the chill off."

I breathe in the festive scent, then take a sip. "Yum. Thank you. And Merry Christmas!"

"Merry Christmas to you too, dear. And I do hope you all managed to get some sleep last night." She winks, making me blush. "Though I can't say I'd blame you if you didn't. It's not every day you have three strapping young men to keep you warm."

"Grandma!" Tristan groans, but there's no real embarrassment in his voice. If anything, he sounds fond.

Meg just laughs, patting his cheek. "Oh hush, you. I may be old, but I'm not dead. Now, who's ready for some Christmas morning pancakes?"

"And bacon?" Beckett asks hopefully.

"Of course," Meg scoffs. "What kind of monster starts the day without bacon?"

Baldwin lets out a sharp yip of agreement, making us all laugh as we follow her into the kitchen.

As we all take our seats around the table, I look around for a moment. This is what family should feel like—accepting and loving, full of laughter and light-hearted teasing. It really is the perfect Christmas morning.

Ryder catches my eye and smiles, as if reading my thoughts. "Merry Christmas, love," he murmurs, pressing a quick kiss to my temple.

I lean into him, watching as Tristan helps Meg with the pancakes while Beckett entertains Baldwin with a new squeaky toy.

My heart feels so full it might burst, and by the time we've all eaten, helped Meg clean up, and settled around her beautiful tree with more mugs of eggnog, there's a sweet ache in my chest, as if the happiness is too much for it.

Then her doorbell rings.

Tristan looks up. "Are you expecting someone, Grandma Meg?"

"Expecting? No," she says, heading for the door. "But hoping? Yes."

When the door swings wide to reveal Caleb standing on the other side, I blink in surprise.

Last night was so emotional that it didn't fully register with me when she invited him to join us for Christmas. And I guess a part of me dismissed the possibility that he'd choose us—me—over continuing to be the perfect son who showed up for our parents.

But he's here, and despite the tension from yesterday, he greets Tristan, Ryder, and Beckett with warm handshakes and back-slapping hugs.

When he turns to me, his eyes are soft. "Hey, Lana. Merry Christmas."

"Merry Christmas," I repeat, my throat tight as he pulls me into a hug. "I'm really glad you came."

"Me too," he says as we separate, squeezing my shoulders. "And I didn't say this before, but I'm really proud of you for standing up to Mom and Dad like that. I had no idea things were so rough for you, that you felt under so much pressure. I wish I'd stood up for you more."

I feel my eyes welling up with tears, but I blink them back, offering him a watery smile. "It's okay. You had my back plenty. And now..." I glance over at Tristan, Ryder, and Beckett. "I've got three more people who have my back too."

Beckett pins Caleb with a hard stare. "We've always had her back."

Caleb nods, a small smile playing on his lips. If Beckett's show of protectiveness is supposed to be a challenge, he's clearly not taking it that way. If anything, he seems pleased, relaxing a little more, like maybe he's coming around to the idea of his three best friends dating his little sister.

"Yeah," he agrees, clapping Beckett on the shoulder. "I can see that."

They hold eye contact for a minute, then Beckett grunts, giving my brother a quick nod.

Caleb snorts and pulls him in for another hug, clapping his back.

"Just don't fuck it up," he whispers, quietly enough that I'm pretty sure I wasn't supposed to hear.

Grandma Meg claps her hands. "Caleb, you look cold, dear.

Get that coat off and let's get you some eggnog. Come on, come on."

"Yes, ma'am," Caleb says, laughing as he shrugs off his outerwear and follows us all back into the living room.

His eyes soften as they land on Meg's tree. It's nothing like the overdone, themed and color-coordinated ones my mother always puts up.

"I remember this," he says, walking over and picking up one of the homemade ornaments. It's a hockey puck, nestled inside a knit sleeve with a date patterned into the yarn. "Our senior year, right, Tristan?"

Tristan laughs. "Winning goal. Grandma wanted to commemorate it."

Caleb shakes his head, smiling, and when he catches my eye I'm almost certain he's thinking the same thing I am. Unlike the designer ornaments on the Christmas trees we grew up with, all the ornaments on Meg's tree commemorate her love for her family and the life they shared.

That kind of joy is so much more valuable than a few shiny, perfectly coordinated baubles.

"All right, I think that's enough reminiscing." Meg waves her hands in the air. "Let's—"

The doorbell rings again before she can finish that sentence. Baldwin races out of the room, barking, to go see who it is.

"Well!" Meg says, getting back to her feet and following. "Good thing I made plenty of eggnog."

I look at Tristan, but he just shrugs. As far as I know, they don't have any family in the area, but it doesn't surprise me at all that someone as welcoming as Meg would have plenty of visitors today.

The moment we hear the door open, excited, childish chatter fills the hallway.

It's Vivian, with Oliver bouncing at her side.

I blink in surprise. Not that I'm not happy to see them, I just... don't understand why they're here.

"It's Christmas!" Oliver announces with five-year-old glee as soon as Meg leads them into the living room.

Baldwin yaps excitedly, dancing around his feet.

Then Oliver catches sight of Beckett and launches himself at the big man, yapping almost as loudly as Baldwin as he starts telling him all about what Santa left in his stocking that morning.

Beckett's face softens in a way I've rarely seen as he scoops Oliver up. "Hey, buddy. Merry Christmas. That sounds like a lot of fun."

The sight of Beckett, usually so gruff, being so gentle with Oliver makes my heart swell. But my attention is quickly drawn back to my sister. Vivian looks... different. Her usual perfect poise is gone, replaced by something raw and vulnerable. Emotions I can't quite name play over her features, all tightly contained as if she doesn't want to let them leak out and spoil her son's magical morning.

"Viv?" I say softly, stepping toward her.

I'm about to ask if she's okay, but the memory of how she rebuffed me at our parents' party stops my tongue. Still, she's here, and since I'm pretty sure she's not part of Meg's knitting circle, that has to mean something since clearly she figured out that it's where she'd find either me or Caleb, or both of us.

"I'm glad you're here," I say honestly. "Um, would you like some eggnog?"

She gives me a stiff smile. "No, thank you, I'm watching my..."

I lift an eyebrow. Watching her figure?

For once, I don't take it personally. If that's what makes her happy, who am I to judge? Then again, maybe we all need a little nudge sometimes.

"Live a little," I say, quickly pouring her a mug. Then, leaning in, I whisper, "It's spiked with the good stuff."

She hesitates, then laughs quietly and takes it, her shoulders relaxing a bit.

"Thank you. I could actually use that right now." She takes a shaky breath, looking around the crowded room. "Actually, can we talk for a second? Privately?"

I nod, leading her to Meg's sewing room. As soon as we're alone, Vivian's composure crumbles, tears filling her eyes.

I take her mug and set it on the coffee table, wrapping her in a hug. "What's going on?"

"I'm leaving Kyle," she blurts out, her voice barely above a whisper.

I blink, stunned. "What? What happened?"

I let her go, and she pushes aside a pile of yarn and sinks back onto Meg's plush loveseat with a sigh.

I sit beside her, taking her hand.

"He's been cheating," she admits, her lips pursing tightly before she goes on. "It's been going on for a while now. I... I knew, but I didn't want to rock the boat. I thought if I just ignored it, I could pretend it didn't matter. That we really were the beautiful, perfect family you complimented me on yesterday."

"Oh, Vivian," I say, my heart aching for her. All this time, I thought she really did have the perfect life, but she was struggling too.

She pulls in a shaky breath, wiping at her face.

"Did something happen this morning to, um..."

I'm not sure how to ask in a way that won't be painful for her, but if she knows Kyle's been a shit for a while now, I'm wondering what changed. What he did to bring things to the point that she'd confess this to *me*, of all people.

We've never been close... although I'd like that to change, if it's possible.

She looks up at me with a small smile. "Something did happen. Not this morning, but last night."

I suck in a sharp breath, feeling slightly murderous toward my brother-in-law. "What did he do?"

Her smile gets a little bigger. "Nothing. It was you."

"What?"

She squeezes my hand, then lets it go and picks up the mug of eggnog, closing her eyes in appreciation as she takes a drink.

"God, I need this," she says with a quiet laugh. "Please remind me to thank Meg for adding the rum."

My heart is thundering in my chest. "Vivian? What did I do?"

She looks me in the eye, her spine getting straighter. "You stood

459

up to Mom and Dad. You were so brave, Lana. It made me realize that I need to start living for myself too. It gave me the courage to admit that my marriage *isn't* perfect, and the strength to... to walk away from it."

My eyes go wide, my throat tight with emotion.

"Oh, Viv. I'm so sorry you've been going through this alone. I'm sorry you've been going through it at all. What a shit-head!"

That startles a laugh out of her, making me grin too as our eyes meet and a connection I've always longed for with her springs into being between us.

It's not the way I'd have wanted it to happen, but it still warms my heart.

All my life, Vivian has seemed like our parents' perfect child, but I guess she's always had problems and fears of her own too. Maybe the two of us are more alike than I ever thought.

She wipes her eyes, taking in a shuddering breath, but looking lighter when she smiles at me again. "I just wanted to thank you for that, but I also owe you an apology."

"For what?"

"All those things you said to Dad..." She shakes her head, squeezing my hand again. "I'm sorry, Lana. I've been so caught up in trying to be perfect that I never realized how much pressure you were under. I should have been there for you more."

I smile at her. "It sounds like we were all going through our own stuff, but I'm glad you're here now."

"Me too," she says, smiling back.

And when she hugs me, something I can't remember us doing in... ever, it feels like we've mended some bridges.

Which is one of the best Christmas gifts I ever could have asked for.

LANA

"I WANTED to bring Caleb's and Lana's gifts by, but I don't want to impose," Vivian murmurs to Grandma Meg when Meg ushers her toward the plush couch nearest the Christmas tree.

"Nonsense," Meg says, enveloping her in a hug. "The more, the merrier. And your timing couldn't be more perfect, because I do believe it's time for presents!"

Oliver cheers, making us all laugh, and seeing how easily Meg welcomes Vivian and my nephew into the fold warms my heart.

This is what family is supposed to be. This is what Christmas is supposed to be.

The fireplace crackles merrily as we all get settled around Meg's lovely tree, casting a cheery glow over the room. Meg has potpourri burning on the mantle next to her nativity scene, scenting the entire room with a sweet, spicy blend of cloves, oranges, and cinnamon. The eggnog flows freely, and we all help ourselves to the platter of cookies and other snacks as Oliver digs through the pile of wrapped presents under the tree.

"Who is this one for?" he asks excitedly, pulling out a beautifully wrapped box with a bright red bow.

"That one is from me, for your mom." Caleb points to a second box with festive paper and a matching bow. "And that one is for you, squirt."

Oliver's grin stretches from ear to ear, but before ripping into his own gift, he brings Vivian's to her.

"Thanks, sweetheart. Do you want to give your aunt and uncle their gifts too?"

Oliver scrambles to get them, and I point out the ones I got for my brother and sister so he can distribute those too.

"What about this one?" Oliver asks, grabbing a larger box with the kind of professional wrapping that screams mall gift wrap center.

Meg laughs, patting her hands in the air as if to tell him to settle down. "How about we spend a little time opening the ones you've already passed around, little elf, before we get on to the next ones."

"Okay, okay," Oliver says, plopping himself down and ripping through the wrapping paper on his gifts from Caleb—a pint-sized hockey set and what looks like a custom jersey with Caleb's number on it—and from me, an age-appropriate art supply set that I half expect Vivian to frown about, since I know her home is all carpeted in white.

Instead, she surprises me by squeezing my hand. "He'll have fun with that, Lana. Thank you."

I beam at her, then quickly finish unwrapping the gifts my siblings gave me as they each do the same. I'm so damn grateful that they both chose to be here with me on Christmas morning.

The guys direct our Christmas elf to the gifts they've brought for Grandma Meg next. She coos over a set of gardening tools from Tristan, laughs delightedly at a risqué romance novel from Ryder, and tears up a little at a framed photo of all of us from Beckett.

She's not the only one. It's a candid shot from a cell phone camera, from the Christmas tree farm we stopped at. I don't know when he took the time to print it and pick up a frame for it, but I already know I want a copy of it for myself too.

Meg wipes her eyes quickly, as if she doesn't want to make a fuss, then grabs a flat box with silly paper on it. "Now, Oliver, this one is for Baldwin, but I think he's going to have a little trouble opening it. Do you think you can help him, dear?"

Oliver grins. "I can do that!"

We all laugh as he dives into his task, sending wrapping paper and ribbon flying. The tiny dog yaps as he's presented with a new sweater—this one adorned with tiny reindeer—and a squeaky toy shaped like a Christmas tree.

Then Beckett clears his throat. "You didn't forget that one, did you, Oliver?"

He points to the larger, professionally wrapped gift Oliver had picked up earlier, and Oliver dives for it.

"Who's this one for, Uncle Beckett?"

Beckett's ears go just a bit pink at the honorary title. "That one's for you, buddy."

"From Santa?"

"Sure."

"But Santa already brought me my gifts at home this morning."

Beckett looks at me with a hint of panic, and it takes everything I have not to laugh.

"I think what Uncle Beckett means is, it's from one of Santa's helpers."

Oliver blinks. "Who?"

"Me," Beckett confesses, and Oliver gapes in awe.

He throws his arms around Beckett's neck, then rips the wrapping paper, letting out a squeal of pure joy when he sees what's inside.

"The Millennium Falcon Lego set! Mom, look!"

Beckett clears his throat. "I, uh, I know it's a bit complicated, Vivian, but he was kind of excited about it the other day. I'd be happy to supervise and help him build it, if that's okay."

Oliver's eyes light up again, and he looks at Beckett like he's just offered him the moon. "Really? You'll help me?"

Beckett nods, a small smile playing on his lips. "Sure thing, kid. We'll make it a project."

"*After* we get through the rest of the presents," Vivian says in a firm voice, but she shoots Beckett a grateful look.

Oliver looks disappointed at having to wait, but he's quickly distracted by Meg asking him to distribute a few more gifts.

I nudge Beckett gently with my elbow. "For a guy who doesn't want kids, you're really good with them," I tease softly.

Beckett's face takes on a faint flush. "Yeah, about that. I might have been rethinking my 'no kid' stance lately."

My heart flutters at his words. I glance at Oliver, who's watching raptly as Baldwin chases the squeaky toy. "Well, I can see why. Oliver could make anyone want to have a kid."

"He's a great kid. But it's not just Oliver. Getting to know him helped, sure, but..." He hesitates, his gaze finding mine. "Let's just say that being with you has made me see a lot of things differently. There are a lot of things I didn't want before that I do now, and I think it's not so much about those *things*, but who I want them with."

My heart skips several beats at his words—but before I can respond, Oliver holds up the three small, carefully wrapped packages I tucked under the tree myself this morning.

"Who are these for?"

I smile at him. "Those ones are from me, for Tristan, Ryder, and Beckett.

Oliver passes them around as I explain.

"I got these at that little shop at the Christmas tree farm. They're not much, but they made me think of each of you."

They unwrap their gifts, revealing three ornaments shaped like frosted gingerbread cookies, just like the ones Beckett picked up for us while we were on the road.

Just like them, but each with one unique difference.

Tristan chuckles, grinning at me as he holds his ornament up next to him. "It's perfect."

The glasses the "cookie" is wearing are just like his. But it's more than just how cute the similarity is.

"It made me think of you because you *see* me," I tell him. "And yours, Ryder—"

"Reminds you of how handsome I am?" he cuts in, posing comically with the little ornament and its rakishly tilted Santa hat.

I laugh. "Exactly. But also how playful you are, and..."

"And?"

I shrug, but can feel myself blushing. "I guess the Santa hat is kind of symbolic. You weren't a big fan of Christmas, but you were willing to indulge my love for it every step of the way. That means a lot to me."

His gaze softens. "*You* mean a lot to me."

"To all of us," Beckett says, his voice gruff as he runs a finger over his ornament's festive knit scarf. He looks up at me. "I can see why you picked this one for me."

"It reminds me of your softer side."

He raises a single eyebrow, and Tristan, Caleb, and Ryder all laugh.

"Softer side, sis?" Caleb repeats with a grin. "You have met Beckett, right?"

Beckett holds my gaze, ignoring their teasing as I smile up at him. I fucking love that this big, gruff man has a soft side—one that has him knitting scarves for sick children and buying my nephew the overpriced toy he talked Beckett's ear off about. And I love that he lets me see it.

"It's amazing," he murmurs. "Thank you, little menace. And we've got something for you too."

Tristan, Ryder, and Beckett exchange a meaningful glance. Then Tristan goes to the tree and pulls a small, shimmering red envelope with delicate gold snowflakes embossed on its surface from its branches.

My eyes go wide. I saw it there, of course, but didn't give it much thought, assuming it was another ornament. The edges are trimmed with a thin border of white faux fur, giving it a cozy, Santa-like appearance, and a sprig of fresh pine is tucked into the corner, secured by a tiny golden bell that jingles softly as Tristan hands it to me.

"What's this?" I ask, my heart filling with warmth as I turn it over in my hands.

"Open it," Ryder urges.

The envelope isn't a standard size. Instead, it's perfectly square and fits in my palm. It's also strangely heavy for such a small thing.

The flap is sealed with a wax stamp in the shape of a Christmas tree, and I slide my finger under it, loosening it carefully.

Once I get it open, I turn it upside down, and a single key falls out, attached to an adorable keychain in the shape of a painter's palette with an address engraved on the back.

"What is this?" I look up at them, my brow furrowed.

"Can I see, Auntie Lana?" Oliver asks, leaning over my shoulder. "Pretty! It's like the paints you got me. Do you wanna paint with me?"

"Sure, honey," I tell him, turning and giving him a butterfly kiss on his cheek.

He giggles, which makes Baldwin yip with excitement and hop around at his feet.

"I'd like to see you do a lot of painting," Beckett says quietly as Oliver gets distracted by Baldwin. "We all would."

"Which is why we bought you an art studio back in L.A.," Tristan adds.

My jaw drops. "You... what?"

"An art studio space," Ryder repeats. "A place where you can create and showcase your work."

I'm speechless. Shocked. My art has always just been a hobby, and they...

"You *bought* it for me? But... why?"

Beckett's deep voice rumbles with emotion. "We wanted you to be able to pursue your creativity the way you've always wanted to. The way it deserves."

"You're incredibly talented, love," Ryder adds, no sign of joking on his face at all.

"But..." I shake my head, overwhelmed. Then I blurt, "You're leaving L.A."

I bite my lip, my heart clenching. Deciding to make this thing real between us is so new, and so much has happened in such a short time that none of us have talked about the future. And as amazing as this gift is, I'm not sure I'll want to be pursuing my art in L.A. once they move to a different city.

Tristan's eyes soften, as if he can read my mind. "We decided to invest in this instead of the new club."

"Wait, *what?*" I clutch the little key to my chest, staring at the three of them incredulously. "You're not opening the new club? The one you've been planning? The one you were going to move for?"

"Nope," Ryder says with a half grin.

Tristan grins too. "Not right now, at least. Maybe in the future, but we've got other priorities at the moment."

"We're going to focus on expanding Radiance in L.A. for now," Beckett rumbles.

"But—"

"No buts," Ryder interrupts me. "Supporting your artistic venture is more important to us right now."

Beckett leans closer, his eyes intense. "You're so talented, little menace. The world deserves to see your work."

I feel tears welling up in my eyes. All my life, my family has dismissed my love for art as a "little hobby," pushing me toward what they considered a "real" job. But Beckett, Ryder, and Tristan clearly don't see it that way.

I swallow, glancing down at the key in my hand—a key to my future, to my dreams. Proof that these men believe in those dreams. In *me.*

"I don't know what to say," I whisper, my voice choked with emotion.

"Say 'thank you,' dear," Meg whispers, patting my hand.

I laugh. "Thank you. That doesn't even feel big enough, but..."

The reality of their gift is sinking in, and I'm overwhelmed not just by their support, but by the knowledge of what they've given up.

"Didn't we say no 'buts'?" Ryder teases gently.

I nod, then shake my head and take a breath. "But... the new nightclub. You can't just give it up. That was your future. I don't want to take that away from you."

Tristan shakes his head, his eyes soft. "No, freckles. *You're* our future."

"I can't believe you did this," I whisper, my voice shaky with emotion.

Ryder takes my hand, his thumb tracing my knuckles. "Of course we did. When you love someone, you want to see all their dreams come true."

I smile through happy tears, wiping at my cheeks as happiness swells in my chest. "They already have."

Beckett grins. "That just means you get to dream *bigger* now, little menace. And we'll be right beside you for it."

"Damn," Caleb grumbles, waving his hand at the four of us as he tries to fight a smile. "You guys are making it kind of hard to have a problem with all this."

"A problem with what, Uncle Caleb?" Oliver asks, looking up from the game he's playing with Baldwin.

"Nothing, sweetheart," Vivian murmurs, giving me a warm smile that's mirrored on Meg's face. "He's just being silly."

Beckett catches a tear that's clinging from my lashes, and the joy inside me bubbles up and spills over all at once. I kiss him, pouring all my love and gratitude into it.

"I take it back," I hear Caleb grouch good-naturedly. And then, when Beckett lets me go and I turn to do the same with Ryder, then Tristan, he gives an exaggerated groan, swinging Oliver up in his arms and covering Oliver's eyes with his hands. "Don't look, squirt. Lana is sitting under too much mistletoe."

Oliver tugs Caleb's hands down, looking up at the empty ceiling above me with an adorably confused expression. "I don't see any mistletoe, Uncle Caleb."

"They don't need any," Vivian says warmly. "Some things are magical all on their own."

LANA

THE MORNING after Christmas is crisp and clear, with a fresh layer of snow blanketing the world outside Grandma Meg's cozy guest house. As we prepare to leave, a bittersweet feeling settles in my chest. This Christmas has been magical, but it also includes a rift with my parents that I don't regret, but which aches all the same.

I pull Grandma Meg into a tight hug, breathing in the comforting scent of cinnamon and vanilla that seems to cling to her. "Thank you so much for everything," I murmur.

She pats my back affectionately. "Of course, dear. You're welcome here anytime." As we pull apart, she winks mischievously. "In fact, I hope to see a lot more of you now that you're in a relationship with my grandson."

I laugh, glancing over at Tristan, who's not even trying to hide his smile.

"I promise we'll keep in touch," I assure her.

Baldwin trots over, his latest hand-knit sweater making him look like a tiny, adorable reindeer. He yaps excitedly, showering me with sweet puppy kisses as I kneel to say goodbye.

Then I stand and turn to my men, who have finished their own farewells with Grandma Meg. It's time to go collect the rest of our things from my parents' house before we get back on the road and head back to L.A.

"Ready?" Tristan asks softly, reaching for my hand.

I nod, lacing my fingers with his. "As I'll ever be."

We pile into the SUV, waving goodbye to Grandma Meg as we pull out of her driveway. As familiar streets pass by, I feel a knot forming in my stomach. I have no idea what kind of reception awaits us at my childhood home. Will my parents have calmed down? Will they even let us in?

Ryder must sense my tension because he leans forward from the backseat, resting a comforting hand on my shoulder. "We've got your back, love. No matter what happens."

Beckett grunts in agreement from behind the wheel, his eyes meeting mine briefly in the rearview mirror.

I take a deep breath, drawing strength from their unwavering support. Whatever happens next, at least I know I'm not facing it alone. Still, as we pull up to my parents' house, I feel my anxiety spike.

Before I can even reach for the door handle, Tristan and Ryder are out of the car, each offering me a hand. Beckett flanks my other side as I step out, the three of them forming a protective barrier around me.

Their housekeeper answers the door, and the house feels unnaturally quiet as we enter. There's no sign of Vivian or Caleb—just my parents, their faces pinched and wary as they watch us file in.

"We're just here to get our things," I say, my voice steadier than I feel.

My father nods stiffly, and my mother turns away, unable to meet my eyes.

There's a pang in my chest as I compare this cold welcome to the warmth we just left at Grandma Meg's, but I don't regret what I said to them. I can't, because it's the truth.

Tristan, Ryder, and Beckett quickly gather their belongings from the guest room, then accompany me to my childhood bedroom. Their presence is a comforting shield as I pack up the last of my things.

It doesn't take long, but when we head back downstairs to leave, my mother's voice stops us.

"Vivian called." Her voice is calm on the surface, but I can hear the shock reverberating in her tone as she adds, "She's... she's leaving Kyle. Kyle *Doherty*."

I turn to face them, seeing the disbelief and disappointment etched on their faces. But the way she emphasized Kyle's family name, as if him being mayor's son is more important than my sister's happiness, makes something inside me snap.

"Good for her," I say firmly. "You should be happy for Vivian. She's making the right choice for herself."

My father's brow furrows. "But Kyle is—"

"Rich? Well-connected?" I interrupt. "What does any of that matter if he's not treating her right? Don't you think being with a man who loves and respects her, who's faithful to her, should be the most important thing in her marriage?"

"I don't think you're seeing the big picture here," my father says with a scowl.

I take a deep breath, feeling Beckett's reassuring hand on my lower back. "No, I think you're looking at the wrong picture, Dad. The picture-perfect version of this family that only exists in your head, based on your standards. But these are the children you have. Not picture-perfect ones, but me, Vivian, and Caleb. We're all different, we're all making our own choices, and if those choices don't meet your expectations, it's up to you to accept us or not. But if you don't..." I pause, steeling myself. "If you don't, that picture might start to look pretty empty."

Mom's lips pinch. "I don't know what you're trying to say, Lana. Your father and I have always wanted nothing but the best for all three of you."

"No, you've wanted your version of the best. And what I'm saying is that you might not have us in your lives anymore if you can't support each of us living the lives that make us happy. Us, not you."

My parents exchange a look, something unreadable passing between them, but if I'm hoping for them to have some kind of epiphany, or suddenly declare their understanding and devotion, I'm disappointed. All I get is a stiff nod from my father and my mother telling us that the housekeeper can see us out.

"No need, I know the way," I say softly, searching both of their faces for any sign that I've gotten through to them.

I don't find it, and as we walk away from my parents' house, I feel a strange mixture of sadness and relief wash over me. I may be disappointed, but I have no regrets. I've said what needed to be said, drawn my line in the sand, and established boundaries that actually feel healthy for once.

And I feel... free.

The moment we're out of sight of the house, Tristan pulls me into a tight hug. "You were amazing in there," he murmurs, pressing a kiss to my temple.

Ryder joins in, wrapping his arms around both of us. "That's our brave girl," he says, his voice filled with pride.

Beckett hangs back a bit, but when our group hug breaks apart, he catches my eye. There's understanding there, a shared pain that doesn't need words. He opens his arms, and I step into them, burying my face in his chest.

"It gets easier," he rumbles softly, his words for me alone. "Choosing yourself hurts like hell at first, but it gets easier."

I nod, grateful for his understanding, and by how open about his emotions he is with me now. It does help to know that he's been where I am now, having cut ties with his own abusive father years ago. His strength gives me hope, and his support and understanding mean everything.

We load up our things and pile into the SUV, Ryder taking the first driving shift. As he adjusts the rearview mirror, I notice he's donned his Santa hat again. He adjusts it to the same jaunty angle as the ornament I gave him, then catches my eye in the mirror and grins.

"All aboard the Christmas Express!" he announces cheerfully.

I laugh, feeling some of the tension melt away. "You do realize it's December 26th, right? Christmas is over."

His grin widens. "We make our own rules."

"I thought you hated Christmas," I tease him.

Ryder shrugs, a mischievous glint in his eye as we hit the road again. "What can I say? I'm coming around to it. In fact, it might just be my new favorite holiday."

THE TRIP back to L.A. goes by much faster than the one that brought us all together.

Several days after leaving New Hampshire, the gentle brush of lips against my forehead slowly pulls me from sleep.

"Wake up, freckles. We're home," a soft voice murmurs.

I blink, feeling groggy, and it takes me a moment to realize I'm still in the SUV, my head resting on Tristan's shoulder.

The guys set a harder pace as we headed for home, staying on the road a lot longer each day and covering the ground more quickly. They also did the majority of the driving, insisting I rest and recover from the whirlwind trip.

"What time is it?" I mumble, stretching as best I can in the confines of the backseat.

"Just past eleven," Ryder answers from the driver's seat. "December 31st. We made it back for New Year's Eve after all."

I perk up at that, the fog of sleep starting to clear. "Really? We're in L.A.?"

Beckett chuckles, already out of the car and opening my door. "See for yourself, sleepyhead."

As I step out, the familiar warmth of a California night wraps around me. The air smells of jasmine and distant ocean, so different from the crisp winter we left behind in New Hampshire. It feels surreal to be back, like waking from a vivid dream.

"Come on," Tristan says, his hand finding the small of my back. "Let's get inside."

I nod, a thrill going through me as I look up at the gorgeous house the three of them share. We still haven't made concrete plans about how this relationship will look, but when they invited me to stay at their place tonight, I was more than happy to say yes. With

473

them, wherever they are, is exactly where I want to be, and knowing they want that too energizes me even more as we all walk through their front door.

It's the first time I've been here, and it's so... them. Distinctly masculine, yet comforting. I smile as I take in the spacious living room, a perfect blend of modern aesthetics and cozy touches.

As we settle into the house, dropping bags and shrugging off jackets, the banter flows easily between us. Tristan teases Ryder about his questionable playlist choices during the drive, while Ryder retorts with a jab about Tristan's lead foot.

I'm laughing at their antics when Beckett's deep voice cuts through the chatter. "Lana, come upstairs with me for a second. I want to show you something."

He leads me up to his room, a gorgeous space filled with warm earth tones, well-worn leather furniture, and a few personal touches that hint at the gentler side beneath his gruff exterior. A skein of yarn on the dresser, a pair of reading glasses on the bedside table, and a small potted succulent on the windowsill.

I take a moment to appreciate the view from the window—the lights of the city sparkling against the night sky. Then I turn back to Beckett, running my hand over the soft black comforter on the massive bed that dominates the room.

"Is this what you brought me up here to show me?" I tease lightly.

He shakes his head, unzipping his travel bag instead of reaching for me.

"No, it's something else."

He hesitates for just a moment, piquing my curiosity, then pulls out a handful of rumpled paper.

Not *just* paper. There are napkins and a few receipts mixed in with sheets of hotel stationary and the thicker paper I recognize from my own sketchbook. Because that's what he's got there. Every sketch, drawing, and doodle I did during our road trip. Every single one of them, even the ones I crumpled up and tossed aside after finishing.

"You... you kept all of these?" I whisper, reaching out to touch a sketch I made on the back of a gas station receipt. It's a rough image of Ryder laughing, his head thrown back in joy.

Beckett nods, his expression serious. "Every single one. They're too beautiful to throw away, Lana."

I shuffle through them slowly, overwhelmed by the memories each sketch brings back. There's Tristan, his glasses slightly askew after our epic snowball fight. And one of Ryder, dramatically posing with an axe at the Christmas tree farm. Looking at it, I can almost hear his laughter echoing through the chilly air.

Then there's one of Beckett, his strong hands working on his knitting and a look of peace on his normally gruff face.

But best of all, I find a quick sketch I made on a napkin that shows all three of them, huddled over an actual paper map at a rest stop when we passed through a remote area that had really crappy cell service. It's a simple line drawing, but it captures the easy camaraderie between all three of them, and the way they fit together so naturally—with each other, but now with me too.

"It's like a scrapbook of our trip. I can't believe you saved them all." I smile up at him, cupping the rough stubble on his jaw. "Thank you."

"Thank *you*," he says, emotion shining in his eyes. "I love that you documented all these memories for us."

I laugh, shaking my head. "Is that what I was doing?"

"That's what you always do." He hesitates for a moment, then turns to his dresser. "Let me show you something else."

He opens the top drawer and pulls out another stack of mismatched papers, holding them against his chest for a moment when I reach for them.

"Beckett? What is it?"

"It's..."

He laughs softly, shaking his head, then finally hands them over with a shrug.

"These are mine," I whisper, my eyes widening as I take them. This stack of sketches is even more eclectic, and it goes back *years*—quick doodles I made at family barbecues, holiday gatherings, lazy summer afternoons when I was just Caleb's little sister hanging around with him and his friends. All things I did just to entertain myself. All pictures I tossed in the trash, convinced by my parents that there was no value to my "hobby" other than that.

My heart swells as I flip through them, memories flooding back. "You kept these?" I breathe, my voice barely audible. "All this time?"

Beckett rubs the back of his neck. "Yeah," he admits softly. "I guess... some part of me always knew."

"Knew what?"

I look up at him, and he meets my gaze, his gorgeous green eyes both intense and vulnerable.

"It's always been you. Even when I didn't realize it, didn't want to admit it, and even when I tried to deny it... it's *always* been you, Lana."

My heart stutters in my chest, emotions rising so fast in me that I don't know what to do with them. But instinct takes over, and I rise onto my tiptoes and kiss him, pouring everything I have into it.

He groans, his arms wrapping me tight as he surrounds me with the scent of cedar and leather that's uniquely him, and with something else too. With safety and belonging and love... and home.

As the kiss deepens, I hear Ryder and Tristan come into the room.

"Now that's a sight to come home to," Tristan murmurs as both men approach.

"That's a sight to ring in a New Year to," Ryder corrects him, heat in his tone.

As if on cue, we hear the distant sounds of fireworks starting, and Tristan glances at the time on his phone. "Ten seconds to go. Should we count down?"

We gather in a tight circle, arms around each other, and it feels like the very same fireworks lighting up the sky outside Beckett's window are going off in my heart too. This moment is perfect. No big parties, no elaborate celebrations— just the four of us, in this quiet room, on the cusp of a new year and a new chapter in our lives.

"Three... two... one... happy new year!" we all say in unison, laughing at the muffled sounds of a city celebrating from out in the street.

As the clock strikes midnight, I'm passed from one set of arms to another as they all kiss me. Their hands start to wander as the air heats up around us and my clothes start coming off.

"You up for this, little menace?" Beckett murmurs, lips trailing down my throat.

The care he's always taking with me makes my heart feel two sizes too big, and a giddy kind of joy fills me, taking my arousal and turning it into something almost magical.

"I agree with Ryder," I breathe. "It's the perfect way to ring in the New Year. After all, they say you start the year the same way you intend to go on."

"In that case," Ryder says with a wicked grin, "I vote that we spend the first several hours of this year fucking our girl."

I like the sound of that.

And I like it even better when they follow through.

EPILOGUE

LANA

The soft strains of Christmas music fill my studio as I add the final touches to my latest piece. Sunlight streams through the floor-to-ceiling windows, bathing the space in a warm glow that highlights the colorful canvases adorning the walls. It's hard to believe it's been almost a year since the guys gifted me this incredible space.

I step back, surveying the painting with a critical eye. It's a large-scale abstract inspired by our road trip last Christmas—all swirling colors and dynamic lines that capture the whirlwind of emotions from that life-changing journey.

As I clean my brushes, I smile at how far I've come. My first gallery showing last spring was a surprising success, and I've been steadily building a name for myself in the L.A. art scene ever since. It's more than I ever dared to dream, yet here I am, living it.

Because of them.

I glance at the clock and realize it's time to close up. I've got a hot date tonight at Radiance with my men, and I can't wait. Literally.

As I lock up the studio, my mind drifts to this morning's wake-up call. Ryder's talented fingers tracing patterns on my skin, his lips following the same path, and his cock buried inside me.

Waking up to the feeling of him fucking me has become one of my favorite ways to start the day.

I smile to myself as I navigate the L.A. traffic toward Radiance. Any guilt I had over the three of them putting their dreams of expansion on the back burner have been laid to rest by seeing what their focused attention has meant for the club's success over the last year.

"Lana!" The club's manager greets me as I walk in, bustling over to take my coat and air kiss my cheek. "Mr. Stone told me we were expecting you. Can I get you a seltzer water?"

I smile at him. "Nothing tonight, Stephen. Thank you. All I need is my men."

"I believe Mr. Callahan and Mr. Whitmore are in the back, and I saw Mr. Stone heading for the back corridor a moment ago."

"Thank you."

I'm about to turn away when he stops me with a light touch to my arm.

"If I may say so, Ms. Reeves, the new piece you delivered last week is exquisite."

He nods toward the main demonstration room, where one of my newest paintings hangs above the St. Andrew's Cross.

I grin. "Thank you."

That particular painting was inspired by a mind-blowing exhibitionist scene the men surprised me with on my birthday, and like my other kink-inspired art that they display around the club, it gives me a thrill to be able to share this side of myself with people who appreciate it.

A shiver of anticipation runs through me as I head for the dimly lit staff-only hallway Stephen referred to, hoping I'll catch Beckett there. It's behind the bar I sat at so nervously during my first visit to this club, when he stepped in and scared off an admirer.

Its entrance is neatly camouflaged to blend into the decor, and as soon as I slip into the hallway, large, tattooed hands grab me and press me against the wall.

"What are you doing here?" he demands, dipping down and dragging his nose along my throat.

I clutch his shoulders, tipping my head back to give him easy access.

"Why does anyone come here?" I answer playfully, my breath hitching when he nips at the sensitive pulse point at the base of my throat. "You do own this place, right? Which means you know what people come here to do?"

He lifts his head and raises a single eyebrow, giving me a look that sends liquid heat rushing through my veins.

"Are you sassing me, dirty girl?"

"What if I am?"

He gives me a slow, sexy smile that promises all sorts of sinful punishments if I don't give my Dom what he wants—an answer.

"I'm here to fuck my boyfriends." I drag my hand down his firm chest, then hook my fingers into his waistband. "But I forgot my panties. Do you think I should go back and get them, or...?"

He groans. "Fuck, you really are a little menace. We've been waiting for you."

He scoops me up in his arms, gives me a filthy kiss, then carries me down the hall with ease. Tristan and Ryder are waiting for us in a private room that's off-limits to the public.

"She claims she forgot her panties," Beckett announces as soon as we get there. "One of you want to check that for me?"

"I volunteer as tribute," Ryder says, sliding his hands up my thighs and pushing the skirt up to my waist as Beckett holds me against him. "Bare, wet, and almost ready for us," he confirms, a rasp in his voice.

"Almost?" I repeat breathlessly.

He flashes a wicked grin. "You're still wearing way too many clothes, love."

So are they, and as soon as they get me naked and set me down on the wide, plush couch we've all fucked on so many times, their clothes start coming off too.

"What's that?" I ask, popping to my feet and running my hand over Beckett's chest. I know his body like the back of my hand, and while he's already decorated with quite a few intricate, beautiful tattoos, I know for a fact that this particular spot—right over his heart—was blank.

Now it's not.

He smiles down at me, holding my hand to his chest, then using my own finger to trace the new ink.

"I drew this," I whisper.

It's from a silly drawing I made when we were snowed in at the hotel during our road trip last year. We'd been joking around about whether or not every snowflake could truly be unique, and to prove my point, I sketched out a whole series of intricate, unique snowflakes on a piece of the hotel's stationary. That led to the men all voting on which one was best.

This is the one Beckett voted for.

"Did you know that snowflakes can represent transformation and change?" Tristan asks, stepping closer.

I suck in a breath as I look over at him. He has fresh ink over his heart too. Another one of my snowflakes.

"You've changed us, love," Ryder murmurs. "You've transformed our lives in more ways than you can ever imagine."

He has new ink too.

"I can't believe you guys did this," I whisper. Then I laugh, shaking my head. "Actually, yes I can. You are nothing if not persistent in showing me how much you love me. Thank you. You mean everything to me."

"Persistent, hm?" Ryder says, pulling me against him and tipping my chin up for a kiss. "You want us to prove just how persistent we can be when it comes to showing you how we feel about you?"

"Yes, please."

"Let me start," Tristan murmurs, turning my head while Ryder still holds me, kissing me deeply as well.

"Not before I get a turn," Beckett rumbles, stepping in and devouring my lips until I'm dizzy.

"You're so perfect for us, freckles," Tristan whispers, stroking his thumb over my lower lip before stepping away. He comes back with a blindfold. "Trust us?"

481

"Always. *Green.*"

I'm breathing hard, my chest rising and falling rapidly as Tristan covers my eyes. Ryder guides me to the edge of the bed, then turns me so that I'm facing it.

"Lean over," he murmurs.

He helps me position myself, bent over the bed, legs spread wide and ass in the air.

"Good girl," he murmurs, stroking a hand down my back. "Now let's make sure that pussy is nice and wet and ready to take all of us."

Then he's on his knees, big hands holding my thighs apart as he eats me out until I come on his face.

"Guess you didn't need those panties after all," Beckett rumbles, running his thick fingers through my hair. Then he guides his cock to my face, rubbing his shaft over my cheeks.

I instinctively turn toward it, running my tongue over the row of piercings running up its length. Then, as Ryder enters me from behind, Beckett pushes his thick cockhead into my mouth.

"Do you have any idea how fucking beautiful you look when you're stuffed full on both ends?" Tristan murmurs, stroking my back. Then he slips his hand beneath me, tugging my clit piercing as Ryder groans and drives into me, and I come, my scream of pleasure muffled by Beckett's cock.

"Oh fuck, so good, love," Ryder, pants, pulling out and letting Tristan take his place.

It's not long before I'm lost in the sensations as all three men pleasure me, bringing me to one orgasm after another. Filling every one of my holes until I'm floating, filled with their cum and riding on a sea of bliss that only they can bring me. I'm breathless and euphoric by the time they've all finished, and they wrap me in their arms, still blindfolded, and gently bring me back to myself.

"Drink something, love," Ryder murmurs, holding a bottle of water to my lips.

Beckett pushes my sweaty hair back from my forehead, then presses a lingering kiss there. "Beautiful," he murmurs.

Tristan turns my head as the other two move away, kissing me softly. Then I'm alone on the plush couch.

"Can I take the blindfold off now?" I ask, feeling as relaxed and languid as a cat in the sun.

"That's our job, little menace," Beckett says, his voice low and husky and filled with a smile I'm eager to see. "Close your eyes."

I do it, and he carefully unfastens the blindfold, removing it and running his thumbs over my eyelids and stepping away.

I open my eyes... and gasp.

All three of them are down on one knee in front of me, each holding a small ring box.

My heart races.

Tristan speaks first, his voice soft but steady. "This past year has been the best one of my life. And just like this..." He brushes the fingers of his free hand over his new ink. "I want to make it permanent. Will you marry us?"

He opens the ring box he's holding, a stunning white gold band with a uniquely shaped diamond.

My breath catches as I meet his eyes and nod, tears springing to mine.

Ryder grins, a hint of mischief in his eyes. "Christmas isn't the only thing you've taught me to love. And there's nothing I want to do more than keep doing that for the rest of my life. Marry us."

When he pops his ring box open, it's a gorgeous platinum band with another uniquely shaped diamond in the center.

I nod, wiping at my cheeks as the tears start flowing down my cheeks.

Beckett's expression is intense, his words gruff but sincere. "Lana, we're better with you. All of us, but especially me. You're already ours, but I want to make sure you're ours forever. Marry us."

"Yes!" I laugh, wiping at my cheeks as my face splits into a joyful smile. "Oh my god, yes, yes, yes!"

The ring Beckett chose has a titanium band, and it's only after all three of them slip them onto my ring finger, marking me as theirs, taken, loved, that I realize the uniquely shaped diamonds on each ring all fit together to form a huge, stunning stone that reflects every facet of my love for these men.

And their love for me.

THE SCENT of cinnamon and pine fills our home as I put the finishing touches on the dining table. It's Christmas Day, and we're hosting for the first time in our new house.

I smile as I take in the festive wonderland around me. It's not a white Christmas, not here in L.A., but my men have still helped me turn our home into our own private winter wonderland.

A little more enthusiastically than I expected.

"Ryder, did you add *more* tinsel?" I call out, noticing a fresh sparkle on the tree.

His head pops around the corner, grinning sheepishly as he adjusts the rakish Santa hat on his head. "Maybe."

I laugh, shaking my head. It's hard to believe this is the same man who once claimed to hate the holidays. This year, he's been the driving force behind our home's transformation into a winter wonderland, and I honestly don't know if it's because he's grown to love it too, or just because he loves me so much.

Either way, I love it. Every surface seems to twinkle with lights or shimmer with ornaments, and I can't wait to welcome the family we have flying in from New Hampshire here to share it with us.

The doorbell chimes, and I hurry to answer it. Vivian stands there, looking happier than I've seen her in years, with Oliver bouncing excitedly by her side. Behind them is James, Vivian's new boyfriend, looking a bit nervous but smiling warmly.

"Merry Christmas!" I exclaim, hugging each of them. "Come in, come in!"

"Is Uncle Beckett here?" Oliver asks eagerly, trying to peer around my legs.

Vivian ruffles his hair with a laugh. "I think you meant to say 'thank you for having us, Auntie Lana,' isn't that right?"

He nods enthusiastically, mumbling the required greeting, then races past me to throw himself at Beckett.

Beckett's face softens in that private way that still gets me every time, and scoops the little boy into his arms for a quick hug. It ends with Beckett dangling my nephew upside down and making him giggle like a maniac.

He sets him down and points him toward the plate of gingerbread cookies I set out earlier as Vivian, James, and I enter the room, their luggage in tow.

All three of my men instantly straighten up, their gazes zeroing in on James as their smiles drop away and they go into protective older brother mode.

I bite back a laugh, exchanging a look with Vivian.

"Oh boy," she murmurs. "They're not going to—"

"So, James," Beckett rumbles, crossing his arms. "What are your intentions with Vivian?"

James looks startled, and Vivian rolls her eyes.

"Oh lord, they are," she whispers.

I laugh. "They love you too, you know. You're family."

Her cheeks turn pink, but she still puts her hands on her hips and shakes her head at them. "Really, guys? He's not some teenager picking me up for prom. Back off."

They grumble, but relax and come over to welcome James with handshakes and smiles just as the doorbell rings again.

"I'll get it," I call out, leaving them to get to know Vivian's new man.

When I open the front door, I'm greeted by Caleb's broad grin and Grandma Meg's kind smile. Baldwin yaps excitedly from her arms, his festive hand-knit sweater making him look like a tiny, adorable reindeer.

"Merry Christmas!" I exclaim, pulling Caleb into a bear hug before turning to Meg. "Thank you so much for coming. How was your flight?"

"It was just lovely, dear. I can't thank you enough for upgrading my ticket to first class."

"As if we'd let you fly any other way," I tell her, hugging her tightly after she sets Baldwin down.

He dances around our feet, and I scoop him up, laughing as he showers me with puppy kisses.

I'm happy to see that the guys have quit giving James a hard time when we join the others in the living room. Everyone looks happy and relaxed, the atmosphere warm and inviting and everything I've always wished for Christmas to be.

Caleb immediately starts teasing Ryder about his ugly Christmas sweater, while Tristan greets his grandmother warmly and settles her into a plush armchair we all picked out specifically with her visit in mind. Oliver chases after Baldwin excitedly, while Meg accepts a mug of hot chocolate from Beckett with a fond smile.

After we help our guests get settled, I find myself sandwiched between Caleb and Vivian on the couch, and as we chat and laugh together, I'm struck by how different this Christmas feels from any other. Not just because of my men, but because of how close I feel to my siblings now, and how full of happiness and love my home feels for the holiday.

Caleb chuckles, throwing an arm around my shoulders. "I sure didn't see it coming. But I've got to admit, sis, you've put together one hell of a family here."

I look around the room, smiling so widely that my cheeks hurt. The room is filled with laughter, love, and the perfect amount of chaotic energy. Leaning into Caleb's side, I rest my head on his shoulder as I watch my three fiancés interact with the people who mean the most to me.

"You're right," I tell him softly. "I really have."

As if sensing my gaze, Tristan, Ryder, and Beckett all look up, their eyes finding mine across the room. The love I see reflected there makes my heart expand like a balloon.

Ryder adjusts his flopping Santa hat, Tristan pushes his glasses higher on his nose with a smile, and Beckett taps his heart right over his new ink and mouths, "Merry Christmas."

I mouth it back as I play with the interlocking rings on my finger, taking a moment to appreciate just how lucky I am.

This is home. This is family. This is where I belong.

And now it's mine forever.

BOOKS BY EVA ASHWOOD

Filthy Rich Santas

**Clearwater University
(college-age enemies to lovers series)**
Who Breaks First
Who Laughs Last
Who Falls Hardest

**The Dark Elite
(dark mafia romance)**
Vicious Kings
Ruthless Knights
Savage Queen

**Slateview High
(dark high school bully romance)**
Lost Boys
Wild Girl
Mad Love

Sinners of Hawthorne University

(dark new adult romance)
When Sinners Play
How Sinners Fight
What Sinners Love

Black Rose Kisses
(dark new adult romance)
Fight Dirty
Play Rough
Wreak Havoc
Love Hard

Dirty Broken Savages
(dark new adult/mafia romance)
Kings of Chaos
Queen of Anarchy
Reign of Wrath
Empire of Ruin

Filthy Wicked Psychos
(dark new adult romance)
Twisted Game
Beautiful Devils
Corrupt Vow
Savage Hearts

Pretty Ruthless Monsters
(dark new adult/mafia romance)
Princes of Carnage
Crown of Lies
Bonds of Obsession
Princess of Vengeance

Magic Blessed Academy
(paranormal academy series)

Gift of the Gods
Secret of the Gods
Wrath of the Gods

Made in the USA
Las Vegas, NV
15 November 2024

11822143R10272